JACK HAD NO JACK.
No job. No prospects. No hopes. No dreams. No beliefs.

HE OWED A LOT.
To Anne, for taking him into her life and her bed, so at least he knew where his next drink and night's sleep were coming from. And to Parry, who had even less than he, yet had enough to save him from being torched by fun-loving kids.

AND NOW IT WAS PAYBACK TIME.
Anne needed a man. Parry needed a woman. And somehow Jack, past master of the one-line put-down, had to cast his line to come up with both. . . .

THE FISHER KING

THE FISHER KING

A Novel by
Leonore Fleischer

Based on the
Motion Picture by
Richard LaGravenese

PENGUIN BOOKS

PENGUIN BOOKS

Published by the Penguin Group
Penguin Books Ltd, 27 Wrights Lane, London W8 5TZ, England
Penguin Books USA Inc., 375 Hudson Street, New York, New York 10014, USA
Penguin Books Australia Ltd, Ringwood, Victoria, Australia
Penguin Books Canada Ltd, 10 Alcorn Avenue, Toronto, Ontario, Canada M4V 3B2
Penguin Books (NZ) Ltd, 182–190 Wairau Road, Auckland 10, New Zealand

Penguin Books Ltd, Registered Offices: Harmondsworth, Middlesex, England

First published in the USA by Signet, an imprint of New American Library,
a division of Penguin Books USA Ltd 1991
Published in Great Britain by Penguin Books 1991
3 5 7 9 10 8 6 4 2

Printed in England by Clays Ltd, St Ives plc

One

Everything you've ever heard about New York City—forget it. What they always feed you is lies. New York isn't a State of Mind, or a Wonderful Town, or the Big Apple, or the City That Never Sleeps, or any of the song lyrics or bullshit mythologies that are fed to a gullible public. Well, maybe the City That Never Sleeps is a fairly accurate description, because New York is not unlike the great white shark, endlessly circling, always awake, searching for prey, constantly on the attack. New York is a giant maw filled with many rows of serrated teeth, a territory devoted to kill-or-be-killed, you devour me or I devour you. You gotta be rich and clever to survive. If you happen to be one of the have-nots, then step back. Take a hike. Get lost. Ain't nobody come here lookin' for you, and we don't take messages.

On the other hand, if you're one of the haves, there's probably no more exciting place on earth to work or live than New York. It has everything—a glittering nightlife uptown and downtown, expensive shops, incredibly snobbish restaurants, the most exclusive hairdressers and couturiers, the best sex and the hottest music, the newest dances, the most beautiful women in the world, the most successful men. New York City is like the appetizer table at a Jewish wedding, loaded with salt and spice and cholesterol and flavor, with a waiter holding out pleasure in his right hand and indigestion in his left. If you've got the bucks, this burg has the bangs.

Fortunately for Jack Lucas, he was one of the haves, actually a supreme and shining example of a have. He personified You Are What You Own, Wear, Drive, Eat, You Are Where You Live, You Are Who You Sleep With, and—most important of all—Jack was a man whose own success he happily measured by the failure of others. The field of endeavor that had endowed him so richly with a good address, a gorgeous lover in her twenties, and other such hip worldly possessions was his own show on talk radio.

The *Jack Lucas Morning Show* was a smash success, the station's big leader. Jack had taken a moribund wake-up time slot on a moribund radio station and, using only his angry wit, his sharp talent for the spontaneous putdown, and his characteristically black outlook on life, had parlayed it into one of the most-listened-to programs on the air. Within a short time, he had become a cult personality with a large following. People tuned in to Jack with mingled curiosity and titillation just to listen to the feeble mews of the poor schlub Jack would be insulting next. In the bloody arena of talk radio, the listeners were the Romans, the callers were the hapless Christians, and Jack himself was the hungry lion.

Alone in his studio, he created a fantasy world for people who couldn't get themselves a life. At home or in their cars on the way to work, his audience couldn't see him, but they could imagine, through the rough masculine sound of his voice and the image of swaggering self-confidence he projected, that Jack Lucas was a superior kind of being who'd been handed the divine right to freely demean lesser beings.

From talk radio to insult radio wasn't really that much of a leap; Jack Lucas made it without straining a well-toned muscle. From insult radio to humiliation radio is a much longer stretch; even so, there were no beads of sweat on Jack Lucas's upper lip when he jumped over that barrier. As the clever centerpiece of one of Manhattan's most popular morning programs, Jack specialized in the humiliation and verbal annihilation of anybody dumb or desperate enough to call in. There were actually a surprisingly large number of wretched men and women who were so needy, so frantic to have their voices heard on the air, to have this master of stand-up contempt fling insults at their unprotected heads, that hundreds of them picked up their phones and literally invited their own belittlement, some on a regular basis.

For every sadist there's a whole bunch of eager masochists. Go figure.

So Jack Lucas, who viewed life from the bottom up, for whom the wineglass of life was perpetually half-empty, whose strongest emotion was discontent, managed to turn his pessimism into celebrity, his distaste for the human race into a large paycheck, the misfortunes of others into a plush life for himself, and all with the collusion of his victims. Hey, why not, this is the nineties, right? To make it in New York in the nineties, you've gotta have an edge, and Jack Lucas's edge was the carbon steel of impatience honed by the sharpening stone of egotism and held to the throat of a shivering humanity.

Strange, because he lacked neither intelligence nor education. Jack was a reader and a thinker. But since he'd become a cult figure and his fame and income had soared, somehow he'd lost the sense of the ridiculous he'd always had about himself and what he was doing. Ambition had put a halt to humorous self-examination.

His prime motivation was ambition, and what kept his ambition fueled was his lack of involvement with anybody but himself. Jack Lucas kept a comfortable distance from and a patronizing attitude toward every other life-form on the planet. His soul, or what passed for his soul, was housed in a glass isolation booth, for which his little broadcast studio was the perfect metaphor. His listeners could hear him, but they could not see him; above all, they could not touch him. All in all, not a very nice guy, but a very successful one. As Jack himself would say, "Fuck nice."

Jack had been nice once; when he was a young man, his deep-set blue eyes had beamed whenever his wide mouth had broken into a broad grin. There was a time when the expression on his handsome face hadn't yet hardened into a permanent sulky, bored grimace with turned-down lips. Once upon a time he'd even had a few ideals, one or two youthful altruistic impulses to maybe make the world a little better than he'd found it. So what had happened to change him?

Years had gone by and Jack didn't see the world getting any better. In fact, it got a helluva lot worse, and no effort of his seemed to make any difference. Maybe it was the greed of the eighties, that me-first decade of junk bonds and junk people. The trash track can be very seductive when you're running on it. It doesn't like to let go. Maybe because life itself had laughed at Jack more than a couple of times—it made him swear to have the first laugh from now on. Maybe it was the fact that never, in all his forty-one years, had he found another human being to love, really love.

There were girls, of course; oh, my God, yes! There was an apparently endless procession of beautiful women parading through Jack Lucas's life— models, actresses, even writers and painters, if they were gorgeous enough, if their legs were long, their thighs were narrow, and their butts as round as

MacIntosh apples. But although they touched his body, they hadn't touched his heart.

Now, at forty-one, where was his heart? Certainly not where you could get near it, or even where Jack himself was conscious of its existence. Jack had attained just about everything he wanted—fame, money, a great pad overlooking Manhattan from three directions, an apple-butt girlfriend. He traveled by stretch limo with one-way glass windows, he wore Italian designer suits at nineteen hundred dollars a pop; his feet sported custom-made three-thousand-dollar snakeskin boots with silver tips, cold-blooded creatures. If he couldn't feel joy, well, who the hell needs joy? Jack Lucas wasn't feeling pain, either. And that was about all you could ask for in this crummy world. No pain.

Yet, as popular as his radio program was—and it had captured the morning drive-time audience—he was finally getting bored with it. Getting out of bed at four to wake up the yahoos and morons of the five boroughs at six A.M. was no longer his idea of bliss. It was time to move upward and onward.

But his career seemed to have stalled right here, in this small studio, too hot in the summer and too cold in the winter, smelling of stale cigarette smoke, with the "On Air" sign flashing and the phone buttons lighting up. If the broadcast studio kept the world locked out, it also served to keep Jack locked in. That made Jack Lucas feel even more bitter, and his bitterness poured out like toxic waste all over the poor defenseless assholes who called in to his board.

Most of Jack's callers were kookaburras, of course, because the kookier they were, the easier it was to attack them and the more laughs his attacks won for him; the more laughs, the more ratings. These men and women were the ones desperate to let the world know they'd spotted UFOs, or were being followed by the IRS or the phone company, or they had the real skinny on exactly which section of the West Side Highway Jimmy Hoffa's bones were cemented into. Jack would string them along for a little while, let them get their weirdness across to the audience, and then . . . crash! He'd pull the rug out from under them and send them tumbling back down into the vortex of near madness from which they'd sprung.

Jack Lucas's equipment was minimal—a wicked wit, a microphone, a broadcast booth, a couple of sound engineers, and a rack of tapes that held an assortment of bizarre noises. The tapes were sound effects of cheers, and boos, and "awwwws," and corny inspirational music, and any other effect that enhanced the humiliation of the caller. Jack could put his hands on any tape at any given moment, slap it into his control board, and it sounded instantly like a large studio audience was backing up his insults with heckling cheers and jeers.

"Hi, this is Monday morning, and I'm Jack Lucas, and we're discussing personal pet peeves. You're on the air, caller."

"Okay," said an uncertain and fluttery female voice. "Well, it's my husband."

"Uh-huh," Jack answered encouragingly, but he glanced at his Rolex, wishing he could make time move by pushing the hands of his watch around the dial.

"He drives me crazy!" the woman complained. "I'll be talking and he'll never let me finish a sentence. He's always finishing my—"

"Finishing your thoughts," said Jack wickedly. "That's awful."

"Oh, it absolutely drives me—"

"Drives you crazy, huh?" Jack beat her to the end of her sentence. "He's a scoundrel."

"Jack, you hit the nail on the head." His caller sighed.

"Yeah? Well, somebody ought to hit you on the head." He pressed the next phone button, cutting off not only her next sentence but her call. In the control booth, the engineers snickered.

Although he relied on callers to keep the ball rolling, from time to time Jack Lucas actually sought out his own victims. As, for instance, now, when he was hassling on-air the female half of the most recent Washington sex scandal, a young woman whose unlisted telephone number Jack had obtained through a clever bit of bribery.

". . . This is disgusting. I don't have to talk to you," the girl was saying resentfully. It was a good connection; every nuance of her ashamed unhappiness would be clear to the audience.

"Yes, yes, you do," responded Jack, reaching for one of his tapes, "because you see, today you're our—"

"Spotlight Celebrity" echoed from the tape. The home audience sat up and took notice. Spotlight Celebrities were a sensational highlight of every show.

"And in the spirit of fairness," Jack continued, with nasty glee, "we want the public to hear your side of things. So, now, how long were you and Senator Payton having this sleazy affair?" He was rewarded by guffaws from the engineers' booth.

The young woman bridled, her voice thick with indignation over the telephone. "I'm sick and tired of the public thinking they've got the right to invade a person's private life."

"Oh, please!" Jack scoffed, heavy sarcasm dripping from every word. "You had sex with a United States senator in the parking lot of Sea World! You're telling me now that you're a private kind of person? No, you're our—"

"Spotlight Celebrity!" The tape again.

"That's still all anybody talks about." The young

woman sighed sadly. "Nobody even thinks to ask whether we loved each other."

"Because nobody cares about that, sweetheart. Nobody wants to hear about your romantic love. No, we want to hear about the backseats of limos . . . the ruined lives of people we want to be . . . new and exotic uses for champagne corks—"

"Listen, I've been humiliated enough already!" She was becoming really angry under Jack's eager probing.

"Perhaps not." Jack grinned. "We need those details!"

But no details would be forthcoming. With a snarled, "You're a pig, Jack," the young woman had broken the connection by slamming down her receiver. Jack laughed out loud in disparagement and pressed down another one of his phone's lit buttons.

Please, God, let the next caller not be so fucking boring! Jack prayed silently. Let's get a little action going. I'm dying in here! Just give me some lamb-o I can sink my teeth into!

"Hello, Jack, it's Edwin."

"It's Edwin!" The answer to his prayer, in spades. Jack greeted him joyfully, and in the sound booth the engineers cheered. Edwin Malnick was one of the program's regulars, another big loser at the game of life, always good for a few laughs. Jack slapped in a fanfare tape, and a swell of music announced Edwin.

"Edwin, we haven't heard from you in, what, a day? I've missed you." The poor schmuck couldn't afford a shrink, but he looked on Jack Lucas as some kind of benevolent God of Good Advice.

"I've missed you, too, Jack."

The "Awwww!" tape was appropriate here.

"So, Edwin, baby, this is Sunrise Confession time. What have you got for us?"

"I . . . I went to this bar . . . this very, ya know,

hard-to-get-into place, called Babbitt's,'' the man's voice began shyly.

"Yeah, I know the place.'' Jack grinned, and his grin was tinged with malice. "It's one of those chic yuppie gathering holes.''

"Uh, okay, I know, but . . . I met this beautiful girl.''

Music welled from the south booth, drenching the airwaves with syrupy lyrics. "Goin' to the chapel, and we're gonna get maa-aried. . . . ''

"Now, Edwin''—Jack laughed—''if you start telling me you're in love again, I'm going to have to remind you of the time we made you propose to that checkout girl at Thrifty's that you liked so much. Remember her reaction?''

Jack slipped the ''AAAAArrrrrgggggghhhhh!'' sound tape in swiftly and then choked off the scream. It was a great effect, one of his favorites.

"I wasn't serious about her, Jack,'' Edwin answered defensively. "That was just a joke for you guys. She was just a girl. This is a beautiful woman.''

Jack Lucas had a momentary visual flash on the caller, drippy Edwin Malnick, even though he'd never seen him. He could picture pale thinning hair, a large Adam's apple, and protruding ears that went red with embarrassment, weak blue eyes behind thick glasses, knobby knuckles. A virgin, he'd swear to it, the kind of dimwit that even the most desperate old maid wouldn't go out with. What a loser!

Edwin continued, unfazed, just happy to have Jack's attention. "I think she likes me. She gave me her number. But she must work a lot, 'cause when I call she's never home. But I think we'll go out this weekend. I've—''

"Yeah, Edwin, sure, and Pinocchio is a true story,'' Jack interrupted harshly, his patience at an end. This hopeless asshole was a complete cipher;

he would never, never have any effect on anybody's life. Jack felt he'd strung the nerd along long enough; time to lower the boom. "Edwin, wake up! This is a fairy tale!"

"No, Jack," protested the caller, his voice going thick as his defensiveness grew. "No, it's not . . . she likes me!"

"She gave you the old brusheroo, kiddo," Jack scoffed into the microphone as he reached for his cigarettes. "Believe me, this tart will never make it to your dessert plate." He snickered a little at his own wit.

"She likes me, Jack." Edwin was stung, but he came bobbing up for more. "She said for me to call."

Lighting up, Jack Lucas drew the harsh smoke deeply into his lungs. "Edwin . . . hey, c'mon, Edwin . . . Edwin . . . I told you about these people," he said with phony cameraderie. "They only mate with their own kind. It's called yuppie inbreeding. That's why so many of them are retarded and wear the same clothes. They're not human. They can't feel love. They can only negotiate love *moments*. They're evil, Edwin. They're repulsed by imperfection and horrified by the banal, everything America stands for. Everything that you and I fight for." Jack warmed to his topic, allowing the bile of his own prejudices to wash mockingly over his listeners. He had absolutely no grasp of what effect his words might have on others; all of Jack Lucas's thinking was one-way, like the window glass in the studio limousine that took him everywhere. He could look out, but nobody else could look in. "Edwin, they have to be stopped before it's too late. It's us or them."

There was a brief silence while Jack's words sank in, then Edwin said quietly, "All right," and hung up.

Jack Lucas's lips twisted in a sneer and he ground his cigarette out in the already-filled ashtray. Edwin Malnick! Quel dork!

The morning dragged on, with crank call after crank call, with every variety of dingbat and moron the city could provide from its overflowing coffers of lunacy. The hands of Jack's criminally expensive wristwatch crept with tortured slowness around its face, and the large studio clock with its sweep second hand taunted him at the same molasses pace. And yet, time did in fact pass away, minute by agonizing minute, until it was time for sign-off. The next slot would be filled by encapsulated headline news and ten minutes of weather and traffic, then the next talk-radio host, a fat, genial robust fellow whose idol was Arthur Godfrey.

"Well, folks, it's been a thrill, as always. Have a perfect day. Everyone here on the *Jack Lucas Morning Show* says 'bye." Jack ground out the last cigarette butt and threw the empty pack on the floor. His throat was a little sore; he'd have to start cutting down.

"This is Jack Lucas . . . so long . . . *arrivederc* . . . I'll be sure to send you a thought today as I lie in the backseat of my stretch limo, having sex with the teenager of my choice. And that thought will be—thank God I'm me!"

TWO

"You know, some of this is very funny." Lou Rosen chuckled, waving the script of the pilot of a new TV sitcom, *On the Radio*, at Jack. Lou Rosen was Jack Lucas's talent agent, from one of the two most high-powered agencies. Jack might be one of his smallest clients at present, but he was up-and-coming, and ambitious, so Rosen coddled him. "Cheever told me they've even secured the rights to the Donna Summer song to play over the credits."

"Ooooh, I have chills," Jack replied sourly, but his sarcasm bounced right off the professionally ebullient Rosen. "Are you sure they want me?" he continued. "I won't read it unless I have an offer."

Lou Rosen looked sharply at his client. They were all the same, performers. Babies, toddlers. All of them neurotically insecure, all demanding to have their nervous little hands held. In his best fifteen-percenter tones of reassurance, he said smoothly, "Jack, of course. Not even a question. When I spoke to him on the phone this morning, I could actually smell how much they want you for it. I could smell it over the phone." He made a little sniffing grimace to demonstrate, and it seemed to Jack that between his large round eyes, small balding head, and twitching nose, the agent looked like a cross between Bugs Bunny and Elmer Fudd.

The pair were seated in the spacious back of the stretch limousine the station had put at Jack's disposal. It was the ultimate status symbol—a city-block long, with a wet bar and TV in the back, one-way glass windows, the latest magazines and fresh newspapers in the door pockets, and the driver even wore a cap. It was Jack's pride and joy; he loved his limo with a passion, although he was too cool to say so out loud. He was always Joe Cool, as though the car and driver and all his other status symbols were just things, only possessions about which he couldn't care less.

Now the limo stopped at a traffic light. A street bum, unwashed and ragged, shambled over hopefully to the limo, tapping with filthy fingers on the one-way glass, trying to peer in. Lou fumbled in his jacket pockets. "I don't think I have any change," he said apologetically to Jack.

Jack glared at his agent through his costly Vuarnet sunglasses. "I am not opening this window," he snapped. "A couple of quarters isn't going to make any difference anyway." He had no idea how the future was waiting to make him pay for those words.

The light changed and the limo pulled away into traffic, as sleek and polished as a rifle bullet. The have-not panhandler looked after it sadly, too wretched, too forlorn even to be angry.

For an apartment to rent for $4,500 a month it has to offer extras, even in midtown Manhattan. Jack's apartment had lots of extras. It was a two-bedroom duplex in a brand-new building, at a good address. Ceilings were higher than usual, and the closets were generous. The space was vast; the living-room windows were two stories high, the view unobstructed on three sides. In the second bedroom Jack Lucas had created his own private playground, a media room cum gym, with state-of-the-art sound and visuals and the ultimate fitness equipment. If a man is known by the price of his toys, then Jack Lucas must be famous indeed, because his toys had set him back many tens of thousands of dollars.

Coffee. He had to have coffee. Jack walked over the expensive Pirelli industrial rubber tiles imported from Italy, picked up an expensive stainless-steel kettle designed by architect Michael Graves, and took it to the kitchen sink to fill. As the water splashed into the kettle he scowled. There was black ink in the sink again. If he'd told her to be careful once, he must have told the bitch a thousand times. . . . Angrily, he rubbed the ink off with paper towel, squinting to make certain that no black stains remained, and flushed the water down the drain.

Carrying the kettle to the stove, he stared into it, checking out his reflection in the shiny steel, and the scowl deepened. "I hate my cheeks," he growled, his customary discontent eating at him.

Jack slammed the kettle onto the burner and stalked angrily into the dining room, where Sondra, his live-in girlfriend, was sitting at the table, sketch pad open, making careful ink drawings of the oat-bran box, drawings she would later embellish with genitalia. Jack couldn't figure it, but the girl was represented by a fairly well-known art gallery, and she actually did sell some of her work, weird as it was.

Sondra's firm body, as narrow as a splinter, still fascinated him, although he'd long ago lost interest in anything she had to say. Life would be so great for him if Sondra would only keep her legs open and her mouth shut.

"Can I just ask that when you clean your hands, you wipe the ink off the inside of the sink before it stains the porcelain?"

"You can ask," Sondra answered with indifference, not bothering to look up. Six months of living with Jack Lucas and his constant pickiness had inured her to his litany of petty complaints.

"Raoul called before. About dinner," the girl added listlessly.

"About dinner as a concept or about dinner with . . . Raoul?" Jack replied with no real interest in the answer.

"You're so witty. I'm so jealous," said Sondra tonelessly, bored. "I need to get out of here, Jack, and do something other than sit in this apartment and count how many funny lines you have per page."

Jack glared at her. "You know, tomorrow's a very big day for me," he said petulantly. "It would be nice if you pretended like you understood."

"Fine. I'll say no."

"They're putting me on film tomorrow." He was still hoping for some encouragement, a little praise, a reaction of some kind. Fat chance. This relationship had run its course, and all it needed now was to be put out of its misery. If only she didn't have such a tight bod. If it hadn't been for the shape of her ass, Sondra would have been out on it weeks ago.

"Fine!"

"For the first time in my life I'll be a voice with a body. Do you know what that means? What this could lead to?"

"It's a sitcom, Jack, you're not defining Pi."

"I'll remember that the next time you get excited by drawing pubic hairs on oat bran," he snapped back sarcastically. Going to the bookshelf, he removed a copy of Albert Camus's *The Stranger,* and pulled out his stash of sensamilla. Sitting down on one of the Le Corbusier cube chairs, he quickly and neatly rolled a generous joint. He lit it and offered it to Sondra. "Want some?"

"No, I have to work."

Jack toked deeply, held the smoke right down in his lungs, and exhaling at last, answered, "How un-sixties of you."

"I was nine years old in the sixties," Sondra reminded him with relish.

As the high began to kick in, Jack stood up and strolled to the window, staring without seeing at the city spread out twenty-nine stories below him. He was caught up now in his own vainglorious fantasy. "I used to think my biography ought to be entitled *Jack Lucas: The Face Behind the Voice,*" he mused. "But now it can be *Jack Lucas: The Face and the Voice* . . . or maybe . . . just *Jack!* Exclamation point."

He waited for Sondra to say something, but the girl, self-absorbed as usual, didn't appear to be listening. She headed up the stairs to the bedroom above, unbuttoning her blouse as she went. Jack looked up just as she'd shed the blouse. The sight of her small, uptilted breasts gave him an immediate hard-on, and he followed her up the stairs and into the bathroom, where Sondra, now naked, had just turned on the shower and was fiddling with the taps to get the water temperature right.

As she stepped inside, Jack shucked off his pants and shirt and followed her.

"Can't we do this later?" Sondra whined. Then, as Jack's hands busied themselves with her wet body, she grudgingly began to give in. But what was in it for her?

"All right . . . okay. But if we do this now, can I have dinner with Raoul?" Sondra wheedled, knowing she had him by the short and curlies.

Jack grunted his assent, and so another yuppie love moment was negotiated.

Afterward, carrying the other half of the joint and a couple of fingers of good bourbon in a Steuben glass, Jack took the script and some takeout Hunan food into the Jacuzzi with him. "Hey, forgive me!" he practiced while soaking in the tub. He kept trying different readings, looking for the one interpretation that would capture the producer's attention and win him the audition, the reading that would crack everybody up. This could be the tag line that would make him really famous, like Ralph Kramden's "To the moon, Alice!" or Jack Benny's "Welll!" or Fonzie's "Ayyyy!" or Archie Bunker's "Stifle y'self, Edith!" or John Belushi's, "But NOOOO!" Memorable comedy lines like those really had an impact on a TV audience. One good catch phrase could catapult an ordinary man into the stratosphere virtually overnight.

"Hey, for . . . give me! Hey, *forgive* me! Hey, FORGIVE me! Hey, forgive ME! Hey, forgiiiive ME! HEY! Forgive . . . MEEE!"

Each interpretation pleased him better than the last. He could do this. He was really getting a handle on this thing. "HEY . . . FORGIVE ME!" Yeah, that one was really good. He'd go with that reading at his audition for *On the Radio* tomorrow, knock them all dead. They wouldn't be able to turn him down. It would be a lock. He'd be on his way, out of the hellhole of early-morning radio.

"I have this, I really have this!" Jack gloated to himself. "My life is really about to change!"

With a towel wrapped around his waist, he strolled into his den, his private sanctuary. This was the room that contained his Sharper Image toys, audio and video on the cutting edge, his in-wall speakers, his compact disks, his laser-disk projection system, his twin VCRs, his media wall with three television monitors, each screen tuned to a different channel. The sets were all on, but the sound was on mute. Jack loved that, three screens in action with no sound. It gave him a real sense of power to control all their voices, to let the screens speak or not speak, to play God with them.

As he rubbed his long hair dry Jack scanned the

screens idly. Nothing happening. Just the eleven
o'clock news, a collection of earnest men and
women with perfect hairdos sitting at news desks
mouthing silence. Still a little high, he clicked the
remote control and changed all the channels until all
sets tuned to the same picture.

Jack was about to turn away when, suddenly, his
eye was caught by the sight of his own face up there,
in triplicate, like an Andy Warhol silkscreen. Inex-
plicably, surprisingly, there he was—Jack Lucas, on
the eleven o'clock news. What the fuck? Quickly, he
grabbed up the remote, turning on the sound.

". . . Everything America stands for. Everything
you and I fight for. Edwin, they have to be stopped
before it's too late. It's us or them." It was his own
voice Jack heard, his words from this morning's
show, followed by the solemn voice of the broadcaster.

"We go to a live report from Marc Saffron at the
scene."

Channel 10's ace city reporter was shown looking
solemnly into the camera. "It was Mr. Lucas's off-
hand remark that seemed to have a fatal impact on
Mr. Malnick. An after-work hot spot, Babbitt's is
popular with single young professionals." Behind the
reporter, the camera pulled back to show the exterior
of Babbitt's, an attractive watering hole on New
York's trendy upper east side, all stained-glass hanging lamps and lush green plants and a twenty-foot-
long mahogany bar. "Edwin Malnick," Saffron
continued in his deepest tones of serious newscaster,
"arrived at the peak hour of seven-thirty, took one
long look at the handsome collection of the city's
best and brightest, then removed a shotgun from his
overcoat and opened fire."

What did he say? *What the fuck was the man saying?*

Appalled, Jack could only stare at his media wall

in disbelief. His nice warm buzz had evaporated totally, and he was stone sober. Every word of the newscast, every graphic visual, imprinted itself on his brain.

What he saw was a scene out of hell. The screen was filled now with an interior pan of the bar. Black zippered body bags were being carried out, and paramedics were wheeling out gurneys on which a few wounded people still clung to the last remnants of existence. Ambulances stood by, their colored lights rotating, casting weird flickering shadows over the scene.

Jack saw men and women sobbing; a few still screamed in fear as medical workers helped them out of the bar. There was broken glass and blood everywhere; it looked like a war zone—Beirut or Baghdad. It wasn't real; it couldn't possibly be real.

"Fuck," Jack whispered through dry lips.

The news story continued dispassionately. "Seven people were killed before Malnick turned the gun on himself and shot a hole through his head."

Without realizing it, Jack sank into a chair with a small moan. His eyes remained glued in horror to the screens. "Representatives of radio cult personality Jack Lucas expressed regret; however, no formal comment has been made. Neighbors of Edwin Malnick said he was a quiet man who lived alone. 'You scarcely knew he was there,' said a woman who lived next door to Malnick for eleven years. But tonight, few will soon forget this lonely man, who reached out to a world he knew only through the radio . . . looking for friendship . . . and finding only pain . . . and tragedy. . . ."

"This is Marc Saffron . . . Channel Ten News," said the broadcaster, and the channel cut to commercial.

Jack's shock dwindled away, turning to disbelief, then denial, then finally, acceptance, a certainty

mingled with horror. This is my fault, he thought,
my fault. I did this. Seven dead. Seven dead, and
Edwin makes eight. Every word was another nail
hammered into the coffin of Jack Lucas's pampered
life.

For forty years Jack had chosen not to live, but to
skate, like some weightless water bug, on the surface tension of life, never actually getting his feet
wet. Now that meniscus was suddenly torn, and he
was plunged deeply below the surface, where there
was no oxygen. He was drowning.

Jack sat frozen as a dozen different screens chattered on with the latest claims made by an oven
cleaner; he couldn't move, he couldn't speak. Within
the handful of minutes the news item had taken, Jack
Lucas's life had changed finally and forever. The old
life disappeared as though it never was; the new life
was unspeakable to contemplate. As his telephone
began to ring and ring and ring, the comfortably
padded isolation booth of Jack Lucas's soul shattered
into a million brittle fragments. Like the Angel Lu-
cifer expelled from heaven, he went plunging down,
down, down, spiraling headfirst into the yawning
bottomless pit of earthly despair.

Three

Any big city anywhere in the world is exactly like a rotted-out hollow log. It may appear clean and dry on top, but if you kick it over, you'll see blind, white, crawly things slithering out from underneath. These faceless creatures creep away hurriedly, rushing to get out of the painful light. In the last eighteen months since the senseless multiple murders at Babbitt's, Jack Lucas had become one of those scurrying creatures.

Six city blocks west of Jack Lucas's high rise and sixty thousand light-years away is Eighth Avenue. Hooker heaven, druggie delight, it's where runaway children go to earn the price of a meal with their own degradation. At night, Eighth Avenue is home to garbage, overflowing cans of decaying former food, picked over in alleyways by scrawny, starving cats. Human garbage, too, the dregs of life, scuffling and shuffling from one side street to the next in search of the next trick, the next meal, the next fix. Hope for the hopeless.

By the light of day it was only a little better, triple-X-rated porno houses, straight and gay, stood cheek by jowl with small bodegas run by local Hispanics, newspaper stores that sold more lottery tickets and cigarettes than papers and magazines, and Chinese-Cuban restaurants advertising *comidas y criollas*. During the day lunchtime crowds from the nearby office buildings on Seventh and Sixth felt safer venturing onto Eighth to buy a cheap hot meal, browse in a bookstore, rent a video.

"Those people are insane today." Anne Napolitano sighed, coming into the tiny back room that served as her office. "They took insane pills." She waited for Jack to answer her, but Jack said nothing, immersed as usual in a sleazy tabloid he'd picked up at the checkout line of the local superette. He sat with his feet up on Anne's desk, a lit cigarette in one hand, a bottle of Jack Daniel's conveniently standing by.

Anne raised her voice impatiently. "Hey, Mr. Happiness!"

Jack lowered the paper. In the year and a half or so since the shootings at Babbitt's, Jack Lucas had become a changed man. He even looked different, older, thicker, bloated, unshaven, his eyes red-rimmed and bleary. He looked like a man who viewed the world from the bottom of a whiskey glass, and the bottle of bourbon that stood close to his reach confirmed it. He didn't have the job anymore; the *Jack Lucas Morning Show* was history, toast. Gone, too, were the chauffered limo, the fancy apartment, the designer marijuana, the tight-bodied girlfriend, all toast. Swept away. Gone was every vestige of his pampered former life—except one. Somehow Jack Lucas had managed to hold on to one remnant of his glittery past. He still wore the custom-made snakeskin boots with the solid silver fittings. Of course, the boots, like Jack himself, had seen much better days. And, of course, if his creditors had wanted his old shoes, Jack wouldn't have been able to keep even these on his feet.

In his old life, Jack had been a star. In his new life, he was a clerk at an Eighth Avenue videotape rental store, Video Spot. More than that, he lived in a narrow apartment upstairs with the store's owner, Anne Napolitano. Not only clerk, but stud. Hey, it was a living. It was either that or the streets, where Anne had found him and from which she'd rescued him out of the kindness of her heart and an attraction she felt as soon as she laid eyes on him.

Anne Napolitano was very different from the kind of woman Jack was accustomed to. For one thing, she wasn't cool, she was fiery. He never had to persuade her or bribe her to make love; her own passion often outstripped his. Where his preference had always been for ashen-haired thin young women in their twenties with small breasts, Anne was over thirty and as dark as a gypsy, black-eyed, round-hipped, and full-bosomed. She had thick, dark curling hair as tempestuous as she was herself. Where his other lovers had worn casual loose garments of expensive washed silk, Anne wore tight-fitting inexpensive clothing that showed off her voluptuous curves.

Yet, while Anne Napolitano might not be 1990s hip, she was truly street savvy. She possessed both intelligence and a certain kind of wisdom, the common sense that comes through living, tough living.

She was totally uninhibited. When she felt like yelling, Anne yelled. When she felt like crying, she cried. When she was moved to laugh, she threw her head back, and she roared happily until her face got red. In his earlier life as a star, Jack Lucas would not have looked twice at an Anne Napolitano. She wasn't his type. As the daughter of a large, noisy Brooklyn Italian family, Anne was simply too real, too alive, too earthy for the so-called superior Jack to be comfortable with. Now, of course, he had no options. Anne had taken him in, she had fed him, sheltered him, given him a job, made frequent passionate love with him, and mothered him half to death, when she wasn't ordering him around. And there was almost nothing he could do about it.

Now she was standing in front of him, peeved, her fists on her hips, her head cocked.

"Are you going to do a little work today or not?" Anne demanded.

"Out there!" Jack's eyes rolled toward the shop, where a crowd of lunch-hour customers were pawing through the racks of tapes, looking for a movie to keep them company and make the oncoming night less lonely.

"They're not terrorists," Anne pointed out calmly. "Jack, they're just ordinary, normal people, like you and me."

And just how normal was that? Jack asked himself as he took another pull at the bourbon bottle. Who's normal? Edwin Malnick was normal, until, suddenly and without warning, he wasn't.

Anne regarded the whiskey sourly. "Breakfast of Champions, right?"

With a grunt, Jack pulled his ass unwillingly from the chair and made his way into the store. As soon as he hit the selling floor he was confronted and trapped by a fat young woman with frizzy hair and lipstick on her teeth.

"Excuse me. Can you help me, please? I'm at an absolute loss!" The woman spoke rapidly and without taking a breath. "I've been looking for an hour, I'm losing my mind! I'm sort of in the mood for a Katherine Hepburn-y, Cary Grant-y kinda thing, you know, zany? Nothing heavy, I couldn't take heavy. I'm looking for something zany. I need zany."

Jack just stared at her, her anxious babble washing over him without leaving an imprint of meaning.

"Or something modern, maybe," she went on, oblivious. "A Goldie Hawn-y, Chevy Chase-y kind of thing, y'know? I wanna laugh. I have to laugh tonight, really. Oh, oh!" exclaimed the woman, in sudden inspiration. "I know! Do you have anything with that comedian who's on that TV show? What is it . . . you know . . . yeah, *On the Radio*. You know, the guy that says, 'Hey . . . forgive me!' ''

The comic catch phrase woke him out of his lethargy and made him scowl ferociously. *On the Radio* had proved to be the monster hit Jack Lucas had once hoped it would be, only now the star of the show was somebody else. Some asshole whose careless words hadn't cost eight lives.

''I get such a kick outta the way he says that . . . he's so goddamn adorable! Didn't he make a movie? That would be perfect. I need something like that, a funny no-brainy kinda thing. . . .''

Furious, Jack reached under the counter and brought out an adult X-rated video. He handed it to the customer.

''Great!'' She turned the box around to read the title. *''Ordinary Peepholes?''* She threw Jack a puzzled look.

''It's a kind of big titty, spread-cheeky kind of thing,'' Jack explained blandly.

This was too much for Anne, who'd overheard most of it. ''Excuse me,'' she said to the customer. ''I just want to borrow him for a minute.''

''You're gonna love that,'' Jack assured the fat woman, and Anne scowled. Grabbing him tightly by the arm, she led him back into the Video Spot office and closed the door behind them.

''That was a frightening woman.'' Jack shook his head. ''I hate desperate people.''

''Honey, sweetie, you hate people. Period. Are you in one of your moods today, baby?'' Anne demanded, half-amused, half-irritated. ''Is this one of those days when you're in—whaddya call it?—an emotional abyss? Talk to me, 'cause I don't understand these moods.''

''Anne, they're my moods. If you want to understand moods, have one of your own!'' he retorted.

Anne looked peeved, then her features softened.

"Jack, baby," she said quietly, "take the day off, all right? Why don't you go upstairs? I'll cook to-night."

"Okay," he told her grudgingly, going back with a feeling of relief to his tabloid and his bottle.

After dinner, which was lasagna, heavy on the meat sauce the way Jack liked it, they got up from the little dining area and moved over to the only slightly larger living-room area to watch *On the Radio*.

Anne laughed loudly at the sitcom, her dark eyes flashing, her black curls bobbing, her large breasts shaking with enjoyment. Jack threw her a dirty look. He hated her laughing at this show. He hated any-body laughing at this show, but especially Anne. He considered it a form of betrayal.

"Well, it's funny! Whaddya want from me?" She tried to stifle her laughter, but giggles kept escaping.

"It's not funny," Jack growled, furious. "It's sophomoric . . . and mindless . . . and dumb!"

"Then why the hell do we watch it all the time?"

The question, so simple and logical, so painful, stung Jack, and he exploded. He watched it to tor-ture himself, what else? To dwell on what might have been, like a tongue probing into an excruciatingly rotten tooth.

The words flew out of him without punctuation or pause, bitter, envious words that cut him to speak. "Because it makes me feel good to see how not funny it is and how America doesn't know the first thing about funny, which makes it easier not being a famous funny television celebrity because that would just mean that I'm not really talented."

"Hey! For . . . give me!" The actor delivered the line that had made him a star, and the laugh track went crazy with hysterical laughter and applause. This was the moment the home viewers waited for each week, the high point of this top-ten sitcom. The catch phrase that should have made Jack Lucas a household name.

Anne stood up and walked over to Jack's chair, shaking her head in amused sympathy. "You know that you're a sick fuck? I don't know why you torture yourself." She rapped on his head. "Too many thoughts, too crowded in there. You're too self-absorbed." As Jack pushed her hand away in irritation Anne added, "You should read a book." She picked up her plump paperback novel and turned the pages to find her place.

"It's important to think," Jack retorted. "It's what separates us from lentils, and people who read books like"—he glanced contemptuously over at the cover of Anne's book—*"Love Song."* His words came out fuzzy, slurred by drink.

"Great book. Dumb title," Anne said defensively. Jack had hurt her feelings again; he was doing that a lot more these days. What was changing between them? Jack was hiding more and more deeply in the bottle, hiding away from her, too.

"Ya know, you used to like that about me," Anne told him as Jack got up to pour more bourbon into his glass. "You used to say you liked that I didn't make you think all the time. That we could just be together and not think."

He took a deep slug of the booze and threw himself back down on the sofa in front of the television set. "Yeah, well, suicidal paranoics will say anything to get laid."

That did it. Deeply wounded, and really mad now, Anne Napolitano stood up with dignity. "Have another drink," she said bitterly. "It's on the house . . . like everything else!"

And clutching her romance novel, she stalked into the bedroom, slamming the door behind her. Jack didn't notice; he was sunk in gloom, glaring blearily at the tiny screen where some asshole was enjoying the money and fame that was supposed to have been Jack's own, the success that was snatched away before he could even catch a whiff of it. Success that would have been his if some nerd with no life of his own hadn't twisted Jack's own around so fatally. Anne was right; this was self-inflicted torture, but he couldn't pull his eyes away from the television screen or get the idiotic canned laughter out of his ears.

All he could do was drink to dull the pain, so Jack Lucas drank and drank and drank. Yet the pain, instead of dulling, grew sharper and more biting, until he couldn't endure the sitcom or this cramped apartment or his own rotten life for even another sixty seconds. . . .

"Madness!" he yelled, meaning the sitcom, his life, his relationships, and all the shit coming down in the world. He snatched up the bottle of Jack Daniels, now half-empty. Grabbing his coat off the hook on the door, he lumbered down the stairs and out into the night. The front door of the shabby building, with its doorjambs of splintered old wood, caught his favorite Versace raincoat on his way out, a large rotten sliver hooking into it and tearing the preposterously expensive fabric.

Swell. Terrific. As if he didn't look like a bum already, with his long hair uncombed and his face unshaved, a ripped raincoat added that *je ne sais quoi* that made the image complete. Jack Lucas yanked the coat free and the action threw him off balance, which was precarious enough anyway, with all the bourbon he'd been swallowing. He went flying forward, to crash against a garbage can, overturn it, and go sprawling into the garbage-strewn puddle on the wet street.

It was raining, of course. Ugly, cold, wet, pissing rain. What else was missing?

Staggering to his feet, Jack checked the bourbon

bottle to make sure it hadn't broken. Thank heaven for tiny little mercies, it hadn't. He moved away slowly, walking east. East, where the magic of Fifth Avenue beckoned, even though Jack was too drunk to know where he was going. All he knew was that he wanted to get away from Eighth Avenue, as far away as his stumbling boots would carry him. Thunder rumbled in the east, and occasional flashes of lightning eerily lit up the sky.

In a couple of crosstown blocks the neighborhood began to alter dramatically, from Eighth's run-down two- and three-story buildings called "taxpayers"—because all they did was take up room and pay the property taxes—to the gleaming steel-and-glass corporate monoliths of Avenue of the Americas to the pricey real estate of Fifth. Angry and hurting, Jack Lucas could glimpse his old apartment building through the haze of raindrops; lights were on in almost every apartment behind the steel-and-concrete terraces, and the entire building shone like a star. And it was about as far removed from his reach as a star, too. He'd need a spaceship to get back to it. The sight of his old pad depressed Jack unutterably; even looking at it from across the street made him realize just how far from it he'd come, and exactly how low he'd sunk. He was so low, he had to look up to look down.

Jack turned away, heading north, and a few minutes later he found himself across the street from the Plaza Hotel, that classic landmark of the good life. The Plaza, built in the style of a French château on the southern fringes of Central Park, cleverly designed to appear as though the verdant stretches of the park were its own private game preserve.

He knew the Plaza well. Jack was too drunk to really focus, but vague wisps crossed his memory, dim but tantalizing recollections of power lunches in the hotel's elegant Edwardian Room, leisurely and

expensive dinners in the Oak Room, succulent oys-
ters washed down with Muscadet or imported beer
at the Oyster Bar, potent rum drinks and barbecued
munchies at Trader Vic's. Yeah, the Plaza. *His* Plaza.
Jack's shambling feet carried him slowly across the
street to where the patient horses stood hitched to
their fancy ribbon-decked carriages, waiting in the
rain with downcast heads to trot leisured people with
money around Central Park.

As Jack crossed Fifty-eighth Street, the hotel's revolving door turned and disgorged a handsome man
in his early forties, wearing a neat Burberry raincoat
and carrying a crocodile briefcase. Behind him came
a bellman with the luggage, and with him was his
son, a diminutive carbon copy about seven years old,
whose clothing was as expensive as his old man's,
and whose demeanor was exactly as sober. In his
hands the boy was carrying a painted wooden Pinocchio doll with pointed hat, long nose, and staring
eyes. The doll had been acquired at the expensive
FAO Schwartz toy store across Fifth Avenue as a
souvenir of this trip.

They headed for a taxi stand, which usually held
a dozen or more cabs, waiting at the curb for fares
from the Plaza. But tonight, with the rain, the cab
rank was empty, and a cab would be hard to come
by in midtown Manhattan. The man began to wave
his briefcase wildly, trying to hail an empty taxi.

"Hey, buddy? Help a guy out?"

The moment the pair, father and son, reached the
curbside, a homeless panhandler accosted them,
begging for a handout. The man shook his head
brusquely and turned away.

"Help me out with a quarter," the bum insisted.
"C'mon."

"Get away from me," the man demanded, and
the bum, yelling obscenities, reached out and
grabbed hold of the Burberry with his filthy hand.

The personal contact drove the wealthy man into a frenzy. How dare a greasy bum lay a hand on him! Striking out wildly with his briefcase, he caught the panhandler on the temple, but before he could do more damage, the Plaza doorman intervened, driving the bum away and escorting the man into an empty cab his doorman's whistle had summoned.

Jack Lucas stood paralyzed, unable to tear his eyes away from the scene. He didn't see the little boy approaching him until a voice very close to him spoke.

"Mr. Bum?"

Jack looked down. The privileged child stood regarding him gravely for a minute, then he held out the Pinocchio doll. For a moment Jack was confused; what did the kid want?

"Grayson," called his father's voice from inside the taxi. "Grayson, come here at once."

The child thrust the doll into Jack's surprised arms and trotted back across the street obediently. He climbed into the backseat and the taxicab pulled away from the curb with a grinding of gears and disappeared around the corner, heading south on Fifth.

Jack stared after the car until it was out of sight. Then he looked down at the doll in his hands. It stared back at him with wide painted eyes, and its long nose was like some accusing finger. Pinocchio, shit. You know, he almost kind of liked the damn thing. He tucked it under his arm and set off in search of Jiminy Cricket.

It stopped raining, and the homeless were settling down on the wet pavement to fall asleep the best way they could. Some were wrapped in newspapers as a feeble attempt to keep away the cold. Others were better provided for. The lucky ones, or the smarter ones—take your pick—had created beds out of flattened cardboard boxes, and were lying on them instead of on the concrete. For the first time Jack really saw them, this hopeless band of outcast men and women with no roof over their heads. For two years he had lived virtually in the shadow of these people, but had never really seen them before. Even in his drunken state, they made him shudder as he realized how close, how precariously close to them he himself was.

The equestrian statue of Victory leading the horse of General William Tecumseh ("War is hell") Sherman had been recently regilded at enormous public expense. Even in darkness it shone now like a lit beacon made of solid gold. The Union general who had destroyed Atlanta and burned a mile-wide swath through Georgia from Atlanta to the sea sat boldly on his horse, while the goddess of Victory, Nike, held the laurel wreath of the conquerer high. But that war ended more than a century ago; nobody really cared about Sherman except the pigeons, the Japanese tourists with their cameras, and the footsore who sank gratefully down on the base of the statue to rest.

Jack Lucas slumped down below the statue and leaned his back against the cold marble of the plinth. Taking a long swig from his nearly empty bottle, he set Pinocchio on his knee and regarded him with solemn melancholy.

"You ever read any Nietzsche?" he asked the doll, who didn't answer.

"Nietzsche says that there are two kinds of people in the world. People who are destined for greatness, like . . . Walt Disney . . . and . . . Hitler . . . and then there's the rest of us. He called us the Bungled and the Botched. We get teased. We sometimes get close to greatness, but we never get there. We're the expendable masses. We get pushed in front of trains, take poisoned aspirins, get gunned down in Dairy

Queens.'' He took another drink, almost draining the bottle.

"You wanna hear my new title for my biography, my little Italian friend?'' Pinocchio looked back, and Jack perceived a yes in that painted wooden smile. *It Was No Fucking Picnic: the Jack Lucas Story.* Like it? Just nod yes or no.'' He tilted the doll's head up and down to say yes. *"Il Nouva Está Fuckin' Picnicko,''* he essayed in a kind of bastard mock Italian to make the wooden doll understand better. Did it work? Jack thought so.

"You're a good kid,'' he told Pinocchio almost fondly. "Just say no to drugs. . . .'' Raising the bottle, Jack took one more drink. Depressed as he was, that last drink pushed him over the edge from melancholy into desolation. He saw himself now as lost, a stranger to the world, completely cut off and shut out from the rest of humanity, and in his drunken state he knew it with remarkable clarity.

"You ever get the feeling sometimes that you're being punished for your sins?'' Jack asked the silent doll. Punished for my sins, he thought. As though there was enough punishment in this world to pay off what I did . . .

Four

Jack felt calm, bathed in a peace that was almost beautiful. There's nothing like making a decision to give a man's mind a rest. It was such a simple decision, really, he thought as he fastened the heavy-cement block around his right ankle. Such a commonsense answer to all his problems; why hadn't he thought of it before? He wound strips of his trousers around the second block and attached it to his left ankle, tucking dear little Pinocchio inside. At least he wouldn't go alone. He had a friend now, a friend who might be a little short on facial expression and vocabulary, but one who didn't judge him, who didn't argue, who always had a cheerful smile for Jack Lucas. They'd go together.

Jack stood up and moved his feet. Great; the blocks were heavy enough so that, no matter how he might struggle to swim, they would do their job and pull him down to the bottom of the filthy, oily river. The East River. Jack Lucas still had class, no matter what. When he took himself out, he'd go in style, on the snobbish east side, where he belonged. No measly Hudson River for a star.

Somebody once said that to the rational mind, life is a race between natural death and suicide. Jack Lucas was just about to lose that race.

There were a few drops left in the Jack Daniel's bottle, and Jack tilted his head back and drained them. Jack and Jack. The lyric from his program's theme song kept turning around in his head . . . *Hit the road, Jack.* . . . How appropriate, how fitting. He didn't intend to come back no more. He flung the empty bottle away and smiled to hear it shatter on the concrete pavement. Another ending.

In the cold moonlight, under the promenade, the river looked serene and inviting, even beckoning. Here is surcease, it said. Here is rest for the weary. O, come all you faithless. . . . Jack took a step forward, mesmerized by the light reflecting from its surface. It was time to go. He took another step.

There was a harsh grinding of gears and the squealing of heavy tires; car doors slammed, and the sound of ugly laughter broke the promenade's silence. But thanks to his drunken oblivion and his fuzzy focus on suicide, Jack didn't hear any of it.

"What's going on?" demanded a rough voice behind him, and this time Jack turned, only to be blinded by bright white headlights. Lured by the promise of the river, he hadn't noticed the 4×4 that was now parked about ten yards away. Two men got out and started toward him. As his eyes became accustomed to the glare of the headlights Jack could see that they weren't men at all, but boys. Maybe eighteen, nineteen. Maybe only seventeen. One of them wore a leather jacket and carried a baseball bat in his right hand. The other wore a windbreaker.

Both of them were carrying cans of gasoline.

Jack was shit-faced, but not too drunk to comprehend the significance of the gas cans. A chill of fear ran through his veins and he began to sweat ice water.

"I said, what's going on?" the boy in the leather jacket demanded, this time in a louder voice as he came up close to Jack. "What are you doing here, man?" His face was menacing, his eyes hooded and angry.

This was going to be bad; Jack knew it instinctively, but his brain was too befuddled from drink for him to react quickly. Even if he were sober, with the heavy cement blocks attached to his legs, he wouldn't be able to run. Before he could answer, the boy in the leather jacket got him in the gut with the bat, hard, knocking the wind out of him and making him sink to his knees, retching and gasping hoarsely to catch his breath. The other boy set the gasoline cans down and began to unscrew them.

Jack Lucas had read about cases like this, where juvenile delinquents set bums on fire, usually sleeping bums. The boys almost never got caught, but the bums died. Every year at least thirty homeless men died that hideous way in New York, screaming in agony as the flames devoured the flesh from their bones. Now it was going to be his turn. Instead of sinking quietly into the cool embrace of the peaceful water, Jack's death would be literally hell on earth, the fire this time. Punishment for his sins, and with a vengeance. No, he didn't want this, not this kind of death. It was too big a price to pay. Between the terrible fear and the harsh pain from the blow to his belly, Jack's mind was shocked into a state approaching sobriety. His body, though, out of condition, limbs paralyzed by alcohol, continued to betray him.

"You shouldn't hang around this neighborhood," growled the boy in the leather jacket, with a grin of malice. He kicked Jack in the side, just to drive his point home, and because he enjoyed it.

"I . . . I was just leaving," Jack gasped, his arms wound tightly around his body, protecting his belly. His eye never left the lethal cans of gasoline.

"People spend a lot of hard-earned money for this neighborhood," the tough continued, prodding Jack with the end of the bat. "It's not fair, looking out their windows to see your ass asleep on the streets."

"Yes . . . I . . . I agree."

"That's good. That's very good." The hoodlum in the leather jacket grinned and turned to his friend. "You believe this drunk?" The delinquent wearing the windbreaker shook his head no. "Me, neither. Man, get the fuckin' gas." He grabbed Jack by the hair, to keep him from getting away.

Windbreaker handed Leather Jacket the gas can; Leather Jacket lifted it high over his head. The twisted malicious grin never left his face as Leather Jacket allowed a thin stream of the flammable fuel to dribble over Jack's clothing. This was the good part; the fun was just getting started.

"No . . . no, *please,*" Jack whimpered. He didn't want to die this way. In fact, now that he was pretty close to sober, he didn't want to die at all. But certainly not as a shrieking human torch.

The boys were laughing now, and Jack Lucas's body was drenched in gasoline. It was hopeless; he couldn't fight, and even if he could, there was no way he could take them both on. It was the end for him and Pinocchio. Leather Jacket had him tightly by the hair, pulling his head back. Jack closed his eyes while regrets of every kind crowded into his brain, too late.

"Hold, varlet, or feel the sting of my shaft! Unhand that errant knight in the name of Blanche des Fleurs!"

The voice came ringing out of the darkness, strong, deep, clear, and dramatic. The adolescent hoodlums turned in surprise, their eyes searching the shadows. Even Jack opened his eyes, startled.

"What the fu . . . ? Ugggghh!" An arrow came whistling through the air and slammed hard into Windbreaker's groin. It was an arrow with a rubber suction tip, from a child's archery set, but even so it hurt like hell.

Leather Jacket dropped Jack's head with a snarl, ready to rumble. Jack peered into the shadows and a small figure took a step forward. My God, it was someone out of an heroic epic of the Middle Ages! Robin Hood or somebody. Was he dreaming? He saw a long cloak, a hat with a feather, a bow over the shoulder, a quiver of arrows. He had to be dreaming! He must have jumped in after all. This whole episode, even the teenage hoodlums, had to be one last hallucination of a drowning man, sinking to the bottom of the East River with bricks strapped to his legs.

Then the figure took another step forward; now he could be seen much more clearly in the light of the street lamp. The cloak was not a cloak but a filthy, ragged army blanket pinned clumsily at the shoulder, the rakish cap, a woman's discarded sequined beret into which twigs and leaves had been somehow fastened. This was no medieval hero, but an ordinary, common tramp. Only crazier, a lot crazier.

Yet Jack could see that there was nothing common or ordinary about the small man's face. It shone with a calm intelligence and twinkled with humor. The eyes were wide and innocent, the nose long and straight, the mouth smiling, and the chin covered by a dark beard. There was no fear in this face, and no menace, but no mistaking it, there was real insanity there. The man appeared to be fairly young, not more than thirty-five, despite the maturity of his beard.

"It's just a bum," Leather Jacket snarled. He brandished the gas can. "You know, there's enough in here for the two of you."

The small man did not appear fazed by the threat. "You speak English?" he roared. "Let the bum go, dipshit! Mendacity! Why are two attractive city squires like you abusing a knight like this?"

Leather Jacket's lip curled in disgust. "You a faggot?"

"Faggot?" The stranger seemed surprised by the word, and considered it with seriousness. "No, but I do believe in faeries. I advise you to let him go," he added quietly.

"You advise us!" A harsh laughter escaped Leather Jacket's lips. This dumb faggot was gonna get it. Both these bums were gonna get it.

The stranger chuckled. "You're outnumbered, son." He waved his hand.

Other figures slowly materialized out of the shadows behind him. They were homeless vagrants, three of them, each one perhaps harmless, even pathetic, but put them together in the dark and the sight of them was something unnerving. One of them was mumbling to himself, obviously a psychotic. Actually, they were probably all crazy as bedbugs, especially their shabby Robin Hood of a leader. This was very creepy. Even Jack was afraid of them, and the two adolescents kept shifting their gaze to make certain they weren't surrounded.

"It's the fuckin' Night of the Living Dead," whispered one, not without fear. Weapons seemed definitely called for. Both delinquents pulled out their switchblades and snapped them open. Windbreaker appeared nervous; he didn't like what was starting to happen here. This was supposed to be more predictable; it wasn't like it was the first time they'd pulled this stunt. But Leather Jacket made an effort to maintain his macho bravado.

Jack Lucas only stared, mystified and a little alarmed. What was going down here? The delinquents might be homicidal, but at least they weren't irrational. On the other hand, his rescuer definitely appeared to be delusional, possibly psychotic, and maybe even murderous. Was Jack about to go from the fire to the frying pan?

"C'mon," Leather Jacket urged his companion.

"Go for it! What the hell are they gonna do? They can't do nothin'."

"*Nothing! They can do nothing!*" The stranger cried out in pained exasperation at the abysmal grammar. "*Gentlemen!*" He took a step or two backward into the shadows and raised his hand. It was a signal to his little band.

Immediately, and stupefyingly, the bums burst into song, caroling about New York in June and a Gershwin tune. They were a country mile away from the tune, some of the lyrics were wrong, and one of them was totally out of sync, yet the ragtag little chorus put real heart into the old standard. It was the single most surreal moment of Jack Lucas's life.

"Shit!" Leather Jacket spat, infuriated. He had some dim comprehension that his masculinity was being mocked here, and it was time to kick some ass. He brandished the knife, ready to use it. The bums' leader smiled genially, and his face lit up like a kid's at Christmas.

"Oh, look, it's showtime." He beamed. "Y'know, boys," he continued in a benign, almost fatherly voice, taking off the sequined cap he was wearing, reaching into it and pulling out a long sock with a round bulge in the toe. As he continued speaking he twirled the sock high over his head until it formed a perfect circle like a gaucho's bolo, achieving momentum until it was only a kind of circular blur.

"There are only three things in the world you need . . . respect for all kinds of life, a good bowel movement on a regular basis, and a nice navy blazer. Oh, and one more thing! Never . . . take . . . your . . . eyes . . . off . . . the . . . ball!" With the last word and a snap of his wrist, he let the sock fly with deadly accuracy.

The sock whizzed through the air, catching Leather Jacket square between the eyes with the tennis ball that was tucked into the toe. The boy groaned in pained shock and, dropping his switch-blade knife, rubbed at the lump on his head. The merry band's leader smiled with simple pleasure and reached for another sock.

"Of course," he remarked conversationally, starting to twirl his second weapon, "the ability to bean a shithead can be a fabulous advantage." He appeared to be enjoying himself immensely.

Windbreaker had already seen one graphic example of the murderous effectiveness of the crazy's homemade weapon. He didn't need to see another, especially since he appeared to be the target of this one. With a yell, he took to his heels, darting past the bums into the 4×4. With a grinding of gears, he peeled rubber, leaving his friend behind in the hands of God only knew what.

The leader strode swiftly over to Jack, who was huddled on the cold concrete. He bent to retrieve the delinquent's knife and asked Jack with gentle concern, "Are you all right?"

Jack Lucas flinched as though he'd been struck and shrank away from the bum's touch. He was completely disoriented, overcome by the alcohol, the swift turn of events, his fear, and the nauseating reek of the gasoline that covered him head to foot. "Please don't hurt me," he begged.

"Why?" asked Robin Hood, sounding suddenly perfectly sane. "So you can be healthy when you jump? Nah!"

Next to him, the boy in the leather jacket was still groaning and clutching at his head. Working quickly, the leader pulled a rope out from under his tattered blanket cloak and tied Leather Jacket's hands behind him, making neat unbreakable knots. Then he stood and helped Jack gently to his feet. He handed the knife to Jack, who took it with a shudder of revulsion and hurled it away, into the river. Taking Jack's elbow, he began to lead him away.

"You can't leave me tied up out here alone, you fucking faggot!" screamed the boy, panic diluting the anger in his voice. He struggled with his bonds, but the rope held good and tight. The delinquent in the leather jacket had been tied in a deliberately awkward position, kneeling on the sidewalk, his butt up in the air.

"You're not going to be alone. Come and geeeet it," called the stranger invitingly, and two of the bums began to shuffle forward. The boy moaned in fear.

Jack found it hard to stand, let alone walk. His gut was on fire from the blow with the bat, and every muscle in his neck and shoulders ached with tension. "I need a drink," he muttered, more to himself than to his rescuer.

"Hey, I know a fabulous place with great ambience." The small man beamed. Kneeling down, he unfasted the cement blocks from Jack's legs and placed the Pinocchio doll into Jack's arms with an almost graceful tenderness. Once again, he took Jack by the arm, steering him along.

All Jack Lucas wanted now was to see his home, a bathtub, a bottle, and Anne. The last thing in the world he wanted was to go along with this loony derelict who suffered from the delusion that he was some kind of white knight. But, somehow, he didn't seem to have a choice. Reluctantly, still trying to figure out the dizzying events of the past ten minutes, Jack stumbled along behind his savior.

Five

For most of his life Jack had heard and used the phrase "the dregs of humanity" without once giving much thought or understanding to it. Now, unexpectedly, he was right in the middle of them. Real-life low-down dregs, the human sludge left in the bottom of the barrel when the good stuff was all used up. It was not a pretty sight. It was a scene out of Gorky, or worse, Dante. *The Lower Depths* maybe, or one of the waiting rooms of hell. Even drunk, Jack Lucas recognized that these people had not only touched bottom, bottom had become their zip code. Here before his eyes, in the unsavory flesh, was the living personification of Nietzsche's Bungled and Botched.

The forgotten, the nameless, the homeless, the hopeless, the mentally ill, the alkies, the druggies, a ragtag army beyond redemption, people who had long forgotten the ordinary daily commerce of the world, were gathered here, in the litter-strewn area underneath the steel stanchions of the Manhattan Bridge. Above their heads, the bridge's heavy suspension cables sang an eerie wind song while swaying in the gusts of the evening. Below, a cluster of men—mostly men, with one or two women so tattered and filthy that their gender was unrecognizable—sat around on the ground like a defeated army, their generals dead, their troops decimated, their host scattered, their eagles lost, seized by the Goths.

Many of these people owned nothing apart from the threadbare clothing on their backs. Others, equally if not more pathetic, had collected paltry, useless bits and pieces, culled from what the real world had cast aside. These treasures they kept always close by them, tied up in garbage bags on which they slept, or piled high into rickety shopping carts lifted from the local supermarkets, over which they stood a weary, endless watch.

Some of them owned mongrel dogs, who scavenged from fire to fire, begging for crusts. There were even two or three cats who called this place home, exchanging their affection for human warmth. The cats kept a large part of the vermin population at bay.

Athough it was a motley and unrelated assemblage, Jack realized that most of its members had something besides homelessness in common—alcohol. They drank whatever they could get their hands on, mostly pint bottles of cheap fortified sweet wine, which they bought in Korean liquor shops with the dimes and nickels they cadged during the day. By now, almost all of them were drunk or well on their way to being drunk. In this, Jack Lucas found himself their blood brother. If he'd been sober, it might have made him think. Yet he still felt superior to this human refuse; he had class, he had education, and most of all, he had somewhere he could go.

This was the downtime, the night hours when these homeless could gather together here on their turf, light a few fires in garbage cans to provide some semblance of warmth. Here they could drink, argue, reminisce, trade lies, weep, and watch the city rats, some of them bigger than house cats, go scurrying by on their unspeakable night errands.

Grinning cheerfully, Jack's new pal, his cicerone, his personal Virgil, led him right into the heart of this urban jungle and sat him down against the bridge's pillar so that he could socialize and make friends. The river's rankness rose on the night air and assaulted Jack's nostrils. On the East River, the night traffic went by. Old freighters of dubious registry, tugboats, and garbage scows, paddling through the scummy waters. Above them, on the FDR Drive, Mercedes and BMWs headed north to Sutton Place.

For the bearded man, this gathering under the bridge was a gala social occasion, the celebration of his triumph against the juvenile delinquents. For Jack, it was a nightmare from which he struggled in vain to wake up.

What the hell was he doing here, in the middle of the night, with a dull ache in his gut, stinking of gasoline and bourbon, listening to the garbage boats chugging by on the river and to this bunch of board-certified crazies raving on, arguing about the profundities of life? He had to be as nutty as they were. Jack sat as far away from them as possible and tried to tune out, just like his Pinocchio doll, but their loud lunatic words kept drifting into his unwilling consciousness.

"There ain't no justice in life," the large black man in the old Vietnam combat jacket was growling. "There's just satisfaction. And the death penalty's just another violation of my constitutional right to satisfaction, goddamn it!"

The long-haired pimply kid, who looked like a refugee from the flower-child 1960s, leaned forward to make his point. "So you mean, if somebody like killed your mother, you wouldn't want him dead?"

"Sure I would!" The black man's brow furrowed indignantly. "But *I* should get to kill him, goddamn it!"

The Irishman agreed. He nodded his head vigorously, and the ash from his burning cigarette dropped all over his ancient filthy overcoat. "He gets to kill him," he explained earnestly to the hippie. "That's democracy, see?"

Jack Lucas shook his head. "This is it," he mumbled to himself. "I'm in hell. Damned to an eternity of idiotic conversation."

"Great place, huh?" His guide, the perfect host, the poor man's Robin Hood, beamed cheerily at him. He appeared to be genuinely happy here, and at home. He seemed to know everybody, and everybody knew him. Repelled, Jack turned away without reply.

A bloodcurdling scream ripped the air. Jack jumped in his skin and looked around. It was the Irishman, caught up suddenly in the whirlpool of his madness, being sucked into the vortex and screaming his lungs out in horror. God alone could guess what his hallucination might be. Then a second scream rang out. Robin Hood joined him, just to keep him company, and the two men howled together like a pair of starving coyotes.

Then, as suddenly as they'd started, they stopped screaming. "How are you tonight?" the Irishman asked pleasantly, as though nothing out of the ordinary had happened here. The nameless terrors of five seconds ago were history now, forgotten.

"Not bad, John, and you?" Robin Hood's eyes crinkled happily from the warmth of his smile.

"Can't complain." The Irishman took a long drag on his cigarette and flicked off the live ash. It flew through the air and landed on Jack Lucas's gas-soaked sleeve. Immediately, the gas ignited and burst into flame.

"Oh, fuck!" Jack scrambled clumsily to his feet, his face a distorted mask of fear. His raincoat sleeve was on fire, burning merrily, and Jack tore at it, dancing frantically around, yelling and fumbling until he managed to get it off his body and hurl it to the ground. After he stomped the blaze out, he checked for damage. The fire had scorched his hand, which began to throb very painfully.

It was a spectacular break in the evening's activities. Jack had just put on a show for them, and the bums, appreciative, broke into enthusiastic applause. There were cheers and whistles. Only the black man grumbled, because he'd been holding center stage, and Jack's crazy antics had taken the group's attention away from him. "Crazy fuck," he muttered.

"So what do you think of the death penalty?" the hippie kid asked the Irishman. Show was over, and everything was back to normal. Unless Jack Lucas burst into flame again, he was no longer interesting to them.

"Death's definitely a penalty. It ain't no fuckin' gift. Life's too goddamn short."

Their words blurred in Jack's ears. He was really starting to crash now. Fatigue was numbing him and he was a very long way from home. Gathering up his sodden raincoat, he started to take his leave of the little gathering. "I better be going. . . ."

But the Irishman wasn't about to let him get away so easily. "Have a drink." He pushed his bottle into Jack's face, and when Jack waved it away, he roared, "Have a drink, damn it!"

Remembering the screaming, Jack thought it best not to argue the point. Accepting the dirty bottle, he took a pull. The fiery liquor, cheap and rough and totally unlike the smooth expensive bourbon Jack was accustomed to, scorched a painful path down his throat and into his belly. He bent over, hacking, coughing, trying to breathe.

"I think they like you," his new friend said shyly, and raised his hand. At once, as if it was a signal, his little band of bums broke into "that song about liking June in New York" Totally inappropriate and completely out of left field, but they seemed to enjoy it.

By now, the fumes of the cheap booze had risen to Jack's brain, making him dizzy. He had the sudden sinking realization that he was about to pass out, here, under an abutment of the Manhattan Bridge with only the terminally weird for company. As he blacked out, the last thing he remembered hearing was the hippie yelling enthusiastically, "You were phenomenal tonight, Parry. Fuckin' Super-Bum!"

Super-Bum? Jack wondered drowsily, and then the darkness came down and closed everything off.

Six

It was the sound, the drip-drip-dripping of the water, one slow agonizing drop at a time, that made Jack Lucas finally open his eyes. He turned his head to see where the water was coming from. Big mistake. He should not have tried to move. The headache from hell grabbed his eye sockets and the base of his skull and twisted, hard. Nausea made a lump of burning bile rise in his throat, and he shuddered, falling back on the bed. Shit, was he hung over!

Where the hell was he? Bed. He was in bed. Or rather, *on* bed. Only it wasn't exactly a bed, in that it didn't have pillows, or sheets, or even a box spring. Jack was lying on a mattress on the floor. Except for his beloved boots, he was still fully clothed. Floor? What floor? Gingerly, he lifted his head up again, and the hangover kicked in, but he opened only one eye and gradually his vision cleared.

He was in a basement somewhere. Pipes ran overhead; he could hear them banging and gurgling, and one of them was obviously doing the dripping. The floor was concrete. A boiler stood nearby, making the room almost intolerably warm. Every few seconds live steam puffed out of it. Right; he was in the boiler room of a basement. A boiler room, yet it was furnished . . . in a very strange way. Where the hell was he and how the hell did he get here?

"Hi! Welcome back! How are you feeling?" A

cheerful voice, bright blue eyes, a cherubic bearded face, a big dopey smile, and slowly it all came back.

Last night. The narrow escape from those hoodlums with the gas cans. The river. He'd tried to drown himself, but he'd been attacked. His belly still ached horribly from the baseball-bat attack; it must be deeply bruised. He flashed on his companion, with his raggedy cloak and his homemade weapons. This mental case and his merry band of schizos had saved his life. Vaguely he remembered the later scene under the Manhattan Bridge, and Jack realized that he must have passed out there. But why had be been dragged here? What did this lunatic want from him?

"Have I died?" Jack muttered, squinting through his one good eye, the other closed to keep the killer headache at bay. He'd assassinate for a cigarette, even though his mouth tasted like the prop wash of a circus parade.

The small man's eyes crinkled up merrily, and he let out a roar of laughter. "Oh, no, no, nonononono . . . not yet."

The laughter penetrated Jack's hangover like an alarm siren, and the headache escalated to new heights of agony. "If you're going to murder me, fine. Just don't laugh." Shifting his weight on the mattress, Jack decided to try to move. It wasn't happening.

"No, no, sorry. Easy, easy," the bearded man soothed him, taking Jack around the shoulders. "Wanna get up? There you go." With surprising strength, he eased Jack up into a sitting position. "Take it real slow, now. Take a few breaths. Good, that's good."

Jack was surprised to discover that he actually felt a little better sitting up. He swung his legs over the side of the mattress, and his feet touched the concrete. Oh, wonderful. No boots. His precious Tony

Lamas with the real silver toe caps were nowhere to be seen. They'd been ripped off, either by those winos under the Manhattan Bridge or by this friendly, smiling fruitcake.

Making a huge effort, Jack stood up. He felt a little wobbly, but his legs still worked. Slowly, he looked around at the small living space the man had created here in this basement boiler room. He opened both his eyes to see better. Talk about weird!

The place was a mess, dirty and disordered. Garbage and stale food were everywhere, and some of it had rotted beyond color and smell to become something unidentifiable. There was an incredible accumulation of rubbish and trash, obviously collected from the street. In addition to the mattress on the floor, there were a couple of wobbly kitchen chairs and a rickety table with its shorty leg propped up by books. These must also have been rescued from the street before the garbage trucks got there. At the center of this rubbish, propped up against a wall, sat Pinocchio, with his unblinking eyes and his painted-on wooden smile. The only illumination in the room came from a bare bulb hanging from a string, which was probably just as well. Strong light might have destroyed the ambience, the romance of the surroundings.

This seemed to Jack to be the flopping place of a homeless bum, but with three important differences. The first thing was that there were books everywhere, hundreds of them, hardcovers and paperbacks, books that appeared to have been read and reread. The second thing was that the walls were decorated as no bum had decorated a wall before. Jack stared at the walls in astonishment.

On one wall were taped pictures taken from books and magazines and art postcards. They were all medieval in theme—knights, castles, ladies fair, scenes of jousting and chivalry; some Jack recognized as well-known illustrations and famous paintings. What they had in common was a beauty and a serenity and an evocation of a time and place dead for five hundred years, a world no one had experienced except in books in half a millennium.

On the opposite wall was a huge poster of a knight in full armor, helmed, corseleted, greaved, bucklered, shielded, and weaponed cap-a-pie, riding straight at the viewer on an armored and caparisoned war-horse. As though the warrior knight himself were not ferocious enough, someone had taken a red Magic Marker and slashed great crimson streaks over the knight and his horse, streaks that looked exactly like hellish tongues of flame. The effect was menacing, nightmarish, totally surreal. Unconsciously intimidated, Jack took a backward step, away from the picture.

He looked around him again, noticing for the first time that some of the rubbish in the room possessed a definite medieval character. A few hubcaps were fashioned into small shields on straps of old rope, and painted with strange devices. The chrome detail from an old Ford Fairlane appeared to be some kind of crudely fashioned weapon. Even the odd rags of clothing strewn about could be seen to bear the aspect of apparel from the Middle Ages. And then there was the alcove.

The third big difference between this basement hovel and an ordinary bum's room was set apart in a small alcove. In contrast to the mess in the rest of the place, the alcove was pristine, even beautiful. Many candles were lit, as though dedicated on an altar. And there *was* an altar of sorts, although the objects being venerated were bizarre indeed. Among them Jack recognized a Chinese-food takeout carton and a pair of chopsticks, a popular junky romance novel of the kind that women read, some imitation jewels, and the picture of a beautiful, virginal

maiden with flowers in her long flowing golden hair.
It was a print of a very famous Botticelli painting,
one of the treasures of the fifteenth century. This
was obviously some kind of shrine, but to what kind
of deity Jack Lucas didn't know and didn't want to
know. The whole business struck him as really
creepy.

"Where am I?" he asked in a low voice. This
goddamn place was spooking him.

"My domicile, my humble abode, my neck of the
woods," answered the bearded man cheerfully,
perched on one of the kitchen chairs. "Want something to eat? Because your stomach must be a real
tabula rasa after last night." He threw the Latin term
off easily, without stopping for breath. "How about
a fruit pie?" From somewhere, the man produced
something greenish and sticky in his grimy hands
and shoved it under Jack Lucas's nauseated nose.

Jack recoiled instinctively. "No, thanks . . . hey,
listen—"

"You're right about that one." The fellow chucked
the little pie across the room. "I was off by about a
couple of months. It's nice to have company," he
added, rather shyly.

"Uh, where are my shoes?"

"They're—" The man broke off and leaped suddenly off the chair, his attention focusing on the
overhead pipes. "What?" he yelled. "I've got company!"

Startled, Jack looked up but could see nothing.
"Where . . . ?"

"What?" The man was yelling at somebody, but
nobody was there.

"What?" echoed Jack, really unnerved now. The
guy was talking to the air, and from the looks of it
the air was answering back.

"I knew it! I knew it last night! I did, too! He's
the one!"

The one? The one what?

The small man came up close to Jack and whispered loudly, "Can you keep a secret?"

Backing off, Jack shook his head no.

"Good, because do you know what the Little People told me?"

"The Little People?" Jack echoed nervously, humoring the madman until he could make his escape.

"They said you're the One."

"The one what?"

The bearded man whirled and yelled up at the ceiling, "Shut up! Get away from here!" He darted to a shelf and grabbed up a can of air freshener. "This will get them out of here!" He began to spray the room with broad, sweeping strokes of the can. The chemically fake wintergreen smell and the choking spray brought on a wave of fresh nausea in Jack. Unable to breathe, he began to cough.

"Oh, God! I've got a right to say something!" the man was shrieking now, sounding desperate. "Leave him alone! I mean, you're tying my hands here!" He sprayed again, gassing his hallucination. "I'm sorry about this," he apologized to Jack. "They say you're not ready to know yet."

"I'm not," Jack agreed, itching to get out of there this minute. "My shoes—"

"He is, too!" yelled the crazy man, with another sweeping spritz of the air freshener. "Fuck off, now! Beat it! Oh, yeah? Fly up there! Yeah . . ."

Desperate to escape from the deadly miasma of wintergreen, Jack backed into the alcove shrine.

"Heyyyy! You can't be in there!" The note of panic in the other man's voice brought him out of there quickly.

"You're frightening him!" the crazy accused the air. Jack backed away until his back was almost against the red-hot boiler, but the small man pursued him, kneeling down close by and peering into his face.

"Do you know who I am?"

Jack saw that the bearded man was regarding him with an earnest attention tinged with anxiety. Better play along.

"Uh . . . I'm drawing a blank." Gotta get out of here, he thought. Where the fuck are my boots?

"Well, take a guess. *Let him guess!*" he roared at thin air, reaching for the can of air spray again.

Anything but that. "Uh . . . gee . . . well . . . you seem to be some kind of vigilante."

"No, no." The bearded man shook his head vigorously. "I mean, of course, that happened along the way, but no." He leaned closer, and Jack found himself looking into a pair of bright blue eyes that sparkled with delusion. "No, I'm a knight on a very special quest."

"A quest?" echoed Jack.

"Take a look at this!" Grabbing something up, the little man thrust it proudly under Jack's nose. "What's this?"

Jack looked. "A hood ornament?"

"No, it's a sword. For the quest. But I need help, and that's why *they* sent you."

They? Oh, right. "The Little—"

"Yes. The Little People. They work for Him. So do I."

"Him?" Jack asked, certain that he didn't really want to know.

The small man leaned even closer to whisper. "God. I'm the janitor of God." Seeing Jack's horrified face, he added hastily, "Hey, I know how you feel. Hard to believe, right? Well, just listen. . . ."

Settling himself into one of the rickety kitchen chairs, he explained while Jack listened reluctantly, calculating the distance between the small man and the door, wondering if he could make it to the street without shoes.

"*They* came to *me* about a year ago. I was sitting on the john having one of those really satisfying bowel movements . . . you know the ones, that border on the mystical." And here, he screwed up his face to illustrate, straining, straining, then uttering a long, blissful sigh of release while his face looked positively beatific. "And there they were, just floating around. Hundreds of the cutest little fat people. And then they spoke. They said I had been chosen to get back something special that He had lost. But my part might be very dangerous. I said, 'Hold it right there!' You start seeing floating little fat people that tell you you're on a mission for God, that'll slap you with some really heavy thoughts. I said, 'Give me a sign.' Then *they* said, 'Look at *Progressive Architecture,* Feb. eighty-eight . . . page thirty-three.' That's pretty specific."

Leaping eagerly from his chair, the small man raced over to a pile of magazines and riffled through them, finding one and bringing it over to Jack. He leafed through the pages to find the right one, then shoved it under Jack's nose. "And there it was, plain as day!" he finished triumphantly.

Jack Lucas was locked in here with a man who heard voices and saw visions on the crapper, yet somehow he'd been sucked into the guy's story, nutty as it was. Despite himself, Jack looked at the glossy magazine. The caption running across a double-page spread read: *Real Estate Billionaire Langdon Carmichael's Tower of Power.* It was a five-page feature story, complete with color photos, about how Carmichael had acquired a nineteenth-century armory on Fifth Avenue and had spent ten million big ones fixing it up as a fortified mansion to live in.

"Langdon Carmichael?" Jack looked at the other man, puzzled.

"No, no. Right there. See it?" With a grimy finger, the bum pointed. On the page was a photo of the tycoon in his newly furnished library. Carmichael was standing proudly in front of a bookcase holding first editions and other precious objects. One of the objects, a silver goblet, had been circled heavily in black crayon.

"It's the Grail. The Holy Grail." The small man sighed deeply and with passion, and a look of perfect ecstasy made his features shine.

"What?" Jack Lucas could not believe his ears.

"It's God's symbol of divine grace," the bearded man said very quietly and reverently.

This was too much, even for Jack. "The Holy Grail? Some billionaire has the Holy Grail sitting in his library on Fifth Avenue?" he demanded.

"I know! You can't imagine how surprised I was. Who would think you could find anything divine on the upper east side!"

That tore it. With his boots or without them, Jack was outta here. "Listen, I don't mean to enrage you or anything, but . . . I'm not the One. I'm not *any* One." He started to push past the small man, whose face paled in consternation.

"I think you're a very nice . . . very nice psychotic man," Jack continued, looking for the exit. "I really appreciate what you did for me. It was a very brave and noble thing—"

"Oh, please, you're embarrassing me—"

"I wish you all the luck in the world. When you get the Grail, I'm sure I'll be seeing lots of you on various talk shows."

Tears filled the bearded man's eyes. He became visibly agitated. "But I can't. . . . But I can't get it!" he cried, and ran over to the poster of the armed knight. Picking up the red marker, he began to add more crimson streaks to the man and the horse. His arm swept over the picture in frantic strokes. "He

. . . he's out there . . . I don't know if . . . He's always out there, see . . . and—'' He looked pleadingly at Jack. "See, you don't know him, that's why you're the One . . . you can get it—''

"I'm not the One!'' Jack shouted. Then, in a more placating tone, he said, "Listen, forget about the shoes. I'll just take a cab. Good-bye, uh—'' He suddenly realized he didn't know the fellow's name. No, wait a minute. What had that bum called him last night? "Uh, Garry.''

"Parry,'' the small man corrected him quietly. He looked very disappointed, on the brink of tears.

"Parry. I'm Jack.''

"I know.'' It was obvious now that Jack was really going, so Parry ran to a little space behind the boiler and retrieved Jack's silver-capped boots. Picking up the Pinocchio doll, he handed doll and boots to Jack.

"Thanks,'' Jack said, taking the boots. "You can keep the doll.''

"Thanks a million,'' Parry said gratefully, and his mood shifted. "Now that you know where we are, don't be a stranger. And I'll give you a buzz and we'll get together and get this thing off the ground. Take care of yourself, Jack. Give my love to the wife.''

Halfway out the door, Jack turned. "I'm not married,'' he said.

"Really? You look married.''

What kind of thing was that to say? It was an odd remark, even for Parry. In what way did he look married? Jack shook his head and, clutching his Tony Lamas tightly against his chest, made good his escape.

The door from the boiler room led out into the rest of the basement, which was lighted, clean, and well cared for. Jack had no idea where he was, but it had all the earmarks of a high-rent building. Which way out? Ahead of him, down a long hallway, he could see an exit door, which led, he presumed, to the stairs up to the lobby. His head still throbbing from the hangover, his burned hand starting to act up again, Jack pulled his boots on and headed for the exit.

"Hey, hey, where you comin' from?"

The sudden voice took him by surprise. Halfway up the stairs, Jack turned to see an irate black man heading toward him. The man wore coveralls with the name Frank stitched over the breast pocket. Obviously the superintendent, and he was steamed, mad as hell.

"Uh, basement, I think," answered Jack, acutely aware that he looked and smelled like any Bowery bum. He was unshaved, unwashed, uncombed, and filthy.

"I tell him *no visitors!*" yelled the super in the direction of the basement. "Who the hell are you and what are you doin' here?"

The loud voice cut right through Jack's aching head like a searing knife. He saw red spots dancing in front of his eyes and knew he had to get out of there before he was sick all over the stairs.

"Hey, hold it! Hold it!" Frank called after him. "You a friend of Parry's?"

Jack turned back. "No."

" 'Cause I don't allow no entertainin'. I let him stay here out of the goodness of my heart because of the tragedy, but this is no hotel and nobody's takin' advantage of me," Frank continued indignantly.

"Tragedy?" Jack asked.

Frank climbed the basement stairs until he was only one step away from Jack. He lowered his voice, more for dramatic effect than for confidentiality. "He an' his wife were in some bar . . . and some nut comes in with a shotgun and blew the place apart. Splattered her brains all over the walls. She never knew what hit her. You oughta heard about that. The nut who listened to the radio?''

Jack sank back against the wall of the staircase, his face a ghastly white. His heart was pumping so hard in his chest he could barely catch his breath. All he could think of was, Gotta get away from here. Gotta get home. I gotta get home.

Seven

Jack Lucas came out blinking into the street, his aching eyes blinded by the strong morning sunlight, and took a look around. He found himself standing under a canopy in front of a prewar rent-stabilized building on Central Park West in the mid-Eighties. By some miracle, there was still cab fare in the pocket of his jeans; after all his encounters of the previous evening, nobody had rolled him after all. It was tough getting a cab, though, because no sane driver would stop for a guy who looked like a Bowery bum. The way he succeeded at last was to jump into a taxi that had stopped for a red light. Before the driver could lock his doors or throw him out, Jack had waved a few greenbacks in his face and given the address of the Video Spot.

It was an agonizing drive back. Frank the superintendent's words kept resounding in Jack's ears like the dirgeful tolling of a bronze bell. *Never knew what hit her. That nut who listened to the radio.* And the sweet, insane face of a small man called Parry floated into Jack's brain like one of Parry's fat fairies, the Little People, a vision within sight but out of reach.

Parry. I did this to him, Jack thought in anguish. I killed the only person he loved. I made him crazy. It's my fault. This was a new aspect of his guilt, one he hadn't encountered before.

Apart from the gruesome sight on his television

screen that awful evening, Jack Lucas had never faced the actual physical presence of his and Edwin Malnick's victims. Their blood might have been on his hands, but not up in his face. Now this Parry was up in Jack's face—living, breathing, walking, talking, shooting rubber arrows, hallucinating. Living in a basement boiler room was the once sane palpable proof of Jack Lucas's terrible guilt.

For six months, ever since the senseless shootings, Jack Lucas had tallied the body count over and over in his head. Eight dead. Seven strangers and a pathetic psycho named Edwin Malnick. Eight. His sense of guilt could barely handle eight. But it hadn't occurred to him that there might be even more than eight. That there might be an entire regiment of the living dead, the people left behind to mourn. Like Parry. Like crazy Parry. Parry made nine. *Splattered her brains all over the wall. She was a beautiful girl. . . .*

And how many more than nine? Jack might never know, but he was surely as guilty of their misery as he was of Parry's madness. Unconsciously. Jack shrank back against the torn imitation leather of the taxi seat, wrapped his arms around his body, and whimpered. Salty tears squeezed out of his eyes. He wasn't even aware of doing it, but the taxi driver, taking a good look at his passenger in the rearview mirror, put his foot down hard on the gas pedal. The sooner this weeping wino was out of his cab, the better off he'd be. New York! Everybody was a mental case!

When Anne Napolitano first met Jack Lucas, she could see the black cloud hanging over his head. She knew he'd be trouble. He was a man haunted by a terrible misfortune, a man who'd lost every vestige of the good life and was trying to hide from his miseries in the bottom of a bottle. In short, the kind of man who needed the love of a strong and maternal woman. Anne the earth mother. Her favorite role. Without thinking twice, she jumped right into the relationship.

And he was trouble, lots of trouble, but up to recently he'd been worth it. He needed her, and he let her know it. Jack was a passionate, skillful, and enthusiastic lover, and Anne was hung up on his big, strong body. She loved the long dimples on both sides of his mouth, his deep-set, blue, brooding eyes, his intelligence and quick sardonic wit. In short, Anne Napolitano loved Jack Lucas, period.

But lately, things between them had been starting to go sour. Anne was a practical woman who saw things with a realistic eye. Yes, Jack had been through hell. Yes, Jack felt guilty about that terrible night at Babbitt's bar. Yes, a lot of innocent people had died. But Jack himself hadn't pulled the trigger, and no amount of guilt he felt could bring any of those men and women back to life. Guilt didn't put any butter on the bread of life. So why carry it around with you night and day? It was time already to stop brooding, time to start living. You can't go around forever with your chin hanging lower than your ass. It was way past time for Jack to snap out of it and get his shit together.

But Jack Lucas had shown no signs of snapping out of it. On the contrary, his consumption of alcohol had, if anything, increased lately. He seemed content just to vegetate with his bourbon and his ciggies, to let Anne take care of business and take care of him, to relinquish into her care all responsibility for his life. He'd become uncommunicative and unresponsive. Worse than that, as his bourbon consumption rose, hardly anything else did. Like many an alcoholic's, Jack's libido was decreasing at warp speed. No more enthusiasm. No more nibbles and secret kisses in hidden places. Lately he had to be coaxed to make love, sometimes even bribed. This hurt Anne terribly, making her feel unwanted and unattractive. The sex had been wonderful, a ten; now it was close to a zero.

Anne Napolitano was an outspoken woman whose language was the language of the streets of Brooklyn's Little Italy, a good but tough place to grow up. But underneath the surface of her frequently crude words flowed a deep well of wisdom and understanding. What she said was: "Jack, you're flying in smaller and smaller circles. Someday you'll fly up your own asshole and disappear." What she meant was: "Jack, you've got to let go of this obsessive self-absorption or someday you'll self-destruct." And what she meant was: "I care very deeply about what happens to you."

But caring didn't mean that Anne was going to let Jack use her as a doormat to wipe the mud off his fancy boots. Last night he hadn't come home; that had made her crazy, torn between fear for his safety and the near certainty that he was giving to another woman everything he was withholding from her. So when he turned up at last this morning, filthy, bleary-eyed, and stinking like a cross between a brewery, a filling station, and a sewer, Anne turned her face away from him and refused to talk to him. At first.

But Jack looked so miserable, sitting across from her in her crowded office at the back of the store, that Anne relented a little. Besides, one thing she couldn't do was stay silent for very long in any circumstances. Talk was her natural element; it was the air she breathed, the bread she ate, the wine she drank.

"Ya need to pick up a phone and let me know you're not dead," she reproached him. "Why couldn't ya do that?"

Before Jack could stammer out an answer, there

was a tap on the door, and Donna, a clerk at the Video Spot, put her head around it.

"What!" roared Anne, annoyed.

"A guy wants to check out the pornos," said Donna, waving at the wall of pornographic videotapes behind Anne's desk.

"So send him back!" Then, turning to Jack, Anne's voice softened a little. "I need to know that you haven't been attacked, or raped, or God knows what! You disappear last night, I don't know what to think. I was up all night long! Look at you!"

The door opened, and a middle-aged man, neatly dressed in suit and tie, came into the office, and slightly embarrassed, began to peruse the titles on the wall.

"I can't tell you how distraught I was," Anne continued as though there were nobody else in the room with them. "All night long. What the hell happened?"

"I was attacked," Jack mumbled.

"What? Oh, baby," cried Anne. That was all she had to hear. Now she was all sympathy.

"Two kids tried to set me on fire." Jack held up his burned hand for her to see.

"*Oh, my God! What did they do? My God!*" Anne yelled, and got up hastily. She rushed around the desk and grabbed Jack, hugging him hard, making him wince in pain. The businessman stopped reading the porno titles; this little live drama was far more interesting than a videotape.

Pulling away from Anne, Jack jerked his head in the direction of the man and gave her a look that said plainly, Get this guy the hell out of here.

"Are you almost done?" she demanded brusquely, and the man jumped a little.

"I've seen most of these," he muttered defensively.

"Whaddya lookin' for, a story?" Reaching up,

Anne grabbed a tape off the shelf and thrust it at the man. "Here . . . *Creamer Versus Creamer* . . . it won an award. Go."

The guy grabbed the videotape and went. As soon as the door closed behind him Anne turned all her attention to Jack.

"You were attacked! My God, you want me to call the police? Should I call a doctor?"

"No . . . no, I'm fine, really." Jack shook his head, half-touched, half-amused by her concern.

She looked at him sharply, her eyes assessing him for damage. "You all right? You're sure?"

He nodded, and Anne moved along to what was really on her mind. She tried to keep her voice casual, but failed dismally.

"So . . . where did you sleep last night?"

Jack shifted uneasily in his chair. How could he possibly explain to her about Parry? "I . . . I stayed at a friend's. Anne, listen, I—"

But Anne put her hand up to cut him off. "Jack, Jack, I want you to be up-front with me now. If you're seein' somebody else, let me know. You don't have to pour gasoline on yourself and light a match just to break up with me. Just tell me the truth."

It was apparent to Jack that underneath the bravado of her words, Anne Napolitano was hurting. He owed her something. "Anne, I was not seeing anybody else. I really was attacked," he told her sincerely.

She threw him a look out of the corner of her eye and saw that he meant what he said. This brought on another spate of demonstrative sympathy, and she threw her arms around Jack and hugged him hard. Wincing, he pushed her away.

"I got a cut."

"Okay, I see it now. I'm sorry." But it was hard for her to let him go. She wanted to rock him in her arms until he felt better about life and about himself. Impossible wish; it would never happen.

"Okay," Anne said at last, moving away from Jack with a small shrug. "Whaddya gonna do? I love you."

She waited for his reply, but none came. "You don't have to say it back." She sighed. "Although it wouldn't break your jaw. Go, go upstairs and take your bath. I'll cook tonight."

He couldn't shake the thought of Parry, or his desperate feelings of owing him something that he could never repay. All day long, while Anne worked downstairs in her video store, Jack Lucas thought about Parry. He thought about Parry while he bathed and dressed and brushed his teeth and napped and drank some bourbon and smoked some cigarettes and brooded over the events of the night before.

Jack could visualize Parry quite clearly in his memory—small, brave, even gallant, cheerful, insane. Again and again Jack remembered how Parry had saved his life, how he'd nurtured him, and why. To explain to Jack his mission for God. The "Janitor of God" he'd called himself, this lunatic visionary on a chivalric quest to find the Holy Grail. How crazy can you get? In the 1990s, in New York City, somewhere in the mansion of a billionaire, locked away behind burglar-proof glass, was kept the very same cup that Jesus Christ had drunk from at the Last Supper.

Yeah, right. And yet Parry believed it with his entire childlike soul.

Anne's lasagna was delicious, but Jack ate it without tasting it. He might as well have been eating cardboard. He was unaware, too, that Anne was keeping an eye on him, disturbed by his brooding silence and his preoccupation.

As she stood up to clear away the dinner dishes, Jack asked suddenly, "You know what the Holy Grail is?"

"The Holy Grail? Yeah, I know that one. It was like . . . Jesus' juice glass." When Jack stared at her, surprised, Anne added with a crooked smile, "Oh, yeah, I used to be such a Catholic." There was the merest tinge of regret in her words, as though she felt a stirring of longing for those simpler, purer times.

"You still believe in God?" Jack asked.

"Oh, sure, gotta believe in God." Anne set the dishes on the table and sat back down. Her forehead wrinkled with effort as she struggled to put her beliefs into words. Anne Napolitano wasn't used to wrestling with philosophical issues.

"But I don't think God made man in his own image. No. 'Cause most of the shit that happens is because of men. No, I think man was made in the devil's image and women were created out of God. Because women can have babies, which is sorta like creating, and which also accounts for the fact that women are so attracted to men. Because—let's face it—the devil is a helluva lot more interesting."

She lit a cigarette and puffed deeply on it, then let it dangle from the corner of her lips as she continued. "I slept with a few saints, and believe me, I know what I'm talking about. Booooooring! And so the whole point of life, I think, is for men and women to get married so that the devil and God can get together and work it out." Standing up, Anne shifted the cigarette and moved over to Jack for a kiss. "Not that we have to get married or anything. God f-bid!" She uttered a short, unconvincing laugh.

Jack couldn't help himself; he shrank away from her ever so slightly, yet enough for Anne to notice. In the last month or so, if she'd mentioned marriage once, she must have mentioned it a hundred times.

She was beginning to harp on it, and it really turned him off. Besides, as she loomed over him now, he noticed something unappetizing on her face, a blemish on her chin. That turned him off, too.

"You . . . have a little . . . uh . . . something on your face."

Anne pulled away, embarrassed. Instinctively, her hand went up to hide the eyesore from his view. "Oh, I got a pimple. This stuff is supposed to blend with my skin color. Like it really works, y'know."

Standing up from his chair, Jack dodged around Anne and went over to the little makeshift bar to pour himself another drink. Anne came up behind him and coyly removed the glass from his hand and set it down. Jack groaned inwardly; he knew what this meant. It was her signal. She wanted to play.

"I . . . don't think I'm up to it tonight, honey," he began, but Anne was busy massaging his shoulders. "I just had a very traumatic experience."

She nodded to show she heard him, but her hands were making larger circles on his shoulders, then down along his spine to his hips.

"Ow, ow, ow . . . ." Jack pleaded, trying and failing to free himself from her forceful fingers. "I think I'm getting sick. . . . Anne, I spent the night in a boiler room. . . . Anne, I'm tired. . . . I'm upset. . . . I'm just not in the mood . . . okay?"

"Okay," she agreed, leaning her weight against him and pushing him down on the sofa. Then she climbed over him, mounting him and pushing her tongue deeply into his mouth, still caressing him with circular movements of her strong hands. Pressing herself against him, Anne began to undo the buttons of his shirt.

It was too much for Jack. It would be easier simply to give in than to fight her. Besides, he was starting to enjoy it. He could feel the warmth of her opulent body under her tight blouse and skirt, and it was getting to him. He felt himself responding. With a little moan, half of passion, half of resignation, Jack pushed Anne to the floor, and they began to make love.

Afterward, released, his energy spent along with his passion, Jack was able to explain to Anne about Parry, about the mad young man whose wife was blown away in front of his eyes and whose reaction was to leave reality behind. While she held him, saying nothing, silent tears streaming down her cheeks, Jack told her in a low voice of the sorry knight and the insanity of his impossible quest.

It was when he got to the part about his refusal of a role in the quest, and his running out on Parry, that Jack Lucas broke down and cried.

Eight

When he woke up the following morning, Jack Lucas found himself still haunted. He was as haunted by this man Parry as Parry himself was by his hallucinatory vision of the Holy Grail. He couldn't get Parry out of his mind. Like the Ancient Mariner in the poem. He shot a seabird whom the sailors considered lucky and was forced to go around forever with the albatross tied around his neck. Having destroyed Henry Sagan's mind, Jack was now forced to carry the burden of Parry's insanity.

All he knew was that he had to learn more about his personal albatross, the man whose wife had been blown away in front of his eyes. Reluctantly, fearing another encounter with the divine madness that infused Parry's brain, Jack took himself over to the apartment building on Central Park West.

He made his way cautiously down the steps from the lobby to the basement and knocked on the boiler-room door. No answer. Jack pushed the door open. Empty. No Parry. Oddly, Jack felt a twinge of disappointment mingling with his relief. He didn't want to meet him, yet strangely, some part of him wanted to see Parry again.

Jack stepped inside and looked around curiously at Parry's "neck of the woods," searching for clues to the mystery of the bearded man. The first thing he noticed was that Parry had taken the little Pinocchio doll and set it up against the back wall as a kind of never-sleeping guardian of his sanctuary. Funny, it looked right at home there, its painted eyes wide open as though he were guarding the portals of the underworld, that happy smile permanently on its little face.

There were the books, of course; Jack went to these first. He himself was college-educated and he considered himself well read, but almost all of the titles here were unfamiliar to him. They all dealt with the Middle Ages—history, literature, weaponry, religion, daily life, chivalry, the Crusades, Arthurian legend, the Holy Grail. Pulling the Grail book off the makeshift shelf, Jack quickly skimmed over the pages dealing with the Christian legend of the quest by the knights of the Round Table.

It all came back to him now. The Grail was believed to provide an unending source of nourishment and healing; it cured all wounds, no matter how grave, because it embodied God's boundless grace. The legend goes that during the Crucifixion of Jesus, Joseph of Arimathea caught some of the Lord's blood in the sacred vessel and escaped with the Grail to England. It provided him with sustenance all his life and was handed down to his descendants for many generations. At last it disappeared, and thus became the object of a quest by King Arthur's best knights. The holy vessel could be found only by one who was totally pure in heart and mind. Only Sir Galahad, Joseph of Arimathea's last descendant, ever achieved the Grail. His strength was as the strength of ten, because his heart was pure. Sir Percival also completed the quest and was rewarded by the sight of the Holy Grail.

And this symbol of purity and divinity, this stuff of legends, this unattainable and mystical ideal was the very cup that Parry believed he saw in a glossy eight-dollar architectural magazine. Jack shook his head at the many and varied forms dementia takes.

He left the books and walked around Parry's tiny quarters. The small table held a large piece of paper, rolled up. Jack unrolled it and saw with surprise that it was a hand-drawn map, evidently of Langdon Carmichael's armory and the city blocks surrounding it. Nervously, Jack rolled it back up and turned his attention to the walls.

Most of the pictures had been ripped out of Parry's books and taped to the wall. As Jack studied the pictures carefully he could perceive a kind of pattern emerging, a delineation of the medieval parameters of Parry's delusion. There was an iconlike quality to the pictures, a worshipful celebration of chivalry and beauty. But on the opposing wall, the red-marked picture of the monstrous Red Knight, his wickedly sharp lance exploding in flame, the hooves of his war-horse pounding directly at the viewer, seemed to personify the inescapable evil of the world.

There was something chilling about the Red Knight. Jack shivered a little and moved into the alcove, where Parry kept his mysterious shrine. This time, without Parry here to stop him, he was able to look more closely at the strange objects on the altar.

In addition to the Chinese-food container and the romance novel, he saw a package of jawbreakers, a plastic flower, some cheap but glittery earrings— everything arranged carefully as an offering. In the center, with votive candles in front of it, was the picture of the beautiful maiden. She had long, flowing golden hair and a soft, sweet, virginal otherworldly smile. Whoever she was supposed to represent, Jack could tell she was the object of Parry's veneration. His dead wife? The Virgin Mary? The lady fair in peril of the dragon? But this other stuff on the altar, what did it mean? He didn't get it. He didn't get any of it.

"Can I help you?" The voice was sharp and sud-

den, making Jack jump. He turned to see Frank, the
building superintendent, glaring at him.

"I . . . I'm just looking for Parry."

"He's not here." The man stood waiting for Jack
to leave, but Jack wasn't ready to leave. He needed
to know more, to find some key to the puzzle of this
room and its enigmatic contents, and especially to
the man who made his home here.

"What did you say his name used to be?" Jack
asked. There was supplication in his eyes.

Frank hesitated, looking Jack up and down. Then
he nodded, deciding to trust him, and left the boiler
room, gesturing for Jack to follow. His superintendent's apartment was down the basement hall, and
he unlocked the door and beckoned Jack inside.
From a closet he took down a large duffel bag and
began to take Parry's things out of it for Jack to look
at.

Here, tumbling out of a canvas bag, was the sum
and substance of a sane man's life. It was a small
collection of objects, but significant. There were two
framed certificates of master's degrees in medieval
literature and medieval history.

"That's his real name, Henry Sagan," said Frank,
pointing to the degrees. "He was a teacher over at
Hunter College. They kept him in some mental place
over on Staten Island. He didn't say a word for over
a year . . . then, all of a sudden, he starts talkin',
only now he's this Parry guy."

Fascinated, Jack pawed through Parry's things.
Here was a snapshot taken of him in Central Park.
Here was the sane Parry, whose name was not Parry
but Henry Sagan. He stood smiling into the camera,
his short hair ruffled a little in the breeze, his beard
neatly trimmed, his clothing exactly what you'd expect from an academic, a teacher of medieval history—button-down shirt with a Shetland sweater
pulled over it under a favorite old tweed jacket. The

eyes glowed with humor and intelligence . . . and
sanity. It was painful for Jack to see it, and he put
the picture down and picked up a thick sheaf of paper bound neatly into a folder. He opened it to the
title page.

*The Fisher King: A Mythic Journey for Modern Man
Doctoral Thesis by Henry Sagan.*

"He and his wife used to live upstairs," Frank
continued. "So when he got released, they sent him
here. I felt bad. He couldn't work. Nobody wanted
him. So I let him stay in the basement. He helps out,
I give him a couple of dollars. People throw things
away, he gets them."

Jack picked up a wedding ring and turned it in his
hands, putting it back hurriedly as though it had
burned his fingers. Then he lifted a photograph of a
woman and studied it. The young woman in the picture was radiant. Although her features were close
to perfect and she was very pretty by any standards,
there was something more than prettiness in her
laughing face. There was tenderness and sweetness
and warmth, and a brilliance that came up from
within. Jack could understand easily how Henry Sagan must have loved her. He shuddered at the thought
of Edwin Malnick's bullets tearing through that head,
of the blood and brains that must have welled up
over that tumbled light brown hair.

"She was a beautiful girl," said Frank sadly. "He
was crazy about her."

It was finally too much. Jack couldn't take another
minute of this. He'd learned all he wanted, and more
besides. He was choking on his new knowledge; it
was a fire in his chest that threatened to engulf him.

Jack tossed in bed for hours, but sleep eluded him,
mocking him for even trying. Beside him in the large

bed, Anne slept soundly, the sweet, untroubled rest of one whose conscience is clear. At last Jack gave up the struggle. He slipped out of bed and left the bedroom in his underwear. Padding barefoot across the living room, he snapped on only one light, a table lamp. Semidarkness ought to be enough for a haunted man.

Moving slowly, as though he were very old, he pulled his scrapbooks and his tapes off the shelf in the living room and piled them up on the floor. He turned on Anne's portable cassette player and put in a tape of one of his radio shows, selected at random.

Any old tape; what was the difference? They were all pretty much alike. Jack Lucas on top, the callers on the bottom. The Superstar meets the Bungled and the Botched. As the tape played he heard the eager voices of his fans and his own bored and confident voice answering them in that superior tone he always affected to impress them. Oh, he'd given them attitude, all right! Fuck 'em all, save six for pallbearers. Jack Lucas's personal philosophy of life.

But Jack soon lost interest; he wasn't really listening, anyway. He just needed to hear a tape of his show as background noise, as an audible reminder of what used to be. He sat down on the floor, turning the pages of the scrapbooks, rereading the clippings that marked the progress of his successes—the stories in *Billboard* and *Radio & Records* and *Variety*, the reviews of his program in the New York papers, the press releases and glossy photos sent out by the station to hype the *Jack Lucas Morning Show*. A strong feeling of nostalgia tempered his melancholy. It really was as good as he remembered it. He'd led an enviable life. He missed it terribly.

But soon he came to the yellowing front pages that screamed in sensational headlines the shootings at Babbitt's. His own name in thick black letters six inches high, a better billing even than Edwin's. Jack's hand trembled, but he still kept turning pages. There was Edwin Malnick's face looking up at him, as much victim as killer. Edwin, who didn't have an original thought in his head until Jack Lucas had put one terrible one there. Jack shuddered, remembering, regretting, wishing only that he could turn back the hands of time, unsay the words he had said, make those people come back to life, go on living his old life. If only Edwin Malnick hadn't taken him literally! He closed the scrapbook and set it aside.

A sudden shaft of light came in from the bedroom and slanted across the floor, hitting Jack. Anne Napolitano, her bathrobe wrapped around her, walked into the living room with a cigarette in her hand.

"Whatsa matter, hon, can't sleep?" she asked sympathetically. Jack's tapes had wakened her; her voice was still thick with sleepiness.

Jack didn't look up. He was sitting as still as if he were carved out of stone.

"I tell you something, Anne," he said at last in a shaky voice. "I really feel like I'm cursed. I get the feeling like I'm . . . a magnet, but I attract shit. Out of all the people in this city, why did I meet a man whose wife I killed?"

It was an unanswerable question. Anne's big heart went out to him. She knelt down close to Jack and touched his shoulder with a gentle hand. "You didn't kill anybody. Stop it."

Jack shook his head. "I wish there was some way I could . . . just . pay the fine and go home." His voice broke, and he could say no more.

This was the most honest thing he'd ever said to her. Anne slipped one arm around him, and he turned and buried his face in her breast, clutching her to him very tightly. Anne held him with both arms now, hugging him hard, while Jack wept against her body, his shoulders shaking with deep, convulsive sobs. She could feel his tears burning her breasts.

"I know, honey, I know . . . shhh . . . shhhh," she whispered, rocking him in her arms as though he were her own crying child. Anne had never loved Jack as much as she loved him this moment, when he allowed her to look into and pity the black depths of his pain and vulnerability. If only she could hold on tight and never let him go!

Jack left the house early the following day and took the subway and a crosstown bus down to the Manhattan Bridge, looking for Parry. He had something to give him, something to make Parry's life better and ease Jack's guilty conscience a little. If he succeeded, then maybe he'd never have to deal with Parry again.

There were fewer homeless people under the abutment during the day, but Jack soon found Parry's little band of brethren—the Irishman, the black man, and the hippie kid. Of Parry himself, there was no sign.

The guys didn't recognize him at first, because Jack looked so different from the other night. He was sober, for one thing. For another, Jack was clean, shaved, and dressed neatly in fresh clothes. They didn't want to talk to him, and they particularly didn't want to tell him where Parry could be found. But the burn bandage on Jack's hand convinced them of his identity and allowed them to be less paranoid.

"So where can I find Parry?"

"You know the Haagensen Building?" asked the black man.

"On Twenty-Fourth and Madison? That big office building?" Jack countered, surprised.

"That's the place. You can find Parry outside there every weekday. Not on Saturday or Sunday, though. Today a weekday?"

"Yes," said Jack, and it occurred to him that men like these didn't live by clocks or calendars. If anything, time was their enemy. Time had stolen away their years without giving anything back. Time mocked their days and evenings, dragging them out as they hunted like sewer rats for survival.

"Then for sure he's there. But you gotta get there before twelve, or you won't find him."

Jack looked at his watch: 11:35. He had to hustle if he was going to make it. "Thanks." Digging into his pocket for a few bills, he handed them around. Somewhere in his memory, he seemed to hear himself saying to somebody, "A couple of quarters isn't going to make any difference anyway." When had he thought that? Maybe a thousand years ago, give or take a century.

Jack set off uptown in search of Parry. The Haagensen Building, every weekday. What was he doing there?

Nine

Jack climbed out of the Lexington Avenue subway at the Twenty-third Street station with four minutes to spare. He was going to make this fast and get it over with once and for all; a simple cash transaction and then good-bye forever. Anne was right; he couldn't carry this shitload of guilt around with him all his days.

As he approached the Haagensen Building Jack could see Parry, sitting on the roof of a car across the avenue from the skyscraper, his eye fixed to the clock in the tower. He was mumbling under his breath as Jack approached him. Jack couldn't hear most of the words, but he did make out "sovereign princess," "faithful slave," and "who endures such misery for love of thee." The guy was rambling on again.

"Parry!" he called in greeting.

"Hi, Jack," Parry answered without taking his eyes off the clock. It was now less than a minute to noon.

Jack came to the point without preamble. "Hey, listen," he said, rummaging in his pockets. "I thought maybe you could use a couple of bucks."

At that very moment the hands of the clock came together, and a loud, sonorous tolling of the noon-hour bells split the air. Agile as lightning, Parry leaped off the car and grabbed hold of Jack.

"Come on!" he yelled urgently, and half dragged

Jack into traffic and across the avenue to the building. He stopped about six or seven yards away from the revolving doors, with a good view of them, and a breathless and puzzled Jack Lucas came to a halt beside him.

The Haagensen Building is one of New York's great art-deco structures, built in the booming market and optimistic prosperity of the 1920s. It boasts a marble lobby, carved stone, and beautiful deco ironwork inside and out, and its impressive lobby is reached by means of heavy bronze revolving doors. Parry's eyes were glued to the revolving doors. Above their heads, from the building's clock towers, the noon hour was still ringing.

Now that the workday lunch hour had officially arrived, the revolving doors were turning busily as the men and women who worked in the building came streaming out for a meal and a midday break.

"Look, look," Parry whispered urgently. And Jack looked. He saw a bunch of people coming through the doors into the street, and one skinny girl not quite making it. Too slightly built to deal with the weight of the doors and the eager impatience of the people behind and ahead of her, she got revolved right back into the lobby.

"She'll be back," said Parry with confidence.

And, a few seconds later, she was back, out on the street at last, straightening her woolen beret that had become dislodged in her struggle with the revolving door.

"Ahhhhh, there she is, see her?" Parry murmured with passion.

Jack Lucas looked in the direction of his ardent gaze, and his eyes widened in surprise. Nobody, nobody even not in his right mind could call this young woman a beauty. First of all, she was too thin. Jack's own personal taste ran in favor of thin women, but he liked tall, willowy women, with legs that went all the way up to their armpits. This girl was small and scrawny, like an underfed chicken.

She wore a man-tailored suit two sizes too large for her so that she virtually disappeared inside her clothing, as though her garments were her hiding place. The suit was drab and seemed to be made out of that dark-colored iron-hard fabric that you see on Soviet leaders. More than anything, she resembled a child dressed up in her grandmother's clothing.

The girl's face was plain, with a large nose and short hair of no particular color that she kept tucked up inside her woolen beret. The beret, which can make a rakish statement on a person of style, was pulled down formlessly over her head like a cooking pot. She had no makeup on, so her face was pale and her features without definition. The young woman wore thick-soled "sensible" shoes on her feet, but she didn't walk with ease or confidence. Instead, she sidled and stumbled along clumsily, occasionally bumping into someone and mouthing silent apologies. When she bumped into the lamppost on the corner, she apologized to that, too. A timid soul if ever Jack saw one.

"Isn't she a vision?" Parry breathed. There was no mistaking the dopey look on his face for anything but perfect love. Parry looked like a teenager with his first big crush. He obviously worshiped this awkward sparrow of a girl.

"Yeah, gorgeous. Look, I'm going. I just wanted to give you—" Jack began digging in his pocket again, but Parry was off and running, dodging behind the lunchtime crowd to stay out of the girl's sight, yet never taking his eyes off her. Impatient and annoyed, Jack followed.

The two of them stopped at the next corner, to watch the young woman select a book from the paperback rack attached to the newspaper stand. Selecting one book, she knocked down three. When

she picked those three up from the sidewalk, she
knocked down two more. At last she did manage to
pull it all together and get her wallet out and pay for
the book without further damage. As she tucked the
book away into her old lady's black leather handbag
Jack and Parry could read the title. It was the same
kind of florid romantic junk that Anne loved so
much, all cleavage and heavy breathing.

"She buys a new book every two days," Parry
informed Jack. *Love's Lost Found.* She's into trash.
Whaddya gonna do?" He grinned fondly.

The girl, yawing off balance like a small ship in a
large gale, went listing down the avenue and finally
made port in a nearby Chinese restaurant, where she
took a table. Immediately, Parry pressed his nose
against the restaurant window so that he could see
her every move. Both men watched as she ordered
nervously. In less than two minutes her order was
plunked down in front of her in a domed metal dish
with a knob on the cover. Taking the cover off, Parry's lady fair managed to burn her fingers and drop
the lid into the dish. There was a big splash and
dumpling juice mixed with soy sauce splattered all
over the tablecloth.

"Awww, she loves dumplings," Parry purred.
"It's her Wednesday ritual."

Jack shifted impatiently from foot to foot. He was
determined to get this over with, give Parry a little
money, and get the hell out of his life. He had
enough albatrosses hanging around his neck as it
was, without adding a mental case. In New York,
money solves almost anything. It was never Jack's
intention to go trotting down Fourth Avenue in Parry's tow, dogging the footsteps of some homely waif
who didn't even seem to know that she was the focus
of a crazy man's fantasies. The sooner he was out of
here, the better.

But Parry's attention was not to be diverted. This

was the high point of his day, the hour he lived for, when he could actually see his lady love dropping a slippery Chinese dumpling off her chopsticks and into her lap. His eyes squeezed shut in rapture.

"That's so sweet," he murmured to Jack. "She does that every time." He appeared to find every gaffe this graceless young person committed irresistibly adorable.

The couple sitting at the window table had been growing more and more uncomfortable at having to confront the faces of two men staring in at them, particularly when one of them had his nose pressed so tightly against the glass that his features were grotesquely distorted. Angrily, they rapped on the window and made superior little waving-away gestures with their hands.

"We're looking through the window!" Jack roared. "You got some problem with that, buddy? We're looking through the fuckin' window!"

Why was he overreacting so angrily? Partly because he was embarrassed to be caught in this Peeping Tom situation, partly because it was humiliating to be identified, even by strangers, as a bum and a companion of bums. But also, buried somewhere deep, there was perhaps a small core of protectiveness toward Parry that Jack himself didn't recognize. Who were these people to act so goddamn superior, to decree that Parry couldn't look into a restaurant window? Even the craziest bum should have rights.

While his young lady was paying her bill, Parry grabbed Jack again and rushed him away from the restaurant, to a vantage point nearby where they could watch her leaving and follow her back to her office. Any other young woman might have noticed that she was being followed, because it really was something of a circus parade with Parry only yards behind her and Jack trotting angrily after Parry, but this girl didn't seem to be able to tell night from day, or rain from sunshine.

She didn't go directly back to work, but stopped at the newsstand again, this time to drop her purse and buy a package of brightly colored jawbreakers.

"If anybody ever told me I'd be in love with a woman who eats jawbreakers," Parry confided to Jack as they witnessed the purchase from five feet away, "I'd say they were nuts. But look at that jaw!"

It all fell into place now. The jawbreakers, the Chinese-food containers, the love novel—all votive objects placed lovingly on the altar in a shrine in Parry's little boiler room. A shrine dedicated to a pale, unpretty, awkward young woman who didn't even know he existed.

In his mind's eye Jack could see the beautiful portrait of the Botticelli flower maiden with her flowing golden locks. This was how Parry idealized his love, this must be how he perceived this graceless girl he was following like a dog. Jack didn't know whether to laugh or to cry, but if he needed any more proof of Parry's total insanity, he had it right here in Parry's romantic obsession.

Now the girl was trying to get back to work, past the dragons that guarded the revolving doors. It wasn't easy; she kept being brushed aside by other workers moving in and out, but finally she positioned herself so that she was caught up in the moving stream and pulled into the building. She disappeared from sight.

"There she goes," said Parry wistfully, his heart in his eyes.

"Do you follow her every day?" Jack asked curiously.

Parry blushed, and his blue eyes looked sheepish. "It's not like that. I'm deeply smitten."

"Who is she? What's her name?"

Parry looked a little startled, as though he'd never

considered the question. "I don't know," he confessed. "Oh, look! A cooler! Wow!"

He broke away from Jack and ran to a mound of rubbish piled up against the curb. On top of the heap was a discarded Styrofoam cooler that Parry eagerly examined. It had a big hole in the bottom. "Needs a little work," he admitted out loud, but he was still delighted with his new possession. A cooler! His lucky day.

This was the moment Jack had been angling for; maybe now he could get Parry's undivided attention, if such a thing existed. He pulled some money from his pocket, selected a fifty-dollar bill, and held it out to Parry.

"Here. I . . . just . . . would like to help you. I thought maybe you could use some money."

Parry just stared at the bill, making no move to take it. "Fifty dollars?"

Jack misunderstood; he thought that it wasn't enough; Parry wanted more. Digging into his pocket again, he pulled out another bill, his last folding money. "Here's another twenty. Will that do?"

"Seventy dollars?" Totally dumbfounded, Parry looked at the money in Jack's outstretched hand.

Once again, Jack misread the situation. Not enough. Scowling, he sorted through the change from his pockets. "I mean, what's it going to take?"

At last Parry comprehended that the money was for him, a gift from Jack, and he was overcome by Jack's generosity. He lifted the fifty delicately from Jack's hand, leaving the twenty behind.

"No . . . no . . . it's . . . I don't know what to say! This is so nice of you, Jack."

Throwing his arms around Jack, Parry gave him a big hug, filled with gratitude and affection. Embarrassed half to death to be seen hugging a derelict on a New York City street, Jack pulled himself away from the embrace.

"That's okay," he mumbled. He was endlessly relieved that the moment had come and gone. He'd given Parry a little something; he was off the hook now. He wouldn't be haunted any more.

"You're a mensch, Jack. Can I take you to lunch?"

"No, I've got to get back to work. Take care of yourself." He turned away, a free man. No more Ancient Mariner.

At the corner, the light was red. Waiting for it to change, Jack glanced back over his shoulder at Parry. What he saw made him turn pale.

Another homeless man had set up a kind of shelter in the lee of the Haagensen building. He had a shopping cart piled high with a useless clutter of possessions, chief of which was a broken, disconnected telephone. In an earlier life, he'd been a stockbroker, a man who'd taken one high-wire walk too many without a net. When the market plunged, he'd plunged with it, down into madness. Now he spent his days on a telephone call to nowhere, reaching out to touch no one, issuing his orders to "Sell, sell, sell!"

What Jack saw, disbelieving, was Parry walking up to this cemento and handing over the fifty-dollar bill.

A new world of business opened up magically. "Buy! Buy! Buy!" yelled the bum.

"Hey! Hey!" yelled Jack, hotfooting it back.

"Well," Parry was advising the other man, "I think you should be realistic. You can't start an ad agency on fifty dollars." Three totally different people living in three totally different worlds.

"What are you doing?" Jack hollered at Parry, grabbing at the fifty in the other bum's hand. "Give that back!"

A small scuffle took place in which the desperate bum managed to hold on to the money, while Parry tugged at Jack until he got him away. The two men began to move up the street, Jack Lucas still not resigned to the loss of his money and the futility of his gesture. Now he was back on square one with his albatross, and out fifty bucks in the bargain.

"Why did you do that?" cried Jack, utterly frustrated. "I gave that money to you!"

"Well, what am *I* gonna do with it?" Parry asked, puzzled, as though it were the most rational question in the world.

Defeated, Jack shrugged. "I don't know. But I gave it to you, to help *you,* not him!"

Parry stopped and turned to look up at Jack. A mischievous little smile tugged at the corners of his mouth, spread across his face as a grin and wound up shining out of his bright blue eyes. There was a look of cunning on his face.

"You really want to help me?" he asked softly.

No. No, no, nonononono. He wasn't going to get suckered into this, vowed Jack. Nothing would make him get involved in this nutty Grail quest hallucination of Parry's. Nothing. No amount of guilt was going to make Jack Lucas even venture into the neighborhood of Langdon Carmichael's Fifth Avenue mansion. Nothing.

Ten

So, naturally, that's exactly where the two of them ended up, on Seventy-fourth Street and Fifth Avenue, right across the street from Langdon Carmichael's wonderful ten-million-big-ones armory. Jack Lucas had been dragged there kicking and screaming. Not literally, of course, because he was more than a head taller than Parry and must have outweighed him by a good forty pounds. But figuratively, he'd been blackmailed into it, because he knew he owed this crazy little man. Although not this much. Nobody owed anybody this much.

Still, Jack had gone along with the gag long enough to come and look. That was all Parry asked of him, to take a look-see. At least, that's all Parry was asking *now*. But he kept upping the ante. Inside that demented little head there seemed to be a peach pit of sane calculation that recognized that he had a hold of some kind over Jack and wouldn't hesitate to use it. A knight on a quest is wise to employ every weapon put at his disposal.

As they were turning the corner onto Fifth Avenue Parry made Jack shut his eyes, no peeking. He wanted the twentieth-century abode of the Holy Grail to come as a surprise to Jack.

And a surprise it was, no shit.

"Okay, you can open your eyes now," said Parry.

Jack Lucas opened his eyes. And blinked in amazement. The layout in the architectural magazine could not begin to suggest just how impressive the red-stone building really was. For one thing, it was a city block long and four stories high, with watchtowers at the corners of the roof. Built in the 1880s, during the art-nouveau period's reflowering of the Arthurian legend, the armory was erected like a medieval battlement to withstand an assault by the centuries. In style, it resembled closely a color print of a twelfth-century Norman castle out of a boy's book by Howard Pyle.

Instead of windows, there were narrow arrow slits, through which archers could shoot. The roof was topped by crenellations, little parapets of stone that would shield the defenders of the castle as they poured boiling oil down on the besiegers. There was a drawbridge with downward-pointing spikes, although its location on upper Fifth Avenue precluded a moat, which must have disappointed the architects no end. It had been designed as a fortress, it endured more than a hundred years as a fortress, and today it was even more of a fortress.

Impregnable as the structure was by nature, modern technology had made it more so. The arrow-slit windows, so thin that a plump cat couldn't squeeze through them, had been covered with protective bars. Sophisticated laser security systems in every room of the house connected directly to the local police station. It was termed, accurately, "immediate response." Wherever you went inside the house, even in the six luxurious bathrooms, a little red electronic eye followed you, and highly developed miniaturized video cameras surveilled you for posterity.

The Holy Grail might not be in Langdon Carmichael's library, but damn near everything else of value was, including priceless Renaissance objects by Benvenuto Cellini, a Rembrandt drawing, several Picassos, and a magnificent Monet flower painting, which cost as much as a small country, and which

Carmichael had acquired recently in a hailstorm of publicity. So there was plenty there to protect, and no expense had been spared in the protecting. A cockroach wouldn't have a Chinaman's chance of getting in there without setting off the alarms.

"Pretty impressive, huh?" Parry said proudly after Jack had stood there for two minutes saying nothing. "Don't let it scare you. Formidable as it seems, everything has its weakness."

"You can't just break into Langdon Carmichael's house," Jack protested. "This man has done nothing."

"Hey, I'll *deal* with it!" Parry retorted angrily. Evidently, he'd given some thought to the innocent-bystander aspect of his quest, and it still affected him like an exposed nerve. "Jack, just let me go through this one more time. The Holy Grail is in—"

"Listen to me!" Jack yelled, out of patience. This gag had gone as far as it was going to. "Don't start drooling, or rolling your eyes when I tell you this, but you shouldn't be doing this. There *is* no Holy Grail."

Parry chuckled, a rich baritone sound. "Oh, Jack, ye of little faith," he chided with affection. "There *has* to be a Grail. What do you think the Crusaders were, the pope's publicity stunt? Oh, you heathen! There's a Grail, come on!"

But Jack interrupted him. "Wait! Wait! Wait! Look, you're only partly insane. People like you can lead seminormal lives. You could get a job—"

"I have a job, Jack," said Parry earnestly. "I have a quest."

Jack ground his teeth in frustration. There was no reasoning with this maniac. It was like discussing philosophy with a gerbil, or trying to get a good fistfight going with a Mallomar. All one-sided. It made him crazy.

"I take it back!" he shouted, balling his hands

into fists. "You're fucking deranged! And you're going to get yourself killed trying to get in there!"

Parry took a step backward and looked up at Jack, and a sudden gasp of realization issued from his lips. His face suddenly radiated joy.

"Now I know what you're trying to do," he breathed happily. "You're trying to protect me, aren't you? You think there's danger—"

"No," snapped Jack. "I think you're a moron and I don't want to get into trouble."

But there was no convincing Parry. "You care!" he cried ecstatically, and he ran forward to throw his arms around Jack. For a small man he had surprising strength, and he hugged like a bear. "First the money, and now this! You care! Oh, you fabulous guy!"

Jack struggled furiously, but he couldn't break Parry's hold without hurting him, and he didn't want to hurt him. He just wanted him to see reason.

"Oh, you jaded and apathetic city!" Parry crowed, raising his voice for all of New York to hear. "I love this guy, do you hear me? I love this guy! He cares!"

This was too much for Jack, and he pushed Parry away vigorously. "Will you shut up!" he hissed in a choked, angry voice, looking around anxiously to make sure that nobody was watching.

But Parry was completely carried away by his emotion, and now his crow became a shout. "I love this man! You hear me, jaded city? I'm loopy about this guy! You're a real human being, Jack," he yelled loud enough to be heard six city blocks away.

Passersby were beginning to look now, and some of them laughed while others crossed the street so they wouldn't have to walk by the pair. Jack Lucas felt the hairs on his neck prickling. "Will you shut up!!" he growled.

Parry smiled. "You're a true friend."

That stung. "Believe me, I'm not," Jack said in a low voice. "I'm scum."

"I'm not going to listen to this. You're a real honest-to-goodness good guy."

"I'm self-centered, I'm weak," Jack went on, meaning it. "I don't have the willpower of a fly on shit."

"That's why the Little People sent you," Parry said happily. "They knew that. Magic is like that."

The irrationality of it all was beginning to get to Jack, to burn his circuits out. Here he was trying to have a normal conversation with Woody Woodpecker. "I don't believe in little floating people," he growled. "Okay? *There is no magic!*"

Jack's lack of faith rolled right off Parry's back. He'd come around. "You're going to help me. That's what matters," he answered with sunny confidence.

That blew it. Jack reached out and grabbed Parry by the shoulders. Here was a guy whose reality check had bounced twice and was no longer negotiable. Jack Lucas was determined to get reality across to him if he had to force-feed it down Parry's throat. It was for his own good, he told himself, so that the little guy wouldn't get hurt trying to make his delusions into realities. Actually, he was doing it so that his own guilt might be eased somewhat.

"Listen to me, Parry, or whatever your name is. You know none of this is true—not the Grail . . . not the voices. There's a part of you that knows it's not true!"

"I think we have to start planning now," said Parry, refusing to listen.

"I know who you are—" Jack insisted.

A look of panic entered Parry's eyes, his hands trembled, and he began to pull away. "Jack, come on . . . what are you saying? I know who you are? You're acting . . . really weird—"

'Or who you were. You don't belong on the streets. You're an intelligent man. You're a teacher—''

''No! No! No! . . . Jack! No!'' Parry was struggling now like a little wild animal trying to get out of a trap. Every word of Jack's was a spike being driven into his head. The pain, the pain was . . . agonizing . . . he couldn't stand it . . . unbearable.

''You were a teacher at Hunter College. Don't you remember?''

''AAArrrrgggghh!'' The scream was ripped out of him, and it didn't sound human.

''Parry!''

Parry pulled away from him and threw himself to the sidewalk, writhing. A terrible, terrible screaming kept issuing from his lips, as though he were being torn to pieces alive. As Jack watched, helpless, Parry curled up in a fetal position, his arms thrown over his head to protect himself. And screamed. And screamed.

The Red Knight came. He was here. His face was too hideous even to imagine, but fire was coming out of his helmet, fire was curling the edges of his beard, flames were streaming from his horse's nostrils, tongues of fire were burning along the shaft of his lance and springing hungrily from the razor-sharp head. The Red Knight's chain-mail armor was all ablaze, and sparks of fire exploded from the rim of his shield. He was here for Parry, because Parry must be destroyed. The Red Knight drew his sword, which also burned with streaks of fire. The war-horse's front hooves rose high in the air, twin powerful hammers to dash out Parry's brains.

Oh, God help me, thought Parry, cowering on the ground. This is the end. I'll never see the Holy Grail.

''Parry, are you all right?'' Jack knelt down beside him and held him by the shoulders. Parry opened his mouth to warn Jack away, but no words came out. Now the Red Knight would kill him, too. He shivered, waiting for the hooves to fall, for his brains to be crushed underfoot, for the cruel flaming sword to pierce his flesh, and for his heart's blood to flow along the shaft of the spear.

But it didn't happen. Nothing happened, and nobody died. After a minute Parry dared to open his eyes. The first thing he saw was Jack Lucas's face looking down at him, looking worried. And then he saw the Red Knight. The horse and rider were standing quite still, watching Parry and Jack, from about half a city block away. The horse shook his mane and moved restively, but he took a few steps back, not forward. The knight's mailed glove tightened on the reins. Parry stared in amazement. To him it seemed that horse and rider wanted to attack . . . but . . . *dared* not!

"Parry, answer me, are you all right?"

He turned his face to Jack, and it was joyous. "He knows who you are! I can tell! *We've got 'em! Come on!*"

And, before Jack could stop him, Parry had bounded to his feet and dashed out headlong into traffic, dodging some vehicles, being grazed by others. He ran down Fifth Avenue toward the Seventy-second Street entrance to Central Park, with taxi horns blaring at him and bus drivers cursing and shaking their fists.

"He's afraid!" he called back over his shoulder to Jack. "He's afraid of you! I can tell!"

"Oh, Jesus!" Jack breathed despairingly, and began to run after him. Everything was turning to shit; this was the last thing he wanted. Why the fuck didn't Parry just take the damn seventy dollars?

Parry saw the Red Knight wheel and turn, his horse's hooves pawing at the clouds. Horse and rider turned into the park with Parry running hell for leather after them. Parry's excitement made his feet fly.

Nothing like this had ever happened before. He had

the Red Knight on the run now, because Jack was the One! Courage coursed through his knightly veins as he gave chase. His legs pumped mightily. As he ran through the park he could see the Red Knight ahead of him—now in the bushes, now on a pathway. He could hear the war steed's unshod feet thundering, and the snort of air from its nostrils. The Red Knight was fleeing. He was afraid, and for the first time Parry was not afraid.

"Yes!" he cried in exaltation. "Yes!" Everywhere the Red Knight galloped, Parry followed without tiring. They raced through playgrounds, onto Frisbee fields, through joggers and cyclists, past startled mothers and nannies pushing strollers and carriages. When the Red Knight tried to conceal himself, Parry could see him plainly. At last they met.

On a high rock, silhouetted against the sky, horse and rider stood at bay. A silence surrounded them. Parry could see the war-horse's flanks heaving under its heavy coat of mail, but he couldn't hear its ragged breaths. He couldn't hear the strike of hooves against stone or the clang of sword against shield. They were isolated, horse and rider, encapsulated in stillness, caught in the meshes of their own fear.

Parry had never experienced the Red Knight afraid. His heart swelled to bursting with the wonder and the joy of it, and a roaring battle cry escaped his lips, shattering the protective silence. The horse reared, the rider tugged at the reins, and the Red Knight wheeled and disappeared, with Parry following at top speed.

Jack Lucas's sides ached so much he couldn't take another step. Yelling Parry's name, pleading for him to stop, he'd chased that maniac little fucker over bike path and jogger path, around water fountains, baby carriages, and people walking their Jack Russells and Shih Tzus on fancy leashes. Parry paid no attention, but just kept running. The little bastard was fast, you had to give him that, and it was obvious to Jack that he was convinced he was chasing somebody or something. Ten minutes into the chase, Jack lost sight of Parry, but he kept on running anyway.

Oh, God, Jack silently begged, just let this miserable day be over soon. Just let me survive this and I will never—repeat *never* butt into anybody else's business as long as I live. The path took a turn and Jack was faced by a large rock. Somehow he knew he had to climb it. His calf muscles screamed for mercy just at the thought of it. Boy, he'd no idea how out of shape a man could get without a Nautilus in only six months.

"Ohhhh . . . God . . . I'm dying," he moaned with his last panting breath. "I can't breathe, and I'm dying."

Reaching the top of the rock after enormous exertion, Jack was not surprised to find Parry sitting there, admiring the view of the Manhattan skyline as calmly as though he'd been sitting there on his ass all afternoon. Not a rasp in his breath or a drop of sweat on his brow. Jack wanted to kill him, the son of a bitch looked so goddamn blissful.

"Isn't this a beautiful spot, Jack?"

"Who have we been chasing!" Jack gasped through aching lungs. "Can I ask this question now?"

"He's gone now, but we had him on the run," Parry answered enthusiastically. "If we had horses, we would have had his ass! He's running scared."

"WHO? *Who's* running? Who have we been chasing?"

Parry looked at Jack, puzzled. "I thought you saw him," he said slowly.

Jack was so mad he was ready to detonate. *"Saw who?"*

"The Red Knight," Parry answered quietly.

"The Red . . . ?" Jack couldn't believe his ears. All this running and dodging, climbing and aching in every goddamn muscle, and there would be charley-horse hell to pay tomorrow, and all for a fucking *hallucination?*

That tore it. That was all. No more. Not ever. I hate this. Jack shook his head. "I gave you the money. You want to keep it, fine. You want to give it away, fine." He turned his plaintive gaze up to heaven. "I just want you to know that I gave him the money. Okay? Are we clear?"

"Who are you talking to, Jack?" Parry asked with real interest.

Before Jack could utter the swear word that sprang so readily to his lips, a desperate cry sounded in the distance.

"Do you hear that?" Parry asked eagerly, his whole face lighting up. "Oh, heaven be praised, in giving me an opportunity so soon of fulfilling the duties of my profession." He scrambled to his feet and struck a heroic pose. Jack groaned in dread.

"No! Leave me alone! Get away!" The voice was clearer now, although whether it was a man's or woman's was impossible to tell.

"These cries doubtless proceed from some miserable male or female who stands in need of my immediate aid and protection," Parry pronounced, and he was off and running in the direction of the voice, every cell of his being alive to his next chivalric adventure.

"This is too hard," Jack moaned. This fucking day was never, never going to end. Miserably, he trailed along after Parry.

Eleven

Parry pounded off in the direction of the cries, which had become more of a high, keening wail. Jack followed more slowly. "Over this way!" the high-pitched voice cried. "You're *missing* me! You should be *hitting* me!"

As the two approached the source of the wailing they could hear the neighing of horses and the sound of trotting hooves. A sudden bend in the road revealed a small, ragged man sitting in the center of the bridle path, blocking the way of the riders. Men and women on horseback took great pains to ride around him, but that only made the little guy more hysterical. When he saw Parry and Jack coming for him, the wailing grew in intensity until it was a hysterical scream.

"No! No! Get away, get *away!*"

Jack stopped circumspectly on the edge of the bridle path, but Parry darted directly onto the path and knelt down beside the man. "I'm not gonna hurt you," he soothed.

"That's what the other guy said," the small man wept. Somebody had evidently tried to rescue him earlier. "Please go away." The man had small, regular features and an enormous mustache that took up almost half his little face. On his head was a massive contusion, and it was bleeding.

"I want to help you," said Parry earnestly, examining the bump. There might be concussion.

"No, please, leave me alone."

"Come on now, you can't sit here. Let me help you up." Parry grabbed one arm and began tugging, but the little guy, who couldn't have weighed much more than a Great Dane, resisted furiously.

"No! I want a debutante on a horse to step on me! Leave me alone!"

Parry glanced around at the riders, most of them in jeans and shabby jackets, posting by on steeds rented by the hour from the Piedmont Stables over on West Eighty-third. "Sorry to tell you this, but the days of the debutantes are over."

At once, the man burst into tears of genuine grief. "Isn't that awful?" he sobbed. "Poor little Gloria. Poor Brenda Frazier. They ruined them! They ate them *alive!"*

"Parry," Jack called, itchy to leave. This little guy was obviously a couple of cards shy of a deck, with a few extra jokers thrown in. Even if Parry did succeed in hauling him to his feet, what the hell were they going to do with him afterward?

But Parry was already deeply caught up in his latest knightly deed, doing the so-called duties of his profession, and a knight must never allow himself to become distracted from the job at hand.

"Yeah, but what about Slim Keith? Or that little Guggenheim girl?" he asked very seriously. Parry took everything seriously, never passing judgment on the worth or the triviality of another's passions. But his attempt at consoling his new friend didn't appear to be working. He gave one more sharp tug, but the other man still resisted. Frail and emaciated though he was, that little gay guy was stronger than he looked. He made himself deadweight so he couldn't be moved.

"Imposters!" he sniffed. "Leave me alone!"

Parry kept on pulling, but to no avail. He just wasn't strong enough by himself to lift a man determined not to budge from the middle of a bridle path. "C'mon, Jack, lend a hand!" he called urgently.

Jack Lucas was far from eager to help. It wasn't so much picking this fellow up that bothered him, it was what might come later. They might get stuck with him. He already had one fruitcake on his hands; two fruitcakes were more than he wanted to deal with. "Listen," he said uncomfortably to Parry. "He just needs to sleep it off. Someone will take care of him."

"Who?" Parry snapped. "Mother Teresa? She's retired. C'mon, it's just us. Let's go!"

Jack shifted from foot to foot evasively. "Well, maybe he wants to stay here. Do . . . do you want to stay here?"

"Sure," the little man huffed. "I just love bleeding in horseshit. How very Gandhiesque of you."

He couldn't fight them both. Jack Lucas heaved a deep sigh and came over to take his other arm. Together, he and Parry managed to get him standing. As soon as he was on his feet the little guy with the big mustache uttered a tiny moan and passed out in Jack's arms.

The emergency room of a free city hospital is a scene out of hell. The ER at St. Alphonsus Hospital on Ninth Avenue made the homeless hangout under the Manhattan Bridge look like the Waldorf-Astoria. Jack Lucas's eyes went wide with horror; he could hardly believe what he was seeing. If the bridge was Dante and Gogol, the ER was Dante and Gogol playing Sartre's *No Exit* while rehearsing for *Marat/Sade*.

The large shabby anteroom was crowded with the wounded, looking ghastly under the harsh overhead lights. The benches, lined up against the institutional-green walls, were filled with them. Those who couldn't find seats stood lined up against the walls or squatted on the linoleum floor nearby.

Those who were too agitated to sit or stand still paced about endlessly, in search of something they would probably never find.

Some of the wounded exhibited physical injuries— a stab in the side that had bled through a man's shirt, turning it a cheerful shade of red. An older woman with a broken leg, crying in pain as she waited her turn to be called. A child who'd been bitten by a rat as he slept. A young woman, scarcely older than fifteen, with bruises all over her face and body where her boyfriend had kicked and beaten her.

Others were wounded just as seriously, but somewhat less visibly. These people bled on the inside. A drunk in delirium tremens, screaming horribly as snakes only he could see attacked him. A twelve-year-old junkie hooker coming down from an opiate high, scratching, scratching at her face and arms, begging for something to get her high again. Manic-depressives in the manic state, with a clear-crystal vision of aliens in spaceships. Manic-depressives in the depressive state, wanting only to die. Schizophrenics who were either catatonic and didn't move a muscle or who were hallucinating, their tortured bodies twitching and jerking uncontrollably. Some of them were confined in straitjackets, their arms strapped behind them.

None of these people had any money, or Blue Cross, or Medicare or other necessary social validation. All they had was their desperation, their will to survive. They were all in some kind of emergency, whether physical or mental or both. So they had congregated here, in this aptly named anteroom, bringing their emergencies with them, begging for attention. This place was truly a circus of the Bungled and the Botched. All it needed was the old philosopher Nietzsche as ringmaster. In the air, hovering over everything, was a miasma of harsh chemical odor—a mingling of antiseptic, urine, vomit, blood, iodine—that made it almost impossible to draw a breath. A line from Marlowe's *Faustus* came suddenly into Jack's mind. *Why, this is hell, nor am I out of it.*

The one common bond these people had, besides the fact that all of them were victims of one kind or another, was that they were all here waiting. Waiting to be helped. Waiting for somebody in authority, somebody with schooling and skill, to examine their wounds and suggest a cure. But where were the doctors? Jack realized suddenly that he'd seen no doctors since they'd brought Michael in. And almost no nurses.

From time to time a nurse came out and called a name. Once, twice, perhaps a third time. The name was never pronounced correctly, and it took a minute or so for its owner to recognize it and to shuffle or hobble or limp forward to a curtained cubicle where emergency care was presumably given and received. But it was a slow, tortuous process. Some of the people here had been waiting five hours or more. So what constituted an actual emergency? A nuclear holocaust?

Jack couldn't bring himself to actually enter the ER, but Parry dived right in. He half led, half carried Michael over to a bench that had just had a vacancy and parked him.

"Will you watch him for a minute, Jack?" he called.

There was nothing Jack wanted less than to walk into this room and baby-sit a half-starved derelict queen who identified with Brenda Diana Duff Frazier, the most celebrated society deb of half a century ago. The guy was filthy, bleeding, wore earrings, and he stank. Dragging his feet, Jack got his ass over to the bench, and before he could utter a protest, Parry dumped Michael into his arms and took off.

"Please, no," Michael sobbed. "I was born in a place like this. I don't wanna die here."

The person next to him got up from the bench, and Jack sat down next to Michael. What the hell was he supposed to do now? He looked around for Parry, but Parry was moving through the crowd like summer lightning, saying a big hello to everybody. He seemed to have a kind word for every man, woman, and child in the room, even for those who couldn't speak English. He took one old woman by the hands, looking deeply into her eyes, and it seemed to have a calming effect on her. He lifted a crying baby in his arms, and miraculously it stopped crying. Wherever he went, people seemed to feel a little better. Despite himself, Jack was impressed. Crazy he might be, but Parry knew how to make a difference in people's lives.

"I wanna go. . . ." Michael mumbled. "Just let me go. . . ."

"Uh, where do you want to go?" Jack asked.

"A real nice place I know about," Michael answered softly. "But we can't get there tonight."

"Well, maybe we can go there later."

Jack's answer only seemed to agitate Michael more. "No, no, we can't! We can't!"

Jack felt a sudden and most untypical stab of pity for the little fellow. "Come on," he said more gently. "Maybe we can. Where do you want to go?"

Michael sighed deeply. "Venice," he whispered. "Like Katharine Hepburn in *Summertime*." A sob escaped him, a cry of frustration and utter hopelessness. "Oh, why can't I be Katharine Hepburn?"

Jack stared at him, at a loss for words. He saw the homely thin face, the scraggly mustache, the bags under the eyes, the lines around the mouth of this aging homosexual mental case. Life's loser if ever there was one. A prime example of the grimness of the underclass. The Bungled and the Botched. A guy who had nothing at all going for him, no mojo, no luck.

And then a very strange thing happened to Jack Lucas. For the first time in years he made contact with another person, a contact that was real, not just a trade or a transaction.

He saw beneath the tired aging face to the soul within. Jack saw, not Michael the worn-out and discouraged little queen, but Michael the man, the human being, the person in need of solace and comfort. And, for the first time in his life, he felt the need to give some comfort to another. And he realized sadly that he didn't know how.

Parry knew how. Look at him now, handing out gobs of affection and comfort to every wounded person in the ER. Did that make Parry a better man than Jack? Jack Lucas had to admit that it probably . . . no, almost certainly, did.

"I wanna die," Michael wept. "I just wanna die." He laid his small head down on Jack's shoulder.

Jack felt his arm going around Michael's scrawny body, sort of awkwardly hugging him. He heard himself murmuring things like, "Hey, it's gonna be all right," meaningless comforting words he didn't really believe himself. And, while a little gay bum named Michael cried himself into exhaustion on Jack's muscular shoulder, much to his own astonishment, embarrassed as all hell, Jack Lucas just sat there and held him.

"That's it," sparkled Parry. "Okay, ready? Here we go." He raised up his arms. He sang the first line of the song about liking June in New York.

He cued a man in a straitjacket to give him the next line.

"I'm in the wrong place," muttered the schizophrenic.

"Aren't we all?" Parry chirped. Parry sang the second line himself. He waved his hand at the next crazy, who stared at him blankly, drooling a little.

Parry smiled encouragingly. He then sang the next line. And he pointed to a tattered and incredibly dirty bag lady whose swollen toes were peering out from her torn shoes.

"Where the hell am I gonna put the children?" shrieked the woman in her demented rage. "God-damn daughter-in-law! Comes into my house look-ing for dust balls! Get the fuck outta my dining room, you asshole!"

"That's a wonderful feeling," Parry approved. "But you're stretching. Come on people . . . tempo, tempo. Allegro!" It was hard to get a good choral group going, especially when its members were locked up so tightly in their private hells, but Parry was always willing to give it a try. Sometimes the results surprised even him.

"Well, I'm a singer by trade," Michael was con-fiding to Jack in a breathy voice. "Summer stock . . . nightclub revues . . . that kind of thing. It used to be what I absolutely lived for! I can do every part of *Gypsy,* even backward," he added proudly. Then his voice dropped, and his face saddened. "But one night, in the middle of singing 'Funny,' it suddenly hit me. What does all this really mean?" He looked up into Jack's face for corroboration, and a surprised Jack discovered that he knew exactly what Michael was driving at. When you came right down to it, what the hell did it all really mean?

"That, plus the fact that I watched all my friends die," Michael added, subdued. "God, I sound like a veteran. My dad would be so proud of me!" He giggled, and felt much better. Felt pretty good, in fact.

"Pizza!" A pizza delivery boy appeared in the

doorway of the ER, carrying six or seven stacked boxes. Instantly, he was surrounded by a swarm of doctors and nurses, waving money. Son of a bitch, Jack thought, so there are doctors in this hospital after all! Where the fuck have they been hiding?

"Jack, it's after four." Parry turned up suddenly, and his usually cheery face looked anxious. "We're going to be late. We're going to miss her if we don't go now." He was getting pretty agitated, like his pants were full of insects.

Jack stood up, his shoulders drooping in exhaustion. He looked down at the fragile Michael. "Uh, I've got to run. I've been doing this all day. Are you going to be all right?"

Michael waved one thin hand in a grande dame gesture. "Oh, please! I was born a Catholic in Brooklyn. I've been to hell and back. I'll be fine." He smiled self-consciously at Jack. "Thanks," he said with sincerity. "You're a gem."

Jack smiled back just as self-consciously. Nobody had ever called him a gem before, and he kind of liked it.

Jack Lucas couldn't remember ever having been this tired. He'd had a long day, a full day, an unreal day. Life in the fast lane. In the last six or so hours, he'd traversed most of Manhattan. First, all the way to the bottom of the island, to the Manhattan Bridge. Then north by northwest to Twenty-fourth Street. Next an uptown trek to Seventy-fourth and Fifth, followed by an excursion into Central Park at sixty miles per hour in hot pursuit of a mythical invisible enemy. Then a delightful sojourn into the bowels of a city hospital emergency room. And now, with the ebullient Parry acting as tour guide, Jack was standing in the center of the grand concourse at Grand Central Station, crossroads of a million private lives, gigantic stage on which are played a thousand dramas daily.

All he needed were a pair of Gucci loafers, a Rolex watch, a navy-blue suit, a white shirt with pens in the pocket, a striped necktie, and an auto-reflex talking camera and he could be a Japanese tourist. What did Parry have in mind next? A little swim through the Narrows to Staten Island? A hike up to the Cloisters? Parry not only liked New York in June, but in January, November, April, and August.

They had arrived at Grand Central virtually on the run, to look for the delicious darling of Parry's loving heart, to seek out one small, skinny figure among the thousands of massed commuter bodies that pulsated across the concourse floor at this evening rush hour, human lemmings rushing pell-mell toward the sea of homebound trains.

Jack surveyed the mob scene with some dismay. "We're never gonna find her in this crowd," he told Parry.

Parry smiled confidently. The hands of the large terminal clock showed three minutes to five. "She's like clockwork," he assured Jack. "She's always on time, every day." Then his face fell. "She's late!" His bright blue eyes began to scan the crowd with anxiety.

Jack had never been in Grand Central Station except on his way to somewhere else, taking a train to a Connecticut weekend, for example, or to some rich friend's fancy renovated farmhouse in upstate New York. He'd always get a reserved seat in the parlor car, the one with comfortable chairs and bar service. Now he wasn't going anywhere, thanks to Parry. He had leisure to look around him.

Jack was interested to see that the station had a flora and fauna of its own, an ecosystem apart from the rushing commuters. A large homeless community had taken up residence here. Jack Lucas read the papers; he knew that from time to time the police cracked down on the station, rounding up the homeless and dragging them off to shelters. "Cleaning up Grand Central," they called it. But these were people, not dirt. You can't run an Electrolux over human beings. Besides, the homeless kept coming back. Where else did they have to go at night? In the station they could keep warm and try to eke out a living from begging for money.

Beggars and panhandlers were all over the station; they seemed to have staked out fixed territories, respecting one another's turf. The difference between them was that the panhandlers would accost their marks, asking for money, sometimes even demanding it. The beggars tended to stay in one place and call out to passersby, usually because the beggars were missing at least one limb and couldn't get around that easily. Parry appeared to know them all by name; now, why wasn't Jack surprised to learn that?

They were standing between the ticket windows and the information booth, where Parry could keep one eye on the terminal clock and the other on the pedestrian traffic to catch the first sight of his lady fair. A few feet away, a legless Vietnam vet named Sid sat in a wheelchair, a Styrofoam cup held out in his hand. Every now and then, somebody would drop a coin in the cup and hurry on by without making eye contact.

"God bless you! Have a safe trip home!" Sid would call out, not meaning a word of it. "Ya hear that Jimmy Nickels got picked up yesterday?" he asked Parry. But Parry was too busy searching the passing faces for the only lovely one of his fantasies, and Jack alone was left to answer him.

"Oh, yeah?" He hadn't the foggiest who Jimmy Nickels was, but he was willing enough to make conversation.

"He got caught pissin' on a bookstore. The man's a pig. Thank you, babe, God bless you. Safe trip. There's no excuse for that. We're heading for social anarchy when people start pissing on bookstores."

The man had a unique point of view, and Jack couldn't help but smile. He turned to share it with

Parry, but Parry was all a-tremble, looking like one of those nervous dogs that people tie to street lamps when they go inside to shop. He was starting to pace, three steps this way, three steps back. Four steps that way, four steps back. His eyes were bright with worry, and his brow wrinkled.

"You'll never see her in this crowd," Jack told Parry again, but the little man just shook his head anxiously and kept looking.

A commuter pitched a coin in the direction of Sid's cup, missing it. The quarter hit the floor and began to roll away. Sid bent to retrieve it, but he had no balance, and Jack chased after the coin and brought it back for him.

"The asshole!" he scowled. "The guy didn't even look at you." It didn't occur to him that this was an ironic observation coming from a man who not that long ago wouldn't bother to roll down a limousine window to give a beggar a coin, because "a couple of quarters wouldn't make any difference." Jack Lucas was beginning to change, but the depth and extent of the changes hadn't yet begun to sink in.

"He's paying so he doesn't have to look at me." Sid grinned sardonically. "What he doesn't know is that I'm providing a service for him. Guy goes to a job every day for eight hours, seven days a week, he gets his nuts caught so tight in a vise, he gets to questioning the very fabric of his existence. But one day, about quitting time, his boss says, 'Bob, come into my office and kiss my ass for me.' And Bob is going to think, 'The hell with it. I don't care what happens. I just want to see the expression on his face when I jab this pair of scissors into his arm.' "

Parry was pacing really rapidly now, his eyes darting nervously from the crowd to the hands of the clock: 5:01 . . . 5:02. His world was beginning to fall apart.

"But then he thinks of me," Sid continued. "He

says to himself, 'Wait a minute! At least I got two arms and two legs and I ain't begging for a living. Sure enough, he puts down the scissors and puckers right up.''

Jack laughed appreciatively; this was some philosopher. Old Friedrich Nietzsche had nothing on Sid.

"I'm what you call a moral traffic light. Like I'm saying, *'Red!* Go no further.' ''

There was a small gasp from Parry, and Jack turned his head. Moving awkwardly, pushing with her elbows through the crowd that pitched and tossed against her, was the girl from the Haggensen Building. At once, Parry moved off in pursuit, keeping a distance of about five feet between them. He was perfectly happy now, because after minutes of anxiety that felt like hours, his life was back on schedule. He had the most beautiful woman in the world in sight, and Grand Central Station must be the most magical structure in the world, more beautiful even than Versailles or the Taj Mahal. Everything was perfect. Parry heard the sound of train whistles as a Strauss waltz and saw the pushing and shoving of the commuters as a graceful ballet.

The girl reached her Metro North platform and vanished into a train. Parry stood on the platform in an ecstasy until the train pulled out and dived down into the tunnel. As Jack came up beside him he was watching the last car of the train go around the bend in the tunnel.

"God," Parry breathed. "Just one night with her. I'd die happy."

Yes! said Jack Lucas to himself, with a lifting of his heart. He could hear the albatross stirring back to life, he could feel its wings move, just a little.

Twelve

If Jack Lucas didn't have a spare moment during this
hectic, manic day to give a thought to Anne Napolitano waiting back home for him, Anne certainly had
plenty of time to think about Jack. He'd left the house
early in the morning without telling her one word
about where he was going, or who he was going to
be with, or when he'd be back. So, naturally, when
he didn't show up, first she suspected the worst,
then, hours later, when she'd been waiting for him
all day and part of the night, she was sure of the
worst. No matter how vehemently he denied it, Jack
must be seeing another woman.

For eight long hours Anne worked in the store
renting videotapes while her mind ran a videotape
of Jack with somebody else. Although she didn't
want to, she couldn't help imagining him making
love to another woman—blond, no doubt, and
skinny, without tits. Her emotions veered between
misery and rage, and her rage ranged between fury
at the two-timer and fury at herself for letting him
get away with it, and for caring about him in the first
place.

At six o'clock Anne locked the door of the Video
Spot, pulled down the iron night gates, and went
upstairs to her apartment. Because she was so nervous, she went into her tiny kitchen and used up a
lot of negative energy pounding and breading veal
cutlets. She could pretend that the cutlets were Jack.

Then she spent another full hour preparing an enormous pan of lasagna with meat sauce. Why she was standing on her feet in a hot kitchen cooking Jack Lucas's favorite foods while the bastard was out doing the two-time two-step was beyond her, but the mere thought of it furnished fresh fuel for Anne's anger.

Dinner was on the table at eight, but no word from Jack. Anne sat down to a solitary meal, but managed only to push the food from side to side on her plate without actually tasting any. By nine o'clock, the cutlets were soggy and cold, and the lasagna was congealed rubber in the pan. And still not even a phone call.

"I do not need this!" she said out loud through gritted teeth as she carried the uneaten food from the dining area back to the kitchen. "A woman my age! There's a person in here!" For one moment she contemplated throwing the food into the garbage, but Anne had been raised poor in a house where food was sacred, so she got out the plastic wrap and let the gesture go.

"You come! You go!" she shouted at the imaginary Jack as she scrubbed out the encrusted baking pan. "And all I do is cook like a jerk! You're a waste of good lasagna. I don't need this! Find yourself another dope!" With trembling fingers, Anne lit a cigarette and sank down at the dining-room table, her face in her hands.

"You son of a bitch," she growled at invisible Jack, and then fell silent. They say ventilating your anger, letting it out, makes you feel better. But Anne Napolitano didn't feel any better. In fact she felt rotten, because she knew she was trapped. Trapped by her own emotions. No matter what she said, or how loudly she hollered, Anne still loved the miserable cheating bastard. Stubbing out the smoke, she burst into tears.

Meanwhile, the object of her wrath actually wanted nothing more than to be home scarfing down a good hot Italian meal. He was worn out from a very long day of playing reluctant tail to Parry's manic kite. Darkness had fallen, and here the two of them were still roaming around, a mad Don Quixote and his reluctant Sancho Panza.

They had fetched up at last on the Sheep Meadow in Central Park, a lovely vast lea where sheep really had grazed until the meat shortage during the Second World War had put an end to them. During the day, kids smoked pot and threw Frisbees to their mutts on the Sheep Meadow, mothers put their babies down on the grass to toddle, and old folks took walks here with slow, careful steps. But at night Sheep Meadow was a dark and deserted expanse that could be home or hiding place to almost anything.

"Don't you think it's time to go now?" Jack demanded anxiously. "Running around here during the day is one thing, but at night we could be killed by a wide variety of people."

"Well, that's just stupid," Parry retorted. He wasn't tired at all, although Jack was about ready to drop where he stood. "This is my park just as much as it is theirs. You think it's fair for them to keep us out just because they think we might get killed or something?"

"Yes, I think it's very fair," said Jack, and he meant it.

"Well, I don't."

Jack fished his pack of cigarettes out of his pocket and lit one. It took a few seconds because the night breeze kept blowing out the match. When at last it was lit, and he looked up, he saw an astounding sight. Parry was half-naked, his shirt and outer garments strewn on the grass, and he was in the act of zipping down his pants.

"What are you doing?" Jack gasped, horrified.

"I'm cloudbusting, Jack," Parry answered matter-of-factly. "Have you ever done any cloudbusting? You lie on your back and you concentrate on the clouds, and you break them apart with your mind. It's wild!"

The pants were off now, down around his ankles, and Parry was hopping around to kick them away. He wore no underwear. His muscular little hairy body was completely naked. "But you have to be nude," he continued. "Otherwise, you can't diffuse the psychic energy." Naked, he lay down on the grass in full view of the moon, his head pillowed on his arms, completely at home.

"You can't do this!" a shocked Jack Lucas exclaimed. "This is New York! Nobody lies naked in a field in New York. It's too . . . midwestern!"

Parry got up and danced around laughing. "Wild! It's really freeing! Come on and try it, Jack. You feel the air on your body . . . your nipples are hard . . . your little guy's dangling in the wind. Everybody in the city is busy with their business and no one knows we're bare-assed in the middle of it. Come on!"

"You're pissin' me off, Parry," Jack warned.

But Parry was too caught up in his Dionysian revelry to pay attention. He kept dancing around Jack, yelling, "Free yourself! Free yourself!" Jack kept glancing about nervously. He couldn't decide which would be more welcome now—the sight of the cops or the muggers. This was the stupidest thing that nut case had pulled yet, and Jack Lucas was damned if he was going to let himself be dragged into it.

"C'mon, Jack!" Parry's exuberance was escalating as his dancing became even more frenzied. He resembled some prehistoric savage in the throes of a religious ritual. "Do you know why you should do it? 'Cause it feels good!"

"No! I'm not doing that!"

"Yes! Yo! Get back to your roots! C'mon, Jack, free up the little guy and let it flap in the breeze!" And, throwing back his head, Parry began to yip and howl like a wild dog.

Of all the embarrassing stunts Parry had pulled today, this was by far the looniest. "I'm not doing this!" Jack yelled at Parry. "This is nuts! This is too nuts! I'm leaving! I mean it!"

He walked away a few feet and then turned to look back. Parry was on the ground again, lying on his back in the grass with his arms tucked under his head, staring blissfully up at the moon. With a snort of anger, Jack kept walking.

"Huh, little guy," he muttered scornfully to himself. "I mean, the man talks to invisible people. He sees invisible horses, and he's lying naked in the middle of Central Park. I should be surprised? I'm not surprised. I'm fuckin' outta my mind to even be here!"

Parry raised himself up on one elbow. "Who are you talking to, Jack?" he asked amiably.

"I'm talking to the Little People," Jack snarled back.

"Are they here?" Parry sat up, excited.

"Yes! They're saying, 'Jack, get thee to the nearest liquor store and buy thyself a fifth of Jack Daniel's, that ye may be shit-faced.' "

"They said that?"

Jack turned back, completely out of patience, and yelled at Parry. "You're out of your fuckin' mind!"

"Bingo," Parry said triumphantly.

Christ, whaddya gonna do? With a sigh of frustration, Jack walked back and lay down beside Parry, fully clothed. He stared up into the night sky and the moon shining golden on the clouds. Long moments passed.

"They're not moving," he said at last.

"Concentrate," Parry advised. Jack undid the top

two buttons on his shirt, as a compromise to nudity-in-cloudbusting. Maybe it helped a little. From time to time a wisp of cloud would drift across the face of the moon, but the large masses of cloud formations appeared to be slumbering in the sky.

It was, as Parry said, a beautiful evening, calm and still. To Jack, it was . . . almost . . . pleasant to lie here in the grass beside Parry. The moonlight bathed them both in its radiance and it was a relief to have Parry at rest for once. Jack had never seen Parry when he wasn't darting about like a hungry hummingbird.

"What if some homophobic jogger runs by and kills us to get back at his father?" Jack wondered half to himself.

" 'Jack Lucas Found Dead . . . Beside a Dead Naked Man . . . The Two Were Dead . . . His Companion Was Naked.' "

Jack recited the imaginary headlines, musing out loud. "I hate it when they use the word 'companion,' it's so insinuating. Although, it would probably boost the sales of my biography. The public has a fascination with celebrity murders that involve nakedness." He added bitterly, "Bastards."

"I may be going out on a limb here," Parry remarked, "but you don't seem like a happy camper."

Jack only grunted in reply.

"Did you ever hear the story of the Fisher King?" Parry asked suddenly.

"No."

Parry began to speak very quietly, as though telling the tale to a child to make him sleep.

"It begins with the Fisher King as a boy—who had to spend a night alone in the forest so that he could become a king. While he was alone in the forest, he was visited by a sacred vision. Out of the fire appeared the Holy Grail, the symbol of God's divine grace. And a voice spoke to the boy, saying,

'You shall be the keeper of the Grail, that it may heal the hearts of men.' But the boy was blinded by greater visions, by a life ahead filled with power and glory . . . and beauty. . . . And in this state of radical amazement, he felt . . . for a brief moment . . . not like a boy, but invincible, like God.

"And so he reached into the fire to take the Grail. And the Grail vanished. And the boy's hands were left in the flames, to be terribly wounded. Now, as this boy grew older, his wound grew deeper, until one day, he had no faith left in any man, not even himself. He couldn't love or feel love. And he was so sick with experience that he started to die. As he did, so did his kingdom, and that terrified his people, so they mobilized to find the one thing they knew could save him, the Holy Grail."

Jack Lucas found himself completely caught up in the story, and in the magical eloquent way that Parry recited it in the moonlight. This must have been what it was like when he was sane, he thought bitterly. Henry Sagan must have been a wonderful teacher, in love with his material and able to transmit the beauty and wonder of it into young minds. A pang of regret nibbled at his heart as Jack realized that he would never know the man Henry Sagan, and that he wanted to, very much. He had a sudden sense of grief and loss.

"One day," Parry went on, "a fool wandered into the castle and found the king alone. Being simple-minded, he didn't see a king, he saw a man alone and in pain.

" 'What ails you, friend?' he asked the king. The king replied, 'I'm thirsty. I need a sip of water to cool my throat.' So the fool took a cup from the bedside table, filled it with water, and handed it to the king. As the king began to drink he realized that his wound was healed. He looked at his hands, and there in them was that which he had sought all his life, the Holy Grail. And he turned to the fool and asked, 'How could you find what my brightest and bravest could not?'

"And the fool replied, 'I don't know. I only knew that you were thirsty.' "

The story of the Fisher King came to an end; Parry fell silent. Jack wanted to say something, but he was at a loss for words.

"Very beautiful, isn't it?" said Parry in a half whisper, and Jack nodded.

"I think I heard it at a lecture once . . . I don't know . . . a professor . . . at Hunter—" Parry broke off, confused and disoriented and suddenly frightened.

Jack turned to look at him. The small man was trembling. "Parry, Parry, hey . . ."

"What was I saying?" Parry asked, a look of panic on his face. He was staring straight ahead, and Jack turned to see what he was staring at. There was nothing.

But it wasn't nothing. Jack didn't see the Red Knight, but Parry did. He was sitting on his warhorse only about thirty feet away, watching. His sword was drawn; his lance rested across the horse's back. And Parry knew what the Red Knight was thinking. He was thinking, Soon, Parry, soon. You won't always have Jack around to protect you. Someday soon, I'll come upon you alone. And when I do . . ." A shaft of moonlight glinted off the deadly sword, and Parry shuddered in fear.

Picking up Parry's tattered jacket, Jack wrapped it around the small shivering figure. Parry laid his head back down on the grass, but Jack could sense his continued uneasiness.

"How come you never asked that girl for a date?" he asked, to change the subject.

Parry sat up and took a cautious look. The Red Knight had disappeared. He caught his breath in relief. "I can't *ask* her. I have to *earn* her," he explained, in a tone that implied that Jack ought to know better.

"It's the twentieth century, Parry, you don't have to earn a woman."

Parry nodded doubtfully. "Maybe, after we get the Grail . . ."

Jack's heart sank. "We"? Where the hell did he keep getting "we"?

"Well, see, she can help you get the Grail," he said hastily, trying to recollect what little he knew about the Middle Ages. "Women are great . . . they make homes . . . and they . . . y'know . . . they kill the livestock so the knights can go out and get Grails and . . . slaughter villages with a clear head. I mean, where would Arthur be without Guinevere?"

"Happily married, probably," Parry answered.

Oh, yeah, right, Jack had forgotten how *that* legend had turned out. "Well, that's a bad example. But trust me on this. A woman who loves you keeps you going . . . gives you strength . . . makes you feel like you can do anything."

"Is that what your girlfriend does for you?" Parry asked eagerly.

The question caught Jack by surprise and threw him off balance. Suddenly he thought of Anne and felt guilty. How *did* he feel about Anne Napolitano? He pushed the question out of his mind, unable to deal with it.

"Sure," he lied.

Jack woke up stiff as a board and shivering with cold. The ground was icy and rocky and damp; he couldn't believe he'd actually slept right here for hours. He brought his wrist up to his face and made himself focus on his watch. It was early, not much after eight in the morning, but already the joggers were skittering through Central Park in all directions, like cockroaches when you turn on the kitchen lights.

Why was he sleeping in the park? He hadn't even been drinking. Oh, yeah, cloudbusting. Jack looked over to where Parry had been sleeping, but the little man was gone. Thank God, his scattered clothing was gone, too, so Jack had some grounds for hope that Parry had dressed himself before he took off. Probably didn't want to wake him.

He suddenly flashed on where Parry must be. It was a weekday, Thursday. Parry had to be in front of the Haagensen Building, waiting for the girl of his dreams to show up for work. Right. Jack stood up a little shakily, every muscle protesting, and brushed himself off. Then he walked over to Fifth Avenue, pushed his way onto a crowded downtown bus, and got off a block after the Haagensen Building. He walked back, careful not to let Parry, whom Jack spotted at his customary station, see him coming. Parry was so focused on the revolving doors that he never noticed Jack slipping into the side entrance of the building.

Taking up his station near the elevators, Jack looked at his watch again. Three minutes to nine. If the girl was as predictable in her habits as Parry claimed she was, she'd be here . . . right . . . about now! And there she was, clumsily pushing her way through the nine o'clock crowd of workers to get to her elevator.

Jack maneuvered himself behind her and got into the same elevator. He turned his face away so that she couldn't make out his features, but he needn't have bothered. The young woman was oblivious of everything and everybody, not looking at anybody else in the elevator, but keeping her eyes to the front, waiting for her floor to come up.

Seen up close, the girl Parry was so enchanted by had pure, beautiful skin and fine large eyes, although the rest of her could really stand one of those magazine beauty makeovers. She got off at the eighth floor, and so did Jack. When she turned the corner down the corridor, Jack hung behind, not wishing to be seen following, but he kept his eye on her as she went through a pair of glass doors to an office.

After she went inside, Jack moved forward and looked at the office doors. Printed on them in gold and black lettering was Two HEARTS PUBLISHING, INC. Jack waited a moment, straightening his rumpled jacket and brushing at his unruly hair with the palms of his hands, then he pushed the office door open and went inside.

He found himself in a reception area decorated by a couple of dusty couches, a table with an ashtray, and a reception desk. On the walls were framed paperback covers, presumably from Two Hearts Publishing's own list. They were all romances—busty young women in low-cut gowns shrinking away while handsome men wearing shirts with long, flowing sleeves bent lustfully over them, one hand on the girl's bodice and the other on a pistol or a sword. If Parry's lady loved reading this garbage, she was certainly working in the right place.

"Yes?" A crisp voice from the reception desk challenged him. A mildly attractive girl with a fluffy perm and too much lipstick was glaring at Jack as though he'd come in on the bottom of her shoe.

He knew he looked like a bum. What did she expect? He'd been out all day and all night, running himself ragged around the city, and he hadn't had a chance to shave or bathe. He desperately needed a change of clothes, a toothbrush, and a comb. No receptionist worth her paycheck would let him get a foot in the door. Jack knew that.

But Jack Lucas had a secret weapon. He had charm. He knew he was good-looking, with thick hair, a good body, attractive blue eyes, a great grin and deep dimples, but the big armament, the nuclear warhead, was his infallible ability to turn on the charm. Charm, don't fail me now!

"Could you help me?" he asked sweetly, looking into the receptionist's eyes and letting charm flow out of him like syrup on an Eggo. "What was the name of that girl who just came in?"

Girl? "What girl? I didn't notice," the receptionist said, caught in Jack Lucas's blue-eyed stare like a fish in a net.

How to describe her? "Uh, she was wearing a kind of, that is, a plain . . . she isn't pretty . . . her hair looks like . . ." He made strings of his fingers to indicate stringy hair.

"Oh, Lydia!"

Lydia. Good. He had a first name, and that was a start. "Lydia what?"

The girl fluffed out her curls, to show Jack what real hair should look like. "God, I have no idea. She's worked here for fifteen years and I have no idea. I'll call her."

"No!" Jack said quickly. "No, no, that's all right. I thought I knew her . . . but thanks." Rewarding the receptionist with one of his biggest smiles, he got out of there.

Parry was not on the street when Jack emerged from the side entrance. He felt kind of good. He had a name—Lydia—and a venue—Two Hearts Publishing. Now all he needed was a plan.

Thirteen

Anne was busy writing up an order for a videotape rental when she was certain she heard footsteps in her apartment above the store. That bastard Jack must be home. Twenty-four hours late, but home.

As soon as she could, she ducked out of the Video Spot and ran upstairs. She found Jack Lucas sitting on her sofa, the Yellow Pages open on his lap. He looked like hell, scruffy and none too clean, like somebody who'd been sleeping in Central Park all night. When Anne came into the room, Jack was saying into the phone, "Yes, is this Two Hearts Publishing? May I speak to Lydia, please?"

Anne could hardly believe her ears. The nerve of the bum! "Lydia?" He was calling some bimbette! And on her phone bill, too!

She approached him menacingly, claws out, ready to kill, but Jack wasn't even paying attention. This irritated Anne even more. Fire flashed out of her black eyes, her breasts heaved in anger, and the very curls in her black hair were electric with indignation.

"You are calling *Lydia?* From my apartment you are calling *Lydia?*" she demanded.

"Hello, I'd like to speak to Lydia." Jack had gotten through to the right department.

"Lydia? Lydia who!" Anne reached angrily for the phone, but Jack held it out of her reach.

He put his hand over the mouthpiece. "I don't

know her last name," he said. "I'll be off in a minute."

Some tramp without even a last name? This was the final straw for Anne, and she let her temper fly. Furiously, she began punching at Jack, hitting him in the neck, on the shoulder, wherever she could reach, while he fended her off with his elbows and continued to cling to the phone.

"Son of a *bitch!*" she yelled. "You stay out all night, I don't even get a friggin' phone call!"

"Ow! Don't! Quit it!" Then he spoke into the phone. "What? No, I don't know her last name . . . her name is Lydia. Can I speak to her?"

But Anne was far from ready to quit it. "You stroll in here at noon, without a stinkin' word. I got two people out sick. You think I need this?! I . . . do . . . not . . . *need* . . . this!" Another hefty wallop, this time a lucky punch, connected hard with Jack's ear.

"Forget it!" Jack hollered into the phone. "Goodbye!" He slammed down the receiver and gave Anne his full attention. He was aware that he owed her a decent explanation, but how could he explain Parry and Parry's bizarre obsessions? Or the crazy idea that Jack himself had come up with?

"I was not with a woman last night," he said quietly. "I was with Parry."

Anne's eyes widened in surprise. "The moron?"

"He's not a moron," said Jack emphatically.

"And who's Lydia?" Anne didn't let go easily.

"Lydia is the girl Parry likes. And I thought, if I could get them together, I . . ."

"What?" Anne demanded. "The curse will be lifted? Gimme a break, puh-leeze!" Her lively face registered scornful disbelief.

Jack fumbled to find the right words. "I . . . uh . . . you're not going to understand this—"

"Don't treat me like I'm stupid," snapped Anne. "It pisses me off."

Jack nodded; fair enough. "Sorry . . . you're right. It's just that . . . I feel . . . indebted to him. I thought, well, if I could only help him in some way, you know? Get him this girl he loves? Then . . . maybe . . . things might change for me, too. My luck, you know . . . maybe it could . . . ahhhh, forget it! It's just a dumb fuckin' idea."

Anne regarded him thoughtfully. The last vestige of suspicion still clung like crumbs to the corners of her mind. But consider. Jack was sober, for a change; he appeared to be sincere, and God knows his luck had been terrible. Now the crumbs of suspicion dissolved, and she felt suddenly guilty for having doubted him. Poor schmuck, she'd been so hard on him. Just look at his disappointed face.

"Aww, you big galoot," she said affectionately. "You're such a mess. Well, listen, stranger things have been known to happen. Here, let me do it. What's the name of the place and the phone number?"

Jack dialed the number and handed Anne the telephone. "Hello," she said crisply, "Is that Two Hearts Publishing? Good. This is Mr. Jack Lucas's secretary. Mr. Lucas is attempting to reach one of your employees, a Miss Lydia—wait, let me check my notes. Oh, Sinclair? Lydia Sinclair? Yes, I believe that's the person. Put her on, please."

Grinning, she handed the phone over to Jack, who threw her a grateful and admiring look. When she had a mind to, Anne could be really something.

A woman's voice came on the line. "Hello?"

"Hello, Lydia?"

"Yes, who is this, please?" Her voice surprised Jack. It was not the timid squeak of the mousy little wimp she appeared to be, but a rather loud, abrasive bray.

"This is Jack Lucas," he said in his best radio-announcer voice, "and I'm calling from Video Spot video rentals."

"Yes?" The voice sounded suspicious, as though Lydia Sinclair were going to hang up on the caller if he didn't make his point soon.

Jack thought fast, coming up with a ploy. "Yes, well, you are a credit-card holder, aren't you?" *Please, please, let her be a credit-card holder.*

"Yes, so?" challenged Lydia.

Jack sighed silently in relief. "Well, Lydia, I have some good news for you. Congratulations. Out of several thousand card holders, in conjunction with major credit-card companies—"

"Which ones?" Lydia demanded.

Which ones? What kind of a question was that? "Uh . . . all of them. Which means *you* have just won a free membership at our store on Eighth Avenue!" He pushed the play button on his tape recorder and happy circus music poured into the receiver and out into Lydia Sinclair's ear.

"How did this happen?" Lydia asked brusquely when the music stopped. She sounded definitely suspicious, as though he were trying to sell her something. Which, of course, he was, although she'd probably keel over in a dead faint if she could actually see who it was he was selling. Lydia and Parry, now *there* was an odd couple!

"Your name was picked."

There was a pause on the line, and then Lydia's voice returned, sounding somewhat confused. "Uh, picked? I don't . . . I don't understand. Was I on a list? Did you pick my name off a list or was it out of a hat or something?"

"A list." This was like pulling teeth. Jack was starting to sweat.

"I . . . uh . . . what's going on? Were there a lot of people in the room or just you or what?"

God, this woman was so literal-minded that getting through to her was like ramming a stone wall! Didn't she have any imagination? "Well, there was . . . what's the difference?" Jack asked, beginning to run out of patience.

Lydia began to stammer nervously. "Well . . . I mean . . . I don't know you . . . I don't . . . I never . . . I've never won anything in my life . . . and I don't even have a VCR."

"You get a free VCR with membership!" Jack announced, then Anne punched him really hard in the arm. "Uh . . . for a short time, until you get your own," he amended. "Listen, why don't you just come down to the store and you can check it out. See if you're interested."

"Did Phyllis tell you to call me?" Lydia asked paranoically. "Did Phyllis in Accounting tell you to call me? This is a joke, right?"

"No!" Jack yelled in frustration. *"I told you! You won a contest!"*

There was a click in his ear. Lydia Sinclair had hung up the phone.

Turning to Anne, who was grinning and shaking her head, Jack moaned. "This is going to be rough. Oh, Jesus, is this going to be rough."

The plot that Jack finally devised out of desperation was so absurd that it would have been laughable except for one thing. He himself was the fool who was going to have to see that it was pulled off correctly. Anne went to the store to have the balloons printed, and Jack, cursing his fate, cursing Lydia, cursing Parry, cursing life, went in search of Michael, the gay little crazy he'd last seen in the emergency room at St. Alphonsus.

Strangely enough, Jack located Michael before Anne had finished ordering the balloons. There seemed to be a kind of bum underground, a network of the homeless, and somehow Jack had become, thanks to Parry, a recognizable member of it. With the information he was given, he found Michael not ten blocks away from the Video Spot, cruising Eighth Avenue. By the time Jack had finished explaining his plan, Michael was ecstatic.

"I'll do it. Of course I'll do it. I'd do anything for you, Jack. You're my friend. Besides, it sounds like the funnest thing!"

Funnest for you, maybe, Jack thought as he rode up in the elevator with Michael next to him. But not for me. Michael had rung in some embellishments to the plan, one or two unexpected ruffles and flourishes. Like full drag, for example.

Jack's eyes had popped out of his head when the little man turned up at the Haagensen Building wearing a costume that could only be described as grotesque outrageous—all spangles and flirty hems and off-the-shoulder see-through, plus high heels. It was topped by a wig and a big picture hat, from under which Michael's tiny face appeared in theatrical makeup—eyelashes mascaraed, cheeks rouged, lips a bright red, and that large mustache sitting smack in the middle of everything. When he saw him coming, Jack wanted to turn and run and hide.

Well, it was too late to do anything about it now. Jack shoved the bright yellow balloons into Michael's hands. Anne had had them printed up with "Video Spot," and the store's address and phone number. She'd instructed Jack specifically not to lose them, because they just might come in handy at the store. Two or three more were printed with "Congratulations, Lydia!" and these Anne didn't particularly want to see again.

Together, Jack and Michael rode up to the eighth floor. Thank God there was nobody else in the elevator, because Michael was warming up, getting into the spirit of things by humming and camping and fluffing up his ruffles. Jack stared at the ceiling and hoped fervently that nobody would get on the elevator between the ground floor and the eighth. That was all he needed, for them to be caught in this together by somebody from the real world.

A little hand touched his arm, and a voice sobbed, "I'm Anne Morrow Lindbergh, and I can't find my baby!"

Jack looked down, startled, at Michael, who was dabbing at his eyes with a lace hankie. Despite himself, Jack had to laugh.

"See." Michael grinned. "I knew I could make you smile."

The elevator came to a stop on eight and the doors opened. "Listen," Jack said warningly, "one chorus and out! Got it?"

"I'm a man with a mission, Jack." Clutching the balloons, Michael flounced out and down the hall, his high heels clacking on the vinyl flooring.

Jack shook his head. "I can't believe I'm on a first-name basis with these people," he mumbled to himself as the elevator carried him back down to the lobby.

In less than the space of a week, Jack Lucas had gone from a black, boozy, shitty, depressing, morally reprehensible but relatively normal existence into the Twilight Zone. Crazies were now his bosom buddies and boon companions. One of them, a man who hadn't worn out a pair of shoes since 1964, thought he was Ethel Merman, while the other, who was fixated on the homliest girl in New York, heard fat little fairies telling him to find the Holy Grail. Bums had become Jack's familiars, they recognized him on the street and hailed him as a brother. How the fuck had he gotten himself into this mess? Oh, right, he remembered. All he'd tried to do was kill himself. Was that such a crime?

Upstairs, Michael and his yellow balloons went wafting down the corridor and in through the front doors of Two Hearts Publishing.

The receptionist took one look at him . . . her . . . it . . . and gulped. "Can I . . . help . . . you?"

"Is there a mousy little woman named Lydia working here?"

"Yes. If you'll wait here, I'll—"

But Michael wasn't into waiting. "This is a personalized message. I have to give it in person." He pushed past the reception desk into the office area.

"Hey, you can't go back there! You're really not authorized—"

But it was too late. Michael was already out of earshot, scampering down the rows of cubicles where employees of the publishing company were toiling away.

He passed a cubicle bearing a little brass nameplate reading "Lydia Sinclair." The person inside had her back to him, but when she turned around, he could see that she was drab and pinched looking, with the least chic outfit and the worst haircut he'd ever seen on a woman outside of a prison or a mental hospital.

"You *must* be she!" he exclaimed. Lydia uttered a little bark of surprise when she saw the face, and the drag, and the balloons.

There was a platform piled with books outside Lydia Sinclair's office, and Michael scrambled up on top of it. Then, taking a pose, he began to belt out a medley from *Gypsy*, only with a change of lyrics. For a little man, he had an enormous voice, worthy of the Ethel Merman he aspired to be.

"Lydia, you've won the grand prize. Just think of it, all the movies you'll be watching free now . . . dramas, westerns, comedies, wow! Video Spot has the best selection . . . if you like porno, we're your connection . . . for you, Lydia! For free!"

Michael finished with a flourish, on a loud, long, high note, and jumped off the platform. "Our card," he announced grandly, handing her the whole handful of balloons with Video Spot's address and telephone number. And before the astonished girl could say a word, he was floating out on his high, narrow heels, down the corridor, through the reception area, and into the elevator.

Well, hell, if that didn't bring her in, nothing would. It had certainly been one of his better gigs. Michael personally knew people who would gladly pay $15.60 or more for a performance like that.

As it turned out, Michael's part was a lot easier than Jack's. Jack not only had to locate Parry, he had to convince him to come with him to the Video Spot. Parry could not conceive of leaving Lydia's office building without seeing her go out to lunch, and it took five minutes of red-faced arguing on Jack's part to get across the idea that Lydia would almost certainly not be going to a restaurant today. That there was every chance in the world that Parry would encounter her at the Video Spot.

But Parry was a creature of habit, and his habit was to be at the Haggensen Building every day at noon.

At first Jack argued with him, but in vain. At the end, though, the thing that finally wore down Parry's resistance was the magnificence of this new possession of his—he had Lydia's name. Lydia. Lydia Sinclair. Splendor. Music. Magic. Beauty. Euphony. Armed with this new talisman and the hope of seeing his lady up close, plus the promise of a hot home-cooked meal, Parry was at last content to trot across town to Eighth Avenue with Jack.

To Anne Napolitano, who had grown up in a house where soap was prized above everything except pasta and the Sacred Heart, the sight and the smell of

Parry came as a repulsive shock. You want to make a career as a bum, okay, but why not at least a *clean* bum? This wasn't going to work; what girl would look at a walking trash pile like him? But she kept her mouth shut, not wanting to rain on Jack's parade. She hadn't seen Jack this excited since . . . well, come to think of it, she'd *never* seen Jack this excited.

It was a quarter after twelve. Since Lydia operated like clockwork, if she was coming at all, she was due here in about five minutes. Jack would barely have time to slick back Parry's hair and pull a Video Spot T-shirt over Parry's head.

"See, with the shirt, it'll be like you work here," Jack assured him.

"What am I qualified to do?" Parry asked apprehensively. He was so nervous that his legs were trembling.

"Well, uh, just . . . stack up the tapes . . . sort 'em out . . . you know, in categories."

Parry's smell, though, was still the same. Very, very ripe. Like garbage left out for three days in the hot sun. In desperation, Jack looked around the store and came up with one of those pine-scented air fresheners that people hang in their cars, or in this case, on their cash registers. He held it in his hands, unsure what to do with it, and finally wound up hanging it around Parry's neck.

"This'll be good. This will make you smell like a pine forest."

At that moment the bell over the front door jingled and Lydia Sinclair walked in. Jack heard a gasp and a moan behind him and turned to see Parry swaying on his feet, his eyes closed. He was almost passing out.

"Parry, damn it! Keep it together!"

The small man nodded and forced his eyes open,

fixing them on Lydia as she came up to the counter. He'd never seen anything so wondrous as her beauty.

"Hello, my name is Lydia Sinclair," she said flatly, and Parry trembled all over with joy. He'd listened to her voice for the first time, and to him it was like the sonorous tolling of the bells of the cathedral of Notre Dame, or like the portentous harmonies of a Bach mass.

"Oh, hi, how ya doin'?" Jack was all smiles and affability. "Congratulations. I'm Jack Lucas. Nice to meet you finally. This is Anne Napolitano, owner of Video Spot."

"Hello," said Anne reluctantly. "Congratulations." She eyed Lydia curiously. This was the great beauty that Jack's little nutty pal was so crazy about? Yeah, well, crazy was the operative word here.

"And this," said Jack, drawing Parry forward by force, "is our . . . coworker . . . Parry . . . uh . . . Parry."

"Parry Parry?" Lydia asked, the most literal-minded person in the world. What a perfect companion for a man who saw Grails in magazine articles! They couldn't miss.

"No, just Parry," said Parry in a voice barely above a whisper.

"Oh, like Moses," Lydia said, and Parry gave a little hysterical moan, compounded of adoration and terror.

"So, how do we do this?" demanded the girl.

Jack thought a second. "Well, first you sign an official membership card." He took one from the pile by the register. "Just sign that, and we'll have this laminated for you right here. Parry. Would you like to laminate Miss Sinclair's card? Parry?"

It took him a minute to snap Parry out of his worshipful catatonia, but when the little man understood what was being asked of him, he took the card eagerly. For Lydia Sinclair, he'd laminate his tongue.

Just being in the same store with her, able to hear her speak, see her face up close, had sent him into such euphoria that he could barely function; the laminating machine was completely beyond his powers.

While Parry was reducing the membership card to a laminated tatter Anne was explaining the rules. "This will last you one year, after which you have the option to renew, if you like, at a membership discount."

"But now it's for free, right?" Lydia demanded suspiciously.

"Yeah," Anne admitted grudgingly. "Now it's for free."

"You can pick out up to ten movies—" Jack began.

"Free?" The girl might look like a mouse, but she was a mouth with sharp little teeth and a mighty suspicious mind.

"Yes, they're free."

"Only the first ten," Anne put in hastily. "After that, they're two-ninety-nine a rental."

Lydia turned this information over in her mind, looking for the catch. Then she headed for the shelves to check out the merchandise. Parry handed Jack the pathetic remnants of the laminated card, and Jack shook his head. Then all three turned to watch Lydia—Anne and Jack with curiosity and some amusement, Parry with his heart in his hopeful eyes.

Lydia pulled a videotape off the rack to have a look at it. Two others began to fall. She tried to catch them, and an entire rackful of videotapes began tumbling to the ground. Anne rolled her eyes in exasperation, and Jack nudged Parry forward to help. It took all the nerve Parry could muster to actually approach and speak to his beloved.

"Can . . . can I help you?"

Lydia turned. This odd little man was standing

very close to her, smelling of pine freshener. Proximity to another human being always made Lydia Sinclair uncomfortable. "No, no, I can look myself."

With your eyes closed, you could tell exactly where Lydia was in the store, by the crash of falling cassette boxes. Parry moved timidly behind her, like the sweeper after the circus parade, picking up the debris and stacking them back up. He held out a videotape.

"Hell Merchants?" he offered hopefully. "Good choice."

"I don't like horror movies," said Lydia flatly.

Nodding, Parry rummaged around for another. "How about this one?" He read from the blurb on the box. 'Zbigniew Speizak's *The Purple Bread,* an intensely portrayed tale of love and envy set against the sweeping background of a polish . . . uh . . . Polish . . . bakery. With subtitles."

Lydia Sinclair shook her head decisively. "I don't like Polish love stories. I like musicals."

Musicals! A preference at last! Parry's face brightened. "Well, we have plenty of those. Here's our entertainment center," and he gestured to a large filled rack. "We got Astaire and Rogers, Judy Garland, Al Jolson . . ."

"Got any Ethel Merman?"

"Ethel Merman . . . let's see." Parry pawed through the racks eagerly, then frantically. He came up empty. "Uh . . . we seem to be all out of Ethel Merman."

Lydia's face screwed up and a frustrated little scream came out of her. "What a gyp!" she shouted.

Jack nudged Anne in the side, a nudge that said plainly, Do something.

"You know," Anne lied, "I think I may have ordered some just the other day."

Think? May have? They didn't know whom they

were dealing with here. "Well, did you or didn't you?" demanded Lydia Sinclair.

Anne's eyes narrowed. "Yessss," she hissed. "They'll be in soon."

"Well, I guess I'll come back then," Lydia retorted prissily. She turned to leave.

"Miss Sinclair!" Jack called hastily. "Here's your card. Don't forget it." Anne handed her the laminated membership card. Lydia reached out to take it, and then she noticed Anne's fingernails. They were long, and red, and perfectly manicured. Each nail had a colorful painted star right in the middle of it. They were actually very beautiful, and Anne was quite proud of them.

"I like your nails," said Lydia, and her face softened just a little. "Where did you get them done?"

"Actually," Anne said with no small pride, "I do them myself. I used to work in a beauty parlor."

"I like the stars." Lydia's face was actually a little wistful, and suddenly she looked much younger.

A light bulb switched on over Jack Lucas's head. "You know, Anne does other people's nails, too." This was news to Anne, who gave him a surprised look, but before she could open her mouth, Jack said, "It's sort of a sideline. If you want, she could do *your* nails."

I'll kill him, thought Anne. The minute I get him alone, I'll tear him into tortellini. Then Lydia asked abruptly "How much?"

"Well," Jack began with a big smile, "since you're a member, we could—"

"Forty dollars," Anne interrupted firmly.

"Forty dollars?" Jack squeaked.

Lydia Sinclair scrunched her face up as though she were in physical pain. Her nose twitched like a squirrel, and she muttered under her breath, "Forty . . . uh . . . fort—" The thought of parting with so much money was evidently giving her a severe ache in the gut. She mentally calculated the impact that forty dollars would make on her budget. Parry watched her, not daring to breathe or even blink his eyes.

"Okay, forty dollars," she said at last. Jack's eyebrows went up in surprise, and Parry let his breath out in a whistle. "When will you do them?"

Anne considered. She was already regretting the turn events were taking. She really didn't want to get sucked into this any more than she was already. "I don't know. Maybe next—"

"Tonight?" Parry suggested.

"Tonight?" echoed Jack, and on his face was a look of pleading mingled with hope. Anne shot him a dirty look.

"Tonight," said Lydia Sinclair in her flat voice.

"Tonight," agreed Anne, with a sigh.

Fourteen

"You know, getting your nails done is one thing, but going to dinner with a bunch of strangers and—" Anne broke off and threw a significant glance at Parry. "*This* one, well, Lydia's not gonna buy it. She didn't even look at him."

Parry didn't appear to be listening to Anne's scathing commentary. He held out his plate for more macaroni and smiled winningly. "Thank you."

But Anne Napolitano wasn't won over. She was far from happy about having this certified lunatic sitting at her table eating her out of house and home, and much less than enthused by Jack's crazy plan of getting the four of them together tonight for dinner.

"It won't be like a real date," Jack said over his shoulder. His voice was muffled because his head was in the closet, where he was rummaging for something decent for Parry to wear. "We're going to make it real casual."

"Got any more starchy food?" Parry asked brightly. With a little scowl, Anne got up from the table and went into the kitchen for the casserole dish. Parry's eyes followed her, appreciating the bouncing of her large breasts and the rotating motion of her hips underneath the tight skirt. All woman, his eyes said.

"I mean, I've gone out with bums," Anne added, dumping the remainder of the macaroni from the dish into Parry's plate, "but they were beautiful. It's the only reason to go out with a bum."

"This food's delicious." Parry beamed. "You're a wonderful cook. and you have a lovely set of . . . dishes."

Anne looked startled and repulsed. "Jack, he's trying to start a conversation with me!" she bawled.

"Well, talk back. He won't bite you."

She drew in a deep breath, which made her prominent breasts stand out even more. "Thank you," she said as politely as she could.

"You're welcome," Parry replied with equal ceremony, happily wolfing down the chow. He kept his admiring eyes on Anne. "You know, you're a beautiful woman. You got your own business. I'm surprised some guy doesn't snatch you up all for his own."

Anne sneaked a look over at Jack, but he was still busy sorting through his wardrobe. *"You're* surprised! But I guess I just never met the right guy. Whaddya gonna do?"

Parry put down his spoon. "I'm shocked! With a childbearing body like yours, why, a guy would have to be out of his mind!"

"Most guys are," Anne observed dryly.

Parry warmed up to his topic. "This is outrageous!" he declared. "No! You, this incredible woman, going to waste before my eyes! I will not hear of this!" Rising to his feet, he swept the food, the dishes, and everything off the table with one broad movement of his arm. Anne uttered a little squeak of disbelief and fear.

"Come on! I'm your man! Let's do it right here! Let's go to that place of splendor in the grass!"

"Jack!" Anne yelled in horror. Nothing this insane had ever happened to her before. She began to back away from the table, looking around her wildly for help.

Parry climbed up on the table and unzipped his pants. "Behold!" he cried proudly, about to grab hold of his little guy. "My magic wand! Come, free your golden orbs!"

"Jack!"

"Holdin' my penis," crooned Parry, serenading this beautiful woman. "What a wonderful way of sayin' how much you like me—"

"What are you, out of your mind? Jack!"

"Parry! Close your pants," Jack ordered quietly, coming in holding a suit on a hanger.

"Took you long enough." Parry grinned, zipping up his trousers. He turned to Anne. "But you let me know. You're too good a woman to go to waste."

Anne drew in a ragged breath. Could you believe this guy? One minute nuts, the next minute . . . almost making sense.

Jack paid no attention to any of this. By now he was used to Parry and his wild mood swings. He held the suit up in front of Parry and cast a critical eye over it. "What are you, a size forty in a jacket?"

Gathering up the suit, a shirt, and a tie, Jack led Parry downstairs. The Video Spot was closed for the evening, and the back room would be the perfect place to get Parry ready for his not-like-a-real-date with Lydia Sinclair. And Parry would no doubt take a lot of getting ready.

Anne cleared the crockery up from the floor and carried the broken dishes and the cutlery into the kitchen. She washed them and scoured the casserole and wiped down the table, the sink, and the stove, but her mind wasn't on her chores. She was thinking about Jack, about the amazing effect that this nut Parry seemed to be having on him.

Partly, Anne felt hurt—why did her lover prefer spending his time with a schizophrenic street bum rather than with her? She knew that he felt guilty about what had happened to Parry's life, but some-how she got the idea that Jack actually almost en-joyed looking after Parry, that something other than guilt was operating here.

But, also, Anne was fascinated, both drawn to and repelled by this crazy little man. Underneath all that horse shit there had to be a pony. Parry was obvi-ously intelligent, and not all that bad to look at, if you scraped off the thick layers of crud he was hid-ing under. He had beautiful eyes and a warm, sweet smile. And there was a kind of interaction between him and Jack that intrigued her; this was a side of Jack Lucas that Anne had never seen, a kind of emerging gentleness, as though Parry were a child that needed looking after. And what about Lydia? *There* was a character! A mouse on the outside, a tiger on the inside. And covered with prickly thorns like a little hedgehog. Lydia Sinclair was somebody who couldn't face life unless her back was to the wall, but once she did, watch out, life! Parry found this homely girl with knobby knees and protruding elbows gorgeous. He gazed at her drab face and nothing hair and stick figure and saw a movie star. She hung the moon for him, and Anne, who was under her tough exterior a mushy romantic, found that ineffably touching. Lydia didn't know how lucky she was; if only Jack would look at *her* that way. Naaah, she was dreaming. Never happen.

When she'd finished in the kitchen, Anne laid out all her manicure implements and nail paints on a clean cloth on the coffee table. She was brushing her hair when the doorbell rang, and she opened the door to find Lydia Sinclair standing outside with a suspi-cious, rather fearful expression on her face.

"Hello, welcome." Anne greeted her with as much warmth as she could muster. "Come in."

But Lydia lingered half in and half out of the door-way, as if afraid of what she might find inside. Anne put one hand on her hip impatiently, and Lydia crossed the threshold at last. She looked around the apartment with undisguised curiosity.

"I've never been inside an apartment over a store before," she said in that flat monotone of hers. "You always walk past them when you walk by, but you never think anybody really lives in them."

Stung, Anne opened her mouth to say something sarcastic, then thought better of it. After all, it wasn't as though Lydia was going to make any difference in her life. After tonight, Anne would never see this prickly person again. She could afford to be nice.

"Can I get you anything? A little coffee, a little tea, maybe? Or how about a little tequila?"

"No, thank you." Lydia was eyeing the tools spread out on the table. She saw nail files, clippers, little manicure scissors, all of them gleaming cold steel like surgical instruments. They looked efficient and almost deadly.

"Will it . . . hurt?" she asked timidly.

"That all depends on you. Sure you don't want a drink?"

"Uh . . . maybe."

Fetching the bottle of tequila, Anne poured them both a healthy shot, and she led Lydia to the sofa.

"You'll enjoy this," Jack assured Parry, slathering an Ernest Lazlo mudpack all over Parry's anxious little face. "This is great for you. It'll make you feel good."

Parry fidgeted nervously, his eyes squinched tight shut. "Mud? You just washed that off."

"That was a different kind of mud. This will make you look great."

"Oh, it's good mud." Parry struggled to understand.

"Just leave it on for a while. It's gonna make a big difference, you'll see," Jack told him. "Now, some clothes. How about this?'' He held up a Gi-anni Versace linen suit, white with black stripes, that had set him back close to two grand in his earlier life. It was way too big for Parry, especially in the length of the trousers, but Jack thought he could make it work. A staple gun and a few dozen staples ought to do the trick. ''Just relax,'' he instructed Parry, although he could see that it was an impossible task. The man was so antsy, he couldn't stop jittering.

''Will you hold still so I can do this?'' Jack demanded, trying not to staple Parry's flesh to the linen.

''I'm sorry. I'm just so excited! You must have felt this way when you first met Anne, huh?''

Jack didn't reply. He wished that Parry wouldn't keep harping on his relationship with Anne Napoli-tano. It stirred up guilt feelings in Jack he didn't enjoy.

''Yeah, if I wasn't already committed to Lydia, boy . . .'' said Parry enthusiastically. ''Except Anne would never go for me, though. She loves you too much. And you really love her, huh?''

Jack didn't know how to answer this.

''You love her a lot, Jack,'' Parry reassured him. ''You're crazy about her. It's just that . . . some-times . . . you're a little bit of an asshole.''

Jack looked up, startled, from his stapling. Now why did he have the feeling that Parry had hit the nail on the head?

''So?'' asked Anne, pushing Lydia's cuticles back with an orange stick. ''Anybody special in your life?''

Lydia pulled her hand out of Anne's and took the other hand out of the liquid in which it was soaking. ''Does it look like there's anybody special in my life?'' she retorted defensively. She took another sip of her tequila.

"Don't say it like that," Anne said, grabbing the hand back. "It's not such a crazy idea. You're a healthy woman. You hold a steady job. You're not cross-eyed or anything—"

"Well, there's nobody special," Lydia snapped, but her eyes clouded.

"Okay, fine." Anne shrugged. It was no skin off her ass. She was just trying to make conversation.

Lydia nibbled on her lower lip. "I mean, it's not easy in this day and age."

"What's not easy?" Anne picked up the emery board and smoothed the edges of Lydia's nails.

"Meeting people."

Anne grinned. "Oh, Gawd, tell me about it. I've been dating longer than I've been driving." As the truth of her own remark struck her she laughed. "I can't believe that."

Lydia's voice dropped to a whisper. "I have never really . . . been through a . . . dating period . . ." she confessed.

"It's a disgusting process," Anne assured her. "You haven't missed anything."

Lydia nodded a little dubiously, and Anne could tell that she didn't really believe her, that she thought she'd missed out on a great deal. Both of them raised their glasses again, draining them. Anne refilled them.

The manicure wasn't going so badly after all. Once Lydia was convinced that Anne wasn't going to murder her, and once the tequila began to take hold, Lydia loosened up a bit and began to confide in Anne. They were just girls together, after all, and this was just girl talk, nothing more.

"My mother calls me once a week," Lydia said, hitting the tequila glass again. "Like a recurring nightmare. 'So, have you met anyone?' 'No,

Mother.' 'So, what's going to happen?' 'I don't know, Mother.' I only thank God I moved out.''

"I can't believe you lived with your mother for so many years," said Anne. "If I had to live with *my* mother, I'd stab myself six times."

Lydia sighed and looked thoughtful, rolling her glass in one hand, while Anne worked on the other, and staring down into the depths of the golden liquor. "I think some people are meant to be alone," she said finally. "This is my idea. I was born a man in a former life and I used women for pleasure, and now I'm paying for it." She sighed again. "I wouldn't mind so much if I could just remember the pleasure parts."

Anne finished painting Lydia's right hand and reached for the left. "Mind the nails; they're wet. I think you're getting a little complicated. What in your opinion is the actual problem?"

Lydia thought the question over gravely. "I don't feel like I make any impression on people," she said slowly, slurring her words. "I don't think I have any personality. At office parties all I do is rearrange the hors d'oeuvres while people are eating them so the platters look as though they're still full. I don't start conversations, because . . . I don't know how to make them end or where to make them go."

Shaking her head, Anne advised, "You gotta be a little easier on yourself, doll. A conversation has a life of its own. I mean, look at us. We're having a conversation."

"I'm paying you," Lydia said bluntly.

Hurt and angry, Anne let Lydia's hand fall. "Will you stop it! I'm not like that. I don't do people favors. If I talk to you, it's because I want to. All right, you're not a super-model," she continued, putting it mildly. "We can't all be Jerry Hall. What a boring world it would be if we were all Jerry Hall. So you do the best with what you got." She thought a minute; her brain was a little fuzzy from the drink. "You want to make an impression? You're looking for a personality? Try this on for size. You can be a real bitch!"

Lydia gasped and her eyes snapped open. She struggled with the concept for a moment, and then her face lit up. "A bitch! Me? Really?"

"You bet."

"Wow!"

As he saw the preparations coming to an end Parry became more and more agitated. He couldn't stand still. He kept fidgeting while Jack tried to calm him down, tying his tie again to get a better knot, smoothing the rather crumpled lapels of the linen suit that had been crushed in the closet.

Jack stepped back to get a better look at Parry. Well, *GQ* would never put him on the cover, but he looked a lot better than the old Parry in rags. For one thing, he was clean, as clean as Jack could get him, considering that some of the grime had been there so long it had worked its way under Parry's skin. His face was gleaming from the mudpack, and his unruly wiry hair had been brushed down with a little bit of mousse. The suit still fit him funny; it was way, way too big, but look who his date would be! They'd be two small people hiding in their clothing. All in all, Jack Lucas was pretty proud of his handiwork.

"I'm gonna give you my wallet so you can pay for dinner," he said, tucking it into Parry's breast pocket.

"You're a nice man, Jack, doing all this for me."

Jack only grunted, his eye going over the last details to see if he could make them better. Suddenly he felt Parry's arms wrapped tightly around him, and Parry's terrified voice whispering in his ear, "I'm scared, Jack."

Extricating himself from the embrace, Jack took a good look at Parry. He *did* look scared; in fact, he looked so scared he was almost ill with it.

"I feel so much for her . . . I feel like something awful is going to happen."

"Nothing awful's gonna happen," said Jack reassuringly, patting Parry's shoulder awkwardly. He wasn't much good at this comforting stuff. "Anne'll be there. I'll be there. Nothing awful's gonna happen."

"I'm still scared," Parry whispered.

Jack took a long look at him, and a stab of pity cut through him like a knife. "I know," he whispered back. It's gonna be fine. You're lookin' good."

"Okay." Parry nodded, making an effort to get a grip.

"Just remember to breathe," said Jack.

"I gotta breathe."

"*Big* breaths."

Fifteen

Jack and Parry could hear the sound of women's hysterical laughter all the way up the stairs. It caught Parry off balance, and he lagged behind Jack, uncertain.

Jack pushed the apartment door open and his mouth dropped open in astonishment. Lydia Sinclair was rolling around on the floor. Literally on her back on the floor, her hands held high in the air to keep her nails dry, and she was hooting with laughter. There was color in her cheeks. Tears of mirth put a sparkle in her eye and her drab hair was attractively mussed. Perched on a hassock next to the coffee table was Anne Napolitano, red in the face from laughing so hard. Jack took one look at the half-empty tequila bottle and the two empty glasses, and his face broke into a knowing grin. The girls had been having themselves a party.

"Hi, how's it going?"

At the sound of Jack's voice Lydia started guiltily. She sat up at once and an immediate change came over her. She stopped laughing, becoming the old Lydia Sinclair again, as she retreated into her customary shy, self-protective shell. Her face closed tightly, and her expression was pinched and a little frightened.

"Parry," said Jack, a bit too loudly, "It's Lydia Sinclair, our membership winner."

"I know!" Parry glowed. He was still afraid to

actually come into the apartment, but Jack gave him a tug.

"What are you two up to?" asked Anne, on cue.

"Well," Jack drawled too casually, "everything's locked up downstairs. We thought we'd get some dinner." He raised his voice, as though he'd just hit upon a brilliant idea. "Say! Anybody up for Chinese?" He'd chosen Chinese food specifically to tempt Lydia, because she already liked it. Looking straight at her, he "had" another brilliant idea. "Have you eaten? Would you like to join us?"

Acutely uncomfortable now, Lydia got to her feet. "Oh, no, I'd rather go home." It was the perfect Lydia Sinclair tactless response.

"Me too," Parry said fervently, and Jack dug his elbow sharply into the small man's ribs. This was not the time to chicken out.

"The nails!" Anne yelled, alarmed. "Watch the nails! Listen," she added persuasively, "you still have to eat."

"No, really, I gotta go home." Lydia's face was screwed up into that old sour knot again.

"Hey, what did I tell you?" Anne spoke to her like a big sister; the kid wasn't so bad after all, not when you got to know her. "Why don't you come? It's just dinner." She grinned at the girl. "You'll have something to tell your mother next time she calls."

A small smile attempted to escape Lydia's tightly pressed lips, but it failed. She still shook her head no.

Time to show a little Italian muscle, make the offer that can't be refused. *"You . . . are . . . coming!"* Anne thundered. And it was settled.

It was another lovely evening; the moon played peekaboo with the clouds, and even New York's seamy underbelly didn't look too bad when bathed in moonlight. The four of them cut over toward the river, walking in pairs. Parry and Lydia went on ahead, Jack strolling a few steps behind with Anne, to give the other two a chance to get acquainted.

Jack kept a sharp eye on the couple in front. Lydia hadn't seemed to notice that Parry's suit was way too big for him, or that his sleeves and trouser legs were pinned up with staples, or that his train of thought occasionally jumped the track. Who knows? This date just might work out, after all. As Anne said, stranger things have been known to happen. When Anne rubbed her shoulder against him and slipped her hand into his, Jack gave her fingers a grateful little squeeze.

"What do you do?" Parry asked. It was more than polite conversation. Every scrap of information about Lydia was a tiny little treasure to be stored up, and laid out later on the altar of his heart and on the altar in his room.

"I work in a publishing house," Lydia replied. "Two Hearts Publishing. I . . . uh . . . I get to read some of the books, but mostly I calculate the production costs from first-edition hardcover into softcover. After that, it's basically someone else's problem."

"It sounds exciting," said Parry in an admiring voice. He was transported, in silent raptures, almost unable to contain his joy. To be walking beside the most wonderful, beautiful, intelligent girl in all the world! How did he deserve this? He could almost not stand so much happiness!

"Why does it sound exciting?" Lydia demanded. "There's absolutely nothing exciting about it at all."

Spotting something on the street, Parry bent to pick it up. He thrust the bit of refuse behind his back and kept his hands behind him, busily working.

His answer was heartfelt and earnestly expressed. "Well, you're calculating costs that could have an effect on whether or not a book is published. And if it is published, it could be a book that might somehow change the way that people think or act. A book can do that.''

"We mostly publish trashy romance novels,'' Lydia said matter-of-factly.

"Don't ever say that!'' Parry turned to her, glowing with emotion. "There's nothing trashy about romance. In romance there's passion . . . it's beauty and magic . . . and besides, you can find some wonderful things in the trash.''

Bringing his hands around from behind his back, he held out his palm for Lydia to see. In it was a charming little piece of furniture, no more than two inches high. Parry had found a champagne cork, the real kind—not plastic—but the kind with the thin metal wire wrapped around it. By twisting the wire, Parry had created a tiny chair, a miniature treasure. Smiling, he offered it to Lydia.

She accepted Parry's gift with pleasure, returning his smile, and there was a look of wonderment on her face. In the moonlight, contemplating her little chair, she could almost be taken for beautiful.

The Chinese restaurant was quite large, and much fancier than the one near Lydia's office. This room had red flocked walls and gold wooden trim on the banquettes, and little colored lanterns with gold-and-red tassels hanging from the ceiling. The four of them took a large corner booth and decided that Jack would give the order.

They sat pretty much in silence until the food came; Lydia and Parry were too shy and uncomfortable to speak, and their feelings of anxiety communicated themselves to Jack and Anne. So far, though, everything seemed to be going okay. Parry had not tried to unzip his pants, and Lydia had not run shrieking out into the night. The waiter arrived at last, placed plates and chopsticks in front of everybody, and a tray of covered dishes was transferred to the table.

Anne took the cover off the first dish. "Oh, dumplings!" she exclaimed. "I could eat all of these."

"Would you like a dumpling?" Jack asked Lydia politely.

"Yes, please."

"There we go." He spooned several onto Lydia's plate.

Nervously, the girl picked up her chopsticks. Her experience with dumplings and Chinese chopsticks had so far been all bad. She loved them, but they always eluded her. They were hard enough to handle even when her nails hadn't been freshly varnished. But with the new manicure, dumplings were a catastrophe waiting to happen, and Lydia didn't find it reassuring that this guy Parry didn't take his eyes off her. His staring, and the company of strangers, made her even more self-conscious, and inevitably the first slippery dumpling wound up not in her plate but in her lap.

"Oh, God," she muttered, mortified.

Instantly, Parry picked up *his* dumpling and dropped it deliberately into *his* lap. "Oh, boy. Sorry."

Her face scarlet, Lydia dipped her napkin into her glass and began to scrub at her skirt. Parry scrubbed at his trousers with his wet napkin. When Lydia knocked her water glass over, flooding the table, Parry knocked his water glass over, flooding the floor.

"Oh, I'm so clumsy, please forgive me," he said to Lydia. "I do everything wrong. You're so patient."

Lydia looked startled, then she relaxed a little, relieved that somebody at the table was clumsier than she was and that she wasn't the center of attention.

Jack marveled at the girl's density; Parry's little ploy was so transparent, yet Lydia didn't catch on. She was so nervous and self-preoccupied that she didn't notice that his every clumsy movement was a mirror image of her own.

The meal progressed. Other courses were served, and other problems were encountered by Lydia and countered by Parry. When Lydia put her face in her food and didn't bother to look up or make conversation, Parry mimicked her exactly. When Lydia had trouble separating the lo mein noodles and sat there with them hanging out of her mouth, Parry did the same. There was the most enormous smile all over his face, from his hair to his bearded chin. He was living out his fantasy, the knight coming to the rescue of the damsel in distress.

To Jack, Parry appeared to be having the time of his life. He felt a warm little glow of satisfaction; this was all his idea, and he'd made it happen. He'd done pretty good, he told himself. For once in his life he seemed to have done the right thing.

"What do you think?" he asked Anne in an undertone.

Anne grinned. "I think they're made for each other," she whispered back. "And I think it's scary," she added.

By the time the dishes were almost empty, a feeling of mellowness had settled over the table. Anne had cracked a few of her jokes, and Lydia had actually laughed. Her unexpectedly raucous laughter had a contagious effect on all of them, and soon the four of them were giggling and chuckling at almost every dumb thing that was said. They laughed over the little mottoes in the fortune cookies; they laughed when Parry took out Jack's wallet and fumbled through the bills to get the right amount for the check. They even laughed when Anne picked up half of the outrageous tip that Parry had left and stuffed it back into the wallet. It was one of those uncommon golden moments in life when everything is funny and there are friends around to share the joke.

Now they sat for a minute, replete, satisfied, knowing that they had to get up and leave the restaurant, but somehow reluctant to break this moment off. Then Parry began to sing, in a sweet, low voice. It was a comic song, an old music-hall and vaudeville ditty made popular by the great Groucho Marx, a song about a tattooed lady named Lydia. He sang it directly to Lydia and there was no mistaking his meaning. Even though the lyrics were absurd, it was a love song of the greatest tenderness.

Then the song came to an end. Silence fell over them, but it wasn't unpleasant, only peaceful.

At last, Parry broke the silence. "I'd like to take you home tonight. Would it be all right?" he asked tentatively. Lydia turned her face away, but she nodded.

Jack and Anne walked home very slowly, enjoying the evening. They were in a remarkably good mood, the first time their moods had actually coincided in many weeks. Recalling the meal, and Parry's hilarious attempts to keep up with Lydia's blunderings, they laughed so hard that they had to hold on to each other to keep from falling over.

"When . . . the noodles were hanging out of her mouth . . . I thought I was gonna die. . . ." Anne giggled, wiping tears of hilarity from her eyes.

"How about when Parry was digging in his lap for the piece of broccoli—" Jack gasped.

"Oh, God, yes, the broccoli—" and they exploded in fresh shrieks of laughter. "And, when the lichee nut rolled off the table—"

"No more, I can't take any more," Jack pleaded. "My sides hurt like hell."

They subsided and strolled along together quietly.

Then Anne said, in a wistful voice. "I'm actually very surprised. She seemed to go for him. Guess there's somebody for everybody, huh?"

"You know? I can't believe I did it," Jack mused. He was very tired, but it was worth all the effort and strain he'd put into this stunt. He felt good about himself.

It seemed to him now that he'd made Parry happy. And if Parry was happy, if Parry got what he wanted, then Jack would be off the hook. Free and clear. No more guilt, no more listening to Parry's ravings about the Holy Grail. Jack could get on with his life, Parry with his. Also, the little guy deserved some happiness, and Jack was suddenly glad that he was the one to help give it to him.

But there was something more. Seeing the intensity and the purity of Parry's unconditional love for Lydia had an odd effect on Jack. It made him envious. Who'd think that someone like Jack Lucas would envy a schizo street bum? What irony. Although, since Parry had entered Jack's life, it had become a walking irony.

"Amor vincit omnia," Anne said suddenly. "It's Latin," she explained when Jack shot a questioning look at her. "It means 'love conquers all.' I don't mean us," she added hastily. "I mean everybody else. Not us."

"Do you think it will work out?" Jack asked softly. They had reached the store, and Anne pulled the key to the door to their upstairs apartment from her purse.

Her face grew thoughtful. "Who knows? Two people can be in the same room at a party and never see each other. Two other people can be on opposite sides of the world, and nothing can keep them apart. If a thing is meant to happen, it'll—what?" She broke off as she caught Jack smiling at her.

"You were great tonight," he said softly. "Thanks

a lot." There was more affection in his tone than Anne had heard in a good long while, and it thrilled her. She unlocked the door, feeling warm inside, then she turned to him, and her large black eyes looked seriously into his.

"You did a great thing for somebody tonight," she told him sincerely. "I was really proud to be with you."

Jack reached for Anne's hand and brought it up to his lips. The gesture surprised him as much as it did her; it was so uncharacteristic of him to be romantic. Then he pulled her into his arms, first kissing her tenderly, and then with rising passion. Joyfully, Anne threw her arms tightly around him and returned his kiss. Their ardor increased with the pressure of their bodies, and mingled until it grew too overwhelming for them to withstand. Moaning with pleasure, unwilling to break off their caresses, they barely made it up the stairs and into the bedroom, where they fell on each other with hunger.

"Tell me about yourself," Parry begged. "I want to know everything."

Lydia shrugged. "There's nothing to tell."

"Don't say that." They had almost reached her apartment building.

Lydia turned to look at Parry, one of the few times she'd allowed him to see her face. "No, really, this is it."

"Well, it's enough for me," Parry stated loyally.

"You don't have to say that." Lydia cast her eyes down and turned her face away again.

"I never say anything I have to."

The girl fumbled awkwardly with the strap of her purse, tying it into little knots as she spoke. "I mean, you don't have to say nice things to me. It's a little old-fashioned considering what we're about to do."

"What are we about to do?" Parry asked, genuinely puzzled.

This was very hard for Lydia, and she stammered a little. "Well, you're taking me home. I . . . think . . . you're sort of . . . attracted to me—"

"Yes!" breathed Parry.

"You'll probably want to come upstairs . . . for coffee—"

"I don't drink coffee."

"—and then we'll probably have a drink . . . and talk . . . and get to know each other a little better . . . and get comfortable . . . and we'll . . . we'll . . . then you'll sleep over . . . and then . . . in the morning . . . you'll awake, and you'll be distant . . . and you won't be able . . . to stay for coffee—"

"I don't drink coffee," said Parry again.

But Lydia wasn't listening. She was deep inside her own pain, dredging up the memories of one-nighters, past rejections. "And then we'll exchange phone numbers and you'll leave and never call." Her eyes were haunted by her anguish. "And I'll go to work and I'll feel so *good* for the first hour, and then, ever so slowly, I'll turn into a piece of dirt."

Parry gazed at her, his face tender and soft with sympathy.

"Why am I putting myself through this?" she asked suddenly, snapping out of the past. She turned, running up the stairs of her brownstone, then she turned back to Parry as she remembered her manners. "It was really nice to meet you. Good night." And she headed for the front door.

"Excuse me! Wait! Wait! Wait up! 'Scuse me! Wait!" Parry yelled after Lydia a little desperately.

She turned back reluctantly. "Listen, I'm not feeling well—" she began.

"Well, no wonder. We just met, made love, and broke off all in the space of thirty seconds, and I can't even remember the first kiss, which is the best part.'' Lydia was standing several steps above him, in the light coming from the downstairs hallway of her house. Parry looked up at her face, and it seemed to him even more radiant than ever.

Lydia had never intended to open herself up to this stranger. She wanted desperately to go home now. "Listen, it really was very special to meet you—" she began with some awkwardness.

"I think you should shut up now," Parry interrupted. "Shut up, please. Thank you. I'm not coming up to your apartment," he told her earnestly. "That was never my intention."

The young woman's face reddened with humiliation. "Oh, God, you mean you don't want to—"

"Oh, no, I want to," Parry assured her. "I've got a hard-on for you the size of Florida . . . but . . . I don't want . . . just one night. I have a confession I have to make to you."

"You're married?" A spasm of anxiety crossed her face at the thought of it.

"No."

"Divorced?"

"No."

"You have a disease?"

"No, please stop!" Parry came up two of the steps that separated him from Lydia and laid his hand gently over her mouth before she could speak again. He looked deeply into her eyes and in a voice so quiet she almost missed the words, Parry said, "I'm in love with you."

Lydia gasped.

"It's not just from tonight. I've known you for a long time," he continued softly. Lydia's eyes widened and she listened in astonishment. "I know that you come out of work at noon every day. I see you fight your way out of that revolving door, and you're pushed back inside. And three seconds later you come out again. I walk with you to lunch. I know that on Wednesday you go to that dim sum parlor. I know what you order. And I know it's a good day if you stop and get that romance novel. I see you buying jawbreakers before you go back in to work.''

Slowly, he removed his hand from her mouth, but Lydia remained silent, just staring at Parry in fascination. Nothing like this had ever happened to her before; it was the epitome of every romance novel she'd ever devoured, it was the epitome of every romantic dream she'd secretly harbored. As she listened tears welled up in her eyes and rolled one by one down her cheeks.

''I know you hate your job, and you don't have many friends, and maybe you're a little . . . uncoordinated . . . but . . . alone as you are . . . I love you.'' The joy in Parry's breast was so strong he thought he'd burst with it. This was a moment he never expected to happen. He used to think he'd be following his lady around, half a block behind her, for the rest of his life! And now, here he was, telling the woman he loved what was in his heart, and she was actually listening! He smiled broadly. ''I love you! I think you're the greatest thing since spice racks and I would be knocked out several times just to have that first kiss. But, oh, I'll be back in the morning. And I won't be distant. And I will call if you let me. But I still don't drink coffee.''

The two of them stood looking at each other in a mist of wonder. Parry didn't see a homely, skinny girl, and Lydia didn't see a crazy man in a suit so large it had to be stapled. They looked into each other's eyes and they saw each other's hearts. And what each of them found made both of them happy.

Slowly, Lydia came down the brownstone steps toward Parry. She brought her face close to his and kissed him. It was an awkward, tentative kiss, nothing practiced or erotic about it, but to Parry it was the kiss of an angel. He trembled all over his small body. With infinitely gentle fingers, he brushed the tears out of his darling's eyes.

Then, Lydia being Lydia, she pinched his cheek skeptically, quite hard. He flinched.

"You are real . . . aren't you?" she whispered, lost in amazement.

Parry nodded, and they kissed again, like two innocent children, their lips touching as lightly as butterflies sip nectar from a flower.

She backed away from him slowly, then turned and ran lightly up the stairs of her house. At the top she turned and spoke, and Parry had never heard that abrasive voice utter sounds so sweet. "You can call me," she said.

Then, Lydia being Lydia, she tried to get into her house through the locked half of the door, and it took her a little more fumbling to make a semigraceful exit.

Parry didn't even notice the blunder. He stood there, dazzled. What an historical moment, a time of exaltation! Even if Lydia had forgotten to give him her telephone number, he knew where to find her. And she would be waiting. God, he was happy! He was so happy he could . . . no, wait! What was that sound? Something was watching him. He could feel it; he could almost taste it. Something hideous and terrifying was waiting for him in the darkness. Something knew he was alone; something knew he was unarmed; something was sensing Parry's vulnerability at this very moment and was lurking hungrily to feed on it.

And Parry knew what that something was. It was the Red Knight.

Sixteen

He was out there; Parry was aware of him with all his senses. He was out there, very close by, and he was totally aware of Parry, too. Parry stood, paralyzed with fear. Now he thought he could hear it, the pounding of the war-horse's iron hooves, and a neighing that grew so loud it split his eardrums. His very nostrils could smell the animal's breath. Very, very slowly, knowing what was waiting there, but afraid to look, Parry turned his head.

They'd come. They were on the corner, sitting horse and rider. The Red Knight's sword was drawn, was raised high in his mailed fist. Flames as red as blood streamed from his helmet and down along the iron of his armor, turning it incarnadine. He was the living fire incarnate, the Red Knight, and he knew that Parry was alone. For a long time he'd been waiting for Jack to go away; the Red Knight was afraid of Jack Lucas, but he wasn't afraid of Parry. He was Parry's deadliest enemy. Long ago, he'd sworn to rip out Parry's heart with the point of his lance and to split open Parry's skull with his sword.

Most of all, the Red Knight intended to take away by force anything that Parry needed to survive. They'd met a very long time ago, these two, in another life, and at that time the Red Knight had been triumphant. He'd taken it all, leaving only emptiness and deadly secrets.

Yet Parry had managed to survive, God only knew

how. He'd fled the secrets, going deep down into that emptiness to exist for a while, and out of that emptiness he'd fashioned a new life for himself. It wasn't a good life, or a happy life, but Parry had survived.

When he learned of Parry's survival, the Red Knight had been furiously angry; his war-horse had stamped his feet so loudly the earth had cracked and crumbled; great pits had opened, yawning, beneath those hooves. The raging flames that came issuing from the Red Knight's helmed face and armor had magnified and swelled until they extinguished the sun and exploded into the sky. He swore vengeance; he swore annihilation. Parry would never escape him again.

Since that time, the enemy was never far away; Parry was always conscious of his malevolent threatening presence somewhere at the periphery of his new life. The Red Knight was the very personification of evil and cruelty, those things that Parry tried so hard to combat, but every way he turned, the Red Knight blocked him with his horrific power. Many times he had seen him, and always—except once— Parry had been terribly afraid. Only that one time in Central Park when Jack was with him did the Red Knight give ground, turn, and run away. What a glorious moment that had been!

Over time Parry had learned and devised mysterious rituals for keeping the Red Knight at a distance—magic charms and incantations that usually worked. The most powerful incantation was *Don't think. Don't remember.* There were certain secret things Parry didn't dare to think about, secrets buried so deeply in the core of him that he successfully forgot them . . . most of the time. These were hidden things of such hazardous import that their revelation would destroy his world. The Red Knight was the designated keeper of those secrets; they formed the power of his sword and his lance, they were the fulcrum of his evil might.

Tonight, Parry had made a fatal mistake; he'd been happy. Being with Lydia had made him happy. He'd forgotten the first and most important rule. Never let them see you happy. He'd allowed the forbidden feeling not only to enter his heart, but to suffuse him entirely. He'd radiated with his joy, and the Red Knight had detected the glow and come riding hard to extinguish it. How could he have been so foolish as to have forgotten? It might cost him everything.

Knowing that Parry was weak and vulnerable tonight because he was happy and not on his guard, the Red Knight had come to strike the fatal blow. Parry had been a fool to think that he could hold on to this newfound happiness with Lydia, that the Red Knight had not been out there watching and waiting. Waiting for his chance, ready and armed to take this new joy away, too, and leave only the emptiness behind.

The most fearful thing of all was that Parry knew exactly how it would happen. He could already feel the lance point in his heart, already feel his skull sliced open by the flaming sword, to expose his insides and fill them with the Red Knight's terrible secrets, which Parry had once hurled far away from himself and which he didn't dare remember.

The horse reared, its hooves cracking through the sky, but the Red Knight reined him in and turned his head forward. His flaming spurs bit deeply into the war steed's back, below the chain mail. Horse and rider moved slowly at first, but Parry knew that was deceptive. Very soon now, they'd be galloping, charging directly at him, like the portrait in Parry's room. Flames would billow out of them, obscuring the outlines of knight and steed, so that it would appear as though a juggernaut of pure fire was racing to the kill.

Parry whimpered in fear. "Let me have this," he

pleaded in a whisper. "Please let me have this."
Even though he knew better than to ask.

The trot became a gallop; the Red Knight was
coming closer. *"Let me have this!"* Parry roared in
desperation. Tears came pouring out of his eyes and
down his cheeks, wetting his beard. He fell to his
knees, sobbing.

But he knew it was of no use; the Red Knight was
implacable, he'd sworn an oath to Parry's destruction. Parry was to have nothing, nothing ever again.
He was to die instead. He should run, but his legs
wouldn't move. His mouth opened to scream, but no
sound came out, and his lips formed the circle of a
terrified "no."

Now the Red Knight was much closer, and Parry
could see the shooting flames reflecting off his lance.
The head of the lance was burning brightly, red as
blood . . . as blood. . . .

"No!" Parry shrieked. He scrambled to his feet
and began to run. He ran for his life down the echo-
ing city alleys and streets. His brain was on fire with
pictures of blood . . . of blood. . . .

An ambulance . . . a stretcher . . . the gurney
rolling down the hospital corridor—*no!* He was in
the ambulance with the woman, holding so tightly
to her hand that the paramedics had to force him to
let go. The girl . . . the beautiful, beautiful girl . . .
so still, her face so white . . . the whiteness such a
contrast to the bright scarlet of the blood bubbling
in her brown hair—*no!* He mustn't remember! To
remember was to die.

Parry ran faster, but the Red Knight was closing
fast behind, and the secrets on the head of his lance
were stabbing their way into Parry's soul. The
woman . . . yes .. Elizabeth . . . so much love . . .
a wedding ring . . . she danced in his arms, and his
happiness was so strong that it filled him up and
bubbled over into laughter . . . laughter . . . they

were laughing together . . . they always laughed . . . the honeyed sound of Elizabeth's laughter—*no!*

Don't make me remember, he pleaded as he ran for his life. He felt the tip of the lance at his belly, pressing into his entrails. It burned.

Parry ran into traffic and east across Sixth Avenue, pelting past crowds of people out in the evening doing normal things like talking, walking together, coming out of movie houses, buying ice cream. Some of them snickered, but many of them didn't even bother to turn their heads as Parry ran by screaming. They saw a crazy little bum in a shapeless suit, and what's new about that in New York?

The Red Knight's thrusting lance probed deeper, deeper into Parry's entrails, spilling out the deadly secrets. They came tumbling out now, each one more terrible than the one before, crowding each other past Parry's brain, yelling, *Me! Me! Me! Look at me first! See me! Remember me!*

He remembered that night at Babbitt's. They had tickets to a play, Henry and Elizabeth. They didn't ordinarily go to bars, but they had an hour to spare before curtain, Elizabeth felt like having a white-wine spritzer. The place looked so cozy, with its hanging frosted-glass globes and its gleaming mahogany bar and all the fresh green plants and the happy socializing mob of pretty young people. So they went inside, sat at the bar, and Henry was on a roll, making Elizabeth laugh.

How he loved to make her laugh! She was so beautiful that he could scarcely believe this perfect creature was his wife, and she looked especially glorious when she laughed. She would throw her head back and her loose brown hair went tumbling over her shoulders in fragrant waves; her throat was exposed, long and white and smooth. He leaned forward and pressed his lips against Elizabeth's throat, and his beard tickled her and made her laugh even more.

The Red Knight galloped closer; he had his sword out now. Parry ran faster. There was no escape.

A man came into the bar; nobody noticed. Nobody ever noticed Edwin Malnick. They didn't even see him pull the weapon from under his coat. But the unexpected noise was suddenly deafening, the angry chatter of bullets. People screamed. They ran in frantic fear. They dived for the floor or crawled under tables. And some of them died screaming.

And Elizabeth . . . oh, God, Elizabeth. Her head exploded. Her precious bright red blood spattered across Henry's glasses; it was warm and sticky on his face. Her head fell forward onto his chest, and he could see the giant hole ripped through the base of her skull, see the brains oozing from her head. . . .

"Nooooooooooooo!" Parry screamed. *"Stoooppp!"* His face was wet with tears. And still the Red Knight galloped forward; Parry could hear the horse pounding behind him. The lance had pierced him, and now the sword was reaching out . . . reaching out . . . Parry turned. The Red Knight was nowhere in sight.

Parry was standing on the promenade by the East River; it was the very place where he had rescued Jack Lucas from the two delinquents who tried to set him on fire. Parry had run all the way there and his body was trembling with exhaustion and streaming with sweat. And now the Red Knight had disappeared. It was a trick; he knew it was a trick. The Red Knight was very near, only waiting for the right moment to disembowel him. There could be no defense against him. It would soon be over.

But Parry didn't intend to die without making a stand. With all of his strength, he cried out into the black night.

"Come on! Where *are* you? *Where are you?"* Sobbing with pain and rage, he dropped to his knees. "Where are you?" he wept. He felt very alone and very afraid.

Suddenly he saw his enemy. The Red Knight was riding straight at him, but he wasn't alone. With him were two dark figures, and dimly Parry recognized the same two boys he'd defeated for Jack—the one in the leather jacket and his friend in the windbreaker. They were being led toward him by the Red Knight, although they couldn't see him or hear him. Only Parry could.

Parry stood his ground. He rose up from his knees and took a few steps forward to meet his fate, on his feet. The Red Knight urged the boys on, and flames poured out of his helmet. The boys held open switchblade knives, and Parry could see the fires reflecting off the steel blades.

"We're tired of looking at you people," the boy in the leather jacket snarled. He slashed at Parry's defenseless chest, cutting it open. And the Red Knight's sword bit deep.

With a strangled scream, Parry fell to the ground and lay still. And then the three of them were on him—the two boys and the evil Red Knight. His enemy had him at last.

Anne came out of the bathroom, rosy from her shower, with a broad smile on her face. She hadn't felt this good in a very long time; she felt satisfied all over and well loved, inside and out. Jack had been so wonderful last night, not only passionate, but affectionate, too. Usually, whenever they made love, Jack turned away from Anne soon after his climax, to sleep alone on his side of the bed. Last night, he'd been there for her, holding her in his arms, kissing and cuddling her until they made love again. And again. Her lover loved her. What woman could ask for more?

Jack was on the telephone when Anne came into the

room in her bathrobe. He sounded very up and positive, sitting on the floor surrounded by piles of tapes from his radio show. Coming up behind him, Anne threw her arms around him in a joyous affectionate hug.

"Well, y'know, I'm feeling good, Lou, I don't know how else to put it," Jack was saying. "I had some personal problems to work out, and I have, and . . . Yeah, right . . . well, the thing is, I want to work again, Lou. I want to get back into it. You think that's possible?"

Get back to work? Anne grinned happily. This was the first she'd heard of it. Things were going great, almost *too* great; she crossed her fingers superstitiously.

"I understand, Lou." His voice was more subdued now, but Jack still sounded hopeful. "I am . . . I won't . . . I will. *Great!* When? Tuesday's great, Lou. I'll see you then. Thanks a lot, Lou." He hung up the phone, smiling.

"So, what's going on? Who's Lou?"

"Lou Rosen's my agent. I called my agent."

Anne gave a little gasp of delight. "You're kidding! What did he say?"

Jack looked very pleased with himself. "He says if I want to get back to work, I just come in. No problem. Just come in and talk, and that's it!"

"Oh, honey, that's terrific!" Anne grabbed him in a bear hug, but Jack pulled away.

"I've got to put these tapes in some kind of order, and, oh, have you seen my good jacket?"

"It's in the bedroom closet."

"Oh, yeah, there's coffee if you want."

Anne let out a joyously incredulous whoop. *"You* made coffee? You're going back to work *and* you made coffee? I love this!"

Pouring herself a cup, she sat at the little dining table watching Jack moving around so full of energy and purpose. For the first time since she met him Anne allowed herself the luxury of thinking about the future. When she had lived with Jack the self-absorbed drunk, any thought of a future was ludicrous, a pipe dream. But now things had turned one hundred and eighty degrees. Jack was staying away from the bottle and doing the right thing. Now he had phoned his agent and was even going back to work. He was her lover again, more passionate than ever before. He was her man. Anne's nesting instinct began to kick in. Life with Jack was going to be great!

"It's wonderful to see you like this, honey. I can't tell you!"

Jack had located his good Armani jacket and was going over it with a critical eye and a brush. "Thanks."

Anne took another sip from her mug. "Y'know, I'm just thinkin' . . . with two incomes coming in, I would love to look for a larger place."

Jack's hand stopped, midway up the left sleeve.

". . . I don't want to rush things, but I'd love to start looking, at least." Her eyes sparkled with pleasure at the thought of making a real home for her and Jack. "You know, maybe a two-bedroom . . . or even, maybe the top floor of a house. Like in Brooklyn"—no, Jack Lucas was definitely not the Brooklyn type.—"Heights," she finished. Brooklyn Heights was one of the most desirable, expensive, and fashionable of New York's neighborhoods, almost an adjunct of Manhattan. She glanced at Jack, hoping for his approval of her plan.

But Jack was only looking back at her, saying nothing.

"What? You don't want to commute?"

"No, it's not that." Jack shook his head. "C'mere." He took Anne into his arms, holding her against him, her back against his belly.

"You're an incredible woman—" he began, but Anne pulled herself out of his arms and looked at him sharply. "What?" he asked.

" 'I'm an incredible woman'?" Anne's voice was angry and filled with suspicion. "What is this, a death sentence?"

Oh, Jesus, she was too fuckin' smart. She had senses like a jungle cat. "I want to talk about this," Jack said. "Listen . . . so much has happened . . . and I think it would be a good thing for both of us if we slowed down a little—"

"Slowed *down?*" Anne's voice rose to a shrill pitch. "Where have I been? Have we been going fast?"

Jack bit his lip. This was not going as well as he'd hoped. "Right now I'm just not sure about . . . making definite plans."

Anne's eyes searched for Jack's, but they evaded her. "I'm lost. What are you saying?"

Oh, fuck, Jack thought miserably. She wasn't going to let him make this easy. She wasn't going to let him get away with jackshit. He should have known. Taking Anne's hand in his, Jack led her over to the sofa, and they sat down. "Look," he began gently, "it's been a real . . . difficult time for me . . . and now, for the first time in a long time, Anne, I feel like I'm above water. I feel like I know a lot more than I did, and I don't want to make any mistakes. So . . . I think I need some time . . . to make the right choices—"

"Wait! Wait!" Anne cried. "I'm lost here. What are you saying?"

"I'm saying I . . . should be alone for a while. Now that I know more, I feel that I should focus on my career. Parry's taken care of, and like I said, I know more now, and—"

Anne leaped to her feet to interrupt, her face a mask of outrage and pain. "First of all, let me tell you something! *You* don't know *shit!* Secondly, as far as *we* go, what the hell have we been doing here, except *time?* Have I ever . . . ever pressured you?" she demanded. "Once? Ever?"

"No," Jack admitted. It wasn't true, of course, she'd put plenty of pressure on him, but Anne sin-

cerely believed she hadn't, and he had to concede
that much. He didn't want to fight; above all, he
didn't want to fight.

"No." Anne nodded her head. "So what time do
you need, baby?" she pleaded. "I love you, you
love me, you want to get your career going—I think
that's the greatest thing in the world. I wanna be
there. Shoot me, but I wanna be there when it happens. So what do you need time to figure out alone?"

Jack didn't speak, but he sighed deeply, and the
guilty look on his face told Anne everything she
needed to know. He was dumping her. With only
one foot on the ladder of his old career, he couldn't
wait to dump her. She'd been down this road before,
and she knew all the milestones and signposts.

"All right," Anne said quietly. "So let me ask you
one thing." She took in a deep breath, summoned
up every ounce of strength she could command, and
asked, "Do you love me?"

Jack hesitated, then: "I don't know," he confessed.

You don't know? A short bark of hysterical laughter escaped her lips. "Jesus, Jack, you can't even
give me *that?* What were you gonna do? Just walk
out that door, move in by yourself, and then what?
Drop the news when you find somebody new? What
the hell were you planning to do, Jack?" She threw
back her head, challenging him to meet her eyes, to
tell her the whole God's honest truth.

Jack shook his head numbly. "I don't know. I just
said all I want is some time," he lied.

He was feeling even worse than he'd imagined he
would. He could see how badly he was hurting Anne,
but there seemed to be little he could do about it.
She'd been so good to him, but Anne Napolitano
was . . . wrong . . . for his new life. She didn't have
enough . . . hipness and class. He was impatient to
leave her behind, along with Parry and everything

else that embarrassed him, all the encumbrances that
he no longer had room for. Excess baggage.

"*Bullshit!*" Anne yelled. She was furious now,
and fighting hard to keep from crying. "If you're
going to hurt me, hurt me now! Not some long-
drawn-out hurt that takes months of my life because
you don't have the balls!"

"Okay." Jack shrugged. "I'll pack my stuff tonight."

But Anne wasn't going to let him go so easily. She
knew she'd been manipulated by Jack into being the
one to throw him out, just so he could ease his guilty
conscience. Just as he'd used her, manipulated her
all along. "What have you been doing here?" she
shrieked at him. "Could you just tell me that? I
wanna know. *What have you been doing here?*"

Now it was Jack Lucas's turn to show temper. He'd
been trying to avoid a fight, but Anne was pressing
all his guilt buttons, and he didn't like it. What she
was accusing him of was cutting pretty close to the
bone. "Listen!" he yelled back. "We both got
something out of it, all right?"

This was too much for Anne. "Oh, yeah? What
did I get?" she demanded. "What did I get I couldn't
have gotten from somebody with no name any night
of the week? You think your company is such a treat?
Your moods, your 'pain' . . ." She threw the words
in his teeth with heavy sarcasm. "Your problems?
You think this has been entertaining for me?"

"Then what do you want to stay with me for?"

The stupidity, the insensitivity of the question
drove Anne Napolitano over the edge, and she lost
the control she'd been fighting so hard to hold on to.
Darting forward, her hands forming into fists, she
attacked Jack, hitting him everywhere she could
reach—his head, his face, his chest and shoulders.
And the tears streamed down her face.

"*Because I love you!*" she yelled, trying to make
him understand, trying to force comprehension into

him. *"You stupid . . . fuckin' . . . because I love you!"*

Jack blocked her blows as best he could, finally pinning her arms to her sides. Loud sobs escaped her, and she almost fell. Jack found his heart aching with pity, and he attempted to embrace her, to kiss her wet cheeks, whispering softly, "Anne, Anne, hey, it's gonna be okay, shhhhh."

But Anne would have none of his pity or embraces. She was too proud to sell herself so cheaply, for such tiny rewards. She'd been used enough already, and the only excuse she could make to herself was that she thought Jack loved her. But he didn't; he never had. Anne felt so damn dumb for not having realized it before. She pulled away from him.

"No, no, you don't get to be nice now. I'm not gonna play some stupid game with you where we act like friends so you can walk out that door feeling good about yourself. I'm not a modern woman. If it's over, then let's just call it over."

Jack felt a sudden pang of disappointment, even loss. Life totally without Anne . . . he hadn't thought about that . . . what if they . . . ?

The telephone rang. For the space of a couple of heartbeats, they stood looking at it as though it were an alien thing. Then Jack picked up the receiver.

"Hello? Yeah?" His face looked puzzled. "My wallet? What do you mean?" There was a sharp intake of breath, and Anne looked at him. Jack looked terrible. What was going on?

"What? When?" Jack exclaimed sharply. He listened a minute, then hung up the phone, turning to Anne.

"It's Parry," he said in a low voice, and his face was ashen with fear.

"Oh, Jesus," Anne whispered.

Seventeen

Jack Lucas had never seen anybody who wasn't dead lying so still. It didn't appear as though there was any spark of life in Parry. Bandaged tightly across the chest, both arms in a cast, a thick bandage wrapped around his head, he lay on his hospital bed with his eyes open, not seeing, not hearing. Under his beard, Parry's face was as white as the bandages. There was no flicker of the eyelid, no intake of breath. Yet he didn't look dead, he appeared merely to have . . . gone away.

"Parry?" Jack called softly. He stood at the foot of Parry's ward bed with Anne behind him. As soon as Anne had gotten dressed, they'd rushed over to the hospital. In the taxi Jack told her what little he knew from the telephone call. Parry had been attacked by homicidal muggers, slashed in the chest, and beaten very badly. Both his arms were broken, and he had suffered a head wound. He was alive, but only barely. And he'd lapsed into a coma. The doctors weren't hopeful.

Parry's attackers hadn't bothered to check his pockets for money; what would a homeless bum be doing with money? So when he was brought into the hospital, the ER attendant found Jack Lucas's wallet still tucked safely in the jacket pocket of the slashed and bloody Versace suit and, using it for identification, had tracked Jack Lucas down.

"Parry?" he called again.

"He can't hear you," a voice said behind them. Anne and Jack turned. A middle-aged doctor, his face weary from lack of sleep, his eyes red-rimmed and pouchy with fatigue, was coming into the ward carrying a chart.

"Hi, I'm Dr. Mandeville." He shook hands with them both. "I was on duty when they brought him in. I've been going over his record. He was brought in once before, I understand."

Flipping open the thick chart, Dr. Mandeville read out loud from it. " 'Catatonic stupor' . . . hmmm . . . 'condition rendered him nonverbal for a period of—' "

"Yeah, so?" Jack interrupted defensively. That was then; this is now. "The guy's been beat up. He . . . he probably has a concussion or something, right? He's gonna snap out of it?"

Dr. Mandeville shook his head, frowning. "I'm afraid not. The beating's bad, but that's not the problem. It seems he's reexperiencing the catatonia. So, like before, he could snap out of it in an hour, or in thirteen months, or in thirteen years . . . I don't know. There's no way to be sure."

"But how could that happen?" Jack wanted to know. He looked at Parry again, trying to detect some flicker of movement—an eyelid, something! Nothing.

The physician shrugged. "A person could actually reexperience the full effect of a tragedy long after the event took place. I was reading how he lost his wife. Are you relatives?" He looked sharply at Jack and Anne.

Jack shook his head and Anne said nothing.

"Well, it doesn't matter," Dr. Mandeville said in a resigned voice. "We'll take care of it. He'll have to be sent back to the same institution." He riffled through the chart, looking for the name and address of Parry's former mental hospital.

"What if I was a relative?" Jack asked suddenly, his voice thick.

"Well, you'd have the option of caring for him at home, but I wouldn't recommend it. He needs hospital care. I just thought you could sign the release forms, but the city can do that."

Dr. Mandeville didn't mean to be brusque, but there was really nothing more he could tell them, and more than two dozen patients he still had to see. Besides, there was nothing anybody could do for a case like this one, and the mental-hospital wards were overflowing with the schizophrenic homeless, so the doctor moved on.

For a long moment Jack and Anne looked down at the small bandaged figure on the hospital bed. Then Anne said, with a bitter smile, "Poor Lydia. She finally finds her prince, and he falls into a coma." She raised one eyebrow at Jack. "Some women just have all the luck, huh?"

She turned, and with enormous dignity and renewed self-respect, she walked out of the ward and out of Jack Lucas's life.

"Anne, Anne, I'll call you, okay?" Jack called after her. But she didn't answer, didn't stop, and didn't look back.

Jack turned again to stare at Parry. Great, now they were back to Square One. Nothing that Jack had done for Parry counted now; he might as well have thrown his efforts into the crapper and flushed. Parry was gone beyond anybody's help, reliving the original nightmare that was Jack Lucas's making. Anger, guilt, and frustration tore at Jack, but he refused to give in to them. This isn't my fault, he raged at Parry silently. I'm not to blame. My intentions were good. And it worked, didn't it? You wanted Lydia, God only knows why, and I had handed her over to you on a silver platter. So I'm off the hook now. You can't raise the damn ante on me anymore. We're even. I'm getting my old life back, and there won't be time enough or room enough in it for you. Besides, you don't need me anymore. You don't need anybody anymore. So I'm taking off. Good-bye.

But Parry couldn't see him, hear him or speak to him, and Jack Lucas felt like shit.

"Well, I'm gone. Have a perfect weekend, and remember, if you've often wondered, 'What *is* sodomy exactly?' well, you're in luck. Monday's special studio guest is an expert on the subject. It's Ben Starr, star of the recently defunct hit TV show *On the Radio,* and he'll have the answer to that question and many more when he tells us exactly how and why he was busted in an Atlanta airport men's room. Be sure to tune us in on Monday, and until then, from one of the Botched to all you Bungled cats out there, I love ya, and right back atcha! So long." The theme music "Hit the Road, Jack" swelled up and out and Jack cut a switch. Off the air. Thank God.

Rubbing at his tired eyes with the heels of his hands, he slumped into his seat at the control board. Back on the air six months now, and he still couldn't get used to the grind. Something had gone out of the work—the thrill of power, maybe—Jack wasn't sure. All he knew was that in the old days he had a hard-on for his voice on the air, and now he just didn't seem to give much of a damn. And he no longer saw any percentage in making fun of the weirdos who called in. He let them describe their fantasies without much interruption. Who was he to pass judgment? Even the gleeful satisfaction he would have felt in the past for the downfall of the very TV actor he most envied was tempered by his ennui, by a feeling of "what does it all mean, anyway? Nothing, nothing at all."

The telephone rang in the studio, Jack's private line. Wearily, he picked it up. "Yeah? Yeah, Lou."

He listened for a minute, his face darkening like a thundercloud, then cut in angrily. "Lou, I said I want a firm offer or they can forget it. Well, you tell them I'm meeting with the cable people about a talk show and . . . what? Beth's father set it up. . . . No, he owns it. Yeah, yeah . . . fuck you, Lou. If the network is ready to make a firm offer and they want to send a script, then fine. Otherwise, forget it. . . . All right, see you then."

He hung up. He should get up now and go home to his luxurious new Tribeca loft with its sweeping views of the Great South Bay and the Statue of Liberty. Beth would already be waiting there for him, all sleek perfect blondness with long waxed legs and a flexible body, and a father who had the bucks and the clout to turn Jack Lucas into a superstar. They'd make love, eat a salad with a glass of wine, and get ready for the long drive out to Southampton for a weekend of opulence and sailing with Beth's folks. Yes, he really did have to get up now. He hadn't packed yet for the weekend. His crew of engineers had already gone home. His girlfriend was waiting. A whole new life was waiting.

But Jack Lucas still sat alone in the darkened studio, his hands cupped tightly against his eyes.

The network people didn't have the final script ready for Jack to see, but they were very eager to meet with him and "give him a feel for it," as the production exec told Lou Rosen. It was a "high concept" show, whatever the hell that meant, a comedy, and they wanted Jack Lucas's input.

Grudgingly, Jack donned his new Yohji Yamamoto jacket, stuck his feet into his latest snakeskin cowboy boots, put his Vuarnet shades on his nose, and took in the meeting. He and his agent limoed over to the sixty-seven-story black glass-and-steel office skyscraper that housed the network and dominated its corner of Fortieth Street and Park Avenue. When the two men stepped out of the limousine, a minor scuffle was going on outside the main entrance, on the stepped plaza that led to the doors. A security guard was chasing away a panhandler. Just another crummy New York scene, like a million others. Jack paid no attention as he stalked past the fountains on the plaza, but then he heard his name being yelled.

"Jack! Jack! It's *meee!* Remember me? I have to talk to you! Jack!"

He turned. The panhandler was Michael, the little gay man he'd found with Parry on the bridle path in Central Park, the one who'd sung his heart out in the medley from *Gypsy* to a stunned Lydia Sinclair.

Before Jack could say anything, the security guard had reached Michael and was grabbing him, pushing him away roughly. Next to the guard's uniformed beefiness, Michael looked puny and fragile.

"Get outta here, I said!" roared the guard.

Lou Rosen grabbed Jack by the arm and tried to hustle him into the building, but Jack half turned back, uncertain of what to do. The guard had his billy out now and was poking Michael in the side with it. Every poke drove him a few feet farther away, but Michael continued to bawl out to Jack.

"Jack! Please, you know me! Please, can I talk to you?" He stretched out a pitifully thin arm. "Please . . . please!!"

Suddenly Jack became aware that people were staring at him, connecting him with this pathetic bum. That decided him. Hiding behind his sunglasses, he ducked his head and followed Lou into the network building. Behind him, he could hear Michael's screams dying away, hoarse and desperate.

"Jack! Please, Jaaaack! Why won't anybody talk to me? Leave me alone! Don't hurt me! Leave me alone! Jaaaackkkkk!!"

* * *

"It's a weekly comedy about the homeless," announced the network exec. sounding very pleased with himself. "But it's not depressing in any way."

Jack made an effort not to let his expression change, but he couldn't believe what he was hearing! This pompous asshole was pitching him the single worst, most tasteless, most denigrating and inhuman idea Jack Lucas had ever heard. A comedy about the homeless?

Jack looked around the executive's huge office, furnished in Italian Modern—all polished surfaces like marble and steel—and heavy fabrics by Donghia. This dickhead got paid to think up shit like this? On the ammonite marble coffee table in front of the black leather sofa was a stack of the latest glossy magazines. On top, a copy of *World Weekly,* with its cover story—"Billionaire Langdon Carmichael buys Vincent Van Gogh's *Road with Cypresses* for $20 Million."

What a fucking insane world this is, Jack thought bitterly. Some poor schmuck with a burning genius in his gut is driven insane by manic-depression and the compulsion to paint. Everybody except his brother hates what he paints, and in his whole lifetime he sells only one picture. So he puts a bullet into his brain in a madhouse before he's forty. And today, a real-estate baron buys one of his paintings for enough money to support a third-world country for years. Only the poor schmuck painter, the mad genius, has been dead for a hundred years and will never know that, all along, he was right and everybody else was wrong.

The TV guy was now warming to his pitch. "We want to find a funny, upbeat way of bringing the issue of homelessness to television. So we've got three wacky homeless characters, but they're wise. They're wacky and they're wise. And the hook is"— and here the exec's oily voice sounded more pleased with itself than ever—"they *love* being homeless. They love the freedom . . . they love the adventure. It's about the joy of living, not all the bullshit *we* have to deal with—the money, the politics, the pressures. And the best part is . . ." The exec paused for maximum timing, for the brilliance of the punch line. "The best part is, it's called *Home Free.*"

Finished with his masterly presentation at last, the network honcho looked to the others for their reaction.

"Oooohhh, I'm getting a rush," said Lou Rosen dutifully. He knew how to earn his fifteen percent.

Jack Lucas wanted to vomit. He stood up suddenly, and without a word, he bolted out of the room.

The executive's jaw dropped and his brows drew together in a scowl. "What the fuck . . . ? Where the hell is he going? Lou, is this another disappearing act with this guy or what?"

"Not a problem," Rosen assured him hastily. "Just a bathroom break. I'll check. . . ." And he hurried out in search of Jack.

Jack got an express elevator and was down in the lobby in a matter of forty seconds. He raced out the entrance to the plaza and looked around for Michael, but the little guy was gone, pushed off the edge of the world by security with a badge and a billy club. Shoving his hands deep into the pockets of his criminally expensive jacket, Jack walked quickly away from the network building. His belly churned in disgust. Disgust for the television world and their tasteless sitcoms, disgust for the values of a so-called society that places money above humanity. Most of all, disgust for himself because he bought into the scam, and because he was now beginning to suspect that his own value system consisted of the fact that Jack Lucas had no values.

Eighteen

For six months, ever since they'd moved Parry to Oakbrook Institute, the mental hospital on Staten Island, nobody had lived in the boiler room. There was a heavy layer of dust and soot over everything, but the room was otherwise kept just as Parry had left it. Frank the superintendent had seen to that. Jack came in, closed the door behind him, and looked around the place.

There sat little Pinocchio, still standing guard, his wooden arms straight out like a soldier presenting his rifle, his painted eyes watching without fatigue.

Funny, a lot of Parry's stuff made a kind of sense to Jack now. At least, he understood its significance somewhat better, because he understood Parry somewhat better. Curiously, he examined the strange handmade weapons that Parry had used. He unfolded again the map of Langdon Carmichael's armory and studied it. He saw that Parry had gotten ropes and grappling hooks ready, as though they were actually going to break into the burglar-proof armory. The nut! There was just no convincing him. Deeply depressed, Jack sat down at the small table and tried to put it all together in his mind. He attempted to see through Parry's eyes.

Henry Sagan, historian, thinking man, man of reason and intellect and humanity and goodness, had been dealt the most cruel and sudden blow. Everything he cherished most in the world had been torn to pieces before his eyes, in a split second, and there'd been nothing he could do to prevent it. He'd seen his wife's brains blown out, and he hadn't been able to lift a finger.

What had gone through his mind? First, shock, and then denial, and then an incurable grief. A human life snuffed out in an instant. And not just any human life, but the life most precious and most necessary to Henry's happiness. No, it couldn't be! Denial. Thwarted rage—the killer had taken his own life. Guilt, because Henry Sagan was still alive, while his innocent wife was senselessly dead. All these intense emotions, and all of them boiling through his brain at the same time. Enough negative input to stun an elephant, and surely enough to kill a vulnerable human being.

But the human mind is a strange and wonderful organ. It moves to protect itself, whether the person owning it wants to be protected or not. When an electrical circuit is overloaded, a fuse blows or a circuit-breaker switch throws itself. The power is thereby shut off. The deadly overload in Henry Sagan's brain did much the same thing—it threw his circuits into catatonia so that he wouldn't have to remember or deal with the powerful memories of those terrible events. Catatonia, a state in which electrical activity in the brain is at an absolute minimum. To protect itself, Henry Sagan's brain had shut itself off.

For thirteen months after that night at Babbitt's, Henry Sagan had lain in a hospital bed, not seeing, not speaking, not moving, a catatonic. Yet underneath the stillness, under all the rejection of sensory stimuli, a rather wonderful thing was taking place. Just as a coral reef is carefully built up of organisms too tiny to be seen by the naked eye, all accreting into a living growth of wondrous complex beauty, so Henry Sagan's brain began slowly to heal itself, to turn the power back on, a few volts at a time. His unconscious mind worked to select the necessary elements to construct the intricate coral reef of his new identity.

Out of the pieces of his old life, Henry's sleeping mind chose the mystical elements of the medieval time he knew and loved so much. The focus of his delusion would become the Holy Grail, because, deep in his soul, he was aware that the Grail, if achieved, had the power to heal. It is only the Holy Grail—Christian symbol of God's grace—that could cure the incurable wound from which Henry suffered so deep a pain.

And who can achieve the Grail? Only the One who is pure in thought and deed. Who achieved it in Henry's researches into the legend of the Fisher King? The fool, because a childlike fool is pure, simple, sacred to God. And because only the fool could see what was hidden from the sight of other men. So to the beautiful growing organism in Henry Sagan's catatonic mind the vital element of God's fool was added. In Arthurian legend, Sir Galahad had the strength of ten and won the Holy Grail. Sir Percival, with but the strength of one, was vouchsafed a vision of the sacred chalice, and thus was granted God's grace. Percival, also known as Parsifal. Parsifal . . . Parry.

Jesus! The sudden piecing together of this set of cryptic clues brought an illumination that surprised Jack greatly, yet it possessed a certain kind of logic, if he put a sideways spin on the logic.

After thirteen months in the dark, Parry had opened his eyes. He was insane because his brain knew that insanity would be his protection. He had become the childlike fool with the clear vision. Hallucinations of floating cherubim dispatched Parry upon a quest, to achieve God's grace and healing. But to do that he needed a Galahad. Parry was alone, with the strength of one. He needed the strength of ten. Oh shit, Jack thought, *me*. I'm supposed to be fuckin' Sir Galahad. Isn't that a laugh and a half? Pure Jack Lucas, undefiled, untainted, chivalrous, saintly Jack Lucas. That's how Parry perceived him. Jack didn't know whether to laugh or to cry.

Keep going. Every knight deserves a lady, a damsel in distress. Enter Lydia Sinclair. Something deep inside Parry, some atavistic memory of Henry Sagan, buried deep, told Parry that he didn't dare again to court beauty. Beauty was too dangerously tempting to destroyers and much too easily destroyed. He needed someone made of stronger, more common clay. So he picked out of millions one awkward, homely girl and invested her with the beauty and grace of his fantasy, and he elevated her above all other women. To be his lady fair.

Every knight must fight his dragons. And dragons are evil, spewing forth fire, snatching life and breath away with choking fumes, cruel sharp teeth, and greedy reptilian fingers. They fly swiftly on leather wings and defile whatever they touch, with their smoky breath and scarlet claws. Jack got up, walked over to the wall, and studied the poster of the Red Knight.

For the first time he could recognize that it was flames Parry had scribbled with his crimson Magic Marker. He saw that the Red Knight personified the dragon nemesis, the guardian of everything evil, the enemy that placed itself between the questing knight and the Holy Grail. The Red Knight was the perilous dragon that Parry had to slay. It was a terrible vision he saw.

So this hodgepodge of a room, this unholy mess, actually represented a complex but unmistakably unified private universe. Parry could see it; now Jack caught a glimpse of it, too. And it scared him—the logic of it, the magnetic power of it, scared him.

And what frightened Jack Lucas the most was the overwhelming need that a small crazy man named Parry had for the healing power of the Holy Grail.

Jack paid off the taxi and stood looking at the grounds of the Oakbrook Institute. It had taken him an hour and a half and sixty-five bucks plus tip to get out here to the other end of Staten Island; traffic on the Verrazano Bridge was a nightmare. It seemed like an okay place, nothing special, but nothing too depressing about it. Low brick buildings, built sometime in the 1950s, with bars on the windows. Patients in bathrobes sitting on benches taking the air while other patients were wandering aimlessly or pacing nervously around the grounds. Burly men and woman in white uniforms keeping a professional eye on them. Your average common-or-garden loony bin.

In Parry's ward, there were beds lined up on both sides of the long room. A television set was on, tuned to a channel that was showing cartoons, but nobody seemed to be watching. There were a number of torpid unshaven men crouched on their beds, their hospital gowns flapping open to reveal certain unsavory parts that were better kept covered. By contrast, Parry looked absolutely gorgeous.

He was dressed in what appeared to be brand-new pajamas, lime green, printed all over with watermelons and other fruits in bright incongruous colors. His bed was freshly and tightly made, and had sheets that no hospital had ever issued. These were colored percale, with contrasting hemstitched borders, obviously expensive, and quite beautiful. Fresh spring flowers stood in a vase by his bed.

Parry himself looked like a sleeping prince. His hair was neatly brushed and combed, his beard trimmed evenly. Apart from that, he was out of it, totally and completely out of it. Catatonic. He lay on his back with his arms folded on his chest; his eyes were closed tightly, and he didn't appear to be breathing in or out.

Jack just stood there at the foot of Parry's bed watching him while an enormous tidal wave of emotion rolled over him. Regret, mostly, but also anger, resentment, frustration, guilt. Jack had believed he could go back easily to his good life, but it hadn't worked. Oh, he had everything he wanted—the right address, good threads, a rich and thin girlfriend with an influential father, a booming career. He'd spent the last six months building up his defense mechanisms again, setting new stones and mortar into the wall around him that had been breached that night at Babbitt's. He'd built it strong, sure that this time it would stand.

But seeing Michael today—and turning his back on him like a Judas—had opened a crack in that wall. Forced to listen to that impossible asshole prattling about a homeless sitcom—"they're wacky and they're wise"—had made the crack wider. Afterward, going to Parry's little boiler room and seeing Parry's life with new eyes had blown an enormous hole in the wall, leaving Jack Lucas standing troubled in the ruins. His defenses had crumbled away. His wall had become useless.

A familiar voice outside in the corridor made Jack turn his head. An unmistakable voice, yet . . . perhaps . . . not as abrasive as he remembered. Going to the door of the ward, he looked down the hall to the nurses' station. A young woman was talking to one of the nurses. It was Lydia Sinclair.

"Pardon me, but not long ago I brought new bed sheets for him," Lydia was saying. "They were lime-colored with little watermelons on them? To match his pajamas?"

"Oh yes," the nurse replied. "I'm sorry. They're being cleaned. The doctor had a little accident with a hypo."

"I see. Please just make sure that he does get them when they *are* cleaned. Thank you."

Please? Thank you? Jack grinned in surprise. It sure didn't sound like the old Lydia. Didn't look much like the old Lydia, either. Seeing her start up the corridor, Jack ducked back quickly into the ward so she wouldn't spot him, but he managed to get a good look at her as she walked by on her way out of the hospital.

Lydia was wearing a colorful form-fitting dress that showed off her narrow waist and small rear end. Her hair was longer and brushed back softly off her face and—was it possible? Yes! She was even wearing a little makeup. Nothing heavy, but some pink blusher and matching lipstick that brought color to her face, and a little eye makeup that brought out the large size and fine hazel color of her eyes. She walked with grace and a spring in her step. She looked like . . . a woman in love.

The fancy sheets and colorful pajamas on Parry, the flowers by his bedside, his neatly brushed hair and trimmed beard—all Lydia. She was a woman with a mission now—to take good care of her man. And it had brought out all her womanliness. Gone was the old shy, suspicious, self-protective Lydia. In her place was this new, trim young woman who stepped on by with confidence, who knew what she wanted, and who, incidentally—Jack marveled—wasn't so bad to look at either. He had never noticed them in those god-awful orthopedic shoes she used to wear, but now, in midheel slingbacks, Lydia Sinclair had great legs.

He watched her leave the hospital by the front door, then turned his attention back to the ward. These were evidently the worst cases, the ones who never left their beds or walked on the grounds outside. Whacked-out on Thorazine, these hopeless men mumbled to themselves, or sat rocking themselves as though they were babies, or just stared off into space. In the middle of them was Parry, like the eye of a storm, white and still.

"*Hi!*" said Jack. "It's me, Jack. How are ya doing? You look good. You do."

If he expected Parry to respond, he was in for a big disappointment. But Jack came closer to the bed and picked up Parry's limp hand. He gave it a little shake. "Hey, you gonna wake up for me? Huh?" Dropping the hand, he scowled and leaned over the bed, almost nose to nose with Parry.

"This isn't over, is it?" he asked resentfully. "You think you're going to make me do this, don't you? Well, *forget it!* No fuckin' way! I don't feel responsible for you, or for anybody! Everybody has bad things happen to them. . . . I'm not God!" I don't decide. People . . . survive." Jack looked bleakly at Parry. "*Say something!*"

But Parry gave no sign that he could see or hear. Furiously, Jack began to pace up and down near the bed, arguing more at himself than for Parry's unconscious benefit. "Everything's been going great. *Great!* I'm gonna have my own cable talk show, with an incredible equity, I might add. I . . . I have an incredibly fucking gorgeous girlfriend. . . . I am living an *incredibly fucking life!* So don't lay there in your comfortable little coma, and think I'm going to risk all of that because I feel responsible for you!"

Jack glared around at the other patients as though they were judge and jury. "*I am not responsible!*" he roared.

"And I don't feel guilty," he told the unresponding Parry. "You've got it easy! I'm out there every day. Every fuckin' *day* trying to figure out what the hell I'm doing. And why, no matter what I have, it feels like I have nothing! So just don't think I feel sorry for you! It's *easy* being nuts! Try being *me!*"

Jack dragged a chair up to Parry's bed and sat

down in it, bending over the comatose man and speaking more softly but very intensely. He was bitterly angry.

"So I won't do it. I don't believe in this shit. And don't give me that stuff about me being the One! There is *nothing* . . . nothing special about me! *I* control my own destiny . . . *me!* . . . not some floating overweight fairies. *I* decide what I'm going to do, and I am *not* risking my life to get some *fucking* cup for some *fucking vegetable.* . . ."

Hurling himself out of the chair, Jack knocked it over on its side. "Motherfucker!" he raged in his despair. "What am I supposed to do? What am I supposed to do?" And in a desperate whisper, "What am I supposed to *do?*"

He turned back to Parry. "Okay," he said in a calmer voice, "suppose for the sake of argument I *did* do this. I want you to know it wouldn't be because I had to! It wouldn't be because I feel guilty or cursed . . . or . . . responsible . . . or anything." He began to weep gently, tears filling his eyes and spilling over down his cheeks. "If I do this—and I mean *if!*—it's because *I* want to do this . . . for *you.* That's all! For you!"

Jack bent over the bed, looking deeply into Parry's sleeping face. His tears fell onto Parry's cheeks, wetting them, but Parry didn't move or open his eyes. He kissed the unconscious man gently on the forehead. "Don't go anywhere, huh?" Jack Lucas whispered. "I'll be back."

Nineteen

At this minute Jack Lucas ought to have been sitting in front of a log fire crackling brightly in a big stone fireplace in a three-million-dollar dune house in Southampton, a drink in his hand, a willowy adoring blonde at his side, a day of sailing behind him. Instead of which, Jack, looking like the King of the Idiots and feeling even dumber, was standing in front of Langdon Carmichael's armory on Fifth Avenue at midnight. And there went the fucking weekend. Shit, shit, and double shit.

Only a fool would go on a quest for the Holy Grail; the catch was, only a fool would find it. To find his own salvation, a man must first find the fool locked inside himself and set it free. Jack knew instinctively that to carry out Parry's plan, he'd have to do it Parry's way. The hard way.

So back he went to the boiler room, pocketed the plan of the armory from Parry's table, tore out the page from the glossy magazine that showed Carmichael standing in front of the bookcase with the Grail, and collected the ropes and hooks and other primeval, low-tech no-tech burglary tools that Mr. Camelot had assembled for this lunatic escapade. On the way out, almost as an afterthought, Jack had taken Parry's ragged old blanket cloak and Parry's little spangled hat, too. Now, heaven alone knew why, because Jack Lucas certainly didn't, he was actually dressed in them, looking like a refugee from a cheap school production of *Arthur and His Knights*. Sir Galahad . . . only in your worst nightmare.

Wonderful. Jack was about to break into a famous billionaire's home that was equipped with every known security device except pit bulls. Shit, maybe there *were* pit bulls. And he was going to do it with his bare hands, a hook, and a piece of old rope. Step right up, world, come one, come all, see Jack Lucas make a fucking ass of himself and maybe get killed in the bargain. Well, why not? The weekend was shot anyhow.

He looked around. By the light of the corner street lamp, this stretch of Fifth Avenue was deserted. Across the street were the dark reaches of Central Park; nobody went in there at this time of night. Nobody who expected to come out again, that is. Jack tested the grappling hook, making certain it was attached firmly to the rope. Okay. He might be no Boy Scout, but it seemed to Jack the knots would probably hold a man of his size and weight.

Taking a few steps back, Jack whirled the rope around like a cowboy's lariat and let the end with the grappling hook go, hoping to catch the hook behind one of the roof's crenellations. It flew through the air, hit the building, and bounced back to the ground, a good ten feet short of the mark. Try again. And again. Each time the hook slammed into the ground, it sounded like a car crash. Yet nobody came. Nobody called the cops. What do you expect? New York. Nobody gives a shit.

His arms starting to ache, Jack heaved the hook again. This time, by some miracle, it landed on the roof of the armory and caught behind one of the crenellations. Son of a bitch, what do you know? Now for the hard part, actually climbing the thing. Since he'd stopped drinking so much, Jack Lucas was more fit than he'd been in years, but climbing up a three-story building on a rope was something else again. For that you needed to be more than fit; you needed to be nuts.

"Shit," Jack muttered when he was four feet off the ground. At six feet, he groaned, and he kept groaning as he made his way inch by tortured inch up the stone wall of the armory toward the roof. His arms felt as though they were tearing loose of their sockets. His chest ached and his breath came rasping through his lips. *If I live through this, I have to give up smoking.* All his weight—and Jack stood a couple of muscular inches over six feet—was being supported on an ordinary rope and on the strength in his hands and arms. The higher off the ground he got, the harder it was not to look down. But Jack knew he didn't dare look down.

What could possibly happen? For one thing, the damn rope could break; it was just a piece of crap that Parry had no doubt picked up out of some garbage pile. Or the grappling hook could tear loose of the stone. In either case, Jack would go plunging down twenty-five or thirty feet to a messy splatter the sidewalk, no doubt screaming his fucking lungs out all the way down.

Or the cops could come. Stranger things had happened, even in New York City. They could be cruising by in a patrol car, eyes peeled for trouble in the neighborhood—naaahhh. "Thank God I live in a city where no one looks up," Jack muttered, gritting his teeth and sweating.

He reached the roof at last, but he was still hanging underneath it, the parapet above his head. He was going to have to swing up and over the parapet. He'd seen it done a thousand times in a thousand costume pictures. Up with the legs and over. C'mon, Jack, up and over. You can do it, come on! Easier grunted than done.

There was a noise off in the distance and Jack hung there, hands blistering on the rope, heart thudding in his chest, just frozen, listening. Horses? He could swear he heard the pounding of hooves. Not the gentle trot of a rented saddle horse, but a pounding galloping. It sounded like one horse, one rider, both extremely heavy, as though they were carrying the weight of iron armor. The noise was coming closer . . . closer . . . Jack shut his eyes.

But there was no horse. Just as suddenly as it came, the galloping stopped. It didn't die away; it just stopped. An eerie silence hung over everything.

"Oh, great!" Jack muttered, spooked. "This is great. I'm hearing horses now. Parry will be so pleased." He pictured in his mind's eye the headline "Radio Personality Turns Screwball on Mission from God," and uttered a hollow laugh. "I just hope that when they put me away they find me a bed right next to his!" Pissed off with himself and the world, he gave himself a mighty heave, and suddenly Jack was over the parapet.

His feet hit the roof with a thud, and Jack gratefully hauled the rope up after him and worked the grappling hook free from the crenellation. Okay, that was the easy part. Now he was going to have to actually break into the house.

He knew Parry's plan by heart; there was a skylight window around the bend of the roof. It was the only way he could break in. Naturally, the skylight was wired into the alarm system; Jack would have to be very careful not to touch anything on the perimeter of the glass or the outer edges of the glass itself. The wiring on these new alarms was hair-trigger sensitive. One little finger touch in the wrong place and it would be jeez Louise, all over with.

Yes, there was the skylight, exactly where it appeared on Parry's diagram. Score one for the catatonic. Reaching under the clumsy cloak, Jack managed to get into his pocket and take out a roll of masking tape. Working swiftly, he made three big loops of the tape and pressed them against the glass, well away from the perimeter. So far, so good.

Now he got out the glass cutter and, very slowly, his heartbeat hammering in his ears, he began to cut out a pane of glass, wide enough for him to get his body through. Minutes passed; the cutting took an excruciatingly long time. It seemed like an eternity before the hole was finished, time enough for the alarm to go off, cops to come, and all hell to break loose. But nothing happened. Pressing his arm against the loops of tape, Jack lifted the pane out intact, without setting off the alarm. Hey, it worked! Even Jack was surprised; he was getting pretty good at this. Maybe there was a career in lawbreaking ahead of him.

Jack set the glass gently down on the roof, made sure the grappling hook was firmly in place against stone, and carefully lowered himself down on the rope through the opening in the skylight. Below him was a pitch-black hole; he had no way of knowing how far he had to drop. All he knew was that the rope was too short, his feet were in midair, and he was dangling in space.

He had to take the chance. Letting go of the rope, he dropped to the floor beneath him, about six feet. He landed with a grunt and a thud. Picking himself up gingerly, he felt to see that nothing was broken. Nothing was. He was inside the house; it was too dark to see exactly where, but inside. Risking discovery, Jack pulled the magazine article from his pocket and lit up his cigarette lighter. He studied the article. The Holy Grail was in the library on the first floor. He was up on the third. He'd have to get down to the library without making noise. He had no idea who might be in the house. Maybe Langdon Carmichael. Maybe the servants. Maybe guests. Maybe all of them. Still, he had no other options. He had to take the chance.

Jack made his way cautiously toward the broad curving staircase up ahead. But a movement in the shadows stopped him dead in his tracks. He felt a chill prickling his skin. He wasn't alone. Somebody or something was there, and was moving forward, straight at him. There, where the landing met the top of the stairs. As Jack's eyes adjusted to the darkness he could see it was a human figure.

The figure stepped out of the shadows. Jack Lucas gasped in horror and disbelief.

It was Edwin Malnick, and in his hands was a shotgun.

Jack stood paralyzed with fear, watching Edwin Malnick raise the shotgun and cock it, aiming straight for Jack's chest. His finger touched the trigger. Jack closed his eyes.

The deafening noise of the shotgun blast resonated through Jack's brain. It echoed down the hallways as it must have echoed that night in Babbitt's. In his mind, for the first time Jack could actually hear the screams of those poor terrified doomed people who'd come in for a drink and found death instead. For the first time he *was* one of those people.

He opened his eyes. He was alive. There was no wound in his chest, no blood on his shirt, no blood on the floor, and no Edwin Malnick. And Jack Lucas realized that Edwin Malnick had been his own Red Knight, and that he had inevitably to meet him face-to-face and experience for himself that grisly scene he'd always managed to evade.

Somehow, although he was shaky, Jack felt stronger now. He walked quietly down the stairs to the library, keeping a sharp eye out for the small red electric-eye lights of the electronic surveillance cameras. On the walls of the staircase hung the famous Langdon Carmichael art purchases—the Monet, the Picassos, and now the magnificent new twenty-million-dollar Van Gogh. Jack couldn't take the time to appreciate them. He entered the library. The house was very still; it appeared that nobody was home, not even the servants. This might be easier than Jack had dared hope for.

The library was a huge room, far more impressive than it appeared in the magazine photographs, its walls totally lined with books, and with very high ceilings and a baronial fireplace at the far end. A green leather high-backed chair was drawn up near the fireplace, in which a fire was burning, and a small lamp was lighted on a table next to the chair. The light from the lamp fell directly on the bookcase, illuminating it. On the shelves were the precious objects that Carmichael collected, priceless manuscripts, a Degas bronze, some Cellini gold, and . . . the Holy Grail.

It was incredible. There, on the second shelf of the bookcase, stood a beautiful silver chalice. Jack opened the cabinet and took the Grail reverently into his hands. There was some writing on it. He turned it over in his hands and read the words inscribed in the silver.

"To Little Lannie Carmichael for All His Hard Work
P.S. 247 Christmas Pageant 1932"

Jack smiled. A commemorative loving cup; he should have guessed. Just a treasured souvenir of long ago, nothing mystical or magic about it. Even so, although it might not be *the* Grail, it was Parry's Grail, and he'd take it anyhow. It was what he'd come for. Tucking it under his arm, he turned to go.

That's when Jack noticed something for the first time. Somebody was slumped in the high-backed chair in front of the fireplace. A man, dressed only in expensive silk pajamas and an elegant robe. Jack took a backward step, but the man didn't move. He appeared to be asleep. Then Jack saw the rest of the picture. The empty bottle of Stolichnaya vodka on the table, the overturned glass. And, on the floor, lay an uncapped pill bottle, all the pills gone.

Kneeling swiftly, Jack checked the pharmacist's label on the bottle. It was made out to Langdon Carmichael, and it was Seconal, a powerful barbiturate. A suicide. Was it over, or had Jack interrupted it? He put down the chalice, reached around Carmichael's neck and tried to find an arterial pulse with his fingers. Nothing . . . no, wait . . . yes, there was the faintest pulse. Jack put his hand on the man's chest and could feel a heartbeat that was barely there. Langdon Carmichael was still alive, but only just.

Christ, what should he do? It was evident that Carmichael had sent all the servants away for the evening in order to have the privacy to kill himself. There was nobody in the house to help. If Jack didn't get medical assistance immediately, Langdon Carmichael would die. If he called the police or the paramedics, his own ass would be grass. What was he doing there, breaking into a billionaire's home in the dead of night? No, Jack couldn't possibly summon help. He had to get out while he still had time.

Hey, if the guy wanted to die, if he went to all this trouble to die, let him die, right? Who was Jack Lucas to interfere with another man's wishes? He grabbed up the chalice and ran out of the library, panicked. But he knew he was doing the wrong thing. Life was too precious to waste. A man in despair one day can be happy the next. He had to save Langdon Carmichael's life.

Jack came to a halt in the large vestibule leading to the front door. The main door must certainly be wired for the night, to open it would be to set off the alarm. He turned away; he'd have to go out the way he came, by the roof. Wait, no! *If he opened the front door, the alarm would go off, and the police would come.* If the police came, Langdon Carmichael might be found in time.

Jack looked around; there had to be evidence of the alarm somewhere. Yeah, there it was, down by the baseboard a couple of inches above the floor. Two crossed electric eye beams, focused on the door. Anybody walking through them would trigger the alarm. He stood up, tucking the precious chalice firmly under his arm. Then he opened the front door and walked out.

Hell broke loose, a loud shrieking of electronic sirens. Jack broke into a run, dashing around the corner of Fifth Avenue and east on Seventy-fourth Street. On Lexington Avenue, he came to a halt, three blocks away from Langdon Carmichael's armory.

He was safe, and he'd gotten away with it. Sir Jack Lucas Galahad, whose strength was as the strength of ten because his heart was pure, had finally achieved the Holy Grail.

The ward was dark and silent; everyone in the mental hospital was asleep. Jack came in quietly and waked to the foot of Parry's bed.

"Wake up," he said. He took Langdon Carmichael's loving cup and put it into Parry's lifeless hands, bringing the hands up and wrapping them around the Grail, which now rested on Parry's chest.

"I did my side of the bargain. Are you gonna wake up now?" He looked down at Parry, who didn't move a muscle. "You want to think about it a little more?" Jack asked gently. "Okay, take your time."

As for Jack, he was totally beat. He couldn't keep his eyes open. Every muscle he owned ached, along with a few he didn't know he had. He pulled a chair up to the bed, settled himself into it, put his cowboy-booted feet up on Parry's blanket, and fell fast asleep.

* * *

Light began to trickle in through the large windows of the hospital ward from the breaking dawn outside. The patients still slept. Jack Lucas still slept. Parry opened his eyes.

He lay on his back, looking up at the shadows still gathered on the ceiling. He had no idea where he was or why he was there. He didn't know what day it was, or what year. But there was something in his hands . . . something cold, heavy, metal, silver . . . he felt it, touching it all over. Looking down, Parry saw with an enormous surge of joy what he was holding. It was the Holy Grail, the only thing that could cure the incurable wound.

Close by the bed, crumpled uncomfortably in a chair, was Jack, and Parry knew it was Jack who had brought him the Grail. He'd been right; the Little People had been right. Jack Lucas was the One. Parry smiled happily.

"I had this dream, Jack," he whispered in a tone of wonder. "I was married. I was married to this beautiful woman. . . . And you were there, too."

Jack opened his eyes, but didn't move or speak. "I really miss her, Jack," Parry whispered. "Is that okay? Can I miss her now?" Tears formed in Jack's eyes, but he didn't turn around. He knew what Parry was really saying. He understood that Parry was asking, is it safe to think about Elizabeth? Can I put her into the past without going mad? Is it the knightly thing to do?

Jack didn't reply; he couldn't, he was too choked up to speak. But somehow Parry must have gotten the message. "Thank you," he whispered. And both of them fell asleep again, this time not to dream.

Lydia Sinclair got off the bus in front of the Oakbrook Institute. She was carrying today's newspaper, with its lead story about the miraculous recovery of

Langdon Carmichael, whose suicide had been interrupted by a botched and bungled burglary. The burglar had gotten away empty-handed, but the billionaire would live. She also carried a fresh bunch of flowers and some lovely new towels she'd picked up at Macy's white sale. They'd go very nicely with Parry's sheets. As soon as she walked into the ward she knew something was different. Parry wasn't in his bed. The bed was empty. Lydia's face blanched, and the breath caught in her throat. Where was he?

Oh, my God, there he was, up out of bed and leading the other patients in his favorite song. *He was out of bed!* Lydia gasped, and let the packages fall from her fingers.

Parry turned and saw her, and his face lit up like Christmas. "Hiya, sweetheart! Where ya been?" he called.

She tried to speak, but no words would come. Instead, tears fell hotly from her eyes, yet she smiled at him while she was weeping.

"Hey, what's that face all about?" Parry asked, coming up to Lydia and wrapping his arms around her. "Hey, why are you crying? Don't cry . . . hey!"

Lydia threw her arms around his neck and bawled for sheer gladness while Parry held her lovingly. "Are you my girl?" he asked her gently, patting her back like you do to a baby. "Are you my girl?"

Lydia sobbed and nodded yes, clinging to Parry as tightly as she could. Parry hugged back; Jack had never seen him so happy.

Jack slipped by them unnoticed. They didn't need him right now; they didn't need anybody but each other. He'd come back tomorrow.

Meanwhile, there was something important he still had to do. Compared with it, stealing the Holy Grail was a snap.

* * *

The Video Spot wasn't busy, and Anne Napolitano had taken a few minutes to go into her private office and go over the week's receipts. When she heard the knock on the door, she called out a grudging "Yeah," without looking up. It was only when the door opened and closed and nobody said anything that Anne raised her head from her accounts. Jack Lucas was standing there looking at her. In his hand was a bouquet of flowers. She hadn't laid eyes on him or heard a word from him for six months, and now here he was, bigger than life and looking good, and saying nothing. Just standing there looking at her.

Anne was so shocked that for one long moment she couldn't find the breath to speak. Then, when she did speak, she was both angry and unnerved. "Well, what do you expect me to do, applaud?" Her cheeks and neck were flushed a dull red with emotion.

Jack didn't answer, but he was looking pretty sheepish.

"What? What?" Anne challenged. "What did you come here for? Did you come to get the rest of your stuff? There's no more stuff. It all got burned . . . accidentally. Jack, don't do this," she warned. His continued silence was making her crazy. "Whatever the hell you're doing, don't do this, okay? You don't just show up here out of nowhere and then just stand there like a statue and make me do all the work. What did you come here for?"

Jack drew in a deep breath. "I . . . uh . . . I love you," he said at last, barely audible.

"*What?*" Anne stood up slowly and came from around her desk. Jack backed up in fear, until his back was against the wall of porno tapes, and he had no more room to maneuver.

"I didn't get all that," Anne growled. "Would you run that by me again?"

Jack was sweating bullets here. This was the hardest thing he had ever had to do in his life. He knew what a shit he'd been, and how much he owed Anne, and he knew that Anne wasn't going to make things easy for him. Life with her would be one very long and loud battle. But what the hell? Everybody had a cross to bear in this life and Anne Napolitano's Italian temper would be Jack's cross. If he got over this first hurdle.

"I . . . uh . . . I think . . . uh, I *realize* I love you," and he sighed deeply.

Anne's brows drew together and fire flashed from her jet-black eyes. "You love me? *You love me?* You son . . . of . . . a . . . bitch!" Hauling off, she gave Jack a real crack across the jowls, hard enough to stun an ox. Jack saw stars and heard bells; his knees buckled and he began to slip to the floor.

Anne was on him in an instant, her lips on his, devouring him with her passion, tugging at the buttons and zippers of his clothes. Jack Lucas was too weak to protest, too weak to stand up, too weak to struggle, but not too weak to make crazy love, the best lovemaking of his life, with his woman.

"God, what a beautiful night," said Parry, deeply moved by the moon, and the park, and the joy of being alive.

"Yeah," Jack agreed. He looked up at the clouds that had gathered over the face of the moon. Through the silver moonlight, he could see them moving. "Hey . . . am I doing that?" he asked.

"You know it," Parry assured him.

The two friends lay side by side on the Sheep Meadow, cloudbusting, at peace with the world, just watching the cloud formations scud across the face of the moon.

And oh, yeah, one more thing. Both of them were naked.

Other great reads from **Red Fox**

THE WINTER VISITOR   Joan Lingard

Strangers didn't come to Nick Murray's home town in winter. And they didn't lodge at his house. But Ed Black had—and Nick Murray didn't like it.

Why had Ed come? The small Scottish seaside resort was bleak, cold and grey at that time of year. The answer, Nick begins to suspect, lies with his mother—was there some past connection between her and Ed?

ISBN 0 09 938590 2   £1.99

STRANGERS IN THE HOUSE   Joan Lingard

Calum resents his mother remarrying. He doesn't want to move to a flat in Edinburgh with a new father and a thirteen-year-old stepsister. Stella, too, dreads the new marriage. Used to living alone with her father she loathes the idea of sharing their small flat.

Stella's and Calum's struggles to adapt to a new life, while trying to cope with the problems of growing up are related with great poignancy in a book which will be enjoyed by all older readers.

ISBN 0 09 955020 2   **£2.99**

Other great reads from **Red Fox**

Haunting fiction for older readers from Red Fox

THE XANADU MANUSCRIPT
John Rowe Townsend

There is nothing unusual about visitors in Cambridge.

So what is it about three tall strangers which fills John with a mixture of curiosity and unease? Not only are they strikingly handsome but, for apparently educated people, they are oddly surprised and excited by normal, everyday events. And, as John pursues them, their mystery only seems to deepen.

Set against a background of an old university town, this powerfully compelling story is both utterly fantastic and oddly convincing.

'An author from whom much is expected and received.' *Economist*

ISBN 0 09 975180 1   £2.99

ONLOOKER   Roger Davenport

Peter has always enjoyed being in Culver Wood, and dismissed the tales of hauntings, witchcraft and superstitions associated with it. But when he starts having extraordinary visions that are somehow connected with the wood, and which become more real to him than his everyday life, he realizes that something is taking control of his mind in an inexplicable and frightening way.

Through his uneasy relationship with Isobel and her father, a Professor of Archaeology interested in excavating Culver Wood, Peter is led to the discovery of the wood's secret and his own terrifying part in it.

ISBN 0 09 975070 8   £2.99

Other great reads **from Red Fox**

Enter the gripping world of the REDWALL saga

REDWALL Brian Jacques

It is the start of the summer of the Late Rose. Redwall Abbey, the peaceful home of a community of mice, slumbers in the warmth of a summer afternoon. The mice are preparing for a great jubilee feast.

But not for long. Cluny is coming! The evil one-eyed rat warlord is advancing with his battle-scarred mob. And Cluny wants Redwall . . .

ISBN 0 09 951200 9 £3.99

MOSSFLOWER Brian Jacques

One late autumn evening, Bella of Brockhall snuggled deep in her armchair and told a story . . .

This is the dramatic tale behind the bestselling *Redwall*. It is the gripping account of how Redwall Abbey was founded through the bravery of the legendary mouse Martin and his epic quest for Salmandastron. Once again, the forces of good and evil are at war in a stunning novel that will captivate readers of all ages.

ISBN 0 09 955400 3 £3.99

MATTIMEO Brian Jacques

Slagar the fox is intent on revenge . . .

On bringing death and destruction to the inhabitants of Redwall Abbey, in particular to the fearless warrior mouse Matthias. Gathering his evil band around him, Slagar plots to strike at the heart of the Abbey. His cunning and cowardly plan is to steal the Redwall children—and Mattimeo, Matthias' son, is to be the biggest prize of all.

ISBN 0 09 967540 4 £3.99

*Other great reads from **Red Fox***

Discover the great animal stories of Colin Dann

JUST NUFFIN

The Summer holidays loomed ahead with nothing to look
forward to except one dreary week in a caravan with only Mum
and Dad for company. Roger was sure he'd be bored.

But then Dad finds Nuffin: an abandoned puppy who's more
a bundle of skin and bones than a dog. Roger's holiday is
transformed and he and Nuffin are inseparable. But Dad is
adamant that Nuffin must find a new home. Is there *any* way
Roger can persuade him to change his mind?

ISBN 0 09 966900 5   £2.99

KING OF THE VAGABONDS

*'You're very young,' Sammy's mother said, 'so heed my advice.
Don't go into Quartermile Field.'*

His mother and sister are happily domesticated but Sammy,
the tabby cat, feels different. They are content with their lot,
never wondering what lies beyond their immediate surroundings.
But Sammy is burningly curious and his life seems full of
mysteries. Who is his father? Where has he gone? And what
is the mystery of Quartermile Field?

ISBN 0 09 957190 0   £2.99

In the Path of the Storm

The strength of the wind increased in power with every passing minute. In a patch of woodland, not too far distant, Badger urged his ancient limbs to greater efforts. He had travelled too far from his own set to be able to return in safety. He could think only of the alternative shelter where, unknown to him, his friends were already assembled. He was between the two and he knew he had put himself in the greatest peril.

By the same author:
The Ram of Sweetriver
The King of the Vagabonds
The City Cats
The Beach Dogs
Just Nuffin
A Great Escape
A Legacy of Ghosts

The Farthing Wood Series:

Animals of Farthing Wood
In the Grip of Winter
Fox's Feud
Fox Cub Bold
The Siege of White Deer Park
In the Path of the Storm
Battle for the Park

In the Path of the Storm

Colin Dann

Illustrations by Trevor Newton

RED FOX

A Red Fox Book

Published by Random House Children's Books
20 Vauxhall Bridge Road, London SW1V 2SA

A division of Random House UK Ltd

London Melbourne Sydney Auckland
Johannesburg and agencies throughout the world

First published by Hutchinson Children's Books 1989
Red Fox edition 1991
This edition 1992

Printed and bound in Great Britain by
Cox & Wyman Ltd, Reading, Berkshire

ISBN 0 09 920551 3

Contents

In Memory of Frederick C. Brown,
friend and naturalist

didn't disturb him. He was an old, wise animal who respected all other creatures in the Nature Reserve and he knew when to leave well alone. He knew Whistler was catching fish and he paused to drink with caution, making sure any ripples caused by his lowered muzzle didn't interfere with the bird's occupation. He drank and slowly raised his head.

Whistler came out of his reverie as he saw movement. He turned his head to the stag. As he looked the deer's body was seized by a sort of spasm and, quite suddenly, the legs collapsed and the great beast crashed on to his side. The stag seemed to tremble; then all was still except that, almost imperceptibly, the body began to slide down the muddy bank towards the stream where it became lodged, half in and half out of the water. Whistler launched himself into the air and, with a few flaps of his wings, reached the deer's side. The glassy look of the Great Stag's eyes and the beast's utter stillness confirmed the heron's fears. The leader of the White Deer Park herd was dead.

Whistler was so distressed he did not, at first, know what to do. The Great Stag had been so much a part of life in the Nature Reserve for the heron and for all his friends who had travelled there to seek sanctuary from their ruined birthplace, Farthing Wood, that he had epitomised the very name of their new home, White Deer Park. Not that it was such a new home to them now, for they would soon be entering their fourth season there. And now here was the lordly animal who had welcomed them into the Park on the first day of their arrival all that time ago, and whom all of them revered, lying lifeless at the heron's feet. It was just too

much for Whistler to contemplate alone. He needed to share the burden. He took a last look at the sad sight of the great deer's carcass and flew hurriedly away.

His powerful wings took him quickly to that corner of the Park where his old friends had settled. The first creature he saw was Badger who was busy collecting fresh bedding for his set. Badger looked up as he heard the familiar whistle of the heron's damaged wing. The old animal's sight was very bad now but he knew Whistler so well by his sound that he didn't need to wait until he could see him properly. He called out a greeting in his gruff voice.

'Hallo, Whistler! More rain, more rain. Everything's sopping. My set's waterlogged and –' He broke off as the heron landed beside him and now even Badger could see the look of anguish in the great bird's eyes. 'Why, whatever's the matter, my friend?' he asked kindly. 'You look as if you've seen a ghost.'

'I – I have – almost,' Whistler stammered. He hadn't yet recovered from his shock. 'An awful thing, Badger. The Great Stag. . . .' His voice petered out.

'Well?' Badger prompted him.

'He – he's dead.'

'Dead?' cried Badger. 'Are you sure? I saw him only recently and –'

'He's dead, Badger,' Whistler repeated. His voice was hushed. 'I saw him die. Just a moment ago. It was horribly sudden. He was drinking at the stream and then – he – he just keeled over and lay still.'

Badger was stunned. He could scarcely believe it. 'How dreadful,' he murmured.

For a while neither spoke, lost in their own thoughts.

At last Whistler said, 'I suppose he was a great age.'

Badger said, 'Aren't we all, Whistler?' He was reminded of his own longevity. 'I don't know how I've survived when. . . .' He didn't finish. The rain still beat down relentlessly. 'I suppose I should get this bedding underground,' he mumbled.

'I'll tell the others,' Whistler informed him.

But Badger didn't hear. His thoughts were full of the momentousness of the heron's discovery. How would the Great Stag's death change things? Would the Park become a different place? He dragged the damp bracken and leaves he had gathered backwards into his set entrance. 'Never dry, never dry,' he muttered as he reached his sleeping-chamber. 'My old bones won't stand this for ever. I'm not immortal either.'

Later the rain ceased for a while. The animals from Farthing Wood, together with their friends and relations, had collected to bid farewell to the Great Stag as a mark of respect to an old acquaintance.

'It's the end of the old order,' said Fox. He looked about him. Vixen, his beloved partner, Weasel, Whistler, Tawny Owl and Badger met his eyes. They were all thinking the same thing. How long before they too would succumb? The stag's death seemed to bring their own a little closer.

'It's so sad,' said Vixen. There was a catch in her voice. 'He was a good friend to us all.'

'Who'll take his place?' Leveret asked. The young hare's question dispelled the older animals' gloomy thoughts. 'There will be a new leader, won't there?'

'There'll be a battle first,' Tawny Owl asserted. 'There's no obvious successor.'

'Someone will win through,' Weasel remarked. 'One of the younger stags.'

'Of *course* he'll be younger,' Tawny Owl said impatiently. 'That goes without saying, doesn't it?'

'I wonder who it'll be?' Mossy said anxiously. He didn't like change.

'We won't know that, Mole,' Badger said to him, 'until their breeding season. And that's a long way off.'

The body of the aged leader of the deer herd rocked gently in the rush of the swollen stream.

Owl is Discomfited

The weather continued very wet. Toad and Adder emerged from hibernation to see the Park wreathed in damp mists and the low-lying ground turned marshy. Toad was in his element. He loved such conditions and his warty skin glistened in harmony. But Adder grumbled. He craved warmth.

'We've come out too soon,' he moaned to his companion.

'Nonsense,' returned Toad, jumping up and down in his glee. 'Things couldn't be better.' Adder turned his back on him with a contemptuous hiss.

Toad leapt away to White Deer Pond and found it brimming over. The Edible Frogs were calling lustily to each other. One of them spied Toad and soon told him of the sad demise of the Great Stag. Like his friends from Farthing Wood, Toad was shocked. He remembered how the leader of the herd had befriended

them all and Toad felt he wanted to be amongst his close companions now to share his sadness. He left the Pond without a word and travelled to the corner of the Reserve where he knew he would find his old friends. On the way he overtook Adder who was slithering through the mire with an expression of the utmost distaste on his face.

Toad broke the news to him. Adder halted. Never one to give vent to his emotions, the snake was nonetheless unable to prevent his expression wavering. And there was an unusually long pause before he replied simply, 'I see.' Toad knew Adder better than anyone and he guessed the news had had the same impact on the snake as on all the community. They continued their journey in silence.

They reached the area where their animal friends had settled, near the Hollow. It was a while before any of them put in an appearance. Tawny Owl was the first to see them from his perch in an oak tree where he was alternately dozing and watching. He flew down to greet them after their winter absence.

'Another season,' he remarked.

'Yes, and a sad start to it,' Toad replied.

Tawny Owl blinked sleepily. It was a while since the Great Stag had died. The deer carcass had been removed by the Warden and Owl had almost forgotten about it.

'He means the deceased beast,' Adder lisped.

Tawny Owl stared. Then, 'Ah! Yes,' he nodded. 'The Stag. It was by the stream, you know.'

Toad said with concern: 'There have been no other deaths? I mean –'

'No, no,' Owl cut in. 'None of us old 'uns. Badger's still around. And – well, so am I.'

'Evidently,' Adder drawled.

'And Fox?' prompted Toad.

'Oh yes. Fox and Vixen. And Weasel. And Whistler. It was Whistler who saw the Stag die.'

'He was a noble beast,' Toad said.

'Yes.' Even Adder concurred with that.

'There's another thing about the stream,' Tawny Owl resumed. 'There appears to be a dearth of food in it at present, according to Whistler. He has to go outside the Park to fish.'

The three creatures contemplated this but could come to no conclusions. Tawny Owl decided to return to his roost. He always slept a lot during the day.

'I'm going to find myself a dry spot – if there is such a thing,' Adder said. His red eyes glinted. 'But that won't do for you,' he addressed Toad. 'So I'll leave you to your own devices.'

'All right. I understand,' Toad answered. 'I'll stay around for a bit until I've seen some of the others. I'll give them your good wishes, shall I?'

'Do as you please,' Adder hissed under his breath as he slid away. He headed for Badger's set. '*That'll* be dry,' he told himself.

There were many births that spring amongst the Farthing Wood community and their descendants. The Farthing Wood Fox and his mate Vixen had lived to see their lineage reach the fourth generation. A grandson of Bold (their cub who had left the Park and not survived) was born whom Vixen swore was the

image of his grandfather at that age. She and Fox watched his progress with great interest. He was named Plucky.

Spring turned into summer and everywhere there were rabbits, hedgehogs, squirrels, mice and voles who were White Deer Park animals through and through, but who owed their existence to their doughty fore-fathers who had travelled across countryside and Man's terrain to reach the Reserve. There were moles and weasels and hares. And toads, kestrels and herons. Soon there would be adders. Only Badger and Tawny Owl remained solitary. Badger was ancient now and didn't always know what he was about. He had become very forgetful. The younger animals loved and respected him.

But sometimes they teased Tawny Owl who had not yet entered real old age. Weasel, too, could not resist a gibe now and then.

'Well, Owl,' he said, 'when will you muster up the courage to go a-courting?'

'When I choose to,' replied the bird loftily.

'It seems to me you don't choose to,' Weasel continued. 'At least, not on the evidence of three seasons in the Park.'

'How would you know? Can you fly?' Tawny Owl retorted.

'I don't need to,' answered Weasel. 'Everyone knows you've never been seen in the company of a female.'

Tawny Owl didn't remain to hear any more insults. He flew away in a huff. But there was no relief for him. Pace and Rusty, two of the younger foxes now parents themselves, found his shelter and goaded him cheekily.

'Here's the only old bachelor left of the originals,' Pace remarked to his cousin.

'Poor old Owl – he can't find a mate,' Rusty added provocatively.

Tawny Owl tried to maintain his calm, moving to a higher perch.

'Have all the females been snapped up, Owl?' Pace persisted, raising his voice.

'Stop chaffing me,' Tawny Owl called down irritably. He was becoming ruffled. 'Haven't you got anything better to do?'

'Haven't you?' Rusty gibed.

'Perhaps not.'

'But think of all those lady owls dying for a word from you, the famous Owl from Farthing Wood,' Pace taunted him.

'They'll have to wait then, won't they?' Tawny Owl answered. He knew he was foolish to take any notice but their raillery was impossible to ignore.

'Wait for what?'

'For me to choose to visit them,' Owl said superciliously.

'Oh – oh. Hark at that, Rusty. Don't you think it might be *they* who haven't chosen Tawny Owl?'

'Must be,' agreed Rusty. 'After all, he *is* the only bachelor.'

'I'm NOT the only bachelor,' Tawny Owl screeched furiously. 'What about Badger?'

'Poor old Badger? He's almost senile,' declared Rusty. 'You can't count –' He broke off as he saw his mother, Charmer, approaching.

'What's going on?' she enquired. She sensed the young foxes were up to some mischief.

'They're baiting me,' Tawny Owl complained querulously.

'Why – whatever for?'

'It's only about his bachelorhood,' Pace explained.

'Whatever business is that of yours?' Charmer demanded angrily. 'Haven't you got responsibilities of your own now that are more important than being disrespectful to your elders? You leave Tawny Owl in peace. He deserves all the quiet he can get.' She lowered her voice. 'And why should you want to scoff at another's misfortune?'

The young foxes looked contrite. They hadn't really meant any harm. Unfortunately Tawny Owl had heard Charmer's last remark and was mortified. Misfortune? What did they take him for? He – Tawny Owl, one of the most revered inhabitants of the Reserve? *He'd* show them! He was seething. He flapped up from his perch so impulsively he almost banged his head on the branch above. But he extricated himself and, trying hard to recover his usual dignity, sailed away across the treetops. When he finally perched again he was a long way from where any of his unkind persecutors could get at him. His anger eventually subsided. But, though he could never have owned up to it, he had been well and truly hurt. And now he knew he had to do something to prove them wrong.

The trouble was, he knew most, if not all, of the female owls would already have paired off. However, he needed to find out for sure. So, in rather a half-hearted way, he began to make a tour of the Park and

its nesting sites. He soon discovered that the other male owls were very jealous of their territory and would drive him off if he attempted to approach too close. It was a demoralizing experience for him. At night he concentrated on catching his prey and, while he ate, pondered on his next move.

'Nothing else for it,' he told himself. 'I'll have to extend my search outside the Park.' In a way he was quite relieved at this state of affairs. There would be a wider area to roam, with the likelihood of better opportunities of finding what he sought. And, best of all, none of his old companions – or new ones – would have any way of following his progress.

One night he flew out, over the downland, skimming effortlessly through the air on his silent wings. He looked back at the boundary fence of White Deer Park and the dark silhouettes of its trees. Although he often flew beyond the bounds of the Park, the significance of his flight this time made him feel just a mite apprehensive, since he didn't know for sure how long it might be before he would return there. But he turned his head resolutely and set a course for the nearest patch of woodland.

A Rendezvous

In May and June that season's White Deer Park fawns were born. The young deer were born with the usual dappled coats. It was only as they matured that the animals took on the white colouring that gave the Nature Reserve its name.

The Farthing Wood animals knew that amongst these newborns there was a future dominant male in whose veins the blood of the Great Stag was coursing. But the older creatures knew they would never know him. What they were interested in was which of the present mature stags would assume the role of the Great Stag's successor. At this time of the year the stags separated themselves from the hinds and wandered, sometimes together, sometimes alone. To the watching animals there already seemed to be one obvious contender for the leadership. He was the largest and sturdiest of the beasts and was certainly aware of his

strength. He was cool and self-possessed in the other
males' company and had a superior air. His antlers
were still growing but he already had a greater head
than his companions. He was known as Trey. The
animals were impressed by him and began to wonder
how they would fare in relationship to him.

'He's a proud creature,' Fox remarked when he and
Vixen stopped one evening to watch. 'Look at the way
he carries himself.'

'Yes,' Vixen agreed. 'He seems to realize even now
he has no real rivals. It's in his bearing.'

'There will be some challengers,' Fox answered her.
'It's in the nature of things.'

'My only concern is that he won't interfere with our
way of life or our friends',' Vixen said, voicing Fox's
own fears. 'It's been so peaceful since the departure of
the huge hunting Cat.'

'We'll keep ourselves to ourselves,' Fox vowed. 'No
creature can take exception to that.'

So the Farthing Wood community went about their
business as usual without upsetting anybody.

Badger had had a tenant for much of the spring in his
set, and an unlooked-for one at that. Because of the
long period of wet weather Adder had set up home in a
dry spot near the mouth of one of Badger's tunnels. He
had not asked permission and Badger was too old and
polite a friend to object. But when a drier patch of
weather set in and Adder showed no sign of wanting to
leave, Badger began to make some pointed comments.
It wasn't that Adder was there all the time. He couldn't
be. He had to go out to catch his food. Yet the way he
used the set as his base, constantly returning to it as if

he had some kind of right, really got under Badger's hide.

One bright morning when the snake didn't seem at all disposed to stir Badger said: 'Why don't you go for a sunbathe? I thought you didn't like temperatures too cool?'

Adder grinned enigmatically. 'There's quite enough warmth to suit me here, thank you, Badger,' he replied.

'Isn't it time you ate?' Badger hinted. 'I don't think you've moved for days.'

'I don't need to hunt every day,' was the reply and Adder coiled himself up even more comfortably. 'I suppose you couldn't spare a few more of those dry leaves for this corner?' His tongue flickered in and out as he savoured the smell of the bedding.

'No, I couldn't,' Badger said shortly. 'I'm not your housekeeper. I didn't mind sheltering you during the constant downpours. I like company. But there are times when I also like solitude.'

Adder ignored him. He merely stared straight back at Badger with a blissful expression on his face. Badger lumbered away, growling to himself.

Later Mossy visited his ancient friend via one of the mole's connecting tunnels that led straight into the set. Badger immediately began talking about Adder as if Mossy had been there all day. 'He's taken up permanent residence here,' he complained. 'Snakes should find their own burrows. What am I to do, Mole?'

Mossy didn't consider he was in a position to advise. 'You've known Adder much longer than I,' he replied. 'I wouldn't dream of –'

'And then, what do you think?' Badger continued

without listening. 'He wants his bedding provided. He always had the cheek of all his kind but this time – well!' He lapsed into peevish mutterings.

Mossy thought it best to change the subject. 'Have you seen Tawny Owl recently?' he enquired.

'What? What? Owl? No, I haven't. What of it?' Badger answered irritably.

'I met Weasel earlier. He says he thinks Owl's disappeared. No-one's seen him since – um – well, since. . . .'

'Since what?' Badger snapped.

'Since the young foxes badgered him,' Mossy finished and tittered nervously.

'Very amusing, Mole,' Badger commented humourlessly. But he was interested. 'What's this all about?' he asked.

Mossy explained. 'Weasel told me the tale. He was involved too. He admitted it. They've been goading Tawny Owl because of his solitariness.'

'Nothing wrong with solitariness,' Badger replied at once. '*I'd* relish it.'

'That wasn't quite what I meant.' Mossy went on to describe the circumstances.

'Oh,' said Badger. 'I see. Poor old Owl. Why treat him like that? And he's disappeared, you say? Disappeared where? To another quarter of the Park?'

'Weasel says not. It seems Whistler hasn't seen Owl flying over any part of the Park for ages.'

'Well, we can't let this rest. Perhaps he's keeping to his roost. He could be ill.'

'None of his favourite haunts are occupied. Whistler's been to look. Weasel is convinced Owl's left the Park.'

Badger was really concerned. 'Oh no. That would be awful. Driven out like that! I hope the young foxes have been –'

'They're very upset about it,' Mossy interrupted. 'Weasel told me.'

Adder had heard the voices coming from Badger's far chamber. He put two and two together. 'The bird's gone searching for a mate,' he hissed under his breath. 'How absurd at his age.'

Badger trundled up the tunnel to give Adder the news.

'I heard,' Adder said abruptly. 'Well, Badger, I think we can look forward to a long absence from our friend Tawny Owl.'

'How can you be so unfeeling?' Badger demanded.

'Not unfeeling; just realistic,' Adder answered, quite unperturbed. 'Old Owl's not exactly a glossy-plumed youngster, just out of the nest.'

'I shall speak to Fox,' Badger said determinedly. 'We must do something. Bring Owl back.' He lumbered away.

'And how do you propose to do that? Sprout wings?' Adder called after him sarcastically.

Mossy followed faithfully in Badger's footsteps for a while. Adder watched them go. 'I suppose they'll mount a search,' he muttered. But the topic of Tawny Owl had reminded him of a search he had been contemplating making himself now that there was dry summer weather. He had expected – perhaps had even hoped – to come across Sinuous in his wanderings. But he hadn't done so. Adder had a feeling, though, that he knew one place where he could find her. It was a

favourite spot of the she-viper's, near the stream. So, despite his comfortable surroundings, he issued forth from the set into the sunshine.

Since the death of the Great Stag the stream had generally been avoided by the Farthing Wood animals. Without actually giving voice to their feelings, the stream had become for them a place of portent. That the stag had died on its banks was like an omen. It gave the site an air of mystery. Whistler was unable to fish there. And the long wet spell had made it unnecessary for use as a drinking place. However, all this was immaterial to Adder as he slithered over the ground, bent on his rendezvous.

Sinuous detected his approach before he saw her. She was sunning herself on a mossy patch amongst the new young ferns. She lay on slightly rising ground. She observed Adder a few metres distant, his tongue darting incessantly as he sought for her scent. Sinuous allowed her face to take on the typical grin of the snake; a sort of leer. She was pleased and a little flattered Adder had come looking for her.

When Adder was close by, she said: 'Our trails cross at last. I've been wondering why it hasn't happened before?'

Adder slid to an abrupt halt at the sound. He didn't wish it to be too obvious that he was on a search. He looked up and saw Sinuous on her couch of moss. 'I haven't been in these parts for a while,' he told her.

'I'm well aware of that,' Sinuous answered. 'What brings you here now?'

'Oh well, one has to go somewhere,' Adder said dismissively.

The she-adder's grin broadened. Her tongue picked up Adder's scent. 'Have you been travelling in a hurry?' she asked archly.

'Um – well, not particularly,' Adder fibbed. 'But my movements are always more lively on a warm, sunny day.' He moved closer. 'The wet weather kept me rather under wraps, as it were,' he joked.

'And in all that time, didn't you spare a thought for me, Adder-of-the-blunt-tail?'

The snake pondered his reply. He *had* thought about her, though only intermittently. 'Oh yes,' he said. 'I think about everyone and everything from time to time.'

'Non-committal as ever,' Sinuous summarized. Her tone changed. 'It's been so quiet here. Almost lonely. Ever since the stream. . . .' She did not complete the sentence.

'Since the stream what?' Adder prompted.

'Became out of bounds.'

Adder considered. 'You were going to say something else at first, I think?'

'No – o,' Sinuous said slowly. 'No, not really. Only that it's as though the animals have become afraid of it.'

'Because of the Stag's death?'

'There may be more to it,' she suggested.

Adder held her gaze. Was she giving him a warning? 'I don't plan to swim there,' he informed her.

'No. Nor I. But there are creatures who are more partial to watery pursuits than we snakes. Toads, for instance . . .'

Familiar Terrain

By the time Badger was discussing the bird's whereabouts with Fox and Vixen, Tawny Owl was far away.
He had met with no luck in any nearby woods or copses
and so had flown on further. Prey was easy to find and
so were places to roost during the daylight hours. But
his quest for a partner proved elusive.

It wasn't long before certain features of the landscape began to strike chords in Tawny Owl's memory.
This was because he had travelled over it before, from
the opposite direction, on the epic journey to the
Nature Reserve – oh! so long ago. He began to recall
events that had occurred at certain places which he
now recognized, or what had been said by one of his
friends at a particular spot. It was uncanny. Many of
those friends he remembered were now gone. Yet they
seemed to live on in this countryside. He perched in an
oak and looked up at the gleaming sky. He seemed to

see Kestrel, hovering, keen-eyed, a speck in the blue, spying out the land ahead. What a flier he had been! An aerial acrobat.

Tawny Owl shook the memories away. He must concentrate on the present and on his new purpose. He rested and as he dozed he dreamed. He dreamed of his old home and his birthplace in Farthing Wood. And at dusk he awoke with a jolt and with a new idea. Why shouldn't he fly back there? Retrace the animals' historic journey? Back to their beginnings, to the place of their forefathers. Of course it would be changed, massively changed. He knew that. But whatever was left, whatever was there now, still enshrined the old home they had all shared all those seasons ago. And perhaps there was still a corner with a few trees where he could stay awhile and survey the new landscape. What a story he would have to tell on his return to White Deer Park! And somewhere on his journey, over all that wide expanse, he would be bound to find that special companion to fly with him. . . .

The more he thought, the more excited Tawny Owl became. He felt younger in spirit than he would ever have dreamed possible again. But he needed to be cautious. For he wasn't young. He must fly within his capabilities; not take risks nor indulge in any foolishness. There was plenty of time. He was very pleased with himself and he flew a little loop around the oak tree to celebrate. His stomach, however, soon reminded him of the necessity of keeping his strength up and he set himself without further ado to obey its commands.

His hunting techniques were born of long ex-

perience. He knew where to look and listen for shrews and wood mice. Soon he had caught and eaten enough to sustain himself. Then he flew well above the tree tops towards a much higher landmark that loomed on the horizon, a shape blacker than the dark sky that surrounded it. Tawny Owl had recognized it and now flew unerringly towards it. It was a church tower.

Flying high as he was he naturally headed straight for the open belfry. He landed on a stone sill and glanced around. 'I've been here before,' he murmured. It all seemed so familiar. This church had been the Farthing Wood party's last sheltering place before reaching White Deer Park. Owl's head swivelled round and he looked out at the sky. The stars glittered.

'I'll shelter here again,' he decided. 'It's an ideal spot. No-one to disturb me here.'

He watched the night sky pensively, his thoughts turning once again to those long-ago events inside the church during the animals' previous visit. Presently dawn glimmered in the east. Tawny Owl's head drooped. He shifted his talons, then closed his eyes. He was soon asleep.

But he wasn't allowed to sleep for long. Because there were other occupants of the church belfry who, in the gathering dawn, began to return there from their nocturnal hunting flights. And they objected to the presence of a large bird at their roost.

Tawny Owl half awoke as something zipped past his ear. He opened one eye but saw nothing. Then the little snap! of noise came again. Now he was quite awake. He was curious. He opened both eyes fully and looked around. Against the pale backdrop of the lightening sky

he saw a number of small darting creatures criss-
crossing on their different swooping flights. Occasionally one would dart directly at the church tower, then
veer away at the last second. More and more swelled
these numbers. Some came close enough to Tawny
Owl to glance at him but none of them dared do more
than chatter at the intruder, before they flitted away
again. The big bird of prey unsettled them. They were
angry, but wary of him. Tawny Owl realized he had
usurped the resting place of a colony of bats.

The tiny animals fascinated yet irritated him. He
admired, as only a bird could, their flying dexterity.
But he wanted to sleep and the bats made this
impossible. Evidently they wished to sleep, too, during
the coming daylight, yet none of them was sufficiently
bold to enter the belfry. They chivvied and chided him,
but Tawny Owl refused to be dislodged. They buzzed
around and past him in a miniature aerial bombard-
ment.

'Will you stop this annoyance?' he cried at them.
'I'm staying put.'

The bats paid no heed but continued their dive-
bombing.

'I just want to sleep,' Tawny Owl hooted. 'Can't you
leave me alone? You'll get no rest either!'

'Fly away, begone.' 'Move away, leave our roost.'
The bats shrieked at him in their tiny high-pitched
voices.

Tawny Owl lost his temper. He launched himself
from the stonework and swooped into their midst,
scattering the animals briefly before they resumed their
skimming, skipping flights all around him. Wherever

he flew they followed him. But he could never catch
any. They could turn and bank in a fraction of a second
and reappear a moment later in a different spot. All
around the sky the bats darted in varying patterns and
directions, never colliding and never settling.

Aggravated as he was, Tawny Owl watched their
effortless skill with wonder. He felt himself to be clumsy
and cumbersome by comparison. He didn't relish
being outshone in the field of flying. Disgruntled, he
returned to his perch on the stone sill. The bats
resumed their skirmishes. Tawny Owl moved further
inside the belfry and perched on a rafter. He put his
head under his wing and tried to ignore the animals'
squeals and squeaks. It was in vain. His patience was
now entirely exhausted.

'How dare you keep this up!' he thundered. 'Do you
know who I am? Tawny Owl from Farthing Wood!' He
waited for the expected result of this piece of information.

The bats, however, had either never heard of him or
treated the news with disdain. Their behaviour
changed not at all.

'This is intolerable,' Tawny Owl moaned to himself.
'First I'm driven away from the Park by insults and
goading. Now I'm starved of sleep by puny little
creatures no bigger than a vole. What have I done to
deserve this? I won't be driven out!' he declared finally.
'I want to rest!' he screeched. 'I don't want to eat you. I
want nothing to do with you! If I can ignore you, can't
you all just do likewise?'

For a brief period the bats stayed outside the belfry,
their movements less frantic and antagonistic. They

seemed to be communing with one another. Then, chattering and muttering together, they flew into the belfry and began to hang themselves upside down, one by one, from their favoured roosting spots. Their little long-eared heads turned all in one direction as they gazed at Tawny Owl.

At last one piped up: 'How do we know you won't eat us while we sleep?'

Tawny Owl fixed the tiny furry creature with his enormous eyes. He realized the bat's face was up the wrong way so he tried to accommodate him by twisting his own head as far as he could in order to meet his eyes. In doing so he very nearly toppled from his perch. The sudden movement startled the bats and they began to leave their places and dart about again.

Tawny Owl was beside himself. 'Stop it! Stop it!' he begged. 'Calm yourselves, please. I can't hang upside down like you so we'll just have to talk to each other the – er – wrong way up, if you see what I mean.' He waited until they were more or less settled again. 'Look,' he said, 'I don't eat bats. I couldn't catch you if I wanted to. And as for eating you while you're asleep, how could I do that if I'm asleep myself?'

He looked around at the little bodies, each of which seemed to be swaying gently from one leg. 'I've already eaten,' he rejoined to doubly reassure them. 'I'm not hungry. Only weary. I sleep through the daylight hours just like you. When it's dusk I'll depart. Is that a bargain?'

There was a barrage of squeaky voices. Then one rose above all the others. 'We won't bargain with you,' the bat said, 'because we can't trust you. We don't

know who you are. So one of us will stay awake all day in case you mean to take advantage. That's our answer.'

'You're silly little creatures, all of you,' Tawny Owl said derogatorily. 'I always keep my word. Haven't you ever heard of the Oath of the Animals of Farthing Wood?'

There was silence. Owl took this as assent. 'Well, the Oath can be extended to any other animals we choose,' he informed them grandiosely. 'So if I extend the Oath of Mutual Protection to you, your safety is assured, isn't it?'

None of the bats chose to respond. Most of them hadn't the faintest idea what the bird was talking about. Some of the older animals did have an inkling of the legendary Oath that Owl was referring to, though they didn't understand enough to realize how it could be applied to the bat community. So silence reigned as they tried to puzzle it all out.

Silence was the one thing that Tawny Owl craved. In a trice he had fallen asleep while the diminutive animals kept themselves awake by their perplexity.

The sun rose steadily in the sky. Tawny Owl slept. Many of the bats still fidgeted. The sun reached its zenith. Tawny Owl slept on peacefully. Some bats shifted their skinny wings as they watched him. The sun slipped slowly down to the horizon. In the afterglow Owl awoke refreshed, stretched his wings and awaited dusk. When it was quite dark he prepared to fly on. All around the belfry tower the suspended bats were fast asleep. Tawny Owl left the church behind with a chuckle.

The lights of a nearby town drew him onwards. He flew well above its buildings and when he had crossed it he looked for another landmark to guide him. The distant but steady hum of heavy traffic reminded him of his direction. He flew over some farmland and alighted in a tall ash whose late-opened leaves were still a fresh new green. From here he could see the dazzling lights of the motorway traffic streaking across the foreground like miniature shooting stars. But the terrifying dangers of such a man-made obstacle as this great highway were no barrier to a bird. Tawny Owl looked on almost scornfully. All at once his reverie was interrupted. An owl had hooted from another tree. Or was he mistaken? He strained his ears to catch a repetition above the roar of the machines. Sure enough the call was repeated.

Tawny Owl replied with the answering call. 'Kee-wick.'

The stranger owl's next call was nearer at hand. Tawny Owl located it amongst a stand of poplars planted as a windbreak at the border of a field. He was confident the calling bird was a female and that she had noticed him and wanted him to come closer. So he obliged.

He alighted on the neighbouring tree to where the other owl was perched.

'I've been watching you,' said the bird who was indeed a female.

'Watching me?'

'Yes, for quite a while. I saw you roosting at the church building and your battle with the bats.'

'Battle!' Tawny Owl exclaimed contemptuously. 'There was no battle. Only a minor irritation.'

'Your flight is very purposeful,' was the next observation.

Tawny Owl took this as a compliment. 'I'm on a journey,' he explained.

'A journey? To where?'

'To an old territory of mine.'

'What for?' the female owl enquired. She sounded intrigued.

'Oh, it's a long story,' Tawny Owl replied. 'I'm flying to an old hunting ground I used to frequent.'

'Is the hunting good?'

'I don't know any more. It used to be when I lived there. But there have been changes.'

'Then why go back there? Can't you find what you want round here?'

Tawny Owl was struck by the aptness of her question, innocent though it was. 'That depends,' he answered with a sideways look at her that was intended to be full of meaning.

The female owl didn't notice the significance of his expression. 'Depends on what?' she fluted.

'Well – you know.' Owl ruffled his wings impatiently. 'Certain things. How much of the terrain is occupied and – er – by whom. . . .'

'What difference does that make? Can't you defend yourself?'

'Of course I can!' he answered huffily. 'I meant, is the area fully marked out and – er – claimed?'

The female owl looked at him for a long time before

answering. 'Now I see why you're returning to your old area,' she surmised. 'You haven't paired.'

This was a sore point with Tawny Owl. He shifted his stance and the slender poplar branch rippled elastically. 'No, no, I haven't paired,' he admitted grumpily.

'Small chance round here for you then,' the female informed him. 'You'd better press on.'

Tawny Owl glared. 'But you – you were calling. Where is your mate then?'

'Collecting food, I hope,' she answered. 'He's been gone a long time. My babies are almost fully fledged. They're always hungry. They never stop nagging for food so I've been trying to hasten his return. They've eaten all we've brought them.'

The last thing Tawny Owl wanted to hear about was the details of other owls' family life, especially in his present predicament. He hastened to be gone.

'I must be on my way,' he muttered and leapt from his branch.

'Where do you head now?' she called after him.

'Farthing Wood,' he hooted, 'if it's still there.' He tarried no longer but sped straight for the motorway. The female owl watched with beak agape. Abruptly she concluded just whom she had been addressing. The Farthing Wood Owl!

Trey

Badger's concern about his old friend Tawny Owl's disappearance was shared by Fox and Vixen.

'To think of one of the elders of the Farthing Wood community feeling himself forced to quit the Park!' Fox bemoaned. 'It's outrageous and Pace and Rusty must be reprimanded. They may think they're grown-up foxes but their behaviour shows otherwise. I shan't take them to task myself. Their own parents have that duty to perform.'

'But in the meantime, Fox, what can we do to get Owl back?' Badger wailed. 'I think he's too old to go off scouring the countryside on some fool's errand such as this.'

'Don't worry, my dear friend,' Fox answered. 'We'll think of something.'

'Does Owl actually plan to stay outside the Reserve?' Vixen queried.

'As far as I can tell he intends not to return until he has someone to accompany him,' Badger replied. 'I think Weasel could tell you more about how all this arose.'

'Weasel? Yes,' Fox mused. 'He and Owl always had their differences, didn't they? Seemed to have a penchant for needling each other unnecessarily. But Weasel ought to know better than to joke about vital things like pairing off. You say he's partly to blame, Badger?'

'Yes, I'm sure of it. He couldn't have foreseen the result, of course,' he added, trying as ever to smooth things over.

'I think we should have a word with Weasel,' Fox asserted. 'The onus is on him to help in this matter. Come on; he's bound to be around close by.'

There was no difficulty in finding Weasel but he didn't prove to be very disposed to help.

'What can I do?' he asked them coolly. 'Tawny Owl's simply gone off in a huff. He'll be back soon enough when he's recovered himself.'

'Really, Weasel, I don't know what you were thinking of, talking to him the way you did. You know how touchy he is,' said Fox.

'I wasn't to know he would go to such lengths,' was Weasel's answer. 'Do you think I'd have said a word if I'd known he'd be so nonsensical?'

'You always have enjoyed teasing him,' Fox recalled.

'Yes, but . . . well, he's never reacted so extremely before, has he? It's no use worrying yourself, Fox. Nor you, Badger. We're past the age when we could mount missions of rescue.'

Fox looked at Weasel's grizzled fur with a wry expression. 'Yes,' he said. 'Our colouring complements each other.' He was only too aware of his own greying coat. As for Badger, he hadn't even regained his breath.

'But we can't desert Tawny Owl, can we?' Vixen pleaded.

'We haven't done so, Vixen,' declared Weasel. 'He's deserted *us*, hasn't he? Purely in a fit of pique. There's just nothing to be done – except wait. Even if we were still our young adventurous selves it would be quite impracticable for mammals to go searching for a bird.'

'Oh dear, he could be far away by now,' Badger wailed. 'And I don't think he's any better equipped than we are to deal with the perils outside the Park.'

'Of course he is,' Weasel said kindly, trying to comfort. 'He has wings to carry him above any danger. Now don't fret. I'm certain we shall soon see –' Weasel stopped suddenly. He was looking away over their heads at something in the background. The others followed his glance.

It was Trey the large white stag that Weasel was looking at. And Trey was looking at them. He was on his own. He stood stock still and stared haughtily. Then, with a proud toss of his head, he began to step sedately towards them. He was a fine powerful-looking beast.

'You're some of the old travellers who came here long ago from another place, if I'm not mistaken,' he said without preamble. He had a harsh voice.

'Yes,' said Fox. 'We are.'

'You realize, I suppose, we only tolerate your presence here, we don't invite it?'

'Tolerate? Presence? What are you talking about?' demanded Fox. 'And who's "we"?'

'The herd, naturally.'

'Oh, you've been elected to speak for all of them, have you?' Weasel interjected sardonically.

The stag gave the tiny animal a contemptuous look as if such a midget wasn't even worthy of an answer. 'I am now the natural leader of the herd,' he said, addressing the two foxes and Badger, 'and therefore I wish you to understand your position.'

Fox ignored the last remark. 'I should have thought some of the other stags might have something to say about whether you're the natural leader?' he suggested. 'That's if I have learnt anything about the pattern of a deer herd's behaviour during my time in the Park.'

'Who is there to challenge *me*, Trey?' he asked boastfully. 'I am a royal stag. Have you ever seen antlers as splendid as these?'

'Yes,' Vixen replied coolly. 'The Great Stag, your precursor, had finer ones in his heyday.'

Trey glowered. But he was honest enough to admit, 'He was a superb specimen, it's true. But,' he added, 'his heyday was over long before he died. Now he's gone things will change – and not just in the herd.'

'We'd like to know about these changes,' Badger spoke for all of his friends, 'since we live here too.'

'Exactly,' Trey said. 'You live here too. We deer have allowed all you smaller animals to do just that, whereas in reality this Nature Reserve was set aside for us alone. We gave the Reserve its name. The Park belongs to us. Do you think for one moment, if it hadn't been for such a rare and valuable white deer herd, that

this area of land would have been reserved for paltry common or garden creatures such as yourselves?'

The animals were open-mouthed.

'You don't answer me,' prompted Trey.

'We are dumbfounded by your arrogance,' Fox answered the stag. He drew himself up. 'I'm old now,' he said. 'But I also have authority and am respected in this Park. Your ancestor would never have spoken to me – or any of us – like that. I'd like to see you brought down to earth. You'll have rivals, sure enough, in due season. Then perhaps you'll find brute strength is more than a match for conceit.'

'The only thing I shall find,' said Trey, 'is every foolhardy rival running from my lowered antlers, one by one. And I mean to be not only the leader of the deer herd but Lord of the Reserve. So you must stay in your corner of the Park, all of you. I want no interference with my herd's grazing. The most succulent shoots, the sweetest grasses, the tenderest leaves are ours alone. Smaller creatures must make do with our leavings. Otherwise you'll be permitted here no longer. So tell your friends the rabbits and hares and suchlike to keep clear. You've all had the run of our Reserve for too long. And what have you brought us in return? Nothing but mayhem: a succession of dangers in what was once a place of tranquillity. You Farthing Wood animals are our Bad Luck.' With that he turned on his heel and walked away with a distinct swagger.

The friends were speechless. They could find no answer to Trey's accusation. At last Vixen murmured, somewhat defensively, 'I'm sure the rest of the herd don't see us that way.'

'Of course they don't!' Weasel exclaimed vehemently. ' "Bad Luck" indeed.'

Fox said: 'We're going to have trouble with that animal. I know it. "Lord of the Reserve",' he quoted. 'A rather premature claim, I feel, but it gives us all an indication of his intentions. I don't know what he meant about dangers and mayhem, do you?' He appealed to his companions.

Badger surprised them. 'I have an inkling,' he admitted. 'It's something that's been in my mind from time to time.'

'What, trouble that we've brought to the Park?' Weasel demanded angrily.

'No, no, Weasel, of course not,' Badger pacified him. 'It'd be more true to say that trouble seems to have followed us.'

Fox looked serious. 'Go on, old friend,' he urged. 'Let's hear your thoughts.'

'Well, I've often considered the irony of our lives here,' Badger resumed. 'Maybe you have too. After all, we journeyed here over hostile terrain, at great risk to ourselves the whole way, believing we were coming to a safe haven in the Nature Reserve. All along, during that arduous journey, it was that thought that buoyed us up. Yet it's been far from a safe haven. The first winter after we arrived we nearly starved to death. Then there were the poachers shooting at all and sundry, but particularly the deer. So Trey was right about *that* danger. Somehow we struggled through that winter to find ourselves the following spring involved in a war with other inhabitants of the Park led by Scarface. To cap it all, last summer a huge hunting

animal prowls the Park, picking off its victims at will without any of us being able to mount any resistance to it. If we'd wanted a life of constant adventure and hardship we couldn't have chosen a better site! Quite honestly, I sometimes wonder if it wasn't more peaceful in Farthing Wood.'

'There's a lot of truth in what you say,' Fox avowed. 'The important thing though, surely, is that we've survived all of it. And the reason for that is that we've pulled together; helped one another. It wasn't like that in Farthing Wood. We were all following our own paths. The Farthing Wood animals were brought together by our journey in a unique way. We had one common aim. And that spirit has continued ever since. For that alone we should rejoice we came to White Deer Park. And I think some of our beliefs have been passed on to our descendants. The dangers that have occurred here would have occurred anywhere else. There's no such thing as a sanctuary entirely free of danger for wild creatures. Not anywhere.'

'The stag Trey seems to think otherwise,' Weasel observed.

'He's blaming us for a set of coincidences,' Fox answered. 'We weren't responsible for inviting danger here. The poaching men with their guns came because this is a Deer Park, not because the animals of Farthing Wood chose to take up residence here.'

'The thing is: what do we do about his threat?' Weasel asked. '*I* don't intend to be intimidated. I'll go on roaming the whole area of the Reserve. Why should we be holed up here? It'd be like the Great Cat's thraldom all over again.'

'It won't make any difference to me,' Badger said. 'I hardly venture further from my set than the nearest meal. Unless I need to see you dear friends. But even that I find taxing these days. My sight's so bad. . . .'

'Yes, we know,' Weasel cut in before Badger developed the theme. 'But I really don't think the threat was aimed at an old creature such as yourself.'

'We'll continue to live our lives as we choose to,' Fox said resolutely. 'Trey's a powerful beast and could be a formidable adversary. But his words may all be bluster. His apparent dominance of the herd may have gone to his head.'

'What of the smaller animals?' Vixen prompted. 'He mentioned the rabbits and hares.'

'We'll warn Leveret to be cautious and to spread the word,' Fox answered. 'But we'll call Trey's bluff.'

'We've been diverted, haven't we?' Vixen reminded them. 'We never did decide what to do about Tawny Owl.'

'Yes, we did,' Weasel contradicted. 'Wait for him to return. *That's* what we'll do. I bet he'd love to think he's put us all in a pet by his absence.'

'Perhaps Whistler will sight him somewhere,' Fox said. 'He's such a silly old owl sometimes.' He sighed. 'But Friendly *must* reprimand the youngsters. They look up to him.'

There was nothing more to discuss and the friends parted.

Over on the other side of the Park, Leveret, the young hare, was munching the juiciest stalks he could find, oblivious of the altercation with Trey. Every so often he raised himself on his hind legs amongst the tall

grasses to scan his surroundings. His prominent eyes and sensitive ears were invaluable in detecting the slightest hint of an alarm. His speed, like that of his father, the Farthing Wood Hare, was legendary. Nothing in the Park could catch him, not even the deer. Not that they tried to do so. Prior to the old White Stag's death, the deer herd had lived equably with its neighbours. And it might have been because of this that Leveret was not quite so alert all of the time as he would have been outside the Reserve.

The grasses and vegetation, generally, were particularly lush that year in the Park, thanks to the long rainy spell. So there was more than enough for everyone. The insect population thrived and there was a glut of caterpillars and grubs. The birds found food easily for their nestlings and the Park's inhabitants enjoyed a period of plenty. Trey, however, was not content with this. He wanted to be acknowledged by all as the paramount being of the Reserve's animal kingdom. He therefore lost no opportunity to enforce this idea. Whenever he could make his presence felt he did so in some way, sometimes bullying, sometimes threatening. The animals resented this but there was nothing they could do about it except long for the stags' rutting season.

There came a day when, because of his familiarity with the deer and his belief in their inoffensiveness, Leveret was, quite literally, caught napping. He had made his couch in the softest, greenest area of grassland and, since he hadn't sought out his Farthing Wood comrades recently, he was quite unaware of the risks he was running as he lay amongst that choice verdure.

The sun was warm on his back, the air balmy; he slumbered peacefully. But a movement, a rustle of the grass and Leveret was instinctively awake. He opened his eyes. A huge white head bearing massive antlers confronted him. Leveret at first wasn't disturbed. Just another member of the deer herd, he thought. Then he noticed the stag's expression. It was not a friendly one.

Trey lowered his head and he scraped the ground with a front hoof as he looked at the hare. He looked like a bull about to charge. Leveret didn't wait to find out. He leapt up and bounded through the grasses. Trey galloped after him. He was in an ugly mood. This animal had ignored his ruling. He meant to punish him. The hare must be made an example to deter others. The stag crashed through the grassland area, flattening the succulent stalks he was so determined to save for the herd's sole enjoyment. Fleet of foot as Trey was, Leveret's elastic bounds left the deer farther and farther behind. The hare's constantly veering course was impossible to follow for long. At last, Trey pulled up. He tossed his head, half in frustration, half in bewilderment at Leveret's pace. But he was content that he had driven home his lesson. He didn't think Leveret would be back.

Trey was correct in his assumption. Leveret had been alarmed and frightened. He kept running and leaping long after the grassland was well behind him. He was a highly strung animal and so intent on flight that he almost collided with Friendly, Fox and Vixen's son, who was lapping listlessly from a puddle.

'Hey! Slow down! What's the hurry?' Friendly called out, cheerfully. 'It's too hot for racing.'

The well-known tones of the affectionate animal's voice halted Leveret's career. He turned, relieved to find a companion.

'Whatever's the matter?' Friendly asked. 'You look badly scared.'

Leveret brought his breath and racing heart under control before he attempted to answer. 'There's a mad creature amongst the deer herd,' he explained. He was still distressed. 'He *attacked* me. Charged at me, the great brute, while I was sleeping. A small animal like me! Without a word of warning. If it's some sort of stupid game. . . .'

Friendly recognized the culprit at once. 'Oh, you've encountered Trey, have you? The mighty new Lord of the Reserve!' He sounded contemptuous. 'No, Leveret, this is no game. Haven't you heard? This stag has set himself up as the successor to his great ancestor. Only he's not satisfied with dominating the deer herd. He wants all of us to pay him homage.'

'But – but – a deer?' Leveret spluttered. 'I thought we had nothing to fear from any of them. They've been our friends – allies even – in the old days.'

'Well, these are new days, Leveret. The old order, you see, has passed. And it seems we're to accept it – or go.'

Owl's Progress

Tawny Owl skimmed over the motorway to the open countryside again. Quietness enveloped him. Soon he felt hungry once more. He caught what he needed and ate, comfortably lodged in the fork of a tree. He was quite alone and he was beginning to enjoy it. He thought for a moment about his companions in White Deer Park but then quickly dismissed them from his mind. He was relishing his solitude, away from Weasel's carping comments and the young foxes' teasing that he had endured for too long. He looked forward to reaching his destination, to re-visiting the old haunts and, above all, to the awe in which he would be held as the only Farthing Wood creature to have dared to journey back. Just let those young foxes hear his story! They'd soon change their tune, especially when he arrived on the scene with the missing female they had loved to joke about.

Tawny Owl rested only briefly after eating. He was eager to press on. He felt fresh and full of energy. He flitted noiselessly through the moonlit summer night over the fox-hunting terrain where Vixen had so nearly lost her life. By dawn he was within sight of the river. An ancient hollow oak beckoned him to roost. He fluttered down and settled himself inside.

A short distance outside White Deer Park, Whistler was dutifully beginning his search for the errant Owl.

The next evening Tawny Owl crossed the river. Memories flooded back once again of Fox's accident in the water when he had been carried away downstream, away from his friends. But all that was ancient history. With the river behind him Owl travelled more circum-spectly. He wasn't so sure of recognizing the route. Until he reached Farthing Wood itself, there would be no more prominent landmarks. However he *felt* his direction was correct. His instincts seemed to guide him. What didn't ring quite true was the ease with which he was travelling. Of course the journey of the animals from Farthing Wood to the Nature Reserve had been infinitely more difficult for land-travelling creatures, especially when the whole party had agreed to adapt its pace to accommodate the smallest repre-sentatives such as Toad, who had actively been demonstrating the route part of the time, and voles and fieldmice: tiny creatures who could only go in short stages. Up in the air, problems and barriers to progress that had seemed almost insurmountable on that journey, were as nothing.

The speed with which Tawny Owl covered the

distance surprised him more than anything. The long odyssey which he and his companions had undergone before had seemed at times as if it would never end. Now, alone, and flying at his own pace, it appeared that his journey would be completed in a matter of days. When he picked out from the air a certain copse whose shape was remarkably familiar, Tawny Owl felt he was indeed getting close. The copse was chiefly memorable for its rookery.

Tawny Owl glided in under cover of darkness and holed up in a dead elm. He meant to surprise the rooks by his presence when they awoke in the morning. Some of them would be bound to recognize him. As he had eaten on the way he allowed himself a semi-doze as he watched, fitfully, the gleaming stars begin to pale. But his doze was rudely interrupted.

The rooks began to call harshly and urgently at the first glimmer of daylight. They were not calls proclaiming territory or ownership but calls of alarm and warning. Still perched on their untidy nests of twigs they passed angry calls from one to another that echoed back and forth in the tree tops. Tawny Owl had been spied and he was not welcome. There were young still in the nests.

Owl clung uncertainly to the grey barkless branch of the stricken tree. He wasn't sure what to do. He supposed, in this murky light, he must seem to the rooks to be just another threatening predator. He decided to wait until the full light of day would reveal to them who it was who had come amongst them. The light grew but there was no lessening of the clamour. Indeed the calls became more raucous, more strident.

Eventually some of the angry birds left their nests and flew close to Owl in a mobbing action. They jeered at him, calling him offensive names such as murderer, robber and vandal. Owl was most put out. He tried to recognize amongst these rooks one who would have known him in the past. He and the Farthing Wood animals had spent a while in their copse and had been warmly welcomed by their hosts as heroes. But as he searched the faces with their long pointed beaks and glittering eyes he could see no hint of dawning friendliness in any of them. And they all looked the same. He couldn't have told them apart. Purple-black plumage with an iridescent sheen that reflected the early rays of the sun. Sharp, malevolent features. They span around him, deliberately malicious, hoping to rid their copse of his presence by their unremitting pressure.

'What, isn't there one of you who knows me?' Tawny Owl called out in bewilderment. 'Not one of you who knows the name of Farthing Wood?'

'Never heard of it.'

'No such place.'

'Farthing Wood? This is Rookery Copse. No other stand of woodland round here.'

Their voices screeched at him. They knew nothing of his past.

'Fox, Badger, Toad, Kestrel, Tawny Owl,' the besieged bird cried, desperately attempting to call himself to mind. 'We travelled here. Before. You made us welcome.'

'Welcome? Welcome? *They'd* be welcome, I don't think,' one screeched back.

'No friends of ours.'

'None of them!'

'But you must remember,' Tawny Owl almost pleaded. 'If not you, then your elders. Where are they?'

'What do you want with them? Leave them alone.'

'Get away from our copse!'

'Don't you see?' Tawny Owl wheedled. 'The older birds will recognize me. I was here before.'

They didn't want to hear. An owl was an enemy when young were in the nests. That's all they knew. They flew at him, buffeting him with their wings. They hoped to topple him from his perch. When that didn't work, the braver among them began aiming their beaks at him, stabbing downwards as they fluttered close. Tawny Owl gave ground. It was futile to resist any longer. Times were changed. There was no camaraderie to be looked for here. He flapped away from his branch and even then the rooks chased him, egged on by their success. They screamed their delight at his defeat, trying to make his retreat as humiliating as they could. The disappointed owl found himself putting on speed to rid himself of their deafening cries. At last they fell back, satisfied they had defended their nest sites with great daring.

Tawny Owl flew on dispiritedly. Now solitude didn't seem so attractive. He longed for some creature, animal or bird, to show him a jot of fellow feeling. He had lived for so long among friends he had forgotten what life was like in the usually hostile environment of nature. He thought of Bold, Fox's and Vixen's cub, who must have encountered just the same suspicion and enmity during his bid for independence away from the influence of his father. And what a hard time *he* had had of it. Owl put

the thought behind him. The rooks' unpleasantness had tired him out, even frightened him a little. He needed to sleep and, first of all, to compose himself.

Without realizing it, Tawny Owl was flying back on himself, back in the direction from which he'd come to the copse. His one thought was to find a suitable perch. He didn't enjoy daylight very much except as a time to rest. He found a solitary hawthorn whose branches were almost impenetrable. Inside the thick canopy of greenery he could at last relax. The day passed him by and the few small songbirds who alighted on the thorn soon left again when they saw an owl hiding in its midst.

As usual Tawny Owl roused at dusk. He got himself airborne and immediately felt that he had been thrown off course. But he wanted to avoid the rookery at all costs, so he could not use the copse as a guide again. What he could do, however, was to use the noise of the rooks themselves as a clue. He knew that at dusk there was always a sort of concert of cawing as the birds settled themselves for the night. So he circled for a while until he picked up their sound. Congratulating himself on this brainwave, Tawny Owl flew towards the sound without ever getting too close to give himself trouble. The noise reached a crescendo and then gradually faded behind him and so Owl knew he had passed Rookery Copse and should soon be on the right track again. But it didn't prove as simple as that. He couldn't seem to get his bearings. In his mind he pictured an orchard, a marsh, a road and rows of houses. That was the way back if things were still as they had been before, but he found he couldn't locate

any of these features. Then Tawny Owl berated himself for his stupidity. Of course things weren't the same as before. How could they be? All that time ago. . . .

He broke off his efforts at navigation to hunt. He decided he must then seek guidance. He caught himself a rat that was trying to raid a squirrels' drey. As he disposed of his prey it occurred to him that the squirrels might be able to help. He finished his meal. Then he flew back to the birch tree where the drey was sited. The tree grew alongside a couple of young oaks in a patch of undergrowth.

The squirrels at first scolded Tawny Owl for coming too close, just as they tried to warn off any predator from the youngsters they had to protect. But when the bird pointed out the good turn he had done them they quietened down and listened.

'Do you know a place called Farthing Wood?' Owl asked. 'It's not far from here.'

'Wood? There's no wood anywhere around here,' the mother squirrel replied. '*We'd* be living there if there were. . . .'

Tawny Owl sighed. The same reaction as from the rooks. 'But you must have heard of it, at least,' he suggested. 'There was woodland around here once. I used to live in it.'

'Doubtless there was,' the male squirrel conceded. 'But what's the use of asking us about a place that doesn't exist?'

'I only wanted to know if you'd heard the name,' Tawny Owl said. He decided he wouldn't tell them he was attempting to travel to a wood that they believed was non-existent.

The squirrels looked at each other. 'I've heard the name,' said the female. 'But not for a long time. I seem to recall there was some sort of tale attached to it.'

Tawny Owl perked up considerably. 'Yes, there was,' he said eagerly. 'I – I mean,' he added quickly, 'that I believe the tale would have been about how the inhabitants of the Wood had to leave it. Isn't that so?'

'Yes. Yes, that's it,' the squirrel answered. 'The wildlife all around here used to talk about them. Many of the older ones saw them pass. But they never knew for sure what happened to them.'

Tawny Owl was burning to tell the squirrels. But he fought the inclination down in order to pursue his main objective. With bated breath he asked: 'In which direction would Farthing Wood have been?'

The squirrels flicked their bushy tails as they pondered. 'It must have been,' the father squirrel said slowly, 'where the human dwellings have spread.'

'Yes, yes!' cried Tawny Owl. 'The men built over it, didn't they?' He was becoming excited.

'Well, if you know that, you must know where it was,' the squirrel rejoined in a puzzled way.

'But I haven't seen any human dwellings,' Tawny Owl spluttered. This was so exasperating!

'You can't have been over the hill then,' the female squirrel told him. 'They're all around there. Now then, if you have nothing further to bother us with, we'll go back to our rest.'

'Nothing more, nothing more,' Tawny Owl called. He was already in the air.

'Thank you again for the rat-killing,' the father squirrel cried generously. 'We really are –'

But Tawny Owl was away. He saw where the land began to rise and followed it directly. At the top of the little hill he looked over and there, below, were the bright lights of human habitations and streets.

'So!' he breathed to himself. 'I'm home.'

But he wasn't. Not quite.

Water Rights

Whistler the heron abandoned his search when it was obvious that Tawny Owl had left the immediate environs of White Deer Park. 'I'll keep a look-out for him from time to time,' he told himself. 'But I can't go combing the entire countryside.' On his return he flew along the length of the stream and was distressed at what he found there. At intervals there were dead bodies of small creatures, mainly watervoles, lying either on the banks or at the edge of the water, bobbing on the ripples. There was a pair of coots who had suffered the same fate. Their deserted nest amongst some reeds had two fairly well-grown, but lifeless, youngsters in it.

'This is terrible,' Whistler said. 'I wonder what's caused this?'

He flew up and down, peering at the water for any sign that would give an explanation. But he could see

nothing unusual. Later he noticed Adder and Sinuous sunning themselves in their favourite spot. These days they were always together. Whistler wasn't sure if he should disturb them but he guessed Adder had seen him so he decided in the end to fly over.

'Have you found anything?' Adder enquired without much interest. He knew Whistler had been looking for Tawny Owl.

Whistler mistook him. 'Have you seen them too?' he asked, referring to the dead creatures.

Adder looked at him curiously. 'Them?' he repeated. 'You don't mean to say. . . .' He was picturing Tawny Owl flying back in triumph with his consort.

'Bodies,' Whistler said. 'By the stream. A number of them.'

'I told you so,' Sinuous remarked to her companion.

Whistler waited politely for an explanation.

'She thinks the place has become one of menace,' the snake said. 'Ever since the Great Stag pegged out there.' He was never one to show overmuch respect.

'I'm not the only one who thinks so. Most of you are steering well clear of the area,' Sinuous said to the heron.

'Yes. Except those who live on its fringes,' he said. 'But now it seems they're at risk. I don't know how long those bodies have been there. *I* haven't been near the stream for a long while.'

Adder ventured a quip. 'When Whistler the heron ceases to patrol the stream's banks there's something fishy going on.'

Whistler chuckled. 'That's just it, Adder. There *are* no fish.'

Now Adder was serious. He had remembered Toad. 'Best to leave the place well alone,' he said. 'I wish I'd seen Toad. He sometimes swims there.'

Whistler was surprised at his words. The snake didn't often commit himself to pangs of anxiety. 'The land is damp and humid enough for him at present, I hope,' said the heron. 'And he does spend a lot of time with his friends the frogs in the Pond, I believe?'

'He's a great traveller, our Toad,' said Adder. 'Nobody knows that better than I. There's no knowing where he might turn up.'

'He must look out for himself then, mustn't he?' Sinuous observed primly. She was well aware of the little clique of Farthing Wood animals who continued to concern themselves about each other. The idea bored her as she wasn't party to it.

'I think I'll look out for him as well,' Adder lisped, 'if you've no objection?'

Toad was actually nowhere in the vicinity of the stream. He was enjoying the bonanza of grubs, worms and insects that was all around him. He was a very plump Toad indeed. Swimming wasn't on his mind very much and, in common with his friends, he hadn't much desire at present to visit the stream. The Edible Frogs around the Pond didn't see much of him either. However, they did see a lot of other creatures. Many of the Park's inhabitants were using the Pond as their chief drinking place now. Amongst these were the White Deer themselves as well as those members of the Farthing Wood community who ranged most widely,

such as the younger foxes. So it was only a matter of time before one of them was confronted by Trey.

The young fox Plucky, still barely more than a cub, had his grandfather Bold's liking for roaming far afield. As soon as he was big enough he began to acquaint himself with every corner of the Nature Reserve. It happened one day he was drinking at the Pond when Trey arrived. Trey was suspicious. He knew there were no fox-holes anywhere near the Pond.

'What quarter of the Park do you come from?' Trey demanded.

'None in particular,' Plucky answered him coolly.

'This Pond is the deer herd's drinking place,' Trey announced.

'Yes, it's very convenient, isn't it?' Plucky remarked. 'I believe a lot of animals use it.'

'Do they indeed? We'll see about that,' the stag responded. 'The deer herd needs to have a constant supply of the freshest water. This Pond was always intended as our water-hole. So I'm reserving it for our exclusive use.'

Plucky looked at him in amazement. 'But, surely, it's big enough for every creature to use who wants to?' he questioned.

'Maybe not if we should have a long dry spell,' Trey replied. 'Anyway, you smaller animals can make do with any odd puddle. You don't need the quantity of water a fully-grown deer needs. And there are many of us.'

Plucky knew about the Great Stag. 'If what you say is true, why did your father drink at the stream?'

'He was a creature of habit,' Trey answered. 'He

preferred to drink from running water. And he wasn't
my father. Our relationship was very distant.'

'Grandfather perhaps? You resemble him a good
deal.'

'No. I'm nothing like him – as you'll find out.' Trey
sounded angry and threatening. 'He was always too
tolerant of lesser creatures,' he added scornfully.

Plucky was in no way abashed. He simply stared
back at the beast, then finished quenching his thirst. As
he ambled away the stag called after him: 'Remember
what I've said.'

Plucky did. And he remembered to tell all his
relatives, too. The seniors, Fox and Vixen, were
already incensed by the incident with Leveret. This
was the last straw.

'We won't take this lying down,' Fox said grimly.
'Who does this creature think he is, dictating to us?'

'He'll put himself in a false position,' Vixen
commented. 'He doesn't speak for the rest of the herd.
The hinds are as friendly as ever.'

'He's talking poppycock,' Fox declared. 'He must
have a small mind if he thinks he can push ideas like
this on to us. We must all meet and work out our course
of action. Plucky, I want you to take the word round.
The Hollow. Dusk tomorrow.'

The next night the Farthing Wood elders assembled in
their traditional meeting place. Plucky had gathered
them all. He knew just where to find each one. Badger,
Weasel, Whistler, Adder and Toad had obeyed the
summons. Leveret and Mossy were there, as were Fox
and Vixen's offspring Friendly and Charmer together

with others of their relatives. Plucky was the youngest animal present. The fox clan was the most numerous. They were also the most daring and skilful of the animals. But of the original band of travellers, only Tawny Owl was absent.

'We all know the situation,' Fox began. 'The question is, what are we going to do about it?'

'Just as you said before, Fox,' Weasel replied. 'Call Trey's bluff. What can he do? He can't deal with all of us. We're too many and too scattered.'

'I've seen what he can do,' Leveret spoke up. 'He'll wreak his will on the more vulnerable of us.'

'We can't allow that,' said Friendly. 'He'll find he's got too many enemies to handle.'

'What could you do, Friendly?' asked his mate Russet. 'Attack him?'

'No, he's too powerful,' Friendly admitted. 'But we can outwit him. My father is the shrewdest, wiliest animal in the Park. He's more than a match for the wits of Trey.'

'Thank you, Friendly,' said Fox. 'One plan has occurred to me and it's one that wouldn't actually involve any of us. Not directly, anyhow.' Every eye was on him expectantly. 'We need a champion,' he announced.

'A – champion?' Toad echoed. 'A champion what?'

'A champion fool, I should think,' drawled Adder, 'if he tries to meddle with that creature.'

'You don't understand, Adder,' said Fox. 'I'm not talking about one of us.'

'Do I perceive, Fox, that your thoughts lie amongst

the other stags in the herd?' Whistler asked in his old-fashioned way.

'Exactly that. You've guessed it, old friend. We need to find someone who'll challenge him.'

'How do we do that?' Badger wanted to know. 'Trey already seems to have cowed them all into submission.'

'No, no, Badger, not really,' Fox answered. 'He only assumes he has. They're content to leave him well alone at the moment. But it won't be like that at the rut. Don't you remember how the Great Stag himself had to fight to keep command at those times?'

'Do you have anyone in mind as our ch-champion?' Mossy stammered. He was a little overawed by all the bigger animals present.

'Not yet,' Fox replied. 'But I mean to do a bit of scouting around.'

'Sort of – look over the material?' joked Toad.

'Sort of.' Fox grinned. 'It may be I can drop a hint here and there.' He put his head on one side. 'Perhaps,' he considered, 'we can all help. Stir a few of them up. You know, set them on. We might have quite a few champions at the end of it all.'

'I still think he could defeat all comers,' Leveret said pessimistically. He laid his long ears flat against his back. 'He's a mighty figure.'

'I think you're right,' agreed Fox, 'if it were to be one by one. But what if they should take him on together?'

'Deer never fight like that,' Vixen reasoned. 'We can't change their nature, my dearest.'

There was a long silence. Then Fox said: 'I obviously need to do some more thinking. But in the meantime a word in an ear here and there. . . .'

'They may listen to you foxes,' said Adder, 'but what message is so important that these stags are likely to give attention to a toad or a snake or a mole?' He looked at Mossy so disdainfully that the little animal quailed, not because he was a coward – he was far from that – but because he felt so insignificant.

'Well, that's straightforward enough,' Fox answered. 'You simply tell them that Trey intends to drive all rivals from the Park.'

Farthinghurst

Tawny Owl was bewildered. There were just so many buildings! They were all big and frightening and their myriad lights dazzled him. It was a long time since he had come so close to a mass of human dwellings and now he began to ask himself why he had come here. His original reason for leaving White Deer Park was quite different to the one that had spurred him on to re-visit his old home and birthplace. He hadn't found that suitable companion during his flight across country. And now, as he viewed from the wing this man-built sprawl, he knew there was certainly no likelihood of any owl being found in its alien landscape.

'Can that really be where Farthing Wood once flourished?' he murmured to himself. 'Or have I, after all, taken the wrong direction?'

No, the squirrels had been quite specific. Well, there was no use his expecting to recognize any feature in

that conglomeration. Certainly not by night when the
artificial lights blazed so confusingly.

'I may take a close look in the daylight,' Tawny Owl
said. 'It's just possible there's something down there
that'll trigger a reaction in my poor old brain. I can't
turn tail now without making sure.'

He needed to find somewhere to roost. But where?
He didn't want to go back to the few trees where the
squirrels had built their drey. He examined the nearest
gardens below. There were trees in them – for orna-
mentation – but such puny, immature saplings could
only provide cover and support for the smallest of
birds. The buildings were mostly in tall blocks and
these were flat-roofed so there was no chance of Owl
tucking himself away in a sheltered corner or in the lee
of a chimney-stack. The smaller buildings had sloping
roofs. There was nothing to perch on amongst those.
But he did notice one of them had a gaping and
invitingly dark entrance hole, like an open mouth, high
up on one side of its roof. There were no lights there. All
the lights in that house were much lower down and well
away from the hole which left it in undisturbed
darkness and privacy. Tawny Owl was sorely tempted
to hide himself in there until dawn. But could he be sure
it was quite safe?

He flew down closer to the building. It certainly
seemed quiet enough. Following the slope of the roof he
fluttered awkwardly until he was able to perch at the
opening itself. Although he didn't know it his talons
were resting on the window-ledge of an open attic
window. He shuffled along it and peered inside. His
feet made scuffling noises but they didn't seem to have

caused any disturbance. He waited awhile. The room
was quiet and bare except for a long wall of shelving
filled with books. Tawny Owl saw the racks as
potential perching posts. After a few moments he
entered the room and fluttered across to its far end. On
the top shelf of the book racks there was a perfect gap
between two rows of volumes which was just wide
enough for Owl to wedge himself comfortably in. He
settled himself but remained wakeful.

For some time noises were detectable underneath
this converted loft – human noises. But to Tawny Owl
they seemed distant enough to be overlooked. Eventually they ceased. The night sky grew darker as he
watched. All over the estate lights were being switched
off as the human community retired to rest. The bird
waited patiently for dawn.

As the night wore on a breeze began to blow into the
room. Half-awake, half-asleep, Tawny Owl shifted his
feet and ruffled his feathers. The breeze stiffened. The
open window began to swing gently to and fro. Tawny
Owl couldn't foresee the danger. The wind strength-
ened steadily and, now blowing directly against the
window, pushed it gradually back, closing the gap and
thus the owl's escape route a fraction at a time. Tawny
Owl recognized his danger all too late. As he hurled
himself from the shelf in a frantic bid to squeeze
through the narrowing outlet, a particularly strong
gust finally slammed the window shut. Tawny Owl's
head and wings were battered against the glass and he
dropped to the floor stunned.

It was broad day when he recovered. He struggled to
his feet and fluttered up to the inside sill. The window

was fast closed. He looked out on a scene of alarming activity; alarming because it was human. Cars and other vehicles moved along the network of roads. People seemed to be everywhere – walking, standing, working in their gardens. Children and dogs were running about. Cats sunned themselves in patches of warmth, oblivious of everything including the watching owl, trapped in a garret.

What was he to do? He began to inspect the room. The first thing he noticed which had not been apparent in the pitch dark was that the loft door stood ajar. Was there some other way out for him? Noises in the lower part of the building reminded him that this door was also the way in to the roost he had so foolishly chosen, for any creature, human or otherwise, who lived underneath. He gulped nervously and sought his night perch, feeling more secure between the tightly-stacked books as if in some way they might protect him.

Time drifted past to the accompaniment of human sounds, inside and outside, which deterred the poor bird from making any rash movement. He was both hungry and thirsty. There was dust everywhere and Tawny Owl felt as if a quantity of it had lodged in his throat. Well, he couldn't stay there indefinitely. The window wasn't going to open of its own accord so he must try the other way. He needed to muster up some of that old Farthing Wood spirit: the spirit of adventure. Tawny Owl stretched himself and preened his feathers. He looked towards the door. He was trying to steel himself for action. The noise from beneath increased in volume. He sank back. After all, he told himself, there

was no point in taking unnecessary risks. He would wait until the house grew quiet.

But it didn't grow quiet. In fact the bird soon became aware of something approaching his secret hidey-hole. There were footfalls – soft, cautious footfalls like those of a creature who might be exploring new territory. Tawny Owl kept his great eyes trained on the door. It was difficult for him to keep still as the regular pad – pad – pad of feet approached ever nearer. He tensed, ready for flight.

A black cat came into the room and paused, just inside the door. It raised one paw uncertainly and sniffed the air. Its head turned slowly to Tawny Owl's end of the room. It wasn't a large cat and the bird tried to tell himself it could pose no threat to an owl. But his efforts were unavailing. He was well and truly alarmed for the consequences if he should be discovered. He remained as still as he could, hoping he blended in with his incongruous surroundings. It was an absurd hope. The cat had sensed something was in the room and was systematically searching for it.

'Ah – there you are,' she said as her eyes alighted on the forlorn owl. 'I knew you were here somewhere.'

'I – I'm just leaving,' Tawny Owl hooted ineptly.

'I don't think you can,' the cat, who had noticed the window was closed, replied. 'How did you get in here?'

'Flew in – how do you think?' the bird blustered.

The cat sat down and regarded him coolly. 'You're not making much sense,' she said at length. 'How long have you been here?'

'Since the night. I meant to leave at dawn but –'

'You can't fly through glass,' the cat finished for him.

Tawny Owl was silent. Was the cat playing with him?

'You won't be able to stay here, you know,' the cat resumed. 'This isn't an aviary.'

'I don't want to stay here,' Tawny Owl declared. 'But how do I get out? Can you show me?'

The cat considered. 'I don't know about that,' she answered. 'You see, I'm supposed to be responsible for vermin. There was a problem with mice here. Up until recently. It took me quite a time to round them all up. But they're all gone now. I don't know if you'd be classed as vermin?'

Tawny Owl gaped at the implied insult and now he was angry. 'How dare you!' he screeched. 'Vermin indeed! I am an owl. I *hunt* vermin. I *eat* vermin. I – I –'

'All right,' the cat said smoothly. 'I get the message. You're not vermin. But I may still have to come after you.'

Tawny Owl's anger saved him. His temper was up. 'Try me!' he cried. He flexed his talons. His huge eyes glared at the cat's presumption. He was exasperated that he couldn't open his wings to their full span. That would have shaken the animal.

The black cat stared at the bird, in particular at his talons. She was weighing up her chances. She began to see that this was no ordinary bird.

'Sooty! Sooty!' a child's voice called from below. The cat's attention wavered. 'Sooty! Are you there?' The cat turned away. The child was mounting the stairs.

Tawny Owl heard these new footsteps in great alarm. He wanted nothing to do with humans. They were unpredictable and beyond a wild creature's

understanding. He didn't know whether to stay put or make a dash for the open doorway. The cat had temporarily forgotten his existence as she waited for the child to appear.

'Soo – ty, Soo – ty,' the shrill voice chanted, ever louder as its owner neared the top stair. The cat miaowed, raising her black tail as she saw her seeker.

'There you are!' cried the child triumphantly. A little red-haired boy of about six years came into the room, stooping to give his pet a cuddle. The cat pushed herself against his legs affectionately and nuzzled his eager hands.

Tawny Owl guessed there was no threat to him here and decided it was his best opportunity for escape. He fluttered off the bookshelf, causing the startled boy to scream, and swooped over his head through the doorway, banking sharply to make the tight turn down the staircase. The bird had no idea where he was heading, but was intent on finding the first available opening to the outside world.

The boy's scream had already stirred the rest of the household. Now he was calling out in the utmost excitement from upstairs. 'Daddy, a bird! A bird in the loft!'

The father came running from below. Tawny Owl had skimmed down the first flight of stairs and reached the landing of the first storey. Bedroom doors were open here and Owl lunged for the first entrance he saw and flew straight for the window. A girl shrieked as his wings clipped her face as she sat at her dressing-table. Fooled by the gleamingly clean picture window which appeared to the bird to be open air, Tawny Owl almost

crashed against the glass but managed to swerve at the last moment. The confined space of the bedroom was difficult to negotiate. The girl was adding her cries to the small boy's. It was enough to terrify any wild animal and now the father arrived on the scene, believing his children were being attacked. He saw the great bird and, instinctively protective, tried to knock it to the floor. Tawny Owl veered from right to left and back again to avoid the man's flailing arms. Surprisingly the girl came to his aid.

'Don't hit him, Dad, please,' she begged. 'He just wants to get out. Open the window!'

The man ran to the window. Now Tawny Owl had more room. He flapped through the door and continued along the landing. He ignored the other open doorways, having learnt his lesson. He came to another staircase and followed it down. Now he was in the hall. The front door was closed. He fluttered to the floor and tried to gain breath. His head was in a whirl. But the man and his children, together with the cat, were in hot pursuit. Tawny Owl didn't understand their intentions. He struggled on again into a room leading off to the right. It was full of furniture – fearsome obstacles for Owl. But what he saw ahead of him made his heart leap. An open window!

It was a small window – a fanlight – left on the latch. But he was determined to squeeze through it even if it should mean leaving some of his feathers. He reached the latch and perched on it. He saw the opening was even tighter than he had feared. As the family came into the room, all talking at the tops of their voices and pointing at him, Tawny Owl pushed his head outside.

The feel of the wind on his face, added to the din behind him, encouraged him onwards. His talons grappled the latch. He pushed and thrust his body through the gap. He felt the hard edges of the window gripping his sides, pinching him like a sort of vice. But he refused to give up. A little more discomfort and, with a final heave, he popped out of the window like a cork out of a bottle.

Instantly he soared upwards despite his throbbing sides, enjoying the supreme luxury of spreading his wings in the free fresh air; in unobstructed and limitless space. He looked around him as he rose higher in the air. Human faces pressed against the glass, watching his progress in admiration, almost in envy. Envy of the supreme freedom of the flight of a bird.

The man said: 'That's the first time an owl has been seen in Farthinghurst. You must remember this, children.'

'And he chose us to visit,' said the girl. 'Look, here are some of his feathers.'

Tawny Owl flew on. Hunger and thirst were forgotten as he flew over the houses, the blocks of flats, the shops. For he knew now that beneath him was what was once Farthing Wood. Its soil, its plants, its roots lay under this man-made wilderness of concrete and brick and metal. And he knew it was Farthing Wood because there was just one remnant of it still existing. The remnant was a tree: a solitary, isolated but massive beech. Tawny Owl had recognized it at once as its great sweeping branches beckoned to him like welcoming arms which longed to draw him into their lonely embrace. This great beech, which now straddled the boundaries of two identical plots on the estate and

therefore belonged to nobody, was the very same beech which had served as a meeting-point for the animals of Farthing Wood as they had embarked on their hazardous journey. It was from beneath this very tree, that now enfolded Tawny Owl in its rich greenery, that their long trek had begun. And this was all that the industrious humans and their machines had allowed to stand of Farthing Wood.

Holly

The beech's generous cover hid Tawny Owl for the rest of the day. He didn't dare to venture forth again even to moisten his parched mouth. He waited. And he thought.

He thought of his carefree days in Farthing Wood before the humans had come, when he had been so much younger. He thought of the other creatures who had lived there who had become his travelling companions first and then his trusted friends. What feelings would they experience were they to join him at the Great Beech now? How their world had changed! Yet, oddly enough, Owl didn't feel sentimental about his old home. That life was too far back in the past. He found himself thinking more about White Deer Park. He was surprised at himself. And what surprised him most of all was that he actually felt homesick for it.

By twilight Tawny Owl had come to the conclusion

that he had made a mistake coming to this place. It was barren. Barren of hunting opportunities and barren of company. When he felt ready for it he would begin the flight back. In the meantime his ordeal in the house had exhausted him and he needed to get his strength back.

Under cover of darkness he sought water. A garden pond soon provided him with that. Food, however, would be a problem. Then he remembered what the black cat had said about mice. So there must be prey to be caught somewhere in the area. Of course, mice inside a house were no use to an owl. But mice got into human dwellings from outside and so in that case, thought Owl, there would be others to find.

'And if anyone can find mice,' he told himself again, '*I* can.' So he began to search the gardens; along the fence bottoms, around the sheds, under the hedges. And pretty soon he found them all right. And he also found he wasn't the only one hunting them. From time to time he caught a glimpse of another bird swooping in the darkness, never very close, always keeping its distance. And he heard the squeals of mice *he* hadn't caught, just a few garden plots away from where he was intent on his own quest.

Each time Tawny Owl made a kill he took it back to the beech and ate in seclusion on one of the broad grey branches. He wondered where the other hunter perched to eat. He didn't know that in between his visits to the tree the second bird was using it as well. Finally their trips coincided. Each was aware there was another occupant in a separate part of the tree. Tawny Owl wondered what sort of bird was sharing his roosting site. As it was a nocturnal hunter like himself

he had every reason to suppose it was another owl. He was curious. But the other bird spoke first.

'How long have you been hunting this area?'

Tawny Owl swivelled round in excitement. The voice belonged to a female. 'That depends on how you look at it,' he answered.

'What do you mean?'

'It means that I know the area as well as any living creature and better than most,' he explained grandly. 'But I've been absent for a long while.'

'Then you can't know it as well as you think,' came the reply. 'The area has been steadily changing ever since I can remember.'

'You don't have to tell me,' Tawny Owl said, very much on his dignity. 'I know all about Farthing Wood, believe you me.'

'I believe you,' said the other owl. 'But do you know about Farthinghurst?'

'Farthinghurst?'

'Yes, that's the name of this area now. Farthing Wood is long gone.'

'I can see that!' Tawny Owl exclaimed irritably. 'But, did you know that we are now perching in a part of it?'

'Oh yes. I've known and used this tree for several seasons. I think it's always been here.'

'As long as the Wood itself. And now it's all that remains.'

The owl was intrigued. 'How do you know so much?'

'If you're a good listener, I've a long story to tell you. But for the moment, suffice to say that Farthing Wood was my home from the day I hatched. When its

destruction was imminent I left. And now, as you see, I've returned.'

'I don't pretend to understand your reasons,' said the other owl, 'since your Wood has now disappeared.'

'Ah – that's another matter,' Tawny Owl told her. 'But what about you? Is this your permanent territory? Tell me about yourself.'

'Not much to tell.' The female owl fluttered to a closer branch. She was another Tawny. 'I was hatched on the fringes of the Wood amidst the roar of men's machinery. There was just a tiny patch of woodland then but, from what you say, I think it may once have been much larger. Most of my kin were killed or found other territories. I stayed around, though.'

'Why?'

'Simple. Abundant food. In my early days there was almost a plague of mice who came in from the countryside to raid the humans' buildings. They were attracted originally by a great barn where grain was stored. This was on the edge of the estate. From there they spread all over, getting into the humans' own dwelling-places. So there was never a shortage of prey for me. Of course, the humans got to work to eradicate my food supply. But they could never quite winkle out every last mouse. So I've hung on here. I compete with cats and others but I've never starved. I suppose I've been lazy in some ways.'

'Far from it,' Tawny Owl contended. 'It always makes sense to exploit a constant source of food. And where do you roost?'

'Well – right here, of course. Where else is there?'

'Here? But I was sheltering here myself during the day. I didn't realize. . . .'

'No reason why you should. I saw you, but you were, by all appearances, oblivious of everything.'

'I was exhausted,' Tawny Owl explained. Then he told her about his adventure in the loft.

'That was an error on your part, to go inside a man-dwelling,' the female owl asserted. 'I've learnt to steer well clear of them.'

'You're right, of course,' he agreed. 'But that was nothing compared to my previous adventures.'

'Oh? And when am I to have the privilege of hearing about them?'

'Any time you wish,' Tawny Owl promised. He was eager to impress. 'What do you call yourself?'

'I don't call myself anything,' she answered. 'And there's no-one else around to give me a name. At least,' she added, 'not until now. Perhaps you'd like to think of one for me?'

'Well, I – I don't know if I'm much good at that sort of thing,' he said awkwardly. 'But I'll try.'

'Do you have a name?'

'Yes. Tawny Owl,' he said.

'I can see that.' The female owl was amused. 'But what of your own individual name?'

'Well, that *is* it.' He rustled his wings. 'I've never needed another. My friends always called me that. I was the only owl in the party, you see.'

'Party?' she queried. 'No, I don't see.'

'I think I'd better tell you my story,' he said.

'I wish you would.'

So Tawny Owl related the story of the Animals of Farthing Wood and of their long journey to a new safe home. His companion was an avid listener. She was

thrilled and awed by his descriptions of the adventures they had encountered on the way, so much so that she wasn't absolutely sure whether he might not be embellishing some of them. But he wasn't, of course. He didn't have any need of embellishments. She hardly spoke a word until he had finished. 'A thrilling tale indeed,' she said. 'And so you all made your homes in White Deer Park?'

'Yes, we did. And soon I shall return there.'

'Forgive me, but I don't understand why you ever left it?'

'Aha,' Tawny Owl returned. 'That's quite another story.'

The female owl didn't press him. She was beginning to feel drowsy. She said, 'It seems so strange for a bird to have mammals as his closest companions – and even a reptile, too. I never heard of such a thing.'

'They've been true comrades, all of them,' he said. He had got himself into quite an emotional state during the recounting of his story, even to the point of being prepared to forgive Weasel his teasing. 'Don't you ever get lonely?'

'I hadn't thought about it before,' she answered. 'But now I see the advantage of friends in times of difficulty.'

'I – er – could be a friend, you know,' Tawny Owl offered hopefully.

'Well, I think maybe you already are,' she replied. 'And so really I think you must give me a name.'

'Yes, yes, now let me think . . . I have it!' he cried suddenly. 'I shall call you Holly.'

'Holly! Why?'

'Because it's a good name for an owl,' he answered promptly. 'And besides – I can't think of anything else.'

She was not displeased. 'Holly, Holly,' she repeated, testing the name. 'Yes, I rather think I like it. It's nice to be called something.'

Tawny Owl was thoroughly pleased with himself. Now his thoughts took another turn and he felt glad he had come this far, after all. He hardly dared to hope that all his plans would be fulfilled. Yet Fate had brought him to this tree, the symbol of Farthing Wood, and here he had found Holly, its last survivor. There had to be some meaning to it all. His thoughts were interrupted.

'Where did you roost last?' she was asking.

'Here – on this very branch.'

'Then I shall join you there,' she said purposefully. And she flew over. 'We may as well start as we mean to go on, don't you think?' she added, perching by his side. 'Friends must stick together, mustn't they?'

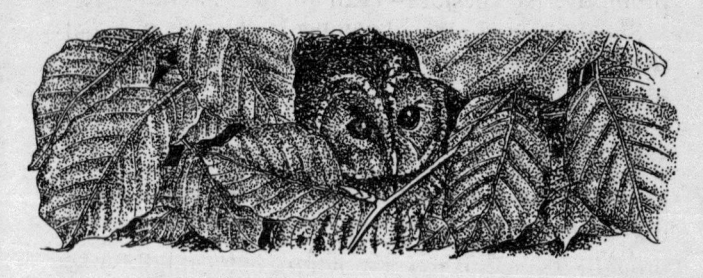

A Rival in the Air

So the two birds roosted together in the beech tree during daylight. At night they hunted mice together. This became the pattern of Tawny Owl's new life and he had no complaints for the moment. He still intended to return to White Deer Park and, of course, he intended to take Holly along with him. But she seemed so content with her lot that he hesitated to broach the subject, fearing she might decline. In this he was quite wrong. Holly had of necessity lived a solitary life. Now she was enjoying the change and would not have wanted to be left alone again. She was a clever bird and also a little cunning. She knew Tawny Owl wanted her to stay with him; she guessed easily enough that he lacked a mate and she took this to be because of his age. From that it was simple enough to surmise that he would be keen to keep her and would therefore be willing to do her bidding. So she decided to make use of

this situation. And, first of all, she would test his feelings towards her.

'I don't think you'll be going back to your Nature Reserve,' she remarked to him coyly one evening as they rested from hunting.

'I certainly shall,' he asserted.

'When will it be?'

Tawny Owl shuffled his feet. 'I – er – I'm not quite sure,' he answered.

'Why leave? Aren't you happy here?' Holly asked next.

'Up to a point, yes,' he had to say.

'We have an abundance of food, we have shelter, haven't we?'

'Yes, but you see, I don't feel this is my home any more. How could I? I belong in White Deer Park.'

'Then why did you come here?'

'I didn't plan to – at first,' he answered.

'What changed your mind?'

'Oh well, I'd already flown a considerable distance away from the Reserve and it occurred to me I might as well come a little further and see what the old place looked like. And, until recently, I wished I hadn't.'

Holly knew perfectly well what he was alluding to. But she pretended otherwise. 'I wonder why you changed your opinion?' she mused.

'Oh, you know,' he said gruffly.

'Do I?' she asked with feigned innocence.

'Well, I had hoped you understood,' Tawny Owl said. 'I mean, most creatures like company of a sort.'

'But weren't you telling me you had plenty of

company in the Park? Your friends the fox and the badger. . . .' She was making it difficult for him.

'Of course,' he said. He shifted up and down. Then he mumbled, 'But one always prefers company of one's own kind.'

'Ah. I see,' said Holly. 'How flattering,' she added softly. Then, 'How important is it to you?'

'Very,' he confessed.

'Then I ought to tell you something. You may lose my company.'

'How? Why?' Tawny Owl blustered.

'I think you may have a rival for it.'

'A rival? Oh, that's of no consequence. He'd soon quit the field when he saw I was around,' Tawny Owl told her self-importantly. He – the Farthing Wood Owl!

'You may be right, I can't tell,' Holly said. She wished to appear impartial. 'But – forgive me for saying it – he seems a much younger bird than yourself. I think I should warn you.'

Tawny Owl's self-esteem was rocked a little by this news. He wondered whether fame alone would be enough to ward off any challenge. And then, if the owl should be really young, would he have heard of the Owl from Farthing Wood? After all, Holly hadn't seemed aware of his status.

'Where have you seen this bird?' he asked cautiously.

Holly thought hard. The story was all invention. How could she make it seem convincing? 'Oh, I've seen him around for a long while,' she answered airily. 'He flits about in the distance, over the house-tops and along the hedge-plants. Sometimes he comes right by

our roost and looks up inquisitively. He watches me, you know. I was aware of his presence before you arrived.'

'*I've* never seen him,' Tawny Owl declared. 'But I'll look out for him from now on!' He sounded determined. In fact he wasn't at all sure he believed her. Holly, however, was pleased with his reaction.

The next time they hunted together Tawny Owl really kept his eyes peeled for the slightest sign. He saw nothing large enough in the air to be an owl. When they were back on their perch he questioned his companion. Had she seen anything?

'Oh yes. He was around,' she told him with the greatest composure.

'But he couldn't have been!' Tawny Owl remonstrated. 'I looked everywhere.' He was becoming suspicious.

'You have to know where to look,' Holly pointed out. 'And besides, he's probably wary of you.'

This remark boosted Owl's ego. It was meant as a compliment and he took it as such. Holly's subtlety had dispelled his doubts for the time being. He didn't mention the other bird again but waited for her to do so. And she did.

Each night she pretended to have seen it, sometimes in one place, sometimes in another. And, according to her, this other male on occasion still flew close to the beech tree while they were resting.

'Not much of a rival, is he?' Tawny Owl remarked sarcastically. 'He never dares to show his face.'

Holly saw she might have miscalculated. She had to retrieve the situation. 'I'm so afraid he's just looking for

his opportunity,' she said. 'When you're asleep, for instance. You always doze off long before I do.'

'Do I indeed?' Tawny Owl returned grumpily. He never liked to be reminded of his tendency to drowsiness. 'Well, I tell you what then. In future I'll stay awake and wait for him.'

For the next few days he did just that. He made a supreme effort to keep his eyes open although a full stomach always made him feel sleepy. He stared through the mass of branches until long after dawn when the beech gradually took on its colours of leaf green and silver grey.

'I saw nothing and nobody,' he kept telling her.

'I think he's waiting till your guard is down,' was Holly's answer. 'He's so clever.'

Tawny Owl was tiring of this game. He decided to bring it to a conclusion. 'Oh yes, he's clever all right,' he said. 'He's so clever at eluding me he's as good as invisible.'

'Oh, Tawny Owl,' responded Holly archly. 'Do you doubt me?'

Owl was sorely tempted to say so but refrained. 'No, no,' he lied. 'Why should I? But I mean to see off this interloper once and for all. So the next time you see him, you tell me straight away where he is and I'll get after him and drive him off.'

Holly was excited. 'Would you? Would you really?' she asked.

'Just see if I don't,' he answered grimly, but inwardly he smiled. He wondered how she would manage the affair.

That night Holly didn't see the elusive bird. Tawny

Owl's inward smile broadened. The next night and the night after that were the same. Owl was beside himself with glee. But Holly was deliberately lulling him into a state of unpreparedness. On the fourth night, as they skimmed together over the gardens searching for mice, he was on the point of remarking that his rival seemed to have given up when she suddenly startled him with cries of: 'There he is! There he is!'

Tawny Owl nearly plummeted to earth in his astonishment, but managed to correct his flight to save himself. 'Where?' he gasped breathlessly.

'There, look! Do you see where those new man-dwellings are being built?' She indicated by changing direction.

'Yes, I – I think I do.'

'He's skulking over there!' she screeched. Her cries were so convincingly raucous that for a moment Tawny Owl almost believed he could himself make out something in the distance. Did he see a fluttering figure?

'Quickly!' Holly urged him. 'He'll be gone.'

Now there was no choice for him. He had to fall in with her plan or appear cowardly. He flapped his wings hastily, increasing his speed, and zoomed towards his objective. Holly watched him with satisfaction.

Tawny Owl was really flying fast. He hoped that if a rival were around the bird would be frightened off by his purposefulness. But there was no rival around and Tawny Owl blundered straight into some almost invisible netting that flapped in the breeze, entangling himself and landing with a thump on a partially laid and unhardened concrete driveway that the netting had been erected to protect. As he struggled to free

himself from the nylon mesh his talons and wings
became daubed with gouts of thick wet cement mix. He
got himself into the air. Now he knew very well there
had been no other owl. He was furious with Holly for
playing games with him. As yet he didn't realize the full
extent of the plight he was in. He only knew his wing
feathers were tacky and uncomfortable and that he
couldn't move them as he wished. He felt strangely out
of balance as if one side of his body was heavier than the
other and it was most difficult for him to steer the
course he wanted. He lumbered awkwardly back to
Holly who had just pounced on a mouse.

'You can bring that back to the roost for *me*!' Tawny
Owl cried imperiously. 'I've done your bidding and
look at my reward.' He exhibited his cement-coated
talons. 'I'll do no more hunting tonight – neither of
mouse nor owl!' He bumbled his way to the beech in a
sort of zigzag motion. He found it impossible to fly
straight. He landed with extreme awkwardness, his
plastered claws encumbering his ability to perch safely.

Holly obediently brought him her most recent kill. She
thought he deserved it. She didn't understand his
predicament yet and believed Tawny Owl was only
grumpy because he had soiled his plumage when he fell.

'You and your stupid stories!' he berated her. 'There
never was another owl, was there?'

Holly replied by meekly laying the dead mouse
within his reach.

Tawny Owl was hungry and tore mouthfuls off the
carcass so that he could continue his tirade in between
swallowing. Usually he disposed of a mouse whole. 'I
don't know what fun you've been having at my

expense,' he snapped, 'but I can tell you it's over. No doubt you think there's no fool' – gulp – 'like an old fool but you'll find out that Tawny' – gulp – 'Owl from Farthing Wood is nobody's fool!'

'Oh, it's not a game,' said Holly. 'You've got me all wrong.' She looked at him with her huge round eyes. 'I only wanted to tell if you were in earnest about me and our keeping company.'

A shaft of brilliant moonlight penetrated the clouds and illuminated the entire tree. Now she saw the sorry state Tawny Owl was in. 'Oh, what a mess,' she commiserated with him. 'I'm so sorry you fell. I had no idea there was such a trap.'

'Neither had I,' Tawny Owl remarked ruefully. He was partially soothed by her words. 'I may as well admit it – I'm too old for such capers. For the time being you'll have to catch enough food for both of us. I feel as if I couldn't fly at present to save my life.'

'I'll go at once,' Holly said willingly. 'I owe you that much. You stay here and rest.'

Tawny Owl watched her disappear over the gardens. She was absent a long time. Once or twice he tried his wings but each time he nearly overbalanced because his encrusted talons prevented him from gripping the branch properly. When Holly finally did return, carrying three mice in her beak, Tawny Owl could hardly move at all. It was as though his wings were encased. He felt weighed down and almost rigid.

'I don't know what I've done to myself,' he blurted out. He sounded scared. 'I seem to have lost the use of my wings. I think I may never be able to fly again!'

The Tainted Stream

Since their meeting in the Hollow the Farthing Wood animals and their dependants had continued to visit the Pond when they needed to. However they were sensible about it and took pains to ensure first that Trey was not in the vicinity. Meanwhile they began seeking out some of the other stags. Fox's message was received with varying responses. Most of the stags were indignant at Trey's presumption.

'Drive me out of the Park? He wouldn't dare go that far,' said one.

'This Reserve is for all the deer, no matter whether one is stronger than another,' said a second.

Some of them were disbelieving. 'How do you know his intentions? He's made no such threat to me,' one questioned.

'Preposterous! The Warden would never allow it. He has to look after the entire herd,' remarked another.

Another saw the impossibility of it straight away. 'How could Trey do it with a fence all around the Park's perimeter?' he demanded.

There were others who were obviously intimidated already by Trey's commanding presence. 'I have no quarrel with him.' 'I'm no contender to be the Great Stag's heir. Trey won't bother with me.'

But all in all the animals succeeded in at least implanting the idea in the male deer's minds that one of their numbers had too low an opinion of his fellows. This naturally rankled and, slowly, a general resentment of Trey's air of superiority began to build up. Fox still hoped that when the time was ripe the haughty stag might find he had assumed too much.

The summer sun shone on the Park and dried out the puddles and pools that had lain so conveniently close to Badger's set since the rainy season earlier in the year. As the stream was still shunned by his friends, Badger realized that before long he too would have to make a trip to the Pond. It would be a laborious journey for the old creature. His sight was now very poor and his legs were stiff and often ached, especially when he tried to be too energetic. But he had to drink like everyone else and one evening he stood just inside his set entrance, sniffing the breezes and vainly attempting to detect a hint of approaching rain.

'It's no use,' he muttered to himself. 'I shall have to make a move. Everything around here's as dry as can be.' And he shuffled off in the direction of the Pond. He hadn't gone far when he halted abruptly. 'This is silly,' he said. 'The stream's much closer. How do we know

there's anything wrong with it? I could go and look for myself anyway.' He didn't turn round at once. He was in two minds about it.

'Suppose I should find something wrong there?' he pondered. 'Then it would be even further for me to go across the Park to the Pond. It's a nuisance the stream's the opposite way. Oh dear, now what shall I do?'

In the end his own curiosity as well as comfort decided the issue. He headed for the stream. It was a close muggy evening and Badger was soon tired. He was glad when he could see the stream in the distance because by then he was very thirsty indeed. When he reached the nearest bank he stood and looked at the water for a long time. The stream was low and slow-moving but, apart from that, didn't appear to be any different from usual as far as Badger could make out.

'Of course my eyes aren't the best judges in the world,' he told himself. 'I'll just go down the bank and see if the water smells as it should.' He grunted as he stumbled down to the stream's edge. He sniffed carefully and methodically. His sensitive snout had lost none of its powers. He raised his striped head. He was still uncertain. There was nothing definite and yet. . . .

'I'll just go a little way along to see if anyone else is drinking,' he decided.

It wasn't long before he did indeed hear the sound of an animal drinking. It was a dainty quiet lapping, not at all like the noisy habit of a fox, for instance. He peered ahead but it was too dark for him to see what creature was there. He hurried on. He wanted to talk to any animal who might know something he didn't. But all at once the sounds of drinking ceased.

'Don't go!' Badger called. 'Whoever's there – please wait. I'd like to speak to you.'

There was silence. Badger didn't think the animal had moved off. He heard no noise of its departure. He guessed it was waiting to see him before deciding if it was safe to remain.

'It's only me – old Badger,' he reassured the animal. He shuffled on.

'All right, I'll wait,' the animal called back. It was obviously satisfied it was not in danger.

Badger could tell from the voice it was a rabbit's, but not one he knew well. The rabbit came into view. When it saw Badger it paused on the lip of the bank. Its body was taut, ready to spring away hastily if necessary. Badger came puffing up. 'You – you were drinking?' he enquired.

'Yes.'

'Notice anything strange about the water?'

'No.'

'No funny taste or – or – anything?'

'No.'

'Well that's a relief,' Badger sighed. 'It'll save me a lot of effort anyway.' He headed straight back to the water's edge and bent his head. He took a couple of laps.

'*He's* not around, is he?' the rabbit suddenly asked nervously.

Badger raised his head. 'Who's "he"?'

'The – the deer,' the rabbit answered. 'The massive one with antlers like oak branches.'

Badger was puzzled. 'No–o,' he said slowly. 'There's

no deer around here. Are you referring to the stag
called Trey?'

'I don't know his name but – he's mean and
aggressive. He drove me off.'

'Off what?' Badger asked.

'Off his territory, he would claim,' the rabbit replied.
'That's why I came here to drink. It's been so dry,
hasn't it? I had to come here. I didn't want to. The
others said it was a risk, but what was I to do? It's
water, at least, even if it is . . . is. . . .' It didn't finish.
Its voice died away.

Badger was alarmed. 'Is what?' he gasped.

'I don't know,' the rabbit said. 'There've been
stories. Birds dying here and – and – I don't know what
else.'

Badger guessed the situation now. 'You were
prevented from drinking at the Pond. That's it, isn't it?
So you came here?' His questions were urgent.

'Of course. I told you. I wouldn't have come here
otherwise.'

'What about the others in your warren? They have to
drink, don't they?'

'They were lucky. They got back from the Pond in
time. I was the last. He – he was standing there like a
sort of sentry as if he'd been waiting for me.' The rabbit
coughed.

'What's the matter?' Badger snapped sharply. He
was on edge.

'Nothing. I – I'm not sure,' said the rabbit. 'Just a
sort of – tickle.'

'A tickle?'

'Yes. My – my throat feels sort of hot.'

'You'd better get back to your burrow,' Badger advised him.

'I will, but now I feel so dry again. I must have another drink.' The rabbit ran towards the stream.

'Don't!' Badger called. He was full of dread. But the rabbit was heedless in its desperation to get to the water. It drank deeply. Now Badger waited for something awful to happen. He was in a turmoil of expectation. The rabbit turned and ran up the bank, seemingly none the worse. It ran straight past Badger as if it had forgotten him entirely. Badger hastened after the animal. He wanted to keep it in sight.

The rabbit, of course, was far fleeter of foot. In no time at all it was lost from sight. Badger forced his aged body into a shambling run. He was desperate to see what would become of the rabbit. His weak eyes probed the darkness. For a while he saw no trace. He didn't even know if he had taken the right direction. But then, all at once, he knew he had. He glimpsed the rabbit ahead. The unfortunate creature had slowed almost to a halt and was staggering about uncertainly as if it had lost its sense of balance. Badger lumbered up, gasping hoarsely.

'What – what. . . .' he wheezed, but he was so short of breath he could manage no more.

The rabbit muttered: 'The burning, the burning . . . I – I'm –' It began to shake uncontrollably. It couldn't keep its feet. It toppled over and lay still. Its eyes stared up into Badger's face. It was dead.

Badger's sides heaved painfully. He stared back at the lifeless eyes in horror. Eventually he got his breathing under control. 'The stream's a killer,' he

whispered to himself in the utmost dismay. 'I've drunk from it too. Oh, why was I so foolish? Better to have tired my legs out going to the Pond than this! What shall I do now?'

He tried to recall how much of the water he had drunk but he was in such a state of shock and anxiety he couldn't be sure. He only knew he was still extremely thirsty, as if he hadn't drunk at all. 'The rabbit had a raging thirst, too,' he wailed. He tried to calm himself but it was difficult. 'Pull yourself together. An old animal like me behaving so stupidly! I can't last for ever anyway. I was lucky to come through another winter,' he reasoned. Yet it was hard for him not to feel frightened.

'It may be too late,' he went on, 'but I must try to get to the Pond. If I drink some clean water it might . . . yes, yes, it might help.' He felt better now he had made the decision and he wasted no more time. With a last glance at the poor dead rabbit he trotted away. He could think only of filling himself up with untainted water. All thought of Trey, and why the rabbit had gone to the stream to begin with, had vanished from Badger's mind.

Several times on the way he stopped to regain his breath. He felt very alone and wished heartily for a friendly face to appear. But he saw no-one until he reached the Pond and then it wasn't someone who was friendly at all.

It was growing light by the time he got to the pond-side. He pushed his way through the sedges and reeds and lowered his muzzle thankfully. He began to drink.

There was a sound of pounding hooves. 'Stop!' bellowed a deep voice.

Badger looked up. The stag Trey was galloping round the far side of the Pond towards him.

'You've no right to be here!' thundered Trey. 'This is not your area. I know where you come from.'

Badger was astounded. But his keen thirst overrode every other consideration and couldn't be denied. He bent again to lap.

Trey was infuriated. 'Do you defy me?' he boomed. He lowered his antlers threateningly.

'I'm an old animal. I have to drink where I can,' Badger reasoned.

'There are other places.'

'No. There aren't,' Badger answered. He was beginning to feel unwell. Why wouldn't the stag leave him alone?

'I know your area. The stream is closer for you,' Trey contended.

'The stream is tainted,' Badger growled. His discomfort made him bold.

Trey took in his words. 'What do you mean?' he asked more evenly.

'Didn't the Great Stag die there?' Badger cried irritably.

'He was old – like you,' Trey replied. 'His time had come.'

'A pity for us all,' Badger remarked. He was tired of bandying words with this domineering animal.

Unknown to the two of them a third animal had appeared on the scene and was watching them carefully. It was Plucky the young fox who was homeward

bound for his earth. He crept closer without being noticed.

Trey bridled at Badger's remark. He thought he would teach this insolent old creature a lesson. As Badger tried once again to assuage his thirst, Trey cried: 'As you're so determined to have the water, perhaps I can help you reach it!' He directed his antlers at Badger's rump and prepared to butt him into the Pond.

Now Plucky guessed the stag's intention and, regardless of any danger to himself, ran up with fangs bared. As Trey ran forwards the young fox caught one of the deer's hind legs in his teeth and gave it a severe nip just above the ankle. Trey's headlong career towards Badger was obstructed but not altogether prevented. The full force behind his antlers was impaired, luckily for Badger. But the amiable old creature still received a considerable clout and he shot out towards the centre of the Pond. Now Trey pulled up and, as the startled Badger struggled to keep his head above water, the stag turned his attention to his attacker. His leg smarted painfully. He saw the youngster whose impudence was beyond belief.

'This time I'll make you pay!' roared Trey.

Plucky raced round the edge of the Pond with the stag on his tail. The fox feinted and changed direction like a hare, dashing this way and that. Trey's bulk was far less manoeuvrable. He couldn't catch the fox any more than he had Leveret and his anger was at boiling point. Plucky kept an eye on Badger in the water while he zipped this way and that. Badger was swimming gamely and was aiming for the opposite side. He had

swum more than halfway across the Pond and the Edible Frogs who inhabited this spot most of the time were urging him on. Badger was so tired he was deaf to all their cries. Now Plucky began calling.

'Come on, Badger! Come over this way. There's a deserted set close by. He can't catch us!'

And Trey couldn't, try as he might. Plucky held him at bay, chasing this way and that and, eventually, the exhausted Badger, his bristly coat pouring water, pulled himself out of the Pond. He wanted only to collapse in a heap in a place of safety. His head was spinning, his throat irritated and his rump throbbed unmercifully but he kept going towards the hole in the ground. It was so close, so close. If only he could get inside it. But now Trey tried to head him off.

Plucky dashed up courageously and, dodging the stag's feet, jumped up to sink his teeth high up in Trey's thigh. Badger made his escape and bolted into the empty set. But even now he couldn't rest. He feared for the young fox. So he turned around in the tunnel and hauled himself back up to the entrance. Plucky was dancing about but now he had risked too much by coming in so close and Trey was aiming blows with his antlers to right and left. It seemed only a matter of time before one would catch him, with severe consequences to the young fox. Plucky's way to the entrance hole was barred by the stag and Badger could see that, despite his own fatigue, he must enter the fray. Trey's back was before Badger and the gallant old creature looked for a way to rescue the youngster whose bravery reminded him so much of his dear friend the Farthing Wood Fox. When the stag stepped back a pace Badger saw his

chance and now he bit deeply into the leg that Plucky had already nipped earlier on. As Trey paused, registering this fresh outburst of pain, Plucky instantly made a dive for the hole and in the next second he and Badger were tumbling over each other in the safety of the tunnel.

Plucky scrambled to the nearest chamber inside the set and Badger crawled after him. He was entirely spent. Outside the set Trey bellowed his fury.

When he could muster up sufficient strength to speak, Badger said to Plucky: 'Once it's dark you must fetch the elders – the Farthing Wood Fox and Vixen.' He gasped agonizingly. 'Bring them here. And my other friends too. All you can find.' He gasped again. 'Tell them,' he panted, 'Badger's finished.'

The Animals Gather

For the whole of that day Plucky sheltered with Badger in the abandoned set. From time to time he went along the exit tunnel to see if Trey had gone. The stag hung around for a long while, hoping for revenge. In the end he realized he was achieving nothing and left with many threats of 'getting even' and 'teaching you not to try and thwart a royal stag' roared down the entrance hole.

Badger hardly uttered a word all day except in reply to Plucky's enquiries about his comfort. Every limb in Badger's body ached unbearably. His rump was sore from the blow of the stag's antlers. But, worst of all, his throat was hot and dry and he knew his drink at the stream might prove fatal. Indeed he expected to die. Every so often he was racked by a painful wheezing cough which was a constant reminder of the sufferings of the dead rabbit. Badger could think only of his need

to survive through the hours of the coming night. It was imperative he give his warning to his friends. He willed himself to hold on.

At long last the late dusk began to descend. Plucky waited a little longer. He was frantic to leave, yet he could not afford the slightest risk. Under cover of darkness he bade farewell to Badger and went up to the entrance hole. He made a thorough check of the Pond's surroundings before actually setting off. There was no scent of deer on the air. He ran round the Pond and, keeping to the shadows as much as possible, made his way to Fox and Vixen's earth as swiftly as his young legs would carry him. There he related to them all that had happened. He knew nothing of the events at the stream.

'We must go to him at once,' Fox said. 'We won't wait for the others. Plucky, I leave it to you to tell them about Badger. Quickly now, explain to me where this set is.'

Plucky gave him the necessary directions.

'Come on, Vixen,' said Fox. 'I hope to goodness we'll be in time.'

The pair of foxes were silent as they picked their way across the Park. They were both deeply worried by Plucky's message. Fox himself, of all creatures, was closest to Badger. Their association and friendship went back such a long way that Fox simply couldn't bear to think what life would be like without him.

Vixen knew as well as if he had told her himself that these thoughts were passing through Fox's mind. Her sympathy for him was intense and, coupled with this, was her own grave concern. For Badger was her friend

too. Next to Fox and her own offspring she had more affection for the kind-hearted old animal than any other creature. So it was a sad and sombre pair who arrived at the pond-side.

They were surprised to find Toad there waiting for them. 'I've been to see him,' Toad told them without preamble. 'The frogs told me what had happened when I arrived for a bathe. He really does look as if he's on his last legs.'

Fox and Vixen looked at each other unhappily.

'The set's this way,' Toad prompted and went on ahead, half-crawling and half-hopping until he reached the entrance hole.

'Is – is he badly injured?' Vixen asked with bated breath.

'I don't think so,' Toad answered. 'He's more concerned about something else. He begged me never to swim in the stream. It's the stream that's on his mind more than anything.'

Fox and Vixen hesitated no longer but followed the tunnel down to the chamber where Badger lay in agony.

'Fox! Vixen!' he croaked. 'Thank goodness you've come. I've managed to hang on for you.'

'Oh Badger, my dear, dear friend. You sound terrible,' Fox whispered. 'What's happened to you?'

'I'm done for, Fox,' Badger wheezed. 'It's all up with me. The stream has been poisoned somehow and I've drunk from it. None of you must ever go near it again. You must promise me!' he gasped insistently.

'Of course we promise,' Fox said. 'But how do you know all this?'

Badger told them about the rabbit and how he himself had unsuspectingly lapped the water before he had realized the danger. The foxes and Toad were unable to speak.

'Where are the others?' Badger asked. 'Where's Mole? And Weasel? They must promise too. I must know they're safe.'

'Plucky will find them. He'll find everybody,' Fox reassured him.

Badger relaxed. He was satisfied for the moment. He lapsed into silence but his friends listened to his harsh breathing with mounting alarm.

'Oh Badger, poor Badger,' Vixen wailed. 'Is there nothing we can do for you?'

'Nothing,' he answered. 'Don't fret yourself, dearest Vixen. There's nothing *to* be done. I've no complaints. I feel calm about it now. I've only myself to blame for what must come.'

Toad took Fox aside. 'Look here,' he said urgently, 'we can't just leave him like this. There's the Warden. D'you remember how he helped Badger before when he injured himself? Perhaps he could –'

'This is no injury, Toad,' Fox interrupted quietly. 'It's something much more serious. Even human help could do nothing. We all have to face this some time but – but –' his voice shook noticeably – 'it's difficult to bear, isn't it?'

'Then all we can do is to stay and comfort him,' Toad murmured sadly.

'Yes,' said Fox. 'We won't leave him now.'

Badger was extremely tired and he fell asleep. His wheezing breaths whistled in the dark underground

chamber. Fox, Toad and Vixen remained nearby. They sat gloomily and scarcely dared to exchange a word. Later they were joined by a very subdued Weasel.

'Plucky is going to look for Whistler and Adder in the daylight,' he told them. 'Friendly and Charmer are coming but I told them to come unaccompanied. Badger could only cope with his oldest comrades, I think? The younger foxes will have to stay away. There wouldn't be room for them and the old fellow might be overwhelmed.'

'Too difficult a journey for Mossy, I suspect?' asked Fox.

'Yes. But Plucky said he's in a terrible state about this.'

'Mossy and Badger almost shared their homes, didn't they?' Vixen remarked.

'Just like dear old Mole in Farthing Wood,' Toad commented.

'I hope Badger won't start asking for him,' whispered Fox. 'I really don't think I could endure it.'

Daylight came but didn't penetrate the general gloom of the set. However Badger's breathing had eased a little. He awoke to find Friendly and Charmer had swelled the numbers. He made the newcomers swear never to visit the stream.

'Is everyone here now?' he murmured weakly. 'No – I don't smell Mole or Adder.'

'Adder's on his way,' Weasel told him, though he didn't know it for sure. 'It's a long crawl here for him and he'll have to be particularly careful now it's light.'

'Yes, yes,' said Badger. 'There mustn't be any

accidents on my account. That crazed stag has sworn to get even with us.' He was thoughtful. 'Perhaps it would be better for Mole to stay out of harm's way.'

'Thank goodness,' Fox whispered to Vixen. Then he spoke up. 'He's doing just that, Badger. No point in his coming, is there? He never visits the stream anyway.'

'Oh dear,' Badger sighed mournfully. 'I should have liked to see Tawny Owl just once before I –'

He broke off as he heard the sound of another animal arriving. Leveret had raced to the set and tumbled into it almost under the nose of Trey who had recommenced patrolling the area.

'He's got us bottled up here all right,' he announced as he joined the others. 'He's only waiting for one of us to make a false move.'

'He'll have a long wait then,' Friendly remarked grimly. 'He hasn't outwitted us yet.'

The animals listened to Trey's angry snorts outside the entrance hole. The stag stamped up and down, first one way, then another.

'He – he's standing guard over us,' Leveret murmured in awe.

They heard his regular hoof-beats. Sometimes Trey called out threateningly although he had no knowledge there was such a large gathering of creatures around Badger.

'This is sheer nonsense,' said Fox. 'Whatever can possess an animal to bear such a grudge?'

'His pride's offended,' Badger said. 'So far we've got the better of him. We've outrun him and out-manoeuvred him. And he's got the scars to prove it.'

'Scars?' Fox asked. 'What scars? I didn't know about this.'

'Plucky and myself left our teeth-marks on him,' Badger said.

'Did you though? My word, Badger, I don't think your days can be over after all. You attacked that huge stag!'

'Yes,' said Badger. 'It's not another animal that's put paid to me, you see, Fox. It's my own stupidity.'

'If Trey's been injured by his encounters with us it does put a different complexion on things,' Fox remarked. 'It's my opinion he'll be determined to redress the balance. He's a vain beast. How belittling for him that he's the dominant deer in the herd yet he's suffered humiliations from creatures far smaller than himself. We'll all have to be doubly cautious.'

It was late in the day when Adder, by subtle and hidden movements, arrived near the Pond. Several times during his journey he had been on the point of giving up. He wasn't known for demonstrations of deep affection or concern. He was, by his very nature, an unemotional animal. But each time he stopped some thought of Badger or some image of him in one of his acts of bravery or kindheartedness compelled the snake to continue. He saw Trey pacing up and down the length of the Pond and it took him an age to get to some cover close enough to the set so that he could get himself into it without trouble when the stag was most distant.

As Adder lay hidden amongst the sedges he saw Whistler fly in and begin a search of the terrain. He was looking for the position of the set where the animals

were sheltering, although there was no possibility of his entering it himself. He seemed to Adder to be in a state of excitement. The whistle of his damaged wing sounded rhythmically over the water. Inside the set the animals detected the sound.

'Whistler's agitated,' Fox observed shrewdly. 'His wing's like a second voice. It's evident he can't settle.'

'The stag must still be around,' Friendly suggested.

'I think our heron friend wants to tell us something,' said Weasel.

Adder was thinking the same thing as he watched the great bird's flight. All at once the heron's sharp eyes picked out the snake's familiar patterned coils amongst the waterside vegetation. Taking careful note of Trey's position Whistler descended and, flapping briskly to steady himself, landed close to Adder's little nook.

'What are you doing?' hissed the snake. 'You couldn't make my presence more obvious if you were to pinpoint me with your bill!'

'Sorry,' croaked the heron. 'But I've made an important discovery about the stream. I can't get into Badger's shelter and I thought *you* could tell the others.'

'Tell them what?' Adder rasped crossly. 'The stag's turning this way!'

'It's the humans,' Whistler confided. 'They've poisoned it. They've dumped –' He interrupted himself and took awkwardly to flight as Trey began his approach. 'I'll be back!' he cried hurriedly.

'Irresponsible chump,' Adder muttered as he buried himself deeper inside some dead leaves. The deer was running to investigate.

Whistler was high in the air by this time and Trey

could find nothing on the ground, try as he might. Adder's camouflage was good enough to fool all but those with the keenest sight. Nevertheless he didn't choose to stay put and afford the heron a second chance of blowing his cover. As soon as Trey had wandered away again Adder emerged from his nest of leaves and slithered determinedly towards the set entrance.

Even then, when Whistler saw his movement, he endangered Adder's dash for safety. 'No, wait!' he called to the snake. 'I didn't finish. It's important!' he bawled at him thoughtlessly.

Adder cared nothing for its importance. Deaf to all entreaties he increased his effort and slid into the hole, cursing the heron roundly all the way.

'Bird-brained, bird-brained,' he hissed to himself over and over again until his anger was cooled by the mustiness of the earthen tunnels.

Weasel came to look. 'It's you!' he greeted him. 'Whatever's the fuss about? Badger needs quiet.'

'It's lucky that dolt of a heron can't get in here then,' Adder observed waspishly. 'He's worked himself into a lather about something and did his best to get me skewered on a pair of antlers!'

'Calm yourself,' said Weasel. 'This isn't the time for recriminations.'

Adder realized he had forgotten himself, though he didn't admit it. 'How is he?' he asked, referring to Badger, as he followed Weasel down the tunnel.

'Hanging on.'

'I'm afraid Badger's made himself an example for the rest of us,' Adder lisped. 'His suffering is our warning.'

'That's exactly why he's called us all here. We've all had to swear not to go near the stream. You'll be made to go through the ritual too.'

Badger was the last to hear Adder's voice though he was listening hard for each new arrival. In his old age he had become increasingly deaf but he was relieved when the others told him the snake had at last joined the throng. Adder dutifully went through the motions of promising never to enter the stream.

'I'm glad I've been able to make you the promise,' he said afterwards. 'I wondered if I'd ever talk to you again. Is the – er – pain very acute?'

'No worse and no better,' Badger answered cryptically. 'But I'm so parched, you see. I think I could drink the Pond dry. And I haven't eaten for an age, either.'

The animals began to murmur together questioningly.

'What?' Adder hissed. 'Are you saying you have an appetite?'

'Yes, I suppose I am,' Badger admitted. 'I don't think my stomach has a scrap of food in it.'

Adder's tongue flickered busily. 'Do you mean to tell me,' he demanded indignantly, 'that I've scraped my scales across the breadth of the Park merely to hear you complain that you're hungry?'

'Well, I – I can't help it, Adder,' Badger mumbled. 'It's only natural, isn't it?'

'No, it isn't,' Adder contradicted. 'Not for an animal who is supposed to be dying, and that's what I was told you were. D'you think I would have come all this way otherwise? There's nothing wrong with you. You're an old humbug, Badger!'

'There *was* something wrong with me. There was,' Badger insisted defensively. 'But, the truth is, I do begin to feel better.'

'How much of this so-called killer water did you actually drink?' Adder asked next.

'Um – I don't remember exactly,' said Badger. 'I was interrupted. I'd begun to lap and –'

Now Weasel cut in. 'So you only took a few laps? Then why all this bother?'

'How can you talk like that, Weasel?' Vixen asked. 'Badger saw the rabbit die. What was he to think? And we should be celebrating, not complaining. Poor Badger!'

'Of course, of course,' Weasel said contritely. 'I'm delighted. You know I am. We all are. I didn't mean . . . oh Badger, forgive me. It's such a surprise, that's all, after expecting the worst.'

The animals all began talking at once, congratulating Badger and each other on a false alarm. Adder remained silent. He was certainly pleased Badger wasn't going to die, but he couldn't quite manage to mask his irritation at the unnecessary journey. Then he remembered Whistler. He waited for the hubbub to die down.

'Listen, everybody,' he lisped. 'There's a message about the stream. Whistler has discovered something. He wants to tell us.'

'We can't leave here till dark,' said Toad. 'Will he stay around?'

'I'll go and see if he's waiting,' said Fox. 'It must be nearing dusk.' He went up the exit tunnel and peered out. The light was indeed fading. He saw Trey standing

by the pond-side at some distance. He was drinking. Fox pushed his head out and called. 'Whistler! Whistler! Are you there?'

There was no answer. Fox waited. But the heron failed to appear.

'He must be planning to return at dark,' Fox said to himself. He looked again at the stag and his anger began to kindle. 'Whatever's the matter with that creature?' he muttered. 'Will he never give up? What does he intend to do? He can't slaughter us all. I refuse to allow ourselves to be holed up like this for as long as he chooses. We can do better than this! We'll soon test his resolve.' He hurried back to the others.

'Badger, are you sure you'll be all right now?' he asked first.

'Yes. Yes, I think so, Fox. If I could only eat something.'

'That's just it. We're not going to stay here. We've all got to eat. What are we thinking of, letting this deer dictate to us?' He was trying to rouse them.

'Oh-ho, this is more like the Farthing Wood Fox,' Friendly remarked to Charmer, his sister.

'We ought to be able to deal with this customer,' said Fox. 'After what we've been through in the past.'

'That's the spirit,' said Weasel. 'I'm with you, Fox.'

'Me too. Goes without saying,' said Friendly.

'I'll back you up,' said Toad, 'though my contribution may be a bit limited.'

Adder brought him down to earth. 'Contribution to what exactly?'

'I – I'm not sure,' Toad admitted. 'What had you in mind, Fox?'

'Oh, only that we're going to leave this little refuge now. We'll go together. We're going to live our normal lives. If Trey has been injured by some of us he brought it on himself. There's every reason to defend oneself in an awkward situation. He must understand that. So – what are we waiting for?'

'I – I don't feel quite ready for a scrap just yet,' Badger said. 'I've got no strength to rely on.'

'Of course not. We weren't intending you to join in,' said Friendly. 'You must stay here and we'll bring you back something to sustain you for a while.'

'I'm so glad I was able to get you all together,' said Badger. 'What a joy it is to have such friends. Now I know we're all safe. There's only one thing I'm unhappy about: Tawny Owl's absence. He won't know about the dangers of the stream and if he should take it into his head to steal back some time without our knowledge we couldn't warn him about it.'

'No good worrying about him, Badger. He's out of reach,' said Weasel.

'If I know Tawny Owl,' said Charmer, 'the first thing he'd do on his return is to find a comfortable spot for a nap! And we all know his favoured places, don't we?'

'All right,' said Fox. 'Enough of talking. Let's face the foe and see just what that supercilious deer is made of!'

He led the way up the tunnel. Friendly, Vixen and Charmer followed directly behind. Weasel went next with Leveret and Toad and Adder brought up the rear. Outside the set it was now almost dark. The first

animal they saw, sitting by the water with the utmost composure, was Plucky.

He leapt up. 'Is Badger –' he began anxiously.

'He's blossoming,' Adder drawled sarcastically. 'He simply loves all this attention.'

Plucky was quickly acquainted with Badger's recovery. He was tremendously relieved. 'What wonderful news,' he said. 'And now I've some for you. I've persuaded Trey to quit.'

'What? How? How could you –' Fox floundered.

'I told him the other stags were rejoicing in his absence,' he answered, 'and that they were becoming extremely friendly with the hinds. I didn't need to say more. You should have seen him gallop. I don't think the dust has settled yet.'

'Well!' exclaimed Vixen.

'*Very* well,' said Friendly. 'Plucky, you're a chip off the old block.'

A Royal Stag

The animals dispersed to follow their own immediate concerns. Chief among these was food. Plucky carried the good news of Badger to Mossy who had been racked by misery ever since he had believed he would never see Badger again. The little mole was so excited he could scarcely wait for the old animal to return to his own home.

'He's got to lie low for a bit,' Plucky told him. 'Get his strength back. Fox and Vixen are collecting food for him.'

Badger lay for a while in the deserted set without moving. The aches in his body were subsiding and the dominant discomfort he felt was still his sore, parched throat. In the end he had no recourse but to stir himself. He lumbered slowly out of the underground chamber and into the tunnel, and from there very, very slowly towards the set entrance. He knew nothing about

Plucky's clever trick on Trey but he was so desperate for water he no longer cared whether the stag was waiting in ambush for him or not. He sniffed at the night air. He could detect no deer odours. Painfully Badger forced his weak, quivering legs over the short stretch of ground to the Pond. He fell on his face in the cool water and gratefully let it wash over him, gulping it down in great draughts. He lay still for a while. It was bliss in the refreshing water. There was no sound nor sight of the stag and Badger was in no hurry to move. What a lucky escape he had had! If he hadn't come across the rabbit he would surely be dead by now. As it was, he had come pretty close to it.

He wondered what Whistler had managed to find out about the stream's danger. Whatever it was, it would be something beyond the scope of mere beasts and birds to rectify. He hauled himself out of the Pond, deliciously wet, and tottered back to his temporary base. Moments later Fox and Vixen returned, carrying roots, tubers and a variety of carrion in their jaws.

'Eat, my friend, eat,' said Fox when he had deposited his load on the hard-trodden earth. 'We want you back with us in our corner of the Park. And your path is clear.' He told him about Trey's abrupt departure.

Badger began eagerly to eat. Fox was amused and approving. 'Badger – the great survivor,' he joked. He and Vixen were supremely happy at their old friend's good fortune.

Badger despatched a succulent root with relish. 'I've had an idea,' he said suddenly as if he had surprised himself. 'There may be a way we can rid ourselves of the stag's threat permanently.'

'We're all ears,' Fox told him interestedly.

'We could make the stream our ally.'

Fox wasn't sure if he understood Badger's suggestion correctly. 'You're not thinking we should persuade Trey to drink from it, are you?' he asked.

'Of course that's what I'm thinking. He's not aware of its danger as far as I know.'

Vixen wouldn't hear of it. 'That's not like you, Badger. It would be an act of betrayal. We've never acted treacherously towards another creature.'

'He's made himself everyone's enemy,' Badger pointed out. 'We had no quarrel with him.'

'That's true,' said Fox. 'But, my dearest Vixen, your heart's in the right place. Trey has no wish to kill any of us; only to dominate the entire Park. So how could we plot his death?'

Badger relented. 'You always were a wise counsellor, Vixen. I bow to your better nature. But I think you're wrong about the stag. After our recent tussles with him I'm sure he'd do anything within his power to avenge himself and it may be some creature will lose its life. I'm not known as a belligerent animal, but if it's a choice between Trey's life and one of my friend's – well, I'd adopt any means to save a friend.'

'It hasn't come to that yet, Badger, thankfully,' Vixen said. 'He's preoccupied with watching the other stags at present. Perhaps we'll have no further brushes with him.'

'I doubt that,' said Badger bluntly. And there the subject was left.

Fox wanted to know more about the stream's mystery and so he sought out Whistler.

'I've been trying to locate some of you,' the heron said petulantly. 'Adder was little help, though I asked him to be. I'm afraid I'm not as stealthy as he and I alarmed him. I wanted you all to know that I've found a clue to the stream's impurity.'

'What is it?' Fox barked. Whistler's long-winded manner could sometimes be infuriating.

'Outside the Park where the stream is joined by a ditch, humans have left their debris. We all have good cause to know how careless humans are about tainting the land. No doubt they're as mindless about water. The rubbish, whatever it is, has contaminated the ditch and the water from the ditch flows into the stream. So it seems very likely to me that –'

'Yes, Whistler,' Fox cut in. 'I understand your drift, and it all sounds very feasible. What made you investigate this?'

'The stream was my chief source of food,' the heron explained. 'Naturally I've wondered why there have been no fish. Now I have to fly a distance to feed. It's very inconvenient. But I think the damage to the stream must be irreparable. It's completely devoid of life.'

Fox pondered the cruel thoughtlessness of humans. 'They poisoned the Great Stag,' he murmured. 'Thanks to them, we have Trey in his place.'

'Countless smaller animals have died there too,' Whistler remarked. 'The entire surroundings have become barren.'

'Even Badger was nearly killed,' Fox growled.

'Wildlife is helpless in these situations,' Whistler said. 'We're at their mercy.'

'I wonder the Warden isn't suspicious, with all these deaths occurring,' Fox mused. 'The carcasses are removed, aren't they?'

'I believe so,' Whistler said. 'The larger ones, certainly.'

'Then he must know something is wrong. *He'll* come to our aid. He cares for us.'

'A heartening notion,' Whistler commented. 'But what of the smaller carrion, such as mice and voles? And songbirds?'

'What do you mean?'

'I don't think the Warden would gather *them* up. They'd be less detectable. So they may be taken by predators such as yourself.'

'I don't hunt or scavenge anywhere in that vicinity,' Fox told him. 'Nor do any of my relatives. But I see what you're driving at. If the little animals are poisoned they in turn may poison those that feed off them?'

'Exactly,' Whistler intoned solemnly. 'So the deaths could become more widespread.'

Fox shuddered. 'All because of one act of carelessness,' he said angrily. 'Will they never learn?'

'Learn?' Whistler echoed. 'You said it yourself, Fox. They don't care.'

The animals became more discerning than ever in their eating habits. The time of the rut was approaching and Trey's main concern continued to be potential rivals amongst the other stags. This allowed the hunting animals a breathing space which enabled them to

range across the safer parts of the Reserve without fear
of hindrance.

Badger recovered sufficiently during this time to be
able to return to his old set. Mossy was so delighted to
have him back as neighbour that he made Badger a
present of a large heap of the plumpest worms and then
they celebrated together.

The animals' enjoyment of complete freedom of
movement again was to be short-lived. By September
Trey's challenging bellows began to boom through the
length and breadth of the Nature Reserve. The Farthing Wood community, like all the other inhabitants,
listened and marvelled at their power. And they
wondered. They wondered if there would be any
answering challenges. They recalled the other stags'
responses to their suggestions that Trey wanted to
drive them out and most of the animals were not very
hopeful.

However, as autumn advanced, there *were* other calls
and challenges. Other stags roared because it was in
their nature to do so at this time. If a challenge was
offered them, they had to take it up. Now Trey came
into his own. His calls were defiant, scathing, dis-
missive of any competitor. His were roars of confidence
and supremacy. And, pretty soon, the crash of tangling
antlers marked the beginning – and end – of the stags'
rivalries. Those bold enough to respond to Trey's
taunts became acquainted with his massive strength
and force. None fought for long. Even as they locked
antlers they were pressed backwards, pushed aside,
tumbled, glad to wrench themselves free and be chased
far away from the proximity of the hinds. The

dominance that Trey had threatened and of which he had long boasted was confirmed. The hinds were his for the taking. He was a royal stag.

The Park fell quiet again. The mists of early autumn rose in the evening and in the still air the Reserve was shrouded secretively. An atmosphere of expectancy pervaded the whole area as if it were on edge, waiting for something to happen. . . .

Trey paced his domain in lordly manner. White Deer Park was his kingdom and the inhabitants his subjects. He really believed all were under his rule and he meant to have none stepping out of line. He hadn't the sense to realize that the birds who nested in the Park were as free of his decrees as the air they flew in. As for the animals of Farthing Wood, they were free in another sense. They had freedom of spirit and no creature, not the Great Cat who had terrorized the Reserve, nor even Man himself, had ever managed to break that. And, as White Deer Park held its breath, it was to be Nature who would demonstrate to all her creatures the real meaning of dominion.

13

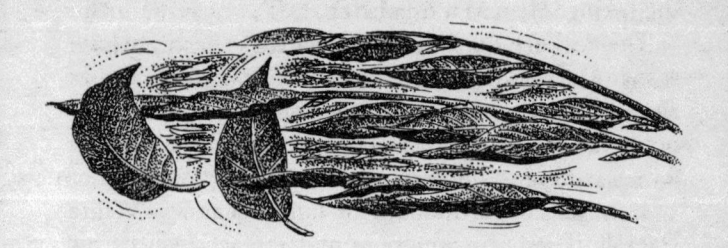

The Hurricane

Tawny Owl was trapped in Farthinghurst. He was unable to stir from the protection of the Great Beech that had, through force of circumstances, become his permanent home. His movements were restricted to an awkward shuffle along the branch he used as a perch. Weighed down by his cement shackles he couldn't fly and it was as much as he dared do to put one foot in front of the other as he waddled miserably along the branch and back again. Even those exercises had to be rationed as he was constantly afraid of toppling over and plunging to the ground. And that really would have been the end of him. But there was one blessing for poor Owl and her name was Holly. The female owl may have led him a bit of a dance at the outset, and indeed had unwittingly brought about his present dreadful situation, but since then she had more than made up for it. All through the remainder of that

summer she hunted and caught food for both of them.
She never questioned the necessity for this, nor did she
complain about the labour of it. Tawny Owl in his
misery was not always as appreciative as he might have
been. And this was because in his heart of hearts he
blamed her for his misfortune.

'I don't feel like a bird any longer,' he would
complain to her. 'A bird who can't use his wings is no
more than a – a freak!'

Holly tried to comfort him. He was always most
miserable when the weather had been dry for a long
spell. Since he couldn't leave the tree to drink from a
pool or puddle, he had to rely on catching raindrops or
dew as it dripped from the leaves of the beech. His
thirst was rarely satisfied adequately and he suffered a
great deal.

'My body's drying up,' he would moan. 'I should be
stuffed and put in a glass box.'

'There will be more rain in the autumn,' Holly would
say soothingly. Sometimes she gathered earthworms
for him as the moistness of their bodies helped to keep
him lubricated.

Tawny Owl had given up all hope of ever seeing
White Deer Park again. The ironic situation might
have amused a more cheerful creature than he. For he
had found his mate, yet was unable to return home with
her in triumph. To Owl the bitterest irony of all was
that he alone of all the Farthing Wood party who had
travelled to the Nature Reserve had actually found a
mate from Farthing Wood itself. All the others who had
paired long before had found theirs in White Deer
Park. Even Fox had found his Vixen during the

journey. And Tawny Owl, after the taunts he had received, was beside himself with exasperation that he wasn't able to boast about this to his friends. He longed to triumph over them.

Holly had tried to remove some of the cement from his wings by pecking and tearing at it, but this had proved very painful for him and when he had attempted to do this to his feet the discomfort was so intense he had to give up. Filled with anguish, Tawny Owl had eked out his existence from day to day and week to week with only Holly's companionship to comfort him.

By early autumn one problem at least was alleviated. There were frequent outbursts of heavy rain allowing plenty of water to drip from the tree. There was so much water in fact, that Tawny Owl was often unpleasantly wet. There was nowhere he could take shelter and he yearned for a hollow oak and wings that could carry him there. As time went on he became more and more disconsolate.

'Why bother to bring food for me?' he said to Holly one evening. 'You're only prolonging the agony. I might as well starve and get it over with.'

'That's no way to talk,' she told him. 'Things are bound to get better eventually.'

'Oh yes? And how will they?' he demanded. 'Am I suddenly going to shed these old wings and grow some new ones, like Adder sloughing off his skin?'

Holly had no answer. She simply wished to cheer him up. It was becoming increasingly difficult to do so.

While she was hunting, Tawny Owl used to shuffle up and down the branch that had become his prison.

He ceased to be so careful with the way he placed his feet. 'What difference would it make if I did fall?' he would mutter to himself. 'It would be an end to this misery.' But somehow he never did tumble off and, despite his words, he still preserved deep inside a faint hope that one day, some way, he and Holly would enter White Deer Park together.

The periods of rain increased in length and intensity, exceeding even those during the wet spring. Underneath the beech the ground was sodden. Pools of water appeared in the gardens nearby. The soil couldn't absorb them. The pavements and roads of the Farthinghurst estate streamed with water. Tawny Owl, hunched and shivering, wondered how much more he would have to bear. Holly found the mice were thin on the ground.

'Better try your luck at fishing,' Tawny Owl joked feebly. 'It would be more suitable.'

Holly began to catch more small birds and sometimes insects. She was very adaptable. During the day she sheltered elsewhere from the incessant rain. But at dusk she faithfully returned to Tawny Owl, and during the dark hours she kept him supplied with a share of her catch.

One night, after the two birds had eaten frugally, Holly kept flitting from one branch to another restlessly. She couldn't keep still.

'What's the matter with you?' Tawny Owl asked her testily.

'I feel ill at ease,' she replied.

'Why?'

'I don't know. There's something. . . . Something's going to happen,' she finished.

Her unease eventually communicated itself to Tawny Owl. And there *was* something in the atmosphere. It was charged with a kind of menace. They noticed other birds – starlings and songbirds and suchlike who would normally be safely roosting – stirring from their sites and calling and moving about in a jittery way. The gregarious starlings bunched together as if for reassurance. But it didn't help them to settle and they wheeled about, coming to rest around the roof-tops, then taking off again uncertainly. Sparrows chattered nervously. Small nocturnal mammals scuttled for cover deep inside their bolt-holes. They sensed a great danger was hovering and they instinctively tried to bury themselves away.

It began as a breeze that rustled the vegetation. It was a steady rustling that made the leaves and twigs of the Great Beech quiver. The owls listened. The breeze didn't die away, then return in fits and starts like the usual night breezes to which they were so accustomed. It persisted, as if it were toying with a few ideas before really making its mind up. Then it stiffened, growing rapidly in strength until, with a sudden explosion of force, it roared with a malevolent snarling anger. The beech tree rocked and shuddered. Holly fluttered to a new perch. Tawny Owl could only cling on grimly. But the wind hadn't yet reached its full fury. It expanded into a whirling, devastating violence that battered everything in its path, contemptuous of any resistance. The noise of it was terrifying – a high strident howl that every so often rose to a scream as a gust of un-

precedented power tore at the landscape. There had never been anything quite like it before. It was a wind of hurricane force.

The human population of Farthinghurst awoke in darkness as their homes buckled and shuddered. Glass shattered, tiles crashed; fencing, sheds and outhouses were ripped to pieces. Chimneys toppled, roofs caved in and some old or badly constructed buildings collapsed entirely. Everywhere, through the roars and shrieks of the wind, was the sound of destruction. Human ingenuity counted for nothing in the face of this onslaught. Man-made things were as vulnerable as those of Nature's making, rooted in the soil. All life, from the lowliest insect to human beings themselves, were reduced to the same insignificant level before such elemental ferocity. Each could only cower helplessly while it raged.

In the early hours of the morning the storm reached its height. Animal cries of panic were drowned by the deafening roar. Every building rattled and vibrated. Broken materials were bowled along or hurled through the air like pieces of paper. Small plants were flattened. Saplings whip-lashed demonically. Only bushes and shrubs with tightly-knit masses of twigs and leaves could partially withstand the blast. Into their midst burrowed countless terrified birds. In Farthinghurst there were no large trees remaining save the Great Beech. The beech bore the full brunt of the storm's force. Its great branches with their heavy load of foliage bent and groaned and cracked beneath the weight. The roots, loosened by days of rain that had drenched the ground deep down, began to lose their grip. As the tree

swayed and shifted, then leant before the assault, Holly abandoned it altogether. She was too frightened to think about anything except her own preservation. She knew the tree was no longer safe. As she left her perch she was caught up in the storm's cruel grasp and tossed like a speck through the air. Her wings spread, she was driven along at tremendous speed until finally she was dashed against a tall hedge. Shaken but otherwise unhurt, she pushed herself into the hedge's denseness like any tiny wren or tit.

Tawny Owl, talons locked as best they could on the splintering branch, waited for the end. The great tree which had withstood scores of lesser storms without damage seemed to heave a last great sigh. Then slowly it gave way. It was as if a giant hand had been plunged into the beech's glossy green hair and was pulling and tugging at it until the whole body underneath lost its balance. The tree toppled, the roots torn from the earth and, with a mighty crash, the last survivor of Farthing Wood prostrated itself on the soil that had nourished it for so long. Tawny Owl was hurled to the ground, yet the force of the wind blew him away from the colossal weight of the beech. As his body struck the soft earth the breath was driven from his lungs. But the brittle cement that had trapped his wings and talons was shivered into pieces. Bruised and gasping for air, it was some time before the bird realized he was free. He lay like a piece of rubbish himself amongst the miscellaneous debris scattered by the hurricane. At last he stirred and instinctively struggled to his feet, flapping his wings as he did so. His shackles had been unloosed. He found he could fly once more. Yet, ironically, flight

now would put him into greater peril than before. He scurried for shelter, bumbling into a small conical cypress that grew in a corner of one of the neighbouring gardens.

Towards daylight the hurricane passed, leaving a scene of destruction in its wake. There was damage everywhere and the countryside round about was changed forever.

Thus the last vestige of Farthing Wood was finally obliterated from the map. Now the Wood only lived in the memory of those who had known it.

14

Dependency

Tawny Owl's first thought, as he nestled amid the thick feathery foliage of the cypress, was for his friends in White Deer Park. He wondered how they had fared during the great storm. Now he knew he could fly back to them, he was eager to begin the return journey and this led him to his second thought which was for Holly. He was glad she had left the Great Beech in time, and could only hope she had managed to find safe shelter somewhere. The wind gradually eased and Tawny Owl looked out through the greyish light at a bruised and battered world. The beech lay motionless along the ground like a slaughtered Goliath. Only the dead leaves on its boughs rustled in the strong air currents that were the aftermath of the hurricane. People were already out of doors, surveying the damage to their property and their neighbours'. Tawny Owl decided to quit his refuge.

He flew up and away and began to call for Holly from the wing. Fragments of cement still clung to his plumage and talons but he was oblivious to them. Soon his cries were answered and he saw Holly emerge from her hedge and fly up to meet him. They were both filled with relief to see that the other had survived. Holly began to question Owl about his miraculous return to flight.

'I have the storm to thank for that,' he told her, 'but there's no time to explain now. We mustn't loiter here any longer. We have a journey to make. Follow me.'

Holly willingly tucked herself into his slipstream and they flew away from Farthinghurst and its shocked and dazed human occupants. Tawny Owl led the way back to the countryside, high across the roads and the marsh towards the place where he had conversed with the squirrels. Everywhere there were changes. Everywhere trees were down; others leant at crazy angles against sturdier neighbours; others again had remained upright but with gaping wounds where huge branches had been ripped off by the butchery of the storm. Tawny Owl couldn't recognize the tree where the squirrels had had their home. It may have survived; it may have fallen. It was impossible to tell. He wondered how much White Deer Park would be altered.

The birds continued to fly throughout the early part of the morning. Tawny Owl wanted to press on while there were not too many humans around. Their numbers were increasing all the time as the morning grew lighter. Tawny Owl knew he and Holly would have to hide themselves away before too long. He was able to steer them towards the orchards, despite the

changed aspect of the terrain. Many fruit trees had
been uprooted or damaged. The two owls sailed
overhead. Neither passed a word to the other. Tawny
Owl needed to concentrate on navigating their route.
He was searching for Rookery Copse. Holly was
content to be led for the moment. She had no regrets
about leaving Farthinghurst and considered they had
both been very fortunate to emerge from the ordeal of
the storm without mishap.

The first clue Tawny Owl had that they were near
the copse was in the sky itself. Ahead of them in the
distance a dark cloud of uncertain shape moved
erratically, now in one direction, now another. It didn't
take Owl long to realize that the cloud was made up of
birds. They were rooks, dispossessed and disorientated
by the events of the night. They wheeled about
uncertainly, crying their harsh cries of distress and
lament. And soon Tawny Owl saw what was left of the
copse. At least half the trees in which the rooks had
faithfully built their nests season after season were
flattened. The old regular outline of the group of tall
trees was punctured by great gaps where the storm had
wrought its work. The rooks were in turmoil. Their
world was turned inside out. Some of them from the
living cloud landed briefly on a branch here and there
but took off again almost immediately. The others
would follow suit and this descending and ascending
and wheeling about went on continuously. The rooks
were caught up in a mass panic where none of them
knew what had happened or what to do. Rookery
Copse had become something different and it was
something they didn't understand.

Mindful of his reception there on his previous journey Tawny Owl decided to leave the troubled birds to their own devices. Despite his rough treatment by the rooks he felt a tremendous sympathy for them. All over the countryside, he now realized, wild creatures would find their homes destroyed; their territories strange and unfamiliar. Now, more than ever, he longed to reach White Deer Park again. He was afraid of what he would find but he knew he wouldn't be able to rest properly until he saw it with his own eyes. A little further on he flew down and landed in a dead elm which, killed long ago by disease, had with a strange irony withstood the blast of the hurricane when so many healthy trees had succumbed. Holly perched beside him.

Tawny Owl spoke first. 'You may as well discount what I've told you about White Deer Park,' he said, 'because it will probably look quite different now.'

'Yes,' Holly agreed. 'I've been thinking the same thing. Unless the storm missed it?'

'I don't think we can depend on that,' he answered morosely. 'How I wish we could!'

'It'll still be a Nature Reserve, though. Won't it?'

'Oh yes. *That* won't have changed.' Tawny Owl was about to add that his friends would still be there, too, but he choked the words back. How did he know if they would be? He had been away a long time. And the hurricane must have claimed lives wherever it had passed. 'I'm eager to get back just as quickly as we can,' he told Holly instead. 'But it's a long journey and we have to be wary, because there are bound to be many humans about. I think we should look for a place to

roost soon; then we can continue when it's dusk.'

'I'm not a bit tired,' Holly informed him. 'We can fly for as long as you like. I leave it to you as the senior.'

'How very diplomatic,' Tawny Owl remarked wryly. 'Well, come on, then.'

The two birds left the bleached skeleton of the elm tree and continued their flight. Tawny Owl was bemused by the tortured features of the scenery. He felt as if he were flying over a new land. He tried to ignore the devastation beneath them. He knew they were on the correct course for the river: he had been able to gauge their direction from the ruined copse. But every so often the cries of wounded or homeless beasts and birds could be heard as the owls travelled past. Sometimes they saw bodies crushed by the force of the storm, lying where they had been hurled. He saw a badger who had been trapped by a fallen tree. And birds – birds everywhere bemoaning their lost nest sites and broken communities. It was then that Tawny Owl feared for his friends and wished fervently that he had never left them. For, whatever horrors they had suffered during the storm, at least he would have been there to share them. That was how it had always been. They had shared all kinds of experiences and hardships and had been able to help each other through their difficulties.

Holly guessed the content of his thoughts every time they became witness to some fresh tragedy. She had no-one to mourn for; she had lived a generally solitary life. Companionship was a new enjoyment for her and the more she appreciated it the more she understood Owl's concern.

'Look out for a likely spot to rest,' Tawny Owl called behind him. He knew the river was not too distant. They were flying over meadows.

Holly scanned the area. There were few trees of any size. But she spied an elder tree which, though not tall, was festooned with a thick cladding of ivy. She thought this might suit their purpose. She flew alongside Tawny Owl. 'Down there,' she indicated. 'There's plenty of cover.'

'Perfect,' he said and they skimmed down together.

There was plenty of space amongst the thick tendrils of the creeper to hide themselves, and they were confident they would be secure. Not that there were any humans in the vicinity. It wasn't a time for people to be out sauntering and taking the air. There were far more important and pressing concerns that day for everyone.

Tawny Owl could hardly wait for dusk. For the first time in many weeks he was looking forward to hunting for himself. Holly had fed him like an invalid for so long he had come to feel quite subservient. He dared not tell her that after their long flight he was well-nigh exhausted. His wing muscles ached abominably. But he told himself he would be more than ready after a good rest. So Holly's next words came as a shock.

'I'll carry on being the provider,' she announced. 'You don't need to pretend any longer to be a bird of prey.' It sounded as if she thought he had become actually incapable of hunting.

'But – but –' he spluttered, so taken aback he couldn't find an adequate response.

'No "buts",' she said firmly. 'I can easily catch

enough for both of us, as you know. You need all the rest you can get. It's a wonder a bird of your age has come through such experiences as you've had at all.'

Tawny Owl was dumbfounded. He couldn't conceive that Holly spoke from kindness and suspected she was insulting him. This was not the sort of association he had wanted to impress his friends with. Why, it was worse than solitude.

'Look here,' he finally managed to say, 'I'm not quite in my dotage yet, you know. I'll admit I'm very tired. It'd be surprising if I weren't. But my hunting days aren't over by any means.'

Holly was amused. 'It's all *right*,' she insisted. 'I understand how you feel. It must have been a humbling episode for you in the beech when you couldn't fly. But it really doesn't matter. I don't mind in the least. I'm younger, fitter, and I can do all that you used to do.'

Used to do! What did she think he was – senile! Oh no. He'd show her. But he smothered his indignation for the present. He decided actions were more telling than words. However, in a short while, both he and Holly were asleep.

Holly awoke first and left the mantle of ivy without disturbing Tawny Owl. It was quite dark and she spread her wings and began to search the meadows. A light shower of rain was falling. Eventually the raindrops which penetrated the ivy aroused Tawny Owl. Realizing his companion was absent he pushed his head out of the creeper and looked for her. At that moment Holly was swooping on a shrew. Tawny Owl saw her pounce and he struggled free of the ivy tendrils

and launched himself into flight. He wanted to get clear away before the female owl might return with her kill.

He was surprised to find his flight muscles were painfully stiff. After such a long period of disuse, he had overtaxed them on the first lap of the journey from Farthinghurst. But he bore the aches and soreness with determination. He had to make it clear to Holly at the outset that he could resume catching his own food. The trouble was, his whole body felt incredibly tired and feeble. It was as much as he could do to flap his wings occasionally, merely to keep airborne. So how was he to hunt? He had no speed now and no agility to rely on. Even if he saw some likely prey he doubted if he could direct his exhausted body with sufficient accuracy to make a kill.

'This is absurd,' he spluttered, angry with his physical shortcomings. 'Am I to remain dependent on another? Unthinkable, unthinkable. . . .'

He had to try. Fortunately his eyesight had lost none of its sharpness. He flew over some fields well away from where he had seen Holly pounce. There was no dearth of small creatures running on their habitual paths through the grass-stems. He looked hard for an animal that might be a little slower, a little older, a little more accessible. The diminutive creatures scurried about busily, pausing occasionally to sit on their hind legs to nibble at a tasty morsel or to look and listen for danger. Tawny Owl flew up and down, unable to decide on his target. His wing-beats became more and more laboured and gradually decreased in frequency. His body dropped steadily nearer ground level. And the nearer to the ground he became the more detectable

was his presence to the voles, shrews or wood mice he was hoping to catch. He soon realized that, unless he selected his quarry quickly, he would lose all opportunity of a capture. Most of the animals were running for the shelter of their tunnels. He did see one, however, who was very absorbed with some particularly appetizing seeds. Tawny Owl lowered his talons and plunged towards it. The wood mouse seemed unaware of his approach. Tawny Owl struck it, grasped it in his beak and prepared to take off again. The mouse was dead. He had made his kill and he was filled with a mixture of pride and relief. But now he found his wing muscles were too stiff for him to achieve lift-off. He needed to beat his wings quickly to get airborne, using what air currents were available to do the rest. But the muscles were so tired and sore that he could only manage a couple of quick beats and these were no use at all. Tawny Owl realized he couldn't get off the ground.

He dropped the mouse. 'Now I really am stuck,' he murmured to himself. 'I can't even get back to the roost.' He began fatalistically to tear at the mouse carcass. At least he could eat where he was. Then all at once he stopped. He knew Holly would eventually come looking for him. He would need a longer rest before he could fly again. And it was important to him that Holly should see that, although he had over-stretched himself, he had not entirely wasted his efforts. So he left the rest of his kill untouched as a sort of trophy to display to her.

Holly was a long time making her appearance and Tawny Owl had grown horribly hungry in the meantime. So when he finally saw her gliding above he called

to her in all humility, desperate to break his fast: 'Here! Here I am!'

Holly's scolding began before she reached the ground. 'What did I say to you, you silly old bird? I've been searching for you for ages. I've caught enough mice to feed a brood, let alone just the two of us.' She landed and noticed Owl's catch. 'And is that all you exhausted yourself for? Some other predator's leavings? Now what is to happen? Are you going to stay here in the open in broad daylight?'

'I caught this, I caught it myself,' Tawny Owl protested feebly. But it was no use. Holly wasn't listening.

'I'll go back and fetch some better food for you,' she told him. 'You'd better eat heartily and build up some strength. You'll need to exercise those wings before much longer or I don't know what might happen to you. And in future,' she nagged him, 'you want to pay more attention to what I say. You've made a real fool of yourself – and at your age too! I shall have to keep watch over you now, just as if you were a helpless chick.'

She flew away, back to the elder tree, to fetch the food. She didn't wait for a reply. Tawny Owl groaned. By trying to assert himself he had ended up becoming more dependent than ever.

No Contest

In White Deer Park, in the last few days before the hurricane reached it, Trey had followed up his triumph by establishing his rule over the whole herd. The other males largely kept their distance but the dominant stag couldn't be in all places at all times and so they were able on occasion to rejoin the hinds. The females were quite content with the situation. When Trey was around, which he generally was, each seemed happy enough to be part of his harem. He was the finest of the stags by far and they recognized his superiority.

The other animals often saw him leading the herd to drink at the Pond. The hinds grouped around its fringes and drank together whilst Trey kept watch for any possible interference. At these times it was not advisable for any creature of the Park to approach too closely. Trey would exercise his self-appointed authority over the Nature Reserve by chasing it away.

He was very jealous of his herd's rights to have exclusive and uninterrupted use of the water. The other inhabitants wondered how much further he would attempt to rule their lives when his present absorption with the hinds was over. He had given them plenty of indications and they tired of seeing him stepping regally along the boundaries of the Park, his head with its heavy burden of antlers held high, and his haughty glance sweeping over the length and breadth of the Reserve.

'It seems his vanity knows no limits,' Fox remarked when the animals were gathered one evening. 'But his legs bear the toothmarks of Plucky and Badger. He's not unassailable.'

'Let sleeping dogs lie,' Vixen counselled. 'He doesn't impose himself on us at present.'

'We've always been free to visit the Pond whenever we needed,' Fox replied. 'All of us. These days, Toad's the only one who's allowed free rein because he's small enough to be overlooked.'

'If only Trey would go and drink from the stream,' Weasel growled, 'it would solve all our problems.'

'It's hardly likely,' said Friendly, 'when every other creature in the Reserve avoids it.'

Adder was bored with this continuous topic of water, perhaps because as a reptile he didn't understand the mammals' preoccupation with the need to drink. 'There's plenty of rainwater lying around now,' he hissed. 'Enough for all the animals in the Park to make use of. Why this constant obsession with the Pond?'

'It's symbolic,' Weasel told him.

'Symbolic of what? Only of unending chatter as far as I can see,' the snake contended.

'It's symbolic,' Weasel intoned slowly, 'of the way our freedom to roam has been blighted by this stag.'

'Oh – oh. Round and round we go,' Adder rasped and coiled himself up as he spoke, so that the others weren't sure if he was being sarcastic or commenting on his own activity.

Weasel, however, was goaded. 'He's right, you know,' he said. 'I can remember days not so very long ago when we did more than just talk.'

'Yes,' said Fox. 'We were young and vigorous then.'

Weasel drew himself up. 'We're still the Animals of Farthing Wood,' he said proudly. 'We've got the better of many a foe in our time. And you said yourself Trey isn't unassailable.'

Fox was interested. 'What do you propose, Weasel?'

'I propose,' he answered, 'that we stand up for ourselves, just like Plucky and poor old Badger.'

'We don't want to meddle with Trey,' Vixen cautioned. 'He's a youthful beast and a strong one and all our wisdom and guile may count for nothing against that.'

'I'm not advocating meddling with him,' Weasel assured her. 'I don't want anything to do with him, personally. But if he continues to meddle with our liberty within the Reserve then, as I say, I think we should stand up for ourselves.'

'Bravo, Weasel. Well said,' Friendly commented. 'Father, why don't you lead our party down to the Pond to drink, just as the stag does with his herd?'

'That's provocation,' said Charmer.

'That's right,' agreed Friendly happily. 'Well, Father?'

'All right,' said Fox. 'It's worth a try. We'll browbeat him. He can't intimidate a whole group of us. He'll have to concede. And, once he's done so, perhaps we shall be allowed to carry on our lives without this constant fear of hindrance.' There was the old authority and determination in his voice.

'We can't travel around in a big group all the time,' Leveret pointed out. 'Supposing he tries to pick us off one by one?'

'We've no reason to fear that,' Fox encouraged him. 'He's shown no sign of it so far. I don't think he's vindictive enough.'

'Nor sufficiently clever,' Weasel added.

'Well, no time like the present,' Fox said confidently. 'I feel two seasons younger already. Who's coming?'

There was a general chorus of support.

'Good,' Fox said. 'Only Badger must stay behind. And Mossy can keep him company.' He turned to the mole. 'Will you make certain he remains in his set?'

Mossy assured him he would.

'Apart from you, then, it's the whole party?' Fox summed up.

'Except for Tawny Owl,' Whistler reminded him.

'I begin to believe we shall never see old Owl again,' Fox said sorrowfully. 'I'm afraid something must have happened to him.'

The younger foxes looked uncomfortable as they always did when Tawny Owl was mentioned.

Fox noted their discomfort and relieved them of it. 'Follow me, then, all of you,' he cried and, quitting the Hollow, set off in the direction of the Pond.

Beside himself and Vixen, only Weasel, Whistler and Leveret were also of the old Farthing Wood contingent. Toad was already at the Pond, Tawny Owl was absent, Badger too feeble, while Adder showed no sign of wishing to uncoil himself. So it was just as well there was a good number of Fox's and Vixen's descendants to bolster the throng: Friendly and Charmer, Pace, Rusty, Whisper and Plucky. Mossy hurried to Badger's set to acquaint him with the animals' move. His short legs were not any swifter overland than his father, Mole's, had been. So an appreciable period had elapsed before he dug himself into the familiar darkness of his labyrinth of tunnels that connected with Badger's home. The old animal took the news badly. He was hurt.

'So they don't think I can contribute anything any more?' he mumbled. 'How could Fox be so unkind?'

'No, no, he meant to be quite the opposite,' Mossy asserted. 'He wants to protect you, I'm sure.'

'Protect me? Nobody needs to protect me,' Badger declared. 'I can look after myself.' He began to lumber up the tunnel.

'Where are you going?' cried Mossy in alarm. 'Fox is relying on me to –'

'To keep me out of it? Oh no. That'll be the day,' Badger growled. 'Where the Farthing Wood animals go, *I* go.' He was quite obstinate. He turned his back on Mossy and headed for the exit. Mossy was powerless to stop him.

'Oh dear,' said the mole. 'I've done this all wrong. Whatever will Fox think of me if Badger's hurt?'

But Badger had no intention of getting hurt. He'd already survived one brush with the royal stag, as well as a near poisoning and he didn't think Providence was against him. As he passed the Hollow he saw Adder enjoying his solitude.

'What are you doing here at such a time?' he demanded.

'Being more sensible than you, by the look of it,' the snake answered, quite unruffled.

'Come on, Adder. We're all together in this.'

'Oh no, Badger. Quite the reverse. We're *not*.'

'Have you forgotten the Oath?'

'No, of course not. But whatever happens at the Pond would have happened anyway long before I could have got there.'

Badger saw the sense of this and realized the same could apply to himself. 'All right,' he said. 'Well, I'll see you later.'

'I certainly hope so,' Adder replied. 'But if you must go, go carefully, Badger. There's something in the air tonight.'

Badger's senses, blunted by age, had not detected anything unusual, besides which his thoughts were thoroughly absorbed with the affront dealt him by his friends. He stumbled along on the trail of the other animals, determined to play his part in the Pond scenario.

The night was well on when the others brought themselves within sight of the expanse of water. As if Fate had ordained it, the first thing they noticed was that the Pond was ringed by the ghostly white blur of deer jostling for positions to drink. Fox's eyes searched

for Trey's figure. And there he was, a short distance
from his minions, keeping watch over the area. Fox saw
the stag's head turning this way and that as he craned
his long muscular neck for intruders.

'He's there all right,' he remarked needlessly, for all
of them had seen Trey.

The animals bunched together. Whistler landed in
their midst. 'What – what do we do now?' Leveret
whispered nervously.

'We go forward, of course,' Weasel snapped. 'To
drink.'

'Yes, but we won't go blundering straight in,' Fox
qualified his answer. 'We've got to be clever about it.
The most important thing is that we stay in a tight
group.'

'There's room at the far end of the Pond for us all,'
Whistler pointed out. 'Well away from where the stag's
taken up his station.'

'No, Whistler, that's just what we don't want,' Fox
told him. 'It would be too blatant and would only
stimulate Trey into immediate action. He'd come
charging at us at once, assuming we were out to
challenge his authority.'

'But we are – aren't we, Grandfather?' Pace asked.

'There are ways, Pace, of doing these things,' Fox
told him patiently. 'An animal of Trey's size galloping
at full-tilt would scatter us irretrievably. He'd have
won his argument before we'd even begun. No, we're
going to, quite literally, fox him.'

The animals enjoyed the pun.

'How do we do that?' Whisper asked.

'By doing what he'll be least expecting,' Fox replied.

'We're going to march right up to him and confront him. He won't be quite sure how to take us.'

'Lead on then, Fox,' said Weasel. 'If anybody can pull this off, you can.'

The animals trod quietly but deliberately forwards, heading directly for the imposing figure of the royal stag. In the darkness it was a while before Trey picked them out. He began to toss his head in a threatening manner. But the collection of animals kept on coming. From the edge of the Pond, amongst some rushes, Toad watched their progress. 'It looks like a deputation,' he marvelled to himself.

'What's this?' Trey bellowed to the approaching group.

Fox waited until they were near enough for him to answer without being required to raise his voice. 'It's a drinking party,' he replied quietly.

Trey's eyes roved over the animals appraisingly. He wasn't sure why they had gathered together but he didn't see anything to test his strength. 'Where are you heading?' he enquired, though he knew the answer.

'To the water,' Fox said.

'There are many suitable puddles all around you,' Trey told them.

'Ah, but they're not suitable for the deer herd, it seems,' Fox said coolly.

'Of course not. The Pond's our source of water.'

'Well then, it shall be ours too,' Fox stated. 'There's plenty of room for each of us and we shan't disturb the hinds. Come on, everyone.'

The band of animals followed Fox and Vixen without a word. They passed Trey and went on

towards their destination. For some moments the stag stood stock still. The presumption of the motley group took his breath away.

As they reached the Pond Fox whispered: 'Get in amongst the hinds.'

The animals did as they were bid and pushed themselves between the bulky bodies of the deer as they drank. Some of them got underneath the long legs of the females and in that manner threaded their way through to the water. By this time Trey had identified Plucky, the young fox who had dared to intervene when he had been teaching the old badger a lesson. The sight of this particular animal boldly defying his presence and actually mingling with his hinds galvanized the stag into action. He dashed across the short distance to the Pond, intent on proving his mastery once and for all. But all the animals in Fox's band had become so intertwined with the female deer that Trey was unable to attack. He snorted furiously and galloped up and down looking for an opening.

The hinds had made no objection at all to the smaller animals' presence at the waterside. They were quite used to the existence of foxes and other creatures in the Park. They had always been around and they had no fear of them. Indeed Fox and Vixen, Badger and Tawny Owl were well-known to them and held in high esteem. Trey was unique amongst all the deer in his arrogant attitude and the antipathy he aroused in the other inhabitants of the Reserve. So, while he sought angrily for one of the Farthing Wood band who might have exposed himself to attack, the female deer were

welcoming their company at the pondside and docilely engaging them in conversation.

Trey's exasperation was overwhelming. Toad watched his antics with the greatest enjoyment. 'Trust old Fox,' he chortled to himself. 'He's left the stag helpless.'

The animals were free to drink for as long as they chose. Yet many of them were not drinking at all. Their trek to the Pond to confront Trey had been a gesture of independence and the fact was that they hadn't really needed the Pond's water to quench their thirst. Led by Fox, they had been out to demonstrate that they meant to go on using it when the need *would* arise. When the stag realized that they were not drinking, his anger bubbled over. Ironically, the very thing he had been trying to prevent now incensed him the most. He knew their intention had merely been to best him. He roared at his females who were displaying every token of friendship to the other beasts.

'Cease your prattling,' Trey boomed, 'and step away!' He wanted to get at Fox himself now. He knew all about his legendary cunning and he couldn't allow Fox to make a fool of him in front of his harem. The stag was simply seething with rage. Flecks of foam flew from his lips.

The hinds turned to look. Trey pranced about, unable to keep still. Some of the other stags who also used the Pond were hovering not so far off, relishing their conqueror's discomfiture. The females were in no hurry to move. Nothing would have persuaded them to put Fox and Vixen in danger.

'Step away, I say!' Trey roared. 'Or you'll rue the

consequences!' His threats were idle. He couldn't harm his own herd.

A wind blew across the Park, a wind of ill-omen. All the animals – the hinds, the other stags, the Farthing Wood community and its younger relatives – were aware of it. They paused from their activities, raising their heads to look for its meaning. The foxes snuffled the air. Whistler flew over the Pond croaking a warning and birds clustered in the sky in nervous knots. Only Trey, obsessed as ever by his own importance, failed to notice. But his bellows and ranting were ignored.

'We need to find shelter,' said Vixen. 'There's a storm brewing.' Even as she spoke the wind began to moan in the nearest tree tops and send wide ripples chasing each other across the surface of the Pond.

Fox quickly began to round up his group, heedless of the fact that they had now to leave the protection of the clustered female deer. There was a greater danger to pay attention to. The hinds milled around uncertainly.

'Remember the place where Badger thought he was dying?' Fox asked his friends. 'We must go there now. There's no time to get back to our own homes.'

Plucky knew the way to the deserted set better than anyone. It was he who had first discovered it. He trotted off, calling over his shoulder. 'It's in this direction.'

Trey saw his opportunity. 'You've taken one chance too many this time,' he said savagely and began to charge at once, his great antlers lowered.

'Plucky! Plucky! Take care!' Vixen cried and she was only just in time.

The young fox sidestepped the stag's impetuous rush

which carried the foolish animal some distance past him, towards the rest of the group.

Fox was scornful. 'The mighty stag!' he scoffed. 'You call yourself the overlord of the Reserve. Yet you don't seem to have any regard for the danger your own herd is in.'

Now the wind was beginning to howl and strong gusts whipped at the sedges and rushes by the Pond. Trey's anger was cooled, despite himself, by the jittery behaviour of the hinds. They sensed the storm and were fretful, lacking direction.

Fox turned his back and led the animals after Plucky. One by one they entered the set, gaining comfort from each other's company. Whistler joined Toad amongst the rushes.

'No contest,' Toad remarked. 'The Pond's ours again.'

They watched Trey gathering the hinds. Presently the herd moved away from the water's edge.

'They'd be wise to stay in the open,' Whistler commented. 'I hope he has the sense not to lead them under the trees.'

The other stags moved away as Trey approached. The strength of the wind increased in power with every passing minute. In a patch of woodland, not too far distant, Badger urged his ancient limbs to greater efforts. He had travelled too far from his own set to be able to return in safety. He could think only of the alternative shelter where, unknown to him, his friends were already assembled. He was between the two and he knew he had put himself in the greatest peril.

Storm Over the Park

In the teeth of the wind the deer herd stood on the open
grassland. The other stags wandered ever closer,
desiring the reassurance brought by a mass of animals.
Trey, however, would only allow them within a certain
radius of the hinds. If they overstepped this invisible
boundary he corrected them. Some of the males lay
down. The vicious wind grabbed at their heavy antlers,
threatening to pull them over. The females milled
about uncertainly. Trey planted his feet farther apart
as he battled to withstand the full force of the wind.

The hurricane quickly reached a crescendo. It
became impossible for any of the deer to stand against
it. The hinds lay down and gritted their teeth, sheltering their youngsters as best they could. Even Trey
succumbed and now all thought of rivalries and
possession was forgotten in the maelstrom of air that
whirled across the Park. The herd, including the other

males, instinctively bunched into a tight-knit group. They listened to the crack! crack! of shattering branches from distant trees. There was a creaking, tearing, ripping cacophony, punctuated by crashes as the root systems of mature specimens in the patches of woodland were loosened from their moorings in the saturated soil and their trunks and branches hurled earthwards. One after another was destroyed. Above the boom of the trees smiting the earth like blows from a steam hammer, the screaming, shrieking wind was the dominant sound. It seemed to laugh and mock at the havoc it caused. The terrified wildlife population of the Nature Reserve cowered in their tunnels and holes or took shelter where they could. Some of them left the Park altogether for the open downland as portions of the boundary fence were torn down, leaving escape routes to the world beyond for those who were driven to take them.

In the abandoned set the community of Farthing Wood animals huddled together, almost too frightened to speak. Every tunnel, every chamber of the underground system was occupied. Fox managed to voice his thoughts to Vixen. 'I'm so thankful that Badger is safe inside his own set.'

As he said it, in that other part of the Park, Mossy dug deeper into the ground while the tempest raged and roared. He had waited for Badger's return when the wind first sprang up, thinking to return would be the old creature's first reaction in the storm. But, as time went on and the storm increased in intensity with no sign of Badger, Mossy began to fear the worst. How he rued his own action in Badger's departure. For,

innocent though it was, if he hadn't brought the message from Fox, Badger would have known nothing of the animals' expedition to the Pond and would have been quite happy staying put. So Mossy trembled for Badger so exposed to the power of the elements and longed for a miracle to preserve him. The little mole buried himself deeper and deeper to escape the terrifying noise. As he paused from his efforts, suddenly the whole labyrinth of tunnels and passages shook under the most almighty blow which reverberated underground like an earthquake. Mossy thought the world had fallen in on top of him and indeed, in some respects, his own subterranean world had done so. One of the larger trees in the wooded area where Badger had constructed his home had fallen directly on the set and smashed through the system of passages into the heart of his living quarters. Thus unwittingly Badger had saved himself by his determination to defy Fox's advice.

Yet now, with every faltering, stumbling step he took across the Park, Badger was still risking death. All around him heavy branches, snapped by the wind, were falling to the ground with their heavy loads of twigs and leaves. As he scuttled free from one dangerous spot another bough would break and bar his way. When the trees themselves began to fall he knew he must attempt to get into the open. But his progress was constantly impeded by the huge obstacles which littered every portion of the woodland.

'It looks as if I escaped being poisoned only to be flattened by an oak,' he muttered grimly. 'If that's to be

my fate I wish I'd died earlier because now I'll never know if the others survive.'

Somehow he struggled on. The horrific howl of the storm accompanied him every step of the way. Badger pulled himself over or under branches, making a circuit of the larger uprooted trees. Some of these had not been torn entirely free from the soil and still quivered as if in their death throes. At last he saw light ahead at the edge of the woodland. It was so dark under the trees that even a slight lessening of the gloom was markedly noticeable. Clouds raced at breakneck speed across the sky, obliterating the moon and stars. But as Badger – panting, exhausted, terrified – pulled himself over the last hurdle of a mass of flattened vegetation, the hurricane strength of the wind was dropping. Badger forced himself on, putting sufficient distance between himself and the horrible sound of crashing trees. Eventually he could go no further. His shaky legs gave way beneath him and he lay, quite helpless, with the storm roaring overhead. The worst of it, however, was past.

When Trey became aware that the storm's force was slackening he scrambled to his feet to survey the herd. A few metres from where the deer were gathered was a crumbled piece of fencing which had once marked the limit of the Nature Reserve. Next to it a hefty Scots Pine, not quite ripped from the earth, leant at a crazy angle and swayed threateningly with every gust of air. Trey saw the wide gap in the boundary fence and he saw the males of the White Deer herd dotted amongst his hinds. He tossed his great head, almost in defiance at the storm's diminishing power. He was once again

the royal stag, jealous of interference. The other males stirred as they saw him towering over the herd. Some of them remembered the tales of how Trey had sworn to drive them from the Park. One by one they stood up, uncertain of their next move. They were not long in noticing a ready-made exit close at hand.

Trey now decided to rid himself of their competition for good. He began to see a way of doing it, thereby fulfilling Fox's prediction, though without realizing it himself. It was growing light. The wind still buffeted the males' antlers, making it hard for them to keep their balance.

'Begone,' Trey ordered the stags. 'The danger is over. Move away from my hinds, I say.'

The males extricated themselves from the herd and wandered off a little way. Trey wasn't satisfied. They hadn't moved far enough. Something about the way the other stags still seemed to be hovering in hope near his females aroused his anger once more.

'*That's* the way, over there, through that gap!' he ordered them.

When they looked at the broken fence and back at Trey in disbelief he began to hustle them.

'I want no rivals near, do you hear? Go now of your own volition or be driven out!' And, to hasten their departure, he cantered towards them with lowered antlers.

Some of the inferior stags took him at his word and actually ran through the gap out of the Park. The hinds watched in amazement. The stouter males saw no reason why they should be forced from their home. But Trey meant to do just that. As they hesitated he singled

one out and charged at him. The animal put up no resistance. In a moment he had joined those who had already left. The remainder were not so easily cowed. They realized that if they didn't make a stand now Trey would have the Park to himself indefinitely. As he ran at them they ducked and weaved and sidestepped in any direction but the one in which he intended they should go. His temper flared. He managed to connect with one stag, butting him and bowling him over. The deer leapt up and ran for the opening. Trey scented victory. He chose another target, a particularly sturdy animal, and gave chase. The two stags went round and round, this way and that. The others looked on in suspense. Trey drove the other male close to the leaning pine. The stag stumbled over the broken fencing, was momentarily overbalanced, and a gust of wind did the rest. He went sprawling. As he fell he smashed against the pine tree which began to rock ominously. Trey, carried forward by the impetus of his charge, was unable to pull up. As the huge tree teetered Trey was underneath it. Even as he turned to avoid it the pine lost its tenuous grip on the soil and fell. It fell directly on to the royal stag, pinning him down beneath its weight. The mighty overlord of White Deer Park lay motionless. The other stag regained its feet. Then the herd mingled around Trey, looking in horror and awe at his stricken body. The males outside the Park returned to gaze at the sight. Trey looked at them helplessly through glassy eyes. His tongue protruded from his muzzle. Blood flowed from his open mouth and collected in a pool under his head.

Dawn broke over the shattered Nature Reserve.

Many trees had fallen. Many lives had been lost. In the Hollow, Adder uncoiled himself and slid away. During the passing of the storm he had not stirred a fraction.

Homeless

It was a while before the animals were sure it was safe to leave the shelter of the abandoned set. They had listened to the moan of the wind for so long that the quietness now seemed unreal and they expected the storm to return at any moment. Eventually, when it grew light, Friendly went to the end of the exit tunnel and looked out. Everywhere there was evidence of the path of the storm. Around the Pond the rushes and sedges were flattened as if by some mighty haymaker. At one end a birch tree had fallen into the water, its branches and leaves trailing under the surface. Some of the Edible Frogs were sitting on its trunk. Friendly wondered how many more were squashed underneath. As he looked further afield he could see a wooded area thinned out by the hurricane's savagery. He hurried back to the others.

'It's – it's changed,' he whispered. 'Everything's changed.'

Now all the animals wanted to look. They left the abandoned set and sat in a group around the entrance hole, not quite believing what they saw. The older animals were reminded of their past.

'It's just like Farthing Wood when the bulldozers came,' Fox said sorrowfully.

Weasel tried to raise their spirits. 'But there are many trees still standing or – or – leaning. . . .'

Fox recognized a new danger here. 'We must avoid the wooded areas as much as we can now. Listen! I can hear them creaking.'

Leveret, whose home was in the open grassland, said: 'What about your homes under the trees?' Most of the foxes' earths were amongst the woodland.

'We may have to make new ones,' Vixen answered him. She shook her coat. 'Let's go and see if Toad's all right.'

The animals went to the Pond's edge, calling his name. Toad came crawling eagerly from his rushy bower.

'What a night,' he croaked. 'I thought it would never end. Whistler kept me company. But he's gone now to examine his nest. Fox,' he enthused, 'it's marvellous to see you all safe. I watched you with the stag. How cool you were!'

'Hm. No sign of the deer,' Fox answered. 'I wonder how they fared?'

'The main thing is, *we've* all come through,' Toad said happily. 'But where's Badger?'

'No need to worry about him. He's safe in his own set,' said Friendly.

The animals realized that their priority now was to see how their own homes had suffered.

'Remember, everyone,' said Fox, 'the trees! Tread carefully and avoid creakers. Good luck.'

They left Toad by the water and went their own ways. It was Fox and Vixen who found Badger. The old animal had rallied with the daylight and was creeping about, not sure whether to continue on to the Pond or retrace his steps. The sight of the pair of foxes put new heart into him. He was eager to know whether they had encountered Trey, but first he had to explain to his astounded friends what he was doing there.

'Foolish but loyal creature,' Fox commented warmly. 'And there we were, all of us, congratulating ourselves you were out of harm's way.'

'I did take a bit of a risk,' said Badger. 'Mole tried to prevent me, but I thought you might need me. Did Trey make an appearance?'

'Oh yes, he was there. But we soon dealt with him.' Fox described their tactics. 'I don't think he'll be bothering us so much from now on.' He didn't know how right he was.

'Are you heading homeward?' Badger asked.

'Yes.'

'Will you walk with me? It may take you a little longer because we have to avoid that stretch of woodland – it's full of debris – and, well, I may be rather slow.'

'Of course we'll go with you,' Vixen answered. 'What an unnecessary question. We'll see you to your set.'

'No need to come all the way,' Badger said, keen to

retain some semblance of independence. 'Just as far as your own earth.'

They set off. Badger was indeed slow but the foxes were patient and made no attempt to hurry him. As they progressed they constantly saw new areas of destruction. They discussed the changed aspect of the Park. At one point they spied the Warden in the distance doing his own round of damage inspection. The sight of the man always inspired confidence amongst the animals.

'He'll make it all right again,' Badger murmured trustfully.

'It'll never be quite the same,' Fox contended. 'Remember Farthing Wood. When trees are down. . . .' He left the rest unsaid.

'It's still the Park,' Vixen commented. 'The animals' Park. No human dwellings. We'll get used to the changes.'

As they travelled Whistler was flying to meet them. He had seen Trey's body from the air and so, for the second time in a season, the heron was the first to bring news of the fall of a dominant stag. He scoured the Reserve for a sight of Fox. Presently the three animals heard the well-loved whistle of the bird's punctured wing. With a few mighty flaps Whistler came to rest on the ground a metre or two ahead of them.

'Astonishing news,' he greeted them. 'Our tormentor is a victim of the storm. He's lying by the perimeter fence, crushed under a tree.'

'Trey?'

'None other.'

'Is he dead?'

'Not dead, but utterly helpless.'

Fox and Vixen exchanged glances. They were stunned. Yet they had mixed feelings about the news. Badger, however, had a look of satisfaction.

'The stag has made his last patrol of the Park,' he remarked. 'So that's one of our troubles removed.'

Fox looked doubtful. 'Where is the rest of the herd?' he asked Whistler.

'Milling around the fallen leader,' the heron replied. 'They seem to be in some sort of confusion.'

'Well, it's no concern of ours,' said Badger. 'We have other matters to think about. We don't even know if our homes have survived.'

'Whistler, forgive us,' said Vixen. 'Your news drove every other thought out of our heads. Did your nest survive?'

'No. It's wrecked,' he replied. 'But nests are easy to replace. Not so the trees that supported them.' He left them then to give the news to others of the community.

'Many homes must have been destroyed,' said Badger. 'The birds and squirrels will have fared worst.'

'I – I wonder if Owl survived,' Fox murmured. 'I don't think we'll ever know. Oh, I do yearn to see that poor pompous old bird!'

'Me too,' Badger echoed. 'It just hasn't been the same without him. Even if he is so quarrelsome at times.'

Fox was amused in a sad kind of way. 'I bet Weasel misses their arguments,' he ventured to say.

The sun was well up when they approached Fox and Vixen's earth. They went very warily under the trees. But the foxes were fortunate. Their earth was situated

in a copse of immature trees which, with their more flexible trunks and branches, had survived very much better than many of the larger specimens.

'We're lucky,' Fox said to Vixen. 'May you have the same luck, Badger, old friend.'

'We shall see, we shall see,' Badger replied as he trudged on, leaving them behind. He crossed the open space between the foxes' copse and the sloping piece of young beech woodland within which his set had been excavated. He soon noticed that, just as elsewhere in the Park, this patch of woodland was altered beyond recognition. Many well-grown trees had met their deaths during the hurricane's brief but imperious rule. They lay, spanning the ground amongst the litter of branches and brushwood. Badger paused to listen for the tell-tale creaks that might herald the imminent fall of those weakened trees not yet entirely prised from the ground. There was nothing immediately noticeable. He loped his way anxiously around the obstructions in his path. He was not far now from his set. A little farther – and he stopped dead in his tracks. He stared at the crater in the ground which was all that was left of his home, crushed beneath the impact of the fallen tree. Badger was rooted to the spot.

'My – my home,' he whispered. 'I have no home.' Over and over again he muttered the last words. Then, all at once the realization came to him of his narrow escape. He knew that there was no question but that he would have been killed had he stayed where Fox had wanted him to. He recognized the irony of Fox's parting wish. For, despite his new homelessness, Badger *was* lucky. Very lucky indeed. He continued to

gaze at the smashed set, wondering how or where he would be able to construct a new home at his advanced age. The thought was not in his mind for long. He had suddenly remembered Mossy.

'Oh! Oh!' he wailed. 'Mole! What's happened to you? Are you buried in there or – or – there at all,' he finished in a whisper.

But Mossy was above ground. After the tree's crash he had surfaced from one of his network of tunnels and he had been timorously waiting and keeping a look-out for Badger ever since. Now he heard his voice and he slowly struggled over the broken and cluttered terrain towards it.

He began to call. 'Badger! Badger! You're safe!'

Badger's head turned at the sound. He saw the little velvet-clad creature pushing through the debris. The two animals rejoiced at the sight of each other.

'Oh Badger, thank goodness you didn't listen to me,' Mossy said fervently. 'Your stubbornness saved you.'

'It did indeed,' Badger replied. 'And your tunnels and home – are they intact?'

'Pretty well,' Mossy said. 'But, poor Badger! Where will you live now?'

'I've no idea,' the old creature admitted. 'I'm a bit long in the tooth to be digging a new home.'

Mossy was silent. He couldn't offer any comfort.

'There's one consolation, though,' Badger went on. 'The Park's ours to roam again. With the threat of Trey removed, I could live – well, just about anywhere. Only, I'd like to be near you, Mole. And *you* live here.'

Mossy was eager to hear about the stag and the rest of the animals. Badger soon told him what he knew.

'Now, what do you think about my idea?' the old creature prompted as soon as the mole was acquainted with events.

'I – I – don't know,' Mossy answered, 'if it would be possible for me to – er – move home now.'

'Oh.' Badger looked crestfallen.

'You see, I have family ties like everyone else – well, *almost* everyone else,' Mossy corrected himself hastily, 'and – and –'

'Of course, I'd forgotten; don't give it another thought,' Badger said at once, kindly. 'I'll manage. Don't worry.'

But Mossy did worry. 'We could stay close anyway, couldn't we?' he offered.

'Well, no, I don't see how we can really,' Badger replied doubtfully. 'You see, the only place I think I can go now is back to that empty set by the Pond. Ah me, I seem to spend all my time going from one end of the Park to the other.'

Mossy was at least cheered by Badger's prospect of ready-made quarters. But he knew they would be distant from each other now and that there was no help for it. The two animals looked at each other sadly.

'Well, well, I'd better be going, Mole,' said Badger. 'I wish I'd stayed where I was, out in the open. I was more than halfway there already.'

'Oh Badger, won't you rest awhile?' Mossy beseeched him. 'You look *so* tired. I'll bring some worms for you. I've plenty to spare. You could at least wait until nightfall before setting off yet again?'

Badger didn't need much persuasion. 'Yes, yes, it would make sense,' he agreed. 'I'll just lie down here

for a bit against this tree' – he referred to the one that had smashed his set – 'and have a nap while you rustle up some titbits. And thank you, Mole.'

Fox and Vixen had not been able to put Trey out of their minds. He had made himself their enemy, yet the thought of the stag lying in agony under the crushing weight of a tree niggled at their consciences.

'I suppose he will be found by the Warden,' Vixen conjectured.

'Maybe not for hours – or days,' Fox commented. 'He may be examining quite another section of the Reserve. Look, Vixen,' he said with sudden resolution, 'we can't leave it like this. I feel I want to see for myself what can be done.'

'I'll come with you,' Vixen said, almost with relief.

They headed in the direction they thought most likely to bring them to the wounded stag. They knew he was by the perimeter fence and they guessed it would be at a place not too far from the Pond. In the end they were guided to him without difficulty because they came across the rest of the deer.

Trey had been lying in anguish for a long while. The herd had been unable to help him and he watched the foxes arrive (as he thought) to gloat, with a bitter expression. 'You!' he gasped. 'Couldn't you have . . . left me . . . to my doom?'

'We may be able to help,' Vixen said. 'It's not our way to turn a blind eye to any creature in such terrible distress.'

'What can . . . you do?' Trey panted. 'Puny creatures. . . .'

Vixen ignored his gibe. 'What do you think, Fox?' she asked her partner. 'He'll surely die if that tree isn't moved.'

Fox was racking his brains. He glanced at the other stags who stood about, none of them offering any suggestions. One of them said, 'He's as good as done for. It's only a matter of time.'

'Perhaps not,' Fox said slowly. He was studying the size of the males, their likely strength and the possibility of their using their great antlers. He came to a decision. 'There's only one chance,' he said briskly. 'You males must line up here by the felled tree. Then you must bend your necks and press your antlers against the trunk – all of you, together. You have to try and push it off him.'

The stags muttered amongst themselves.

'Why should we?' asked one bluntly. 'Trey was no friend to us. His day is over.'

'What's *your* interest in helping him?' another one challenged Fox. 'Why do you ask this of us?'

'I'll tell you why,' Fox answered softly. 'Because I picture myself under that tree. It's not difficult to imagine how the poor beast must be suffering.'

His words had a noticeable effect on the male deer. They looked crestfallen; some, a little ashamed. They came forward. Trey watched them in disbelief. He didn't know what to make of Fox, but his pride came to the fore.

'Leave me . . . be,' he whispered. 'I don't ask . . . your help.'

Fox ignored him. The stags hesitated, then continued. Even now some were still in awe of their

maimed leader. They set their heads to the bole of the pine and, each straining to his utmost, pushed against the weight of the upended tree. Trey groaned, then bellowed with pain as he felt it shift.

'Harder!' Fox urged. 'It's moving!'

Suddenly the tree half-lifted and then rolled over, leaving Trey free, his gashes and wounds exposed to the onlookers' gaze. He struggled to raise himself but, racked with a terrible agony, fell back again. His crushed and broken limbs could no longer support him. His efforts had exhausted him and he was unable to stir. The other deer backed away, appalled at what they saw.

'We can't leave him like this,' said Vixen.

'Only human intervention can help him now,' Fox replied grimly. 'We must search for the Warden.' He turned a look of compassion on Trey and a flicker of recognition momentarily lit up the stag's glassy eyes.

The foxes moved away. They had not gone far when the human figure they knew so well suddenly confronted them. The Warden had heard Trey's roars of pain and was already on his way to investigate. He recognized the pair of foxes and, for a second, three pairs of eyes met. Then the man went on, leaving Fox and Vixen with a strange feeling of comfort and well-being. They saw he was heading for the wounded beast.

'Do you think there's anything even he can do?' Vixen whispered.

'He has his means,' Fox said. 'Humans have great powers.'

Later, that evening, after his rest, Badger left the

regretful Mossy and stumbled away into the darkness. Mossy wondered when he would see him again and Badger, for his part, had much the same thoughts in his own mind. The old animal didn't hurry himself. A new, lighter wind had sprung up, but a chilly one with the feel of late autumn about it. Badger was wary of any wind now that might dislodge the 'creakers' Fox had warned about, so he kept to the open as far as he could. It was a sensible precaution but one that, unfortunately, made his journey to the substitute home much longer, and this delay was to prove crucial.

The Missing Ones

The damage caused by the hurricane throughout the Reserve was extensive. Badger, of course, was not alone in having his home destroyed. And, by the time he had hauled himself to the Pond and crept round its edge to the abandoned set, a whole family of badgers had forestalled him. The set was already tenanted. Badger smelt the smell of his own kind as he snuffled the air. He guessed at once what had happened. At the entrance hole he stopped and listened. Animated badger voices – some young, some older – were all chattering about their luck in finding this new home. Badger sighed. They had beaten him to it, and he had to acknowledge that the extensive tunnels and chambers were more suited to a family than to one ancient, solitary animal. He trudged to the Pond to drink.

Lost in his mournful reflections on the situation, he was unaware that another badger was drinking, only a

metre or two away. But she, however, had noticed him and, so familiar a figure was the Farthing Wood badger, she knew at once who he was. She lost no time in trotting to his side.

'It's a pleasure to see you,' she said sincerely.

'Oh!' said Badger with a start. 'Is it?' He looked at the young female.

'What a terrible storm,' said the female. 'I've moved my family here. We lost our old place.'

'Yes. So I gathered. I'm also homeless,' Badger confessed.

'You? Oh no. That's dreadful. But wait – were you –?'

'Yes,' Badger interrupted her. 'I came here on the same quest. But you stole a march on me,' he joked. 'I've no complaints; don't feel bad about it. There's too much space to be wasted on one old male.'

'Oh, but you have to have shelter too,' the female replied feelingly. 'There's plenty of room for one more. Please – we shouldn't care to leave you out in the cold. Do join us. We shan't interfere. You can keep yourself to yourself. And we –'

'No, no, I wouldn't dream of it,' Badger refused. 'You're very kind, I'm sure. I do appreciate it. But I'm not used to sharing. Really, I wouldn't care to start now. I'll be all right. I'll find something.' He had already begun to move off.

'Please,' the female badger called after him. 'Don't go. I'm sure we could work something out quite to your satisfaction.'

'I'm touched by your kindness,' said Badger, but he

didn't turn back. 'Please don't concern yourself about me.' He even increased his pace.

The young female stood looking after him. 'Poor old fellow,' she murmured to herself. 'I do believe he was a little afraid of me.'

'No home now, no home now, not anywhere,' Badger muttered as he wandered about. 'What can I do? I can't live out in the open. Perhaps there's a hole somewhere I can tuck myself into.' That was the best he could hope for. Just a resting-place; a refuge. He didn't expect to find himself a proper set. And, as he wandered and searched and searched and wandered, even the modest demand of a small hole seemed unattainable. The prospect of wandering right through the dark hours without discovering anything seemed a real possibility, as the areas Badger dared to search were limited because of the risks under the trees.

For the first time in his long life Badger came close to despair. He tried reminding himself that, during the animals' long trek from Farthing Wood, he had had to rest and hide in all kinds of unusual places. But he had been younger then, more adaptable and, above all, not alone. Now he was aware of an awful loneliness and he really was too old to cope with this sort of disruption to his life.

'What a way to end up,' he murmured self-pityingly as he sought in vain for a shelter of some kind. He got in such a state that it rather turned his head and he didn't realize where he was going. He wandered through one of the gaps in the broken perimeter fence and out on to the open downland. He didn't know where he was and he went on, blindly searching, as if he were still within

the Park. In the end weariness and hopelessness took their toll of the old creature and he simply lay down where he was and went to sleep. Even the cold wind failed to disturb him.

When daylight broke over the grassy expanse Badger woke up, thinking momentarily that he was safe inside his set. His eyes soon told him differently and, with an awful shock, he realized he was no longer even in the Nature Reserve. He felt as if he were in a sort of daze. Nothing seemed quite real any more. He didn't know why he was standing alone on the downland or how he had got there.

'No point going back to that place,' he told himself as he stood looking towards White Deer Park. 'Nowhere for me there.' The rigours of homelessness and solitude had scattered his wits. 'Only one home for old Badger,' he decided as he remembered the comforts of his ancient family set in Farthing Wood. '*That's* where I'll go. Nobody else knows about it. It'll be just for me, like always.' And at that moment he really did believe the set was there waiting for his return.

'Now, let me see, which direction would it be? It's a long way, I know.' He looked about him and settled on his course. Some dim recollection of the way the animals had travelled prompted his decision. 'Hm, yes. I think this is it,' he mumbled as he set off again. 'Toad will know anyway. When I see him he can remind me.'

The cold wind ruffled his bristly coat. Under other circumstances Badger would have known perfectly well that Toad, in such temperatures, would be driven to begin his hibernation. But that sort of reasoning was

beyond him now and so, in this sorry state of mind, he went on.

During the next few days the animals speculated about the White Deer herd. The Warden had taken charge of Trey and Whistler had reported that the stag had been removed from the Reserve. 'I doubt if he will be seen again,' he said. 'His injuries were so severe.'

'Only time will tell,' said Fox. 'We did our best for him, at any rate.'

'And if he doesn't return, who will be his successor?' Weasel wondered. 'Let us hope it will be one who recognizes that the Park is for all of us.'

'We can almost depend on that,' said Vixen. 'The blood of the Great White Stag, our friend, is in most of the herd. Trey was not typical. The others are unlike him. They're altogether milder creatures.'

The inhabitants of the Park became used to the presence of men brought in to remove dangerous and fallen trees and to repair the all-important Reserve fencing. The sound of mechanical saws became a regular feature, together with that of hammers and motor vehicles. Naturally the animals kept well away from any human activity but, as time went on and much of the wreckage was cleared away, they were struck constantly by the new look of the Park that was their home. New vistas, new clearings were opened up. The familiar terrain became unfamiliar and for a while the Reserve's inhabitants all felt strange; as if in some way they had been displaced. However, there was one piece of good fortune that resulted from the storm.

On his rounds of inspection the Warden had covered

every corner of White Deer Park. In this way he had discovered the poisonous containers that had been dumped some time ago into the ditch which led into the stream from outside the Park's boundaries. In no time at all these dangerous items had been disposed of, yet it would take a while longer for the water to be rid of its pollution and run clean again. All aquatic life in the stream had been killed. It became the Warden's responsibility to monitor the level of toxicity in the water so that eventually, once the stream was healthy again, re-stocking of fish and other small fry, as well as some vitally necessary vegetation – water-weeds and suchlike – could go ahead.

The ever watchful Whistler kept his friends up to date with events. 'He's testing the water,' he guessed. 'He cleared the rubbish out of it. I think he's trying to make the stream well again.'

Another time the heron notified them, 'The Warden's taking some water away with him. If he's going to drink it, it must be pure.'

'Take care,' Fox warned him. 'Don't risk yourself too soon.'

'There's no danger,' Whistler answered. 'I shan't go close to it until the fish return. Then I'll know the stream runs clear once more.'

But the stream was not the animals' main concern. Their chief worry now was the disappearance of Badger.

No-one knew where Badger had gone. Fox and Vixen had soon found the crushed home of their old friend and had been pointed in the direction of the

abandoned set by Mossy. But when they discovered the
family of strange badgers in residence, they turned
their attentions elsewhere. A meeting was held in the
Hollow and everyone was asked to comb each likely
spot for a sign of the missing animal. Of course every
one of them drew a blank.

Fox feared for the worst. 'I'm afraid we've lost him,'
he said to Vixen brokenly. 'He can't be in the Park any
more. We've looked everywhere. There's just nowhere
else. He's gone outside it, I know he has.'

Mossy was distraught. 'He couldn't find a home, he
couldn't find a home,' he kept chanting in his misery.

'*We'll* find him a home all right,' Plucky declared. 'It
only needs a few of us to drive out those usurping
badgers. We'll save the set by the Pond for *our*
Badger.'

'No, no, we certainly shan't,' Fox, his elder,
corrected him. 'Your heart's in the right place, Plucky,
I know. But the set was never Badger's own. The other
animals have just as much right to it. They've settled
there and *we* shan't disturb them. Oh, if I could only
find the dear old creature I'd dig him a home myself.
Yes, if it took all my strength I'd do it.'

'You wouldn't do it alone and you know it,' Vixen
told him. 'I have claws too. Do you think I wouldn't
want to help?'

'Of course you would,' Fox said. 'But what's
happening to us? First Tawny Owl and now Badger.
We're losing each other and – and I don't think I
can put things right this time. I just can't bear it,
Vixen.'

'If Badger's gone outside the Park, then why don't

we go after him?' suggested Weasel. 'He's not so swift-footed that we couldn't soon catch him up.'

'Yes, and which direction would we go in?' Adder demanded. 'Would we all go crawling about over the countryside together? Or take different paths? That way there'd be more than just Owl and Badger numbered among the lost. As it is, if I don't get underground soon I shall be lost anyway. Lost for good if the frost gets to me.'

'Nobody's asking you to hang around,' Weasel pointed out.

'Thank you for your civility,' Adder hissed. 'D'you think I can sleep the winter away without knowing if Badger will be here to greet when I wake again?'

'Well, well, you snakes must become more senti-mental as you get older,' Weasel remarked. 'I've never known you admit to such feelings before.'

'Never you mind about that,' Adder rasped, his demeanour resuming its usual mask of nonchalance. 'I think it was you who was instrumental in driving out Tawny Owl from amongst our company?'

'Never!' Weasel cried. 'Not I! I'd never do such a thing. I acknowledge I may have pulled his leg once or twice but how could I have foreseen the consequences? Why, I've never ceased to rue the day he left. All I want is for us all to be together again especially as – well' – here his voice dropped, even trembling slightly – 'as we all grow older.'

Whistler said, 'I'll fly a reconnoitre now and again. But you know I had no luck seeking out Owl. It may be as unrewarding looking for Badger.'

'There's one advantage,' said Friendly. 'Badger's on the ground. Easier to spot an animal than a bird.'

'I'll do my best,' Whistler promised.

Fox turned to Adder. 'Please don't put yourself at risk,' he advised the snake. 'Toad's already slumbering in his winter quarters. We don't want any more losses.'

'I'll wait awhile,' Adder said firmly. 'There have been no frosts so far. And one thing's for sure. There is no dearth of leaves to bury myself in at night.'

'If you should need extra warmth,' Vixen offered graciously, 'our earth can be the cosiest of places. . . .'

Adder's tongue flickered busily. He was strangely moved. 'D'you know, Vixen,' he said softly, 'that sinking my fangs into that horse's leg, so long ago now, is something I've always considered as one of the best things I've ever done in my life?' The snake's red eyes seemed to glow particularly brightly for an instant and Vixen didn't fail to notice.

'I've never forgotten it,' she whispered, 'and I never shall.'

Whistler began flying over the downland the very same day. His eyes scanned the mass of green for a flash of black and white that would reveal Badger's whereabouts. No other animal had that unmistakable colouring. But while the heron coasted and soared on his broad wings, Badger had paused to rest in the shadow of a large building. He had made uncertain progress but the church under whose walls he now lay sleeping was the first positive reminder to him that he had chosen the correct route. Just like Tawny Owl before him, it was the one recognizable landmark for

him in that region. And, even as he snored in the open with his back pressed against the stonework, Tawny Owl and Holly were heading for the very same building from the opposite direction.

Home

Tawny Owl's journey back to White Deer Park had not been the happy one he had planned. Holly had taken charge of all hunting activities since he had exhausted himself on the first stage of their flight. She had nurtured him with the plumpest of the prey she had caught, almost as if he were a fledgling. Much as he enjoyed these tasty meals, Owl was only grudgingly grateful as, with each day, he felt he was losing more of his independence. Holly also made sure he didn't overtax his stiffened wing muscles, and of this he was quite glad since as soon as his strength returned fully he intended to end his reliance on her. The only function left to Tawny Owl now, over which Holly could exert no control, was his navigation of their route. One by one the major features of the journey – the river, the area of the Hunt, the motorway, the town – were marked and passed. Now Owl set their course for the church.

Sometimes, when Holly had been particularly irksome, he wondered about leaving her in whatever roost they had chosen that day, and then flying away as she slept. There were occasions when he definitely wished to be rid of her. But something always held him back. He would remind himself that he would lose the very thing for which he had left White Deer Park in the first place – a mate. And he was conscious of the fact that he did owe a debt of gratitude to the female owl. She had kept him alive when he had been trapped in the beech at Farthinghurst. So they stayed together and now they neared the end of their journey.

Holly was constantly asking about when they would arrive. Tawny Owl always replied that, once the church was within their sights, they were as good as home. When at last he spied the building ahead, feelings of excitement, relief, anticipation and also uncertainty flooded over him. All along he had dreaded finding what the storm had done to White Deer Park. And now that moment had almost arrived. The two birds flew straight to the church and Tawny Owl, remembering the indignation of the colony of belfry bats, led Holly to the nave roof instead where they perched side by side.

'So this is it at last,' Holly breathed. There was no mistaking her own excitement. The stars shone brilliantly in the wide expanse of sky. It was a perfect night for hunting. 'I'll waste no time,' she said to Owl. 'The sooner we eat the sooner we can complete our journey. And, just think, the next time I hunt it will be in the Park itself.'

Tawny Owl flexed his supple wings. 'Yes,' he said.

'This is the last occasion when you bring me my food. You must stop treating me like an owlet.'

Holly looked at him askance. She guessed his thoughts. 'There's no need for your friends to know about our arrangement,' she said archly. 'I'm sure they don't watch you hunt?'

'Well no, but –'

'Very well then,' she interrupted. 'I can go on looking after you just as before. You should be grateful to be relieved of the tedium of hunting. You'll have a most comfortable and cosseted old age, I promise you.'

'Look, I don't want. . . .' Owl began peevishly, but it was no good. Holly flew away without listening just as she always did. 'How *am* I to get her to understand?' he fluted in exasperation. He watched the bats darting on their aerobatic flights from the belfry. Then he glanced down and, by the south side of the church he saw an animal stirring in the shadows. The striking striped head of a badger was illuminated by the crisp autumn starlight. Tawny Owl gasped. He could scarcely believe his eyes. In his amazement he almost over-balanced from his perch on the roof. He recognized Badger instantaneously.

'Badger! Badger!' he called and swooped downwards.

The old animal looked up with a puzzled expression. Then he saw Tawny Owl who alighted next to him.

'What on earth are you doing?' Owl asked in an astounded voice.

'Oh, Owl,' said Badger who was still very confused, 'you shouldn't have come looking for me.'

'I didn't come looking for you,' replied the bird.

'Whatever are you talking about? I haven't seen you at all for the whole of the summer. And wherever are you going?'

'Going?' mumbled Badger. 'Oh – um – going home, Owl. Going home.'

'I should think so. But why have you left it?'

'Left what?'

'Home.'

'Well, we all left it, didn't we, when we travelled across country to the – to the. . . .'

'You're not making any sense,' Tawny Owl interjected. He could tell that something was wrong with Badger. 'Now, tell me again. Where are you going?'

Badger looked at him as if he thought it was the owl who was out of his wits. 'Well – Farthing Wood, of course.'

'FARTHING WOOD?!'

'Yes, I have to get home, you see, because I can't live out in the open. I need shelter and – and –'

'Badger, stop. It seems there's something seriously wrong. Now, what's happened? What's the matter with you?'

'The matter with me?' Badger echoed. 'Well, I should have thought that was obvious. I'm homeless, Owl. That's what I am. Homeless.'

Tawny Owl was able to put two and two together. He realized there had been destruction in the Park and now he dreaded more than ever what he was going to see. But he tried to concentrate on Badger's troubles. 'Your home is White Deer Park,' he prompted. 'Why have you left the others? Where are they?'

'Oh, they're all right,' Badger answered sensibly

enough. 'They didn't lose their homes like me. So they
– er – they've stayed put.'

Tawny Owl was moved by his old friend's sad plight.
'Dear Badger,' he said. 'You don't understand. There
is no Farthing Wood. So you must turn back and go
along with me.'

But Badger, who had almost lost his reason, couldn't
accept this. 'Of course there's a Farthing Wood,' he
disputed. 'What a ridiculous thing to say about the
place we all grew up in!'

'Oh Badger, have you no memory?' Owl cried. 'The
wood was destroyed! Why ever else would we have left
it?'

'It was being destroyed when we left,' Badger
agreed, 'but most of it was still there. Well, some of
it. . . .' He was beginning to sound uncertain.

'Well, it isn't there now,' Tawny Owl insisted in a
loud voice as though Badger might be deaf. 'I've been
there – all the way back. There's not one stick left
standing. No, not one plant. Everywhere is covered
with human dwellings. So you *must* turn back.'

The old animal seemed to be trying to register this
information. He couldn't quite grasp it. 'You – you've
been there?' he repeated.

'Yes.'

Badger was regaining a semblance of his wits. 'Is
that where you've been all this time?'

'A lot of it, yes. I've a long story to tell you.'

'But why did *you* go there?' Badger asked perplexedly
as he noticed a second owl skimming towards them.

'Here's one reason,' Tawny Owl replied as Holly

arrived, with her bill crammed with food. 'Now, why don't we all eat together?'

Gradually, with Owl's patient help, Badger's understanding began to return. He saw how his foolishness had resulted from the shock of finding himself without a home. When they were ready, they set off for the Park. Badger was very slow, but Tawny Owl was determined not to let the old creature out of his sight and was quite satisfied to fly in short bursts to accommodate his slower pace. As for Holly, for once she was content to take a back seat.

As they went, Tawny Owl was able to piece together from what Badger told him, how the hurricane had devastated the Park. He learnt of the poisoned stream, too, but that despite everything all his old companions had survived. Then he, in his turn, described to Badger his own adventures and the sad fall of the last relic of Farthing Wood.

'So you see, we only have one home, don't we?' he summed up. 'And that's White Deer Park.'

It was broad daylight as they approached the Nature Reserve. Tawny Owl sought out a suitable entry point for Badger where the fencing was not yet repaired. High in the air, Whistler saw the three travellers, flew closer to make sure his eyes weren't deceiving him and then, with a 'krornk' of utmost delight raced to rouse Fox, Vixen, Weasel and Adder.

So when Badger trudged once more into the Park, the group of friends were there to greet him and the long-lost Tawny Owl.

'I hardly dared hope for this,' Fox murmured

emotionally. 'It's a day like no other. How did you come together?'

'There's much to tell,' Tawny Owl answered joyfully.

'My heart beats for both of you,' Vixen whispered to the two lost ones. 'And, Owl, I see you've not travelled unaccompanied?'

Holly was speechless at the sight of the gathered group, so many of them seemed to her like living legends. Tawny Owl wasn't slow to notice this.

'No, I've had good company,' he said, 'though, as you can see,' he added mischievously, 'it's been difficult for me to get a word in edgeways.'

There was much amusement at his remark, though the animals did not, as yet, understand its irony. Weasel was so relieved to see the return of Tawny Owl that he was quite unable to offer him any banter.

'Well, at long last I can retire,' hissed Adder. 'Sinuous has given me up for lost. I've seen what I wanted to see and I don't wish for any more than that. Badger, Owl – I salute you, though you *have* caused me discomfort. Farewell, All. Till the spring!'

They watched him slither hastily away.

'Come, Badger, old friend,' said Fox. 'We have something to show you.' He led the way and eventually they all arrived at Fox and Vixen's earth. Next to it there were new earthworks. While Badger looked on in wonder, clods of earth were thrown up from within this new construction which landed almost at his feet.

'It's not quite ready yet,' Fox said apologetically. 'But there's a company of busy fox paws digging away, as well as others'. You won't have too long to wait.'

'Me?' Badger murmured. 'Is it for me?'

'Of course it's for you. Who else?' said Fox. 'You're to be our near neighbour. And what could be better than that?'

'Nothing,' said Badger. 'Nothing at all.'

'It'll be your home for ever,' Fox told him. 'We shall stay close together for the rest of our lives.'

Just then Mossy surfaced from the new set. 'The foxes dig so furiously,' he said, 'I'm in danger of being buried.' He rushed to be re-united with Badger.

'I think,' said Tawny Owl to Holly, 'we can safely leave them to it for now. Animals have their own habits and we birds' – here he flapped his wings vigorously – 'we have other occupations. The story of Farthinghurst can wait. As for now, I propose we make a circuit of the Park. I haven't seen it for a while and I need to re-acquaint myself with my best hunting terrain. Come on, I'll show you around.'

Holly promptly followed him as he launched into flight.

'Well!' exclaimed Weasel. 'That's something I *never* thought I'd see.'

Other great reads from **Red Fox**

Further Red Fox titles that you might enjoy reading are listed on the following pages. They are available in bookshops or they can be ordered directly from us.

If you would like to order books, please send this form and the money due to:

ARROW BOOKS, BOOKSERVICE BY POST, PO BOX 29, DOUGLAS, ISLE OF MAN, BRITISH ISLES. Please enclose a cheque or postal order made out to Arrow Books Ltd for the amount due, plus 30p per book for postage and packing to a maximum of £3.00, both for orders within the UK. For customers outside the UK, please allow 35p per book.

NAME _____

ADDRESS _____

_____

Please print clearly.

Whilst every effort is made to keep prices low, it is sometimes necessary to increase cover prices at short notice. If you are ordering books by post, to save delay it is advisable to phone to confirm the correct price. The number to ring is THE SALES DEPARTMENT 071 (if outside London) 973 9700.